P.O. BOX LOVE

P.O. BOX LOVE

A NOVEL OF LETTERS

PAOLA CALVETTI

English Translation by Anne Milano Appel

ST. MARTIN'S PRESS 〰 NEW YORK

P.O. BOX LOVE. Copyright © 2012 by Paola Calvetti. English translation copyright © 2012 by Anne Milano Appel. All rights reserved. Printed in the United States of America. For information, address St. Martin's Press, 175 Fifth Avenue, New York, N.Y. 10010.

www.stmartins.com

Book design by Kelly Too

Library of Congress Cataloging-in-Publication Data

Calvetti, Paola.
  [Noi due come un romanzo. English]
  P.O. Box love : a novel of letters / Paola Calvetti.—1st ed.
    p. cm.
  ISBN 978-0-312-62570-2 (hardcover)
  ISBN 978-1-4299-3817-4 (e-book)
  I. Title.
  PQ4863.A38454N6513 2012
  853'.92—dc23   2011033802

First published in the Italy under the title *Noi due come un romanzo* by Mondadori

First Edition: February 2012

10 9 8 7 6 5 4 3 2 1

To my G.'s

Turned to stone, the lovers have been standing there for eons, buffeted by the wind. One day a year, the gentle breath of a fairy releases them from the evil spell. The two lovers become flesh and blood again, but the unwary traveler who might want to spy on their embraces would end up overwhelmed by that impossible, eternal love.

P.O. BOX LOVE

I wake up early now.

But first, that very first blissful moment between sleep and wakefulness is given over to Alice and the bookshop. The *moment* comes around 6:00 A.M., 6:15 at the latest, when the herbal potion that has replaced the dream-suppressing pills has done its job and I find myself riveted to the bed with my eyes wide-open and a unique surprise: It is in the empty silence of my room that my best ideas are formed.

And my heart settles down.

There is an annoying aspect to my precocious awakenings: Right after lunch, I slip into a deplorable state of lethargy and my eyelids lower like shutters. If I could, I would fold my arms on the bookshop counter and rest my head there for a nap, even just a brief one. Or I would stretch out on the Persian rug beneath my feet, nose between my paws and tail lying sideways like Mondo, Gabriella's Gordon setter.

Naturally, I can't, and I restrain myself.

To rouse myself from this torpor, I go upstairs with the excuse of having to refill the thermoses, and take refuge in the coffee nook. Oh, nothing special, not an actual café, just two armchairs and some bistro tables and chairs purchased at the Porte de Clignancourt flea market and shipped at an inordinate cost—you'd think they were the treasured relics of a saint.

At exactly ten o'clock, Dreams & Desires opens its doors to the public.

The schedule was not chosen by chance. One rarely feels the urge to skim through the pages of a romance right after breakfast or just before sitting down to business at the office computer. My artisanal *salle de thé* is not the right place for readers who are insomniacs. Complex moods, such as the euphoria of falling in love, the pain of an inexplicable rejection, regret over a lost opportunity, the languor of the first time, or the urgency of a quickie, cannot be drowned in a latte, despite the reassuring nicety of the porcelain cups and real glass tumblers set out in rows like a battalion of stout soldiers. No paper cups from a vending machine here, but also no croissants, raisin scones, or slices of jam tarts out of a Victorian novel. I don't have a permit to sell solid types of comfort and I have never in my life made a soufflé.

Before opening, I inhale my hour of freedom and apply myself to dusting. A light touch of the wrist, little more than a flick from top to bottom, guides the feather duster as it dances along the spines and dust jackets. With its bamboo handle and swirl of goose down on top, it is a nod of deference to my old nanny. Her name was Maria ("like Callas," she used to say, proud of having a well-established, respectable name), and as she polished the furniture in the small dining room, she would sing popular Sanremo hits like "Grazie dei Fior" and "Vóla Colomba." In the afternoon, I would come home from school and find her and Mama sitting there in the kitchen, chattering away. I would eavesdrop as Maria poured out her wretched life, and in the eyes of a child considerably inclined toward an overactive imagination, Maria seemed to be an untiring model of tolerance in the face of adversity.

As I dust, I sing softly to myself. Pop tunes from the seventies, selections from Lucio Battisti, the Beatles, and Bruce Springsteen. I stay away from operatic arias, too demanding for my frail little voice. Dust motes flutter in the air, causing me to sneeze in allergic syncopation. Still, dusting is a necessary exercise and the feather duster a reliable ally: It comes in close contact with titles and writers, memorizes the covers, steals a peek at the plots from the jacket flaps, finds books that are missing, retrieves those unjustly forgotten.

The morning's silent roll call gladly welcomes new arrivals, affording a kind of intimacy with novels I'm not acquainted with, the possibility of mingling stories and plots without constraints of genre, time period, or setting. From the gloomy dwelling of Thornfield Hall, Jane Eyre confides her hopeless adoration for Rochester to the stony Elizabeth Bennet in simulated flight from the astute Mr. Darcy, while Mr. Stevens, bundled up in the "Love Under Ice" section, pines in obstinate silence for Miss Kenton as he polishes the silverware and broods, green with envy, over *The French Lieutenant's Woman*. The latter, autographed by John Fowles, resides in the display case of the "Untouchables" alongside a letter from Mary McCarthy to Hannah Arendt, a gift from Gabriella for the shop's opening.

This mingling of genres is an infraction, I know.

Manuals for booksellers dictate precise rules about dusting, insisting that the merchandise—as those who don't know any better call it—must be tidied up in the evening, before closing. I, on the other hand, prefer to let the volumes doze on the tables. Let them do what they like, at night, unrestrained, with no one in charge.

It was not an easy step to take.

The alarm bell went off when a guillotine dropped into place at the mouth of my stomach no matter what I ate. Usually in the afternoon, around four o'clock. I tried to keep things light, I reexamined the chromatic solitude of rice with olive oil, I developed a passion for hospital diets, I eliminated red meat, and I gobbled up cooked vegetables, processed and bland. Nothing helped. The invisible blade came back punctually in time for tea. I lived in a vague state of expectancy; I had a presentiment of change, but I had no idea what to do or where to start.

I was seeking simplicity.

I needed space, to start listening, to get out of airplanes. And so, before I ceased to exist, I gave up years of grueling business trips around the world and took off. Alone, in the snow-white anonymity of Arvidsjaur, a village in Swedish Lapland, amid reindeer steaks and pitchers of dark beer, I worked out plans based on the endless possibilities of a decent life. When the blond giant booked by the hotel took me on a "unique and unforgettable" tour of that icy wilderness, most of my five foot, three inches bundled up in a sled, the signal lit up and a single sentence flashed on my internal monitor: IT'S TIME FOR A CHANGE. It was like being born a second time, though I didn't have the slightest recollection of what the first time had been like.

Back in Italy, I found a message from the office of a notary named Predellini, who turned out to be a charming woman of about forty, whom my aunt had gone to. *An opportunity that only knocks once,* I thought. *Grab it without thinking too much, no matter where it leads.*

"You are naïve, rash, and stubborn. I say this fondly, Emma, but you've taken leave of your senses." The statement has the baritone ring of my Faithful Enemy. His name is Alberto, he's an accountant, he's been married to my best friend, Gabriella, for twenty-five years, and he has opposed my plan since its inception. After his lapidary "It won't work," the specter of insolvency, failure, and poverty in which I would plunge within six months haunted me like Banquo's ghost, no doubt partly due to my ignorance in business matters, as abysmal as my incompetence with crossword puzzles, petit point embroidery, the sciences, and any kind of dog breeding.

"It won't work." The Faithful Enemy went on chanting his mantra. I invited him to dinner, just the two of us, to at least show him the photographs.

He was on a diet.

I abandoned the idea of a pasta *al sugo* and set my sights on steamed sea bass with new potatoes, green beans in olive oil, and a Trebbiano d'Abruzzo that cost me a fortune. On the off chance that he might waive his strict regime, I bought a chocolate cake at Cova's to serve with the best dessert wine in the world, a Pedro Ximénez sherry. The drain on my finances was essential to win him over to my project.

"Here, take a look. I photographed the rooms to give you an

idea of the space. As soon as you have time, I'll take you to see it. It's already inviting, and with some touching up, it can become quite charming. All it needs is some fresh paint on the walls, getting the parquet floor polished, moving the counters, adding a couple of tables, and having the shelves restored." When I fear reactions that may go against what I want, I tend to overdo it with the details.

"You're like a little girl playing shopkeeper: 'Good morning, ma'am. What would you like today? Shall I wrap it for you?' and all that crap. It's a midlife crisis, Emma. Sooner or later, we all think that changing our lives has the power to stop the years. It's called second adolescence. Why don't you go and take a nice trip with Gabriella?"

"Right, and maybe a face-lift and liposuction for my thighs. Albi, I'm sick and tired of traveling around the world. I want to stay put. Coach me in the basic rules of business. All I'm asking for is some help."

"The competition is fierce, Emma. You'll have to contend with shopping malls and chain stores, sharks who offer fifteen, twenty, or thirty percent discounts off the cover price. Think about online sales: You pick a title on the screen, you press Enter, and the book arrives at your house in two days. You're getting yourself into a real mess."

"You always see the negative side of things! Not to mention that it will be a specialty bookshop, not just any old bookstore."

"Nowadays, books in their original language are available everywhere."

"That's not what I meant. I mean there are no bookshops that specialize in love."

"Oh please! You're joking, right? Or maybe you've already decided to paint the walls a nice syrupy pink? That's paraliterature, Emma; the bookstalls are overflowing with silly little romance novels."

"This would be something completely new. Look, not even in London or Paris—"

"Exactly. Ask yourself why. Love is too specialized a topic to build a business plan on. A little like bocce, or chess, or horses. Niche interests, for a few devoted fanatics."

"Alberto, the history of literature, the *entire* history of literature, is an uninterrupted river of love. It's not an endangered genre on its way to extinction, like the giant panda, sea lions, and hens—museum creatures or subjects of *National Geographic* documentaries."

"Children know perfectly well what hens are, that they're not on their way to extinction."

"Try going to an elementary school in Milan and ask them to draw a hen. Five out of ten wouldn't be able to, and you know why? Because they've never *physically* seen a live hen."

"Selling books is economically unsound to begin with; opening a bookshop that sells only romances is a surefire fiasco. A crappy idea. Now, don't take offense."

"Alberto, listen to me: No one can compete with the dissolute grace of Count Vronsky, boast the alabaster skin of Prince Andrei, scheme like the Marquise de Merteuil, overturn your life like that scoundrel Heathcliff," I replied with a stab at bravado. It fell on deaf ears.

My accountant did not have the foggiest idea who Heathcliff was.

"Use your brain, count to ten before answering, and explain to me why on earth a customer should buy a book from you rather than at the supermarket while doing her Saturday-morning shopping."

I sipped from my goblet of sparkling water, took my time, and refilled his glass with Trebbiano. As a confirmed teetotaler, I am unfamiliar with the power of alcohol, but I place my trust in it wholeheartedly.

"Try saying to any old megastore clerk wearing a name badge on his jacket, 'Excuse me. I had an argument with my girlfriend. Do you have a book that will give me some advice on how to make up?' He would stare at the computer screen and type in the formula 'girlfriend plus argument plus make up," expecting the monitor to flash an algebraic sum masquerading as an intelligent answer.

Or else, without even looking at you, he would point toward the nonfiction section 'in back to the left.' Nonfiction, get it? Chain bookstores are places no one possibly wants to go to, nonplaces, as Marc Augé would say. My bookshop will be a *place* place. I won't have customers and *consumers,* as you economists call them, but people who will come and find courteous responses. They won't experience that supermarket bewilderment, or the feeling of inferiority that comes over you in those boutiques for bibliophiles run by people who treat books like monuments: Look but don't touch. Mine will be a shop with a human touch. I'll make sure the renovation is inexpensive; I'll resort to used furniture. You'll have to estimate start-up costs and at least one year of operating expenses, but, please, don't slaughter me with your damn numbers."

Though I felt swallowed up in a maze of humiliation, I tried to refute his cynical offensive by wearing him down. I had to convince him.

"Your enthusiasm is touching, my dear, but I might point out to you that the world, life, even the reproductive activity of animals, all revolve entirely around those damn numbers."

"The only alternative is to sell it. It would be like killing her. Voluntary homicide."

A deep breath. A pause. The idea of a crime scared him. Maybe.

"You could make a ton of money; thirty-seven hundred square feet with a loft right in the city center are worth roughly one point five million euros. But okay, I'll try. I'll look into it and prepare a feasibility study at seven hundred thousand. I have a couple of clients in the publishing world, and I don't want to be a cause of depression. I just wish you wouldn't gamble away your savings. You have a son to support and you're in excellent health, my dear."

My precious Alberto—a brother to me now that I no longer have any brothers—stood up from the table with a resigned air and, upon reaching the door, froze me with a sardonic grin—the same one that had led my best friend to the altar. Alberto is tall and charming, and he still has a full head of hair, which makes him look like anything but an accountant. Behind his rational, disenchanted ways lies a gentle, generous soul. He hugged me, his views unchanged. "While you're at it, be sure to devote a shelf to ill-fated romances. They are statistically more common than happy ones."

The "Broken Hearts" section, on the upper floor, is dedicated to him, with a gold-plated plaque. Alberto: the accountant who lets me live peacefully by taking care of bar codes and invoicing and who allows me to keep track of the stock in a ledger where titles, publishers, books sold, and those to be restocked are entered *by hand*. In my bookshop, in fact, there is no trace of a computer. Ever since I read that at least twenty million Italians are affected by stress due to new technologies and that reading e-mails and text messages lowers one's IQ, I have excellent reasons for living without an e-mail address. I'm beginning to enjoy doing one thing at a time. Getting over multitasking was as tricky as learning a new type of exercise. Now I brag about it. I dedicated a section to what Aunt Linda left behind, a treasure trove of pastel-colored envelopes and stationery adorned with borders of violets, bunches of suitably soft Caran d'Ache pencils, three inkstands, a stack of notebooks with black covers and red spines, a sponge finger pad, packets of rubber bands, a set of red sealing-wax sticks, pins and thumbtacks with colored heads, felt blackboard erasers, rubber erasers, tins of paste and bottles of glue, and a unique specimen: a red leather portfolio with a rawhide cover and a built-in pencil case. In the back of the stationery shop, I found an Olivetti Lettera 22, a dilapidated gem, which, thanks to the attentions of the only Milanese craftsman who still cares about that kind of typewriter, is displayed on the shelf that holds the epistolary novels.

Mattia was the sole member of the family who supported me. "The only thing more absurd that can happen to a kid who still keeps his textbooks in plastic covers is a mother who's a bookseller," he said. My son's enthusiasm and a little pair of yellowed cotton gloves that I happened to find in a drawer were the definitive viaticum.

Now I'm really happy here, among the paper romances.

They are fail-safe loves that do not dissolve beneath a web of wrinkles. They have silenced the pitying concerns of friends, ex-husbands, and ex-lovers who are convinced that when it comes to sentimental development, I did not follow what they, the all-knowing ones, call evolution. More simply put, I'm done with that subject. Case closed. And ten months after I fled to Lapland, the bouts of nausea and other ailments disappeared. My daydreaming has a good front: At times of dejection, I remedy the situation by opening a book, and I no longer have to deal with real love.

I am a fulfilled woman.

I pass the duster over the "Romantic Hideaways" section, alcoves and hotels where enduring marriages and illicit trysts were consummated; Marguerite Gautier's "charming little house of two stories, with a semicircular railing"; "the hall paved with coloured marble," belonging to the wheeler-dealer d'Ambreuse; the "secret little hut made of rustic poles" where D. H. Lawrence's Connie waited and waited and waited; the London homes of Thomas Carlyle in Chelsea and John Keats in Hampstead. I haven't sold many during these days of the furnishings expo; who knows, maybe carpenters and designers don't fall in love. It's a few minutes before ten, just enough time for a cup of tea with lemon.

I climb the stairs, proud of the monastic order of the tables and shelves. A small phosphorescent yellow flag sticks out from the pages of *Ballades d'amour à Paris* (the only copy, in the original language, bought from a Parisian colleague). I hate people who tamper with the books, but it's because of my tolerance that customers treat this place as if it's their home. Someone left a place mark. Thank goodness he didn't fold down the corner of the page. I remove the sticky note gently so as not to tear the paper. Written in green felt-tipped pen, a name and telephone number. *That* name. Can it be?

It is.

"I got you a scone. It's still warm. Would you like it up there?"

Alice's face is rosy from her workout and her damp hair smells like vanilla balsam.

"Thanks, I'll just finish straightening up and come down. Meanwhile, you open up; it's already late."

Sitting in this chair, I've been trying to organize my thoughts for the last twenty minutes. I think maybe it's a joke, a coincidence, a chance occurrence. Federico is a common name. I look in the drawer for the calculator that Mattia gave me for Christmas, a never-used radish red plaything with yellow keys that look like coat buttons. I turn it on. It works. I punch in the numbers. It's been 31 years, 372 months, 1,612 weeks, 11,315 days, and 271,560 hours since I've seen him. Give or take. I never heard anything more about him, and even with Gabriella, the only witness to that affair, the subject was relegated to the letter *E,* for Error.

Or Emotions.

Which often coincide.

Dialing this number would be like taking a shot at speed dating, those horrific blind dates that give you just a few minutes to decide if you want to go to bed with someone and if he wants to do the same with you. Federico was never about sex. He exited my life abruptly and his memory was buried away with reckless haste, only to reemerge from our high school days a few minutes ago.

No need to dramatize.

From a certain age on, it is statistically possible, even probable, that among more than six billion people on the globe, an ex might well turn up as if nothing had happened in the meantime. What is disturbing (assuming it's not someone with the same name) is that he would show up just now when, having packed away the past, I am strutting along radiantly in my neospinster Eden. I have the shop, and the books protect me from everything that's out there.

Except that, as of today, he's out there.

After 271,560 hours, I can't call him. I couldn't bear the disappointed look of a man who won't say what's going through his mind (polite, he was always extremely polite) but meanwhile is thinking, *That was a close call.* And what if he has put on weight, or turned into a ridiculous dork, a car dealership manager, a sales rep, a lawyer or notary, or one of those executives who says *slide* instead of *transparency, briefing* instead of *meeting, name tag* instead of the badges Scouts and Brownies earn, or calls a switchboard a PBX? I'm done with slides and I've learned to keep a tiny back room as orderly as a boutique. The only clue is the Post-it note stuck to my right thumb. Why on earth would someone go around with a pad of Post-its in his pocket? Maybe he's an artist, or a meticulous person who takes notes and sticks them on the refrigerator. Maybe he's a long-winded bore by the name of Federico who will buttonhole me and tell me his never-ending tales. Asking Gabriella for advice is not an option. She would weigh the pros and cons, imagine some hidden intrigue, and embellish it. Of the two of us, she's always been the reflective one. After close scrutiny of the available information—phone number, handwriting, the book in which he chose to leave the message, assessment of the past, the time elapsed between his leaving me and the discovery of the message—she would advise an *F*.

File it.

He answers after five interminable rings.

"Hi. It's me," I say.

"Thank God. I had given up hope."

The first six attempts had gone no further than the area code, but now the voice—the piece of the puzzle that kept me undecided all day between taking a chance and prudent hesitation—*that* voice on the other end of the line, is speaking quickly and is not at all mellow, unlike what I was sure I remembered. I resist the urge to end the conversation before it has even begun. Better to sit calmly; there's no reason to get upset.

"How are you, Emma?"

"Fine. I'm fine. Where are you?"

Did I really say that? Me, of all people, the one who goes around proclaiming her disgust for cell phones, not to mention loathing that question to which anyone can reply with any old baloney. Me, who passed the Nokia on to Mattia (in my previous life, I had used it like everybody else), feeling a dull loss at first and later a superior sense of liberation. I admit that the first few days were a disaster, but I had announced my historic decision to half the world and I couldn't take it back; somewhat like when you go on a diet or you decide it's time to quit smoking: You tell everyone you meet. And though the first few hours, the first few days, the first few weeks of abstinence from obsessive conversation are terrible, once your will-power overcomes the compulsion to be constantly in touch, your self-esteem grows by leaps and bounds. The cell phone and the PC had become extensions of my body, so that when the computer froze, I went to pieces; not responding to an e-mail seemed a mark of rudeness; and if I deleted a text message, I lost my identity. I copied the most significant ones in a small notebook covered with Florentine paper. Alice accuses me of "Paleolithic obstinacy." That's not so. I claim the sacrosanct right not to be found and I enjoy the perverse pleasure of being unreachable. Not being always online has its drawbacks—my metamorphosis has left a lot of people by the wayside—but I'm now free to leave no traces. I'm a prototype of new contemporary womanhood: I believe it is possible to live without technology. Those who love me know where to find me. I have a landline at home, and at the bookshop I have a tabletop phone with a bulky receiver and a rotary dial.

So . . . Emma the virtuous asks, "Where are you?"

"I'm at a hotel. I'm leaving for New York Monday morning. I'm living there now." The news of an imminent departure is a relief. "We could have dinner together, but it seems a little late. How about tomorrow?"

"D-dinner?"

Why am I stammering? It's hardly the first time someone has asked me out to dinner. I could kick myself.

"Coffee tomorrow morning? Or maybe lunch? Just to say hello at least . . ."

Federico presses me; from the hurried way his words tumble out, one might think he's overcome by childish euphoria, or that maybe he's afraid his old high school sweetheart will send him packing with a curt "No," or a vague "I can't," or an "I'm so sorry, but I have prior plans for the weekend; it would have been lovely to see each other again after all this time." I have nothing planned for the next twenty-four hours. Nothing other than making myself irresistible, come to think of it. Federico goes on talking, and I can just picture his knobby fingers, the nails bitten and squared off, those asymmetrical hands that moved like fish in a bowl. I saw them a short time ago. Before finding the necessary courage to dial the number, I rummaged through photos of family members, elementary school classes, baptisms, First Communions, and graduation parties until he popped out of the pile, standing in front of a whitewashed house at the shore. On the back, written in ballpoint, a date: "August 23, 1969." I hesitate, not that I'm troubled by any uncertainty. What does he look like, this fifty-year-old man who walked out of my life before he had even turned twenty?

"Federico . . ."

"Emma . . ."

"What if we don't recognize each other?"

It might be the voice or that afternoon's photograph, but I can see his perfect, flawlessly white teeth.

"We can always call our cell phones, right? Besides, I saw you just a few hours ago. Shall I make a reservation? Is the trattoria in Santa Marta still open?"

He sounds eager, enthusiastic.

"The owner's son took over. Okay, let's meet there at eight-thirty. Just in case, my number is 0234934738. Do you have a pen handy?"

"Noted. See you tomorrow."

Click. I hang up the receiver as if in a film, lost in thought.

Now what?

My hairdresser is closed tomorrow, and if I wash my hair myself, my seventy-euro cut will look like a tossed salad. Going to the hairdresser for a weekly trim is one of my addictions, like going to the gym or seeing my aesthetician. The solution to the problem goes by the sweet name of Alice, who because of her love for books has put aside her degree in Romance languages and accepted a temporary job in the retail business.

"I'll do an online search and find a hairdresser you'll like. I'll make an appointment for you. Oh, Emma, do you need a manicure?"

"Mom, I'm late, I'm out of gas, Andrea is waiting for me downstairs, and my cell phone is dead. I have nine and a half minutes to take a shower."

Mattia uses the house as a pit stop, and tonight his rushed, irritating sprint is a disturbance. I am critically focused on the lash-lengthening mascara when I hear him knock at the bathroom door with the impetuous arrogance that usually melts me but right now interferes with the restoration operation I've been engaged in for hours. It took me six hours to feel a smidgen secure about my appearance, and he's hurrying me up.

"You can call him from the home phone, can't you? Andrea, I mean!" I shout. Meanwhile, he doesn't budge from the door.

"Mom, what is this schmaltzy music?"

"It's 'My Girl,' by the Temptations, ignoramus. You can use the small bathroom."

Hygiene, for Mattia, is closely related to sex. If he needs to wash, it's because today, a weekend day, he is likely to find someone to go to bed with him. But if I say "go to bed," he corrects me.

"It's called *fucking*, Mom."

I can't bring myself to say *fuck*, but the night I saw him floss his teeth, devour breath mints, concentrate on his lower body parts, and ask advice about deodorants, I was almost moved. Assuming, despite my ignorance of the sexual habits of today's eighteen-year-olds, that he had hopes for something more complex than a kiss. I open the door, twirl around, and do a credibility check with the only tangible result of my married life: "What do you think?"

"Thanks, Mom. In the smaller bathroom, I have to sit down in the tub. How come you're so foxy tonight? Where are you going all dressed up like that?"

"I'm going to see what kind of girl I used to be," I say enigmatically with the most literary phrase that comes to mind, lowering the volume of the CD player, and secretly hoping he won't ask anything more. We're very close, but I'm still his mother and I can't tell him that I don't want to be outdone by the ghost of who I was at age eighteen. Despite the fact that he encourages me to find admirers, for Mattia, my love life ended with Michele, his father, my ex-husband.

The wavy hair in the photograph is still all there. The brown mane that spilled over his shoulders is now a short, neat bush, sprinkled with dove gray. He keeps his hands buried in his duffel coat. The collar of a Brooks Brothers shirt peeps out from under it; below, wool flannel cuffed trousers and Church's dark brown suede lace-up shoes. Did he do it on purpose? Maybe he never changed his uniform. I take a deep inhalation and a deep exhalation, then . . . off I go. I cross the short distance that separates me from him with my head held high. He'll see me and will surely notice the color in my cheeks. They're hot, definitely red, with eggplant purple spots. I'm shy, but this detail of my character is known only to those close to me. To everyone else, I'm an extrovert with a gift of gab, though with age and experience I've dropped the melodramatic tones and learned the therapeutic value of irony. We petite women don't march forth with a solemn gait; we slowly pick our way along. And even though just a few yards separate me from him, it's as if I'm moving toward an unknown continent and am midway there. Impossible to do an about-face and go back, even if only to decide how to greet someone who stole your heart an incredible number of years ago. A hug might be misunderstood, viewed as excessive familiarity. I could just shake his hand. Good to see you, hello. Basically it's a bit like a first meeting. He might think me too formal and this would make him freeze up for the rest of the evening. Pouncing on his neck is unthinkable; Federico is over six feet tall, and I—if I stand on tiptoe—manage to reach at most a height of five three. The man with the salt-and-pepper hair takes a step toward me. There's not enough time to get used to this new face with traces of the old one, no time to examine—out of purely anthropological interest—how it's changed, because as soon as I'm in front of him, Federico clasps me tightly to him with the most natural gesture in the world. How could I not have thought of it before?

"Hello, Emma."

"Federico . . ."

"Shall we go in?"

My breathing becomes more regular; my heart slows down from the mad gallop at which it had foolishly set off. I walk behind him into the warmth of the trattoria. He hasn't changed his cologne: Eau Sauvage. Evidently it's remained a classic, like my Chamade, a duty-free souvenir from my prior life. Or else he chose that on purpose as well.

Take it easy, Emma. Novels have nothing to do with real life. And this, my Faithful Enemy would say, is a thought right out of a silly romance novel.

Federico is almost old-fashioned in his ways, and his height forces him to hold his body slightly forward. He has not put on weight, and he was already gallant back in school, when others acted rude just to seem important. He slips my little black coat off my shoulders and hands it to the waiter. He moves my chair out and, when I'm all settled, he sits down on my right. He picks up the wine list, as if it's the most normal thing in the world after all this time.

"Red or white?"

Now how can I tell him I don't drink wine anymore?

My ex-husband considers it one of the factors that precipitated our divorce. Plus, Federico was already a wine lover back then, never passing up a glass of house wine when we went to inexpensive pizzerias. I am expecting something to happen, or maybe I'm struck by the absolute naturalness with which he moves, so self-confidently.

"I don't drink wine. Maybe a beer."

"Not the perfect choice for celebrating."

"How do I seem to you?" I ask, getting bread-stick crumbs all over the bright yellow tablecloth in that trattoria where time seems to have stopped at our graduation dinner: the same straw-bottomed chairs, the sideboard with the white dishes and bottle green glasses, the walls covered with movie posters and black-and-white photos of opera singers, stage actors, and showbiz entertainers whom I don't recognize.

"The same," he replaces, with no particular inflection in his voice.

"Say that again," I ask, immensely grateful for that irresistible gesture of generosity and good sense.

"You haven't changed a bit, Emma. You look just the S-A-M-E," he repeats, spelling out the letters and giving me a smile—*that* for sure is the S-A-M-E, that broad lady-killer smile that swept me away in the final year of high school, when we girls had to wear a black smock with embroidered polka dots on the collar, while the boys were allowed to wear bell-bottom jeans and plaid shirts. When we got to the fifth polka dot (Maria saw to it for me, with perfect hieroglyphics in blue thread), we rejoiced: Nine more months and this hell would be over. The ignominy of the black muumuu, which concealed a glorious explosion of kilts, miniskirts, musketeer boots, and skimpy sweaters, was washed away by oblivion on July 17, 1970.

A top score of sixty out of sixty ensured parental permission for the first group trip. Coming from a private high school, Federico had plunged into our class like a meteorite at the beginning of the school year, an appearance that disrupted my life. He drove a wedge into my symbiotic friendship with Gabriella, who, in fact, immediately judged him loathsome and arrogant, the boring son of wealthy parents. Flawed, not to her taste as a girl from a good family, brought up simply, with a hint of huffy snobbishness accentuated by a rounded *r* that helped her in French. Actually, she was jealous. She admitted it many years later, at our English teacher's funeral: to overcome our sadness at the loss of the only person in school who had understood and encouraged us, we tried to take our minds off it by playing who was who and look how he turned out. Gabriella remembered him; she looked around for him among the pews of San Marco, crammed with three generations of students, and said, "I wonder what happened to the beanpole," as she called him.

"It's just another four months."

It's the first thing that pops into my head as I order risotto Milanese and meatballs in sauce with mashed potatoes. I need time. And calories. I lower my eyes like a schoolgirl and look at myself in the empty plate, where the crumbs have formed a minuscule sand-colored dune.

"Another four months to what, Emma?"

"Till I turn fifty."

"Oh, I've just reached it, and I assure you nothing serious happened. Just a more lavish party than usual."

"I'm not having any party. Ignoring my birthday is the best way to avoid falling into depression. Your lips are thinner," I murmur, moving closer to study him, and immediately regretting having used such an unfortunate remark to try to allay my impatience to tell him about me and, above all, to hear about him. One of the annoying things about meeting someone new at my age is that it requires a summary of our respective pasts: university, jobs, wives, husbands, boyfriends, literary tastes, the ten songs you should never split up to.

The advantage, with him—if you don't count the scarring and damage left by 271,560 hours—is that we already know each other. Mentioning that would offer some idea of my current state of mind, yet I can't think of even a single thing.

"It's charming, the store where you work," he says.

"It's not a store. It's a bookshop, and I own it. I inherited it."

"How nice to inherit a bookshop instead of the usual pile of money."

"You should have seen me at the notary's! I felt like an heiress, while she solemnly read the simple letter from Aunt Linda, who died after seventy-nine years spent sharpening pencils, selling note-books, and comforting pupils. She left me her memorable statio-nery shop. I was her only remaining relative, her favorite niece, and she wanted to leave her notebooks in good hands."

"And how did the stationery shop become Dreams & Desires?"

"I visited more shopping malls in one week than in my entire life, and the more books I saw stacked up among the mountains of diapers and cans of peeled tomatoes, the more I became convinced that there was a need for a place where people could come together and browse through books without feeling obliged to buy. I con-ducted surveys among my friends, smothering them with questions, until it dawned on me that I needed to open a bookshop that re-sembled me. A place that would speak of feelings."

"You haven't changed in that respect, either."

"With respect to feelings?"

"You're talking nonstop and your risotto is getting cold."

"I wanted to sell an immortal product: love."

"Well, immortal but perishable."

"Less perishable than a new electronic gadget that has already been surpassed by a *new generation* the minute you take it out of the box."

"It's a delightful place and you're a perfect proprietor. I would have liked to linger just to enjoy the atmosphere."

"Instead, you ran off."

"Ran off, no, but I was . . . I didn't know how I should act."

"You never ran into an old girlfriend before?"

"I avoid them, usually. There's the danger of being disappointed. And you're not just any ex-girlfriend."

"*Ex* is always better than *post*."

"Sorry, I don't care for the prefix, either."

We go on for hours, our student pasts recomposed like *A History of Italy,* tomes that would never find a home in my bookshop.

"Whatever happened to that brownnose in the first row?"

"And Enrico, your best friend? Don't tell me he married that tease Teresa?"

"I got my degree in architecture. I work at the Renzo Piano Building Workshop. Right now, I'm overseeing a project in New York."

"I have a son who's eighteen."

"And I have a daughter, thirteen."

"I'm divorced."

"I'm not."

We are so caught up in the nightmare of class assignments that we don't notice the waiter. With an imploring look, he hands Federico the bill, politely but firmly. We are the last remaining diners, and he must surely have a girlfriend waiting for him somewhere. Federico pulls out a credit card from a slim wallet. No photos, it seems. We leave. The street is deserted. Milan is fragrant with the scent of spring and Eau Sauvage.

"Shall we take a taxi?" I ask.

"Let's walk a bit, if it's okay with you."

"Of course. I'd like that."

We walk all the way home.

"Here we are. This is where I live."

The awkwardness is palpable. Also a kind of gaiety, at least as far as I'm concerned. I'm saying good night to a man at the door and I feel like a debutante returning from the ball. Sort of like Cinderella with shoes, with a different ending. The prince takes her home and vanishes in the night. The strange thing is that I fall asleep without my sleeping potions and without mulling over what happened.

Two days later, I enter from the back door that opens onto the courtyard. The bookshop is set into the building like a bauble around the wrinkled neck of a turn-of-the-century woman. The Philippine caretaker, who lives in a few square yards crammed with plastic knick-knacks and rice-paper chandeliers, comes toward me, holding a stiff scrub brush, and hands me an envelope. My name in green ink is the only thing written on it, the handwriting upright and the capitals rounded like the pinnacles of the Sagrada Família.

Emma Valentini. Private and Confidential.

"A fine gentleman delivered it, early this morning," Emily mutters, as if she is holding a bill that promises to be a nuisance.

A gentleman, of course. Nowadays, an envelope lined with ivory paper is sent only to invite you to a first marriage. For the second or third, they'll give you a call at best, and there isn't even a bridal registry. I open the envelope. Whoever the fine gentleman is, he must have read my mind.

• ——— •

Milan, April 12, 2001
Grand Hotel et de Milan
Via Alessandro Manzoni 29

Dear Emma,

As I write, I'm thinking about your hands. I imagine you as you open this letter and enter your realm "with eyes still swollen with tears or at least covered by an invisible film of sadness" (a sentence copied word for word from a novel that someone left behind in this hotel room). I'm taking my time, but even as a boy, when it came to writing compositions in class, I would ramble on and on, circling around the title. "You did not fully develop the specified theme" was often the teacher's response. Maybe I chose architecture to get to the point. It was a beautiful evening. I'd like to call you, but it's late. I've been in Milan for days and I haven't called anyone. I have no desire to see friends, families of friends, friends' teenage children. I have no desire to be hosted like a guest, even if they all get mad, starting with Enrico, who brags that he has preemptive rights over me. I won't call him because I'd feel like a prick not telling him that I saw you. I thought I would feel homesick. But I don't. Reminiscent of an emporium with sofas and chairs, lamps and tables, festivities, cocktail parties and openings at all hours of the day, Milan no longer seems to have anything to do with me. The other day, I was walking through the area around via Tortona, where the former Ansaldo factory allegedly lends the district the look of an international city. On via Torino, the movie theater where we used to hide out in the morning is no longer there; instead, there's a row of shops, all the same: Loafers with tassels, cowboy boots, and briefs are all authorized porn-shop items. To avoid the clanking of the trams (how much noise they make!), I veered off toward Piazza Sant'Alessandro. The sky loomed overhead like a metal grate, casting its shadow over the facade of the basilica, that magnificent 1601 example of Baroque architecture. Four elderly women, their hair as wispy as clouds, were plodding up the stone steps. The smallest one inadvertently brushed my sleeve. My nostrils picked up the familiar scent of camphor and face powder. I thought about what my mother would have been like at that age. The wrinkly ladies seemed to have agreed on a string of pearls—the same ones she used to wear on her lilac or pale blue cardigans—with a pin on their lapel and fussy hats. I followed them into the darkness of the church, toward the front pew. Dozens of votive candles glowed, burning up endless prayers. I slipped a bill into the collection box and lit one with the help of a candle stub. Around me rose the chanting of those who have been believers for a long time. I would have liked to linger there, but seeing the priest enter, I felt the urge to escape. I bowed slightly, a genuflection caused by conditioned reflex. It's just that I don't know how to speak to God and this makes me anxious, arousing a vague sense of guilt, as if I hadn't tried all the possibilities, as if I had passed over some options. In the dim light of the piazza, a shop straight out of a Victorian greeting card caught my eye. The sign, Dreams & Desires, hand-painted in bright canary yellow on a midnight blue background, intrigued me. In the window, scattered like handkerchiefs, were expensive volumes with photographs of hotels, accompanied by novels. The Grand Hotel Quisisana of Capri and Simone de Beauvoir's letters to Sartre; Agatha Christie's *Murder on the Orient Ex-*

press next to the Pera Palas in Istanbul; a history of the Hotel
Danieli in Venice and a slim blue volume containing the correspondence of George Sand and Alfred de Musset. I pushed open the glass
door and the bell signaled my presence to two flamingo legs peeping
out from under a kilt. The two rooms with wine red walls, and especially the third, smaller room, painted in a delicate apricot, gave
off the pleasant aroma of books. The bleached-wood shelves grazed
the paneled ceilings, flanking two large dressmaker's tables in solid
walnut. At the windows, heavy cotton curtains trailed on the floor.
Magazines and illustrated editions peeked out of wicker baskets.
On the walls, black-and-white photographs with captions useful to
those who, like me, had no idea who all these people were: a woman
with long ruffled hair and furious eyes (a certain Colette) throws
grains of rice out the window to the pigeons, alongside the big ruddy
face of Ernest Hemingway, winking at a pinched-faced Harold Pinter.
It was cozy: That's what I liked about your place. It has the look of
an apartment a bit too *Marie Claire Maison*, a tad too feminine, but
inviting. Whoever your decorator is, he's talented. I went upstairs
and walked through the aisle of shelving, where the "Hopeless
Loves" huddled between the "From Here to Eternity" section and
the "Mission Impossibles." In the back, three small tables, two checkered armchairs, beige and burgundy, an old butcher's counter, on
which an ever-meticulous soul had set out thermoses, tea bags, and
instant coffee. I was wandering around the bookshop when I saw
you perched on your stool, a lofty, impregnable post. You held a
small leather-bound book from which a ribbon dangled. Your face
captivated by the pages, the pose of extreme solitude, moved me. I
felt an absurd sense of panic and anxiety. I went back upstairs and
stood aside, hoping I wouldn't be spotted, but the efficient kilted
sentinel approached. "May I help you?" she asked. "I'm looking for a
gift. I'd like the volume . . . in the window. It's for an architect, you
see." Lying is still one of my specialties for getting out of tight spots.
It's no accident that I like bookshops where you can sit on the floor
or on a couch and leaf through magazines without anyone dreaming
of asking you whether you intend to buy, much less asking what you

might want. "Take your time choosing; we're here," she said. "I'll take another look around, thank you." It was you. I couldn't possibly be mistaken. High-waisted trousers, laced-up boots, a white shirt with men's suspenders, earrings, the unmistakable pageboy just above your shoulders, and the look of someone who takes everything seriously. Your bangs covered half your face. Behind your head, a sign in Times New Roman warned: "The only advice you can give someone about reading is not to accept any advice, to follow his own instincts, use his brain, and draw his own conclusions." I could have started with that warning, chosen a book, and approached the cash register to see if you recognized me. I froze. I hesitated, wavered. Go on, I told myself; at worst she'll throw it at you and that'll be the end of it. I wrote down my number, and I'm glad I did. You know the rest. Before leaving, I'll drop off this letter with a proposal. I went online and opened a post office box in New York (now don't hold this technological slip against me). I'd like it if we could write to each other, and this method, though archaic and perhaps inconvenient, seemed to me to be the ideal way to tell each other about ourselves without infringing on your habits. A private space, the only kind open to a mind like yours, adverse to modern communication means. "Mail for your eyes only" is the slogan that an ingenious adman came up with for American post office boxes. The letters will be invisible to anyone else. If you like the idea (I very much hope that you do), write to me at this address:

Federico Virgili, Post Office Box 772, New York, NY 10002.

A transoceanic kiss,

Federico

. ——— .

By opening the post office box, Federico displays an obvious need to talk to someone.

"I have two pieces of news for you. One good and one bad. Which do you want first?" he asked me at the door to my apartment.

"First the bad news," I replied.

"Actually, they're one and the same," he said, teasing affectionately. "It's been more than thirty years."

"So what's the news?"

"It's been more than thirty years, but it's as though not even a single day has passed."

Can it be that he married a woman who doesn't talk? All he told me was that her name is Anna.

The post office on Piazza Cordusio is just minutes from the bookshop. To get there, I have to make my way along a few narrow streets, and the bicycle wheels get jammed in the cobblestones just like my heels do. I hook the chain to a post supporting a blue street sign with a white arrow pointing up toward the sky. Because I don't have a driver's license and am proud of it, street signs mean nothing to me or, better yet, they tell me whatever I want them to. To me, the arrow indicates a heaven above that I like to imagine as blissful, with puffy clouds and an entire corollary describing a democratic paradise. In addition to siblings and parents, there are quite a few people I love there and I like to know that they are in a comfortable place.

The large hall with the yellow sign is awash in neon lighting. Dozens of people are languishing or fretting at the counters, depending on their age and temperament, awaiting their turn. Others are sitting on metal chairs, gripping a ticket number as though they are at the deli counter in the supermarket. Some are leafing through magazines; two young people are making out, indifferent to the reproachful look of an elderly gentleman muffled up in a loden coat, though it isn't cold. It's spring. Six out of every ten customers are talking on a cell phone. The post office is a place you can count on. People come here and stamp envelopes, pay bills, fill out forms, check the computer, pick up their pension checks. I haven't been here in years. I enter a narrow corridor whose walls are entirely lined with metal mailboxes, each marked by a number. The dim light creates a soft amber-colored cast on the metal doors, which I imagine hold forgotten packages, secret exchanges, shady affairs. Inside a glass booth is a girl who looks bored. She sees me and motions me over. *The Shop Around the Corner* comes to mind, stored away during nights spent in front of the TV; who knows if the young lady has ever heard of it.

"I'd like to open a post office box," I say as nonchalantly as I can. Actually, I'm embarrassed, as if I'm doing something illicit. Unaware of the tempest raging in my mind, the young lady looks up from the magazine resting on her knees. "Do you have an ID?"

"Of course I have an ID. Why?"

Aren't they anonymous, these post office boxes?

"You have to fill out the form. Payment in advance. Each box is numbered, has a security lock, and is available in various sizes. Mail is delivered in the morning; you can retrieve it at any time." In a country where the sacrosanct custom of continuous business hours is unable to make headway, this seems like a miracle of distinction. As if reading a letter at any time of the day or night is more urgent than buying a quart of milk, a head of lettuce, or a packet of cigarettes. As if it's the most natural thing in the world (though for her, it really is the most natural thing in the world), the young lady hands me the key to the P.O. box.

When I get to the bookshop, notably late by my usual Swiss-clock standards, Alice is assisting a tiny, plump woman with flagrant carrot-colored hair, who is browsing in the "Loves and Crimes" section.

"Thank goodness you're here, Emma. I was getting worried."

Right, I hadn't warned her that I would be late. Carrottop has made her selection, Richard Mason's *The Drowning People,* the story of an uxoricide craving vendetta. She pays and goes out in a decidedly brighter mood, unaware of the plot that awaits her.

"Are you familiar with *The Shop Around the Corner,* Alice?"

"Never heard of it. Should I have?"

"It's a film by Ernst Lubitsch, I think. James Stewart works as a salesclerk in a kind of gift store, the shop around the corner, and is madly in love with a girl he's never met in person, though he conducts an intense correspondence with her. Margaret Sullavan works at the same shop. The two can't stand each other, not realizing that love has already blossomed between them: She, in fact, is the girl James Stewart has never met and for whom he's fallen head over heels . . . through their letters."

"That's the plot of *You've Got Mail*! Meg Ryan is a bookseller and Tom Hanks is the arrogant owner of a large bookstore chain, much like the ones you would like to see razed! Meg has inherited a small children's bookshop from her mother. The opening of the huge chain store will force her to close down. She vents her feelings in e-mails to an unknown man who falls in love with her. A hymn to virtual communication. You should see it, to convince yourself that the Internet is not the devil."

"You're talking about the remake, Alice. I'm talking about the original."

"Should I get the book?"

"I don't think it was based on a book; it just popped into my head."

"When I go home tonight, I'll do a search on the Internet."

She says it on purpose, not to miss a chance to point out the lack of a computer in the shop. I ignore the provocation and go upstairs to make a cup of coffee, borrowing Ennio Flaiano's *A Woman and a Night* and pondering titles for the one-night-stands display. "The best kind," insists my ex-husband, who considers a second time with a woman too demanding for his temperament.

. ———— .

Milan, April 14, 2001
Dreams & Desires

Dear Federico,
I'm not used to the sound of pen on paper anymore and I'm trying to be light-handed so as not to make any holes or stains that would force me to have to recopy this on a new sheet. I'm not used to try-ing to write neatly anymore.

It could have been a disaster. We could have felt distant, bored; I might have fled. I'm forgetful. You were talking about how we used to be, and I felt like I was listening to a story I'd never heard before. People change; they evolve or they become fossilized: Have you ever run into a classmate you remembered as a great individual, only to find a person of no consequence with whom you have nothing to talk about? Well, that didn't happen to me. It was a lovely evening; you're absolutely right. Even more exciting was receiving your letter and the idea of the post office box.

Since the other night, I've been frustrated by *l'esprit de l'escalier,* an impairment that has plagued me for years. To overcome it, I've started drafting a list of questions to ask you in a future letter. You are free not to respond, but your answers would reassemble the picture and give me a clearer framework in which to place you. One of my favorite authors, A. S. Byatt, wrote that all human beings tell the story of their lives by selection, choosing and reinforcing some memories, relegating others to oblivion, and that they are all interested in fortuitous occurrences. If you've never read one of her novels, I urge you to do so. Start with *Possession.* If you can get through that, you're ready for all the rest. When you get my list, you can answer all the questions, or only half of them, but not less than a third. It would kill me. This is a great idea you had, really. My mailbox is waiting.

Emma

P.S. *L'esprit de l'escalier* strikes when you're at the bottom of the stairs, on your way out the door, and you realize you haven't said all you would have liked to say. They are the moments when you think of the cleverest comebacks, the wittiest remarks, and . . . it's too late to say them.

• ——— •

New York, April 25, 2001
42 W. 10th St.

"Neither snow, nor rain, nor heat, nor gloom of night stays these couriers from the swift completion of their appointed rounds": derived from the words of Herodotus and read this morning on the pediment of the main post office, which has stood between West Thirty-first and West thirty-third streets since 1913. Just think, Emma, I passed it dozens of times and never bothered to notice it. No small oversight for an architect. The building was designed by Charles Follen McKim, William Rutherford Mead, and Stanford White, names that probably don't mean anything to you but that are legendary to us. William Mitchell Kendall, a colleague in their firm, chose that inscription, drawing upon Herodotus's *Histories*, in which the historian described the Greeks' expedition against the Persians during the reign of Xerxes, around 500 B.C. It was the Greeks who devised a system of postal couriers, precursors of modern-day mailmen.

In line at the airport check-in counter, I wondered how you would react to my proposal. Ahead of me were a smiling, distinguished-looking couple, parents with a set of twins who wore different-color braces on their teeth (a way to tell them apart?), and a pretty young woman, a little too skeletal. *A model*, I thought as I boarded, relieved by my daughter's passion for the natural sciences. I hadn't slept for twenty-four hours. I let the stewardess lead me to my seat, and as the lady in the blue-and-green uniform offered me the fresh glass of orange juice provided to first-class passengers, I gave thanks for Alitalia's frequent-flier points and Row A, at the front of the aircraft. I gazed at the runway through the little window and fell asleep, waking up at JFK. I was relieved to see Anna appear and disappear behind the customs window, hugging Sarah in a way that I've always considered a confirmation of my good fortune. My women were there and all was as it should be. Two weeks have passed. Entering the main post office was like landing on a movie set. I handed my passport to the clerk who gave me a burnished metal key that costs thirty-seven dollars per year.

"Get your mail conveniently with a P.O. box." I felt like a schoolboy on the first day of class, when the kids mingle in the school yard and the teacher is the only loving face in a jungle of strangers; so I followed a lady with braided gray hair, heading for her own mailbox, as if she were a long-lost relative. "They're in numerical order; number seven seventy-two is back there," she said as she retrieved her packet of mail. And here I thought my idea was original! In the U.S., people move around continuously, not like us Italians, who are born and die in the same apartment, and a lot of people have a post office box. I am a novice, milady. I turned around and she was gone.

My first time. A little bit like your first notebook, the first design for a client in a graphic arts studio during the Poligrafico awards, your first trip on your own, your first, and only, daughter. I put the key in the lock and, before turning it, stared at the matte brass box with the same eagerness I would have felt stumbling upon a large seashell hidden in the sand. In it—so they told me when I was a child (and I believed it!)—was the pearl that would make me a rich man. I opened the box. The pale blue Smythson of Bond Street envelope was right in front of my nose. I tucked it safely away in my jacket, climbed on the Vespa, and felt like Gregory Peck, while you, my invisible Audrey, tightened your arms around your prince's waist. I drove around Manhattan as excited as an idiotic kid; the manhole covers looked like medallions set in the cement and the patrician residences along Madison Avenue seemed like abbesses ready for evening vespers. The envelope stayed in my pocket until the afternoon. I always put things off when I have to face something important. What if you had told me to leave you alone, so long and good-bye, it's been nice remembering the good times, and so on? From John's mailbox—that's Renzo's friend, who rented us the apartment from which I'm writing to you—I retrieve his bills, his parking tickets, his credit card statements, the Italian magazine *Abitare*, tons of advertisements and other depressing scraps of paper. The rest, everything else, comes by e-mail. Everything except you. Your technophobia was the blessing that led me to this archaic means of communication, which goes into the yawning blue metal

mouth of the U.S. Postal Service. I'm enclosing a photo of my fiftieth birthday party. As you can see, I look quite content.

I await your list of questions.

Federico

P.S. How long has it been since the last time I mailed a letter?

• ——— •

The dogged indifference I display toward my past is a defensive strategy. Thanks to Federico, heaps of cravenly neglected detritus from a
childhood I recall nothing of and from an adolescence hazardous as
all adolescences are may become an opportunity. Or a trap? I'm reading his letter while curled up among the sofa cushions. On the table,
on top of the piles of books and magazines, I placed two photographs:
the one from the class trip, narrow and vertical, with a reddish tone,
and, next to it, a horizontal shot of his fiftieth birthday party taken by
his older sister. He added a caption, printed in capital letters: IN
WHAT SENSE DO MY LIPS LOOK THINNER? The gap separating
males from females is not ideological; it is quite simply cosmetic. I
must have offended him, underestimating his vanity as well as the
inability of males to grasp innocent jokes. A woman knows perfectly
well that over the years her lips shrink. Men don't. In those early days,
each birthday was a victorious step toward emancipation. Nowadays,
we tend to camouflage the calendar numbers, much like we do other
innocent obsessions. I look closely at the nineteen-year-old with the
full lips. His body radiates indestructible enthusiasm. I barely come to
his shoulder; Federico forms a V with his index and middle fingers.
To his right stand Gabriella and Renata, a classmate with long auburn
hair, and three young men with shoulder-length curls and Cavour-
style goatees. We were attractive, with tanned skin and restless eyes. If
those kids had looked into the future, what would they have seen?

His fiftieth birthday party, in the other photo, is an elaborate affair: Federico is standing in the center of a cascade of yellow and red
flowers, blowing out the candles on a three-tiered wedding-style
cake. To his right, two blondes look at him devotedly, a blend of grace

and pride. The adult has thin lines around her eyes, too much blush on her cheeks, and a hooded gaze. The younger one resembles him, slight, ethereal, fair. Federico married a respectable woman; his is a unified, happy family. And yet, it's as if his lips have surrendered something. I pick up the mirror, holding the photo with the other me in my left hand. I can't say I'm beautiful—too short, breasts that barely fill an A cup, slender wrists, and hair discolored by sand and salt. Impossible to retrieve the thoughts that lie behind those eyes. Those, too, forgotten. Audrey Hepburn and Gregory Peck: I like the comparison; I seem to have passed the exam between past and present, though more and more often it happens that I don't recognize people I meet who may greet me warmly. They ask me personal questions; they mention Michele and Mattia, so they know me. I can't seem to bring their identities into focus; I probably seem like a sorry fool, like that time at Gabriella's wedding-anniversary party. "Maybe we, too, have the same effect on others," I told her when I mistook her brother's former girlfriend for an aunt. "Of course if a woman stops dyeing her hair, she's asking for it," I said, justifying myself, as she dug her fingers into my forearm. I know that in a month there will be other things I won't remember, other faces, other stories I've been told. I erase them. I forget news I hear, good and bad; I even forget things it would be nice to remember. My memory works intermittently: it's sharp when it comes to something relevant or recent. After reading a book, I'm able to remember the page containing a certain phrase or passage, sometimes even a single word that struck me, for about a week. Then little by little all the images and feelings arising from the reading fade and eventually disappear. It's a real problem for a bookseller, even though the customers oblige me to review vigorously. Attorney Pedrini, a civil lawyer in the Milan Tribunal, who stops by the shop once a week, has adopted the method of memorizing lines of poetry. He knows two to three thousand verses and recites them in the morning for at least ten minutes straight, every day of the week, just to keep in form. In my previous job, I did simultaneous interpretation from Italian to French and English, listening and manipulating sentences, words, and concepts. I

had a vocabulary that would make a puzzle enthusiast envious. In
my new life, now, in front of this mirror, I recognize that girl. For
today, that's enough. Raking up the past is not my forte.

. ——— .

Milan, May 1, 2001
Via Londonio 8

Dear Federico,
The list of questions was too long, so I trimmed them down to two.
For a long-winded type like me, it's an effort I hope you will appreciate: What were we like? What did we do? You see, I live with a kind
of anesthetized amnesia. Stored away in my brain and in a part of my
heart is a host of phrases, visions, fragments that I've never wanted
to recompose; a mutilated archive of weeks and months that have
been swallowed into a void. I've tried to focus and collect the images
that have to do with you, like picture cards. Noted here in random
order:
    Final year, homeroom B, at Alessandro Volta high school.
    Me: an orange sweater (horrible, I'd say), short at the waist, with
yellow and apple green horizontal stripes.
    You: a blue polo shirt, moleskin blue pants, a very soft pullover.
    A Ciao bicycle that gets jammed in the tram rails.
    Skinned knees and the embarrassment of entering the class-
room: There was a Latin translation exercise that day, and I didn't
have time to repair the damages (as you can see, I recall the details
but not the general context).
    A gray Vespa. Yours.
    A linoleum corridor scuffed by sneakers.
    Long hair. Both of us.
    The poolroom in the bar on via Lecco (what was it called?) where
you played with Enrico and the others; with the cue in your hand,
your face focused on the little colored ball, you looked like a cowboy.
    Playing darts on the terrace at your house: I never once managed
to hit the bull's-eye.

Soccer tournaments between fifth-year homerooms A and B: I sat on the sidelines, knowing very little about rules and plays, aside from the fact that whoever got the ball in the box the most times won. In an impromptu referendum among us girls, you were voted as having the best legs on the team.

Rock. In my next letter, I'll include a list of songs that I still can't part with, even today.

That's all for now. I'll stamp this and go and mail it.

Emma

. ——— .

New York, May 8, 2001
42 W. 10th St.

Dear Emma,

It's three in the morning and I can't get to sleep. There's a deli down the street, so I went out to get a container of milk. I've become friendly with the clerk and stop to chat with her when I don't feel like going straight home after work, or in the middle of the night, like now. She's always there. You have no idea how many people here work for six dollars an hour, for as many as eighty hours a week, day and night—it makes no difference, since almost everything here is open twenty-four hours a day. The cashier at my deli fled from Nicaragua where the Sandinistas slaughtered her family. I'm drinking a glass of warm milk while writing to you. You ask what we were like, and it seems incredible to me that you've erased the most important months of your education—namely, those spent with me (I'm kidding, though not really). My life was relatively simple: soccer, music, and architecture (not necessarily in that order) in a classic country family, the first generation to become "industrialized," with an absent father who was wrapped up in the cult of money and work: a man we saw a lot of in the summer, when he demanded my presence at the seaside house for at least a month. My mother (do you remember her at least?) died in 1971. From that day on, the trouble started. My father became even more withdrawn. He worked longer hours (I never saw him), worrying a lot about my academic performance and only a little about my frame of mind; he didn't understand that I would make it just the same. You were a break with the world in which I grew up; you were different from all the others, and from what little I've sensed, you still are. I have an interior library that concerns only you, where I can retrieve quite a bit.

How did I capture you (today our kids would say "score")? I saw you lying facedown on the hall table during the break, while I was showing off with a guitar, causing a certain sensation, at least among the girls. I asked you something—I don't remember what—you glanced up from your book (presentiment?) and looked at me as if I had interrupted some kind of masterpiece. Those dark beacons of yours bored into me, making me feel like a pain in the ass. It took me several weeks to break through your defense, but eventually you fell into my arms. Allow me the illusion of being the conqueror, remember it that way. Other postcards from a love story: a night trip to Venice, returning in the wee hours of the morning. I had just gotten my license and swiped the car from my father. I felt like a cool and crazy guy, and buying you a cappuccino at the kiosk in the parking lot of Piazza Roma seemed really romantic to me. Occupying the school of architecture, where we landed as high school greenhorns, wet behind the ears. Lightning must have struck in those classrooms, where the students seemed much more mature than we did. A class trip to Calabria. I think it's the one in the photograph. A folk concert. Someone's eighteenth birthday: You have a toothache; my friend Daniele "bewitches" you; I suffer like crazy with jealousy, though I don't hold that inconsiderate act of insensitivity against that girl you were.

Write to me,

Federico

P.S. Not out of vanity, but I was wondering what effect seeing each other again had on you.

· ——— ·

One of the merits of the bookshop is that it has released me from a guilt complex: that of not remembering all the books I've read. I have forgotten entire plots, beginnings and endings, and I now have an excuse to reread some of those novels, just as if it were the first time. The customers suggest titles and prompt me to this endless pursuit. Today, Mr. Bianchi came into the store, asking for a copy of Guy de Maupassant's love stories to give to his wife's friend, who invited them to dinner. I didn't even remember that this collection of seventy-five love stories—seventy-five, no less!—by one of literature's most tireless seducers existed. Alice found it on the "Latitudes of Love" shelf. She started in again with her litany of the absolute need to enter the books into an electronic database. I cut her off, went out to have a cappuccino, and started writing under the barista's gaze; he must have wondered why I was sitting there when the entire bookshop was available.

. ——— .

Milano, May 19, 2001
Bar Tabacchi,
Piazza Sant'Alessandro

Dear Federico,
I'm reeling. What you've written to me is a roller coaster of revelations. I don't remember the night with you in Venice, but the occupation of the school is impossible to forget. My father was furious; it was the first time I had slept out, and he was convinced that I must have lost my virginity in wild sex orgies with strangers. He died in 1976, from a bone tumor. I don't know much about his illness; my mother was reluctant to speak of it, as if it were something that primarily concerned her. She was madly in love with him and outlived him by ten years. We have that in common: parents who loved each other. I have a vague memory of the class trip to Calabria (the one in the photo). Cute, that story about the hall. I like to think I fell in love with you and novels at that moment, though I

had been obsessed with books since I was a child, when I would imagine the writers (always male—who knows why?) as I chewed my pen or frantically scribbled words on a pad resting on my knees. What has always fascinated me, more so than paintings or sculptures (which Gabriella has devoted her life to—she teaches art history in our old high school) is the nonmateriality of the word, which does not come from a tube of tempera or kneaded clay, nor from designs that are transformed into bridges—I don't think I'm offending your sensibilities by saying this. A word is intangible, yet in my eyes it is more powerful than any physical act. It sprouts from an idea, a thought, from any observation of nature or a street, a building, a face; it materializes from a slap or an embrace and—bam!—it can change your world. Or at least your view of it. Despite the fact that Virginia Woolf explained "how very little natural gift words have for being useful," I can't do without them.

What effect did seeing each other again have on me? The dominant feeling was curiosity; I wanted to see what kind of man you had become. I found you still good-looking (that is, I didn't experience a shock; you haven't turned into a monster, though there was a real risk that it might have happened to both of us, let's face it), and the true surprise was feeling that I knew you even though I didn't remember the particulars that had to do with us. It was like you were someone new, yet I felt an intimacy between us that eliminated the temptation to defend or protect myself, to pretend, as I often do. I was at ease and then some: I trusted you. Back home, I deluded myself into thinking (don't laugh, please) that our two souls had remained on good terms for years while we did other things, and that for some strange reason, once they saw each other again (the souls), they . . . recognized each other. When you left, I needed more time; I'm slow. I wanted to figure out if you were pie in the sky, leaving aside the soap-opera aspect of two people seeing each other again after so many years, etc., etc. Your letter came, and now here I am continuing our conversation.

That's all for now,

Emma

P.S. I am dismayed about that Daniele. Who was he and how did I manage to get lured away from you? I await details on my regrettable behavior.

. ——— .

It's Saturday night; Mattia must have a date. He's been going in and out of the bathroom for more than half an hour. First his shirt is hanging out of his pants; then he puts on a dark shirt, disappears, and reappears with a white one, more fitted, and a narrow tie. Love, and the insecurity it brings, is the same at any age. It's only fair.

"Do you need some advice, darling?"

"I can't make up my mind, Mom. Do I look more trendy with the shirt or with the sweatshirt?"

"Wear them both, layered. You can always take off the sweatshirt," I reply, distracted by the letter from Federico that's waiting in my purse. I haven't read it yet. It's long, and I want to enjoy it in peace, when Mattia decamps.

"Forget it, Mom. A shirt and a sweatshirt don't have jackshit to do with each other. But do you have ten bucks?"

. ——— .

New York, June 7, 2001
University Café

Dear Emma,

I'm sitting at a table in the café adjacent to Beyer Blinder Belle, the studio where I've been working with a group of extraordinary colleagues. I hit it off with them at our first meeting months ago, when the boss presented the plan for the restoration and expansion of the Morgan Library. Beyer Blinder Belle Architects & Planners LLP, established in 1968 (a prophetic date, not only for us Europeans), designs architecture for people and preaches coherence between buildings and individuals. Predictable, you might say, but not everyone views architecture that way. The area to the right of the lobby, where we found some space for our group, is dominated by awards, framed scrolls, and designs for projects built throughout the United States, along with bipartisan praise signed on two different occasions by Bill Clinton and George W. Along the walls enclosing the studio space are pasteboard models that reflect integration between past and present: the Ellis Island Immigration Museum and the South Street Seaport Museum here in New York, the Muhammad Ali Center in Louisville, Kentucky, the Montclair Art Museum in New Jersey, the Red Star Line Museum of Migration (the European version of Ellis Island), and many others. There are 170 architects working at BBB, all of them convinced that people need places where they can gather, be together, and be uplifted. My office mate, Frank Prial, Jr., is a very likable man, crazy about his two children, his wife, and our project. His passion is historic buildings, which he rescues with the fervor of a Red Cross nurse, adamant about preserving the past and giving it new life and new functions. You can imagine how in tune we are about the expansion project for the Morgan, that repository of one of the most valuable collections of manuscripts, books, musical scores, and art in the world. It's the first assignment I've been put in charge of. The Morgan Library project was awarded to us a year ago. I was in Venice with Renzo; on the vaporetto that was taking us to the station, he looked at me dreamily and asked me if I remembered the proposal. "Well, they called again, asking us to do it," he said. The project had been granted to the Renzo Piano Building Workshop by a unanimous vote. Piano's idea is to connect the existing buildings and at the same time increase the library's space by half its original capacity by eliminating nonessentials. The important thing was to agree on what was nonessential, given that the Morgan has already undergone several transformations: It was expanded in 1928 with an insignificant, classic-style annex and connected to the brownstone mansion of John Pierpont Morgan's son, Jack, by a dark glass passageway. They asked us to reconceptualize it and expand its cubic space, but a skyscraper would have ruined the harmony of that graceful corner of Madison Avenue. What to do? "When you can't go up, you go down," suggested Renzo, who has a gift for simplifying complex matters and not complicating simple things; "the essence of the project is not to expand, but to reequilibrate and reconceptualize the institution." If I were not a heterosexual male, I would have fallen in love with him. In fact, I've loved him since he interviewed me, in Genoa, when I was still an undergraduate, offering me my first real job and the chance to escape. For this project, he promoted me to partner in charge for RPBW, and the only one who wasn't happy about it was Sarah. She had just finished middle school when she heard the news that we would be leaving Paris ("It's not forever, sweetheart; in a few years, we'll come back home," I said, trying to reassure her). Instead of congratulating me, she sulked for weeks. Can you blame her? What did she care about the promotion and New York? "All my classmates are enrolling at Richelieu; in New York, I won't know anyone. You can't force me to change my life," she whimpered, making me feel like a careerist asshole. Naturally, she didn't have the slightest idea who Cardinal Richelieu was; I was uprooting her from protective defenses developed in past years to offset the paralyzing crises of a shy, introverted temperament, for which I feel a good 60 percent responsible (the rest, I attribute to fate). Throughout the first semester here in Manhattan, she looked at me as if I were a monster who had shattered her adolescence, but then Ricki came to my aid: a colleague's fifteen-year-old son, who took her dejection seriously to heart. They became inseparable; I just hope (I'm extremely jealous) that the acned adolescent doesn't try to go beyond a great, possessive friendship. I've rambled on at length describing the places in my life. Which for an architect are everything.

Till next time, my dear book lady,

Federico

. ——— .

On October 12, 2000, 508 years after the discovery of America, I raised the curtain on my own new continent. The night before, I ran the vacuum cleaner into the most out-of-the-way corners (needlessly, since the parquet floor was shiny as a billiard ball), stacked the books in piles according to love category, cleaned the windows with alcohol and newspaper, polished knobs and handles. At two in the morning, I headed home through a rather chilly Milan with the firm intention of going to sleep, but despite the drops, I lay awake with a choking anxiety. That feeling of plasterboard around my sternum had returned and I couldn't even turn to Gabriella for help, since she had been thoughtless enough to leave for Avignon just then for a conference on medieval art. Pride kept me from phoning Alberto in the middle of the night, and Mattia was sleeping at his father's house. I was alone with my nightmares.

The solution, as always, was the bathtub. As in the best films and dozens of novels, the liturgy of a relaxing bath has its rules. Sitting on the edge of the tub, her gaze turned inward as she thinks about the only man who has made her happy for a moment, a day, a week, or a good part of her life, she turns on the tap and, when the water reaches the rim, sinks into the foamy bubbles. Amid the warmth and steamy tiles, the vanilla-scented candles, two chamomile cotton pads on her eyelids, she imagines him. Raise your hand if you've never seen such a scene at the movies. That's just what I did, but I was so tired that I fell asleep: The candle wax melted into tiny sculptures; the cotton eye pads shriveled up like dried leaves. I awoke with a start. The water was cold and I felt like letting myself die there, swept away down the drain. I crept between the sheets in my bathrobe and collapsed. A few hours later, I put on my bookseller clothes, a vintage sheath dress in aubergine mohair, laced shoes with three-inch stiletto heels (a gift from Michele, who remains one of the few who know my taste in shoes), Bakelite earrings, light makeup. After a quick stop at the hairdresser, I introduced myself to my neighbors. There aren't many of them, in Piazza Sant'Alessandro, but they all said they were excited about the shop (The only puzzled comment was, "Nothing but romance novels? Only women will come. Men don't like to talk about love.") and had been fond of Aunt Linda. The ruddy, nonsmoking tobacconist, who sells cigarettes with a hint of disapproval on his face; the antiques dealer, who spends his days among the furnishings and odds and ends displayed with erratic disorder in a double storefront; the café owner, to whom I explained that I like my cappuccino without foam; the dry cleaner, Luisa; and the butcher on the corner. I invited Emily, the porter, to have a look around my shelves and rolled up the first shutter of my life. The anxiety did not go away. I paced. I rearranged the stacks. I checked the phone for a dial tone. *You never know*, I thought, figuring someone might call to ask about a title, since I had distributed business cards throughout the neighborhood, including checkout counters at the FNAC electronics store two hundred steps away (I counted them). The doorbell was working. At eleven o'clock, I turned to my magnificent merchandise and embraced the realization of a dream, despite the horde of dissuaders and thanks to a generous backer, who had promised to stop by before evening. To ward off bad luck, I had not planned an opening reception. I had to make it on my own and confront the market squarely. I had made a pact with myself: If that first day turned out to be a fiasco, I would do at least five things that I hated. Since there are many more than five that I detest, I was forced to choose. If no one came in during the first hour, I would go shopping at the supermarket and carry home a six-pack of one-and-a-half-liter bottles of water; if the second hour passed, no bike riding on the sidewalk for a week; after three hours, I would give up the hairdresser for two weeks. Then came more demanding vows and acts of mortification: I would quit smoking for a month; step only on the even tiles; make three odious phone calls a day for one week; jog for half an hour every morning (which for someone who practices gentle yoga is an affront to good sense); go to the bank and avoid arguing with the teller; not get irritated at the inefficiency of any salesperson in any store; read standing up while crushed on the tram; drink an entire glass of wine in just one gulp; not comment on the piles of clothes—jeans, sweatshirts and boxer shorts—Mattia leaves on the floor like sculptures, or the ashtrays overflowing with butts.

One hour and seven minutes after eleven, she walked in. My

first customer. The first in my entire life. She was wearing flat purple elfin boots, pants with roomy pockets on the thighs, and a hip-hugging maroon velvet jacket; her hair was layered over her shoulders, and she had ample breasts (judging by eye, a bountiful D cup), fair skin, and light eyes. Speechless with joy, I left her to herself. As she trailed her fingertips over the stacks of books, her eyes eager, she gave a squeal of congratulations and euphoric excitement.

"How chaaarming," she shrieked, unaware of having instantly banished the pain in my back, achy from cleaning and carrying. "Is it true you sell only romance novels? How insane! And you do gift wrapping, too? You're a genius!"

Really.

"I can't stand those stores that put books in plastic bags—you know, the ones with the logo printed on them—as if they were bagging panty hose! Even when I buy one for myself, I want the book wrapped and tied with a ribbon."

Gushing effusively, she said: "I want." And I, who thought that I had freed myself forever from bosses, realized that my new bosses would be them: the readers. Fine. I would turn them into accomplices, maybe even friends, I thought, with a beginner's delusion of omnipotence.

"I work in the building across the way. I have a degree in statistics. For now, I'm doing market research for a thousand euros per month," she informed me. Concise, but attentive to detail.

"You can come here to get away from your numbers," I replied, overcoming the timidity that kept me hooked to the counter.

This first customer of mine, a truffle dog whose name was Cecilia, cheered me with the purchase of three titles: *Be My Knife*, by David Grossman; *The Love Letter*, by Cathleen Schine; and *Paper Kisses*, by Reinhard Kaiser. Naturally, she insisted on three gift wraps. I got busy, certain that the books were for personal use and that she would unwrap them that very evening. Since that day, Cecilia has dropped into the shop regularly. She sniffs around, leafs through the pages. Her requests for information are interrogations, in fact, since she's wary of bestsellers and advertisements; she doesn't trust hyperbole, exaggerations, celebrity blurbs (usually by writers and friends of writers) that scream "masterpiece" and "highly anticipated novel." She chooses books with that special instinct of a smart reader who isn't fooled by cover flaps, who reads the opening lines, then turns to any page at random and makes her ruling with confidence. In short, she either falls in love at first sight or puts the volume back with no regrets. She generally bursts into the shop during her lunch break, or toward six o'clock, even just to say hello or have some tea. We talk about books and about her mercurial boyfriends. Despite the generation gap, her neuroses as a reader coincide with mine, whereas Alice, who is her contemporary, considers her a bit excessive.

I, of course, adore her.

· ——— ·

New York, June 21, 2001
Barnes & Noble, Union Square

Dear Emma,

Compared to you, I don't know the first thing about novels, and so am reluctant to tackle them. To overcome the sense of inferiority you've sparked in me, today I bought a hefty (798-page) biography of John Pierpont Morgan, the man to whom I indirectly owe my American sojourn. J.P.M. is my employer: It's thanks to his insight that I'm here, and the least I can do is read up on his life. Aside from reading about the lives of architects, I hadn't opened a biography since time immemorial. The Barnes & Noble bookstore on Union Square has become one of my favorite haunts, spread out over four floors, with a large area for DVDs and a teen section, where I look for books for Sarah. You're the only bookseller I know personally (not that I know any others) who welcomes even those who don't buy anything to have a cup of coffee. I'm sitting at a dark-wood table in the second-floor café, where the floor is tiled in black and white. I got a raisin scone and a large coffee; I have a free hour and I'm taking it easy. On the wall in front of me, a parade of authors, not very well painted, in bright colors: George Orwell; Vladimir Nabokov; James Joyce; Mary Shelley; Rudyard Kipling; George Eliot; Henry James, very elegant in a white shirt and tails; to his right, all but reclining, Oscar Wilde in his dressing gown, with a lily in a glass; Mark Twain, looking pensive, with his thumb and forefinger under his chin; George Bernard Shaw; and, last of all, intent on having her portrait painted, the reclusive poet Emily Dickinson. Only three women, which says a lot about their importance in the mind of the dilettante who painted them. At the tables, everyone is reading; or rather, everyone has a book or magazine in front of them. And they all appear to be on the first pages—so untouched, you'd think they were blank. A few people are writing, some studying, others typing on laptops. The percentages will cheer you: four computers in use; for the rest, paper. You'd be pleased with this crowd of fellow readers. I sip the boiling hot swill from the paper cup, despite the fact that the calendar announces the first day of summer. I'm on the first pages of the engrossing human story of an extraordinary man. I'll summarize. Noteworthy ancestors: James Pierpont, one of the founders of Yale University, and the Reverend John Pierpont, abolitionist and poet. J.P.M. was born in 1837 in Hartford, Connecticut, at a time when the United States was breathing a "thin aesthetic air" (in the biographer's words): Anyone who wanted to devote himself to the study of art or architecture had to look to older Europe. Precocious in his passion for paper, at age fourteen he ordered several covers of a special edition of the *Illustrated London News* and advised his cousin Jim to do the same because, he wrote, they were "so much handsomer" than the ordinary issues. His father wrote him letters from England, giving him boring history lessons. Just think, after visiting the tomb of the duke of Wellington, he did not fail to remind his son that the man had "conquered Napoléon at Waterloo." Imagine if we wrote to our kids, telling them about our discoveries as travelers; they would commiserate with us and groan, "What a drag." The tome relates that J.P.M.'s health was never particularly robust: During childhood, he was stricken with rheumatism and his family sent him to the Azores. Joined by his parents, he did a grand tour in Britain, Germany, Belgium, and France, during which he recorded everything: the people he met, the shows he saw, the museums he visited, the admission fee at the Palace of Versailles and Napoléon's tomb, visits to the Gobelins tapestry factory, the École nationale supérieure des Beaux-Arts, and the Louvre. (Sarah doesn't even take notes at school. "There's no need to," she says; "I can find everything on the Internet.") It is likely that J.P.M.'s passion for collecting art was born during those youthful trips, though buying history was a common-enough pastime among nineteenth- and twentieth-century American billionaires. Morgan wasn't the most enlightened among them, nor the most cultured, but certainly the most brilliant. Often he would say, "If you have to ask, you can't afford it." J.P.M. was a philanthropist, and you are my Pygmalion: If I hadn't met the prettiest bookseller in Milan, I would have been reading the newspaper today. My free time is almost over. Ciao for now. Write to me,

Federico

• ——— •

Milan, July 9, 2001
Dreams & Desires

Dear Federico,
I'm familiar with Barnes & Noble—I remember one around Astor Place, I think—although their bookstores are too modern for my taste. In New York, I prefer the Strand, on Broadway, a homier place for volumes that are used but not yet defunct; I saw it for the first time eons ago, when I spent an unforgettable vacation there with Gabriella, Alberto, and Michele. The first thing I look for in any city I happen to be in are bookstores. The malady is not something new. Even as a young girl, I would chat with the clerks; in some unconscious way, I envied them, convinced that they stood behind the counter all day, reading for free. Actually, I've discovered that there

isn't much slack time in bookstores: Between dusting and putting the books in order, tidying up the display sections or arranging new ones, I'm never idle for one moment. At one time, I used to take photos of bookstores, like a Japanese tourist; your letter reminded me of it. Simplifying what was an elaborate adjustment (of schedules, routines, even clothing), I would say that the trip to Lapland transformed an innocent youthful obsession into an occupation. In your next letter, tell me about the Morgan. Although I consider myself a conscientious traveler, I've never been in it, which makes me a dilettante as a bookseller.

Emma

P.S. I don't remember our first kiss. You?

• ——— •

Every little change in the bookshop is a subject of discussion. It feels like being back in the seventies, when assembly was the most common form of confrontation. In school, at home, at demonstrations, at get-togethers with friends, and in the apartment-building garages, which were home to our first home-grown rock bands, everything was challenged just for the sake of argument. But the assemblies of those years were pleasant parlor conversations compared to the contention that has been going on for a week in these humid climes. Milan is being suffocated by a pall of gritty heat, which notably reduces my ability to put up with conversations that cross the threshold of pure conviviality. I would much rather hold forth on the difference between a Coca-Cola with ice cubes and a mint granita, between fresh-squeezed orange juice or a nice glass of sparkling water. Anything else, at these temperatures, is intellectually challenging. The subject on which we cannot agree is air conditioning. Alice insists on the benefit (to the customers) of installing at least one unit. Poring over brochures, she lists the special offers, compares costs and models, and repeats desperately that "if we don't hurry up, supplies will run out." The Faithful Enemy does not agree, and he has countered my assistant's most recent plea by stating, "We don't have the money."

"At most, I'll allow you some ceiling fans. They'd go well with the bookshop's decor, they have a romantic air, and they're inexpensive," he ruled.

A film of sawdust formed like talcum powder on the counters, though I had implored the installers to take care and had protected the books with plastic sheeting. I run the vacuum through; it's half past eight and I have to admit that the Faithful Enemy was right: These metal paddles overhead are noisy, but they cool things off. I'm waiting for Alice, who will bring up the second theme that during the week danced a minuet with the need for air conditioning: book lists. We are in partial disagreement on those, as well: While drafting book lists is pure entertainment for me, Alice takes them terribly seriously. I compile lists of titles read, or reread, those I would like customers to read or those they themselves have recommended. They have free access to the chalkboard and can criticize, review, or leave comments. She says we should take "a broader, more objective view" and not overly personalize the selection of novels that are listed. The Faithful Enemy couldn't care less, though he argues that the chalkboard takes up space and should be replaced with a magnetic bulletin board.

This is a bookshop based on participatory democracy.

Those two don't understand that the lists soothe anxiety like a game of Trivial Pursuit, Monopoly, or rummy, innocent table games perfect for those who have no desire to study the instruction manual as if it were a quantum-physics text. I can't play poker or checkers and I've never even attempted chess, all those clever, intellectual games. Being neither clever nor intellectual, though I can claim several wins at gin rummy, I use the lists as antidotes to boredom. The discussion with Alice usually begins quietly on Monday. The intention is to have the list compiled by Saturday, writing it on a sheet of paper first, then copying it in chalk on the blackboard that I bought at an elementary school auction. Today is Thursday and we're still at a stalemate. My list is supposed to be of "best-selling romances," though in reality I include whatever I want. She's insisting on "beach reads."

"It's only a few days until we close for the month of August, and novels to take to the beach are primarily what's selling," she begins, turning up her nose like a know-it-all.

"And what about those who go to the mountains? And customers in the hills, at the lake, on a boat, in a foreign city—aren't they entitled to a novel? I'd like to know what constitutes a 'beach read.' "

I could compile lists for those who spend their vacation in Paris (Balzac, Zola, Maupassant, Proust). Or, let's say, in Prague, in which case I would include Kafka. He never wrote romantic novels, but I can't ignore him when I think of the bleakness of his heart. And there's Kundera—*Ignorance, The Farewell Waltz, The Unbearable Lightness of Being.* While Croatia, which is very popular as a vacation destination, poses a problem. Too niche, Alberto would object, though he doesn't stick his nose in when it comes to the lists, since they don't cost anything. I can't stand arguing with my pigheaded assistant, although our discussions can't actually be considered quarreling. More like bickering, skirmishes. The generation gap between us in these situations is almost physically noticeable: She wears me down by taking advantage of her mental stamina and my inability to stomach conflicts, including those with a vaguely intellectual flavor. I wait her out, impatiently. By noon, I would like to find a middle ground between pine trees and beach umbrellas, between London and Prague and those well-heeled yachtsmen—sporadic readers but big spenders. Sailing with skipper and mate in tow, the wives or girlfriends always embark with a good supply of books and, at the end of the cruise, abandon them in pitiful condition, their pages curled up from the salt air. In fact, for boat excursions, I recommend paperbacks, which can be left behind without too many regrets. I would also include books for those who don't go on vacation at all—serious readers, who can't imagine a vacation away from books.

This is what we ended up with:

Romance Novels of the Week

1. E. M. Forster, *Howard's End* (twenty-five copies—thanks to a high school teacher who assigned it to her third-year students as vacation reading).

2. Dino Buzzati, *A Love Affair* (for those who remain in Milan for the entire month of August).

3. Emily Brontë, *Wuthering Heights* (even though Heathcliff is a little too vindictive for my tastes).

4. Charlotte Brontë, *Jane Eyre* (equal opportunity—*her*, I like).

5. Marc Levy, *If Only It Were True* (you have to have a good-looking author).

6. Nadia Fusini, *L'Amor vile* (the story of a deserter in love, punished at the end of his life by a certain Lavinia).

7. Jeanne Ray, *Julie and Romeo* (a beach read—the Capulets and the Montagues have respectively become the Cacciamanis and the Rosemans, rival florists in Boston).

8. William Shakespeare, *Romeo and Juliet* (to counterbalance the preceding one).

9. Louisa May Alcott, *Little Women* (I always include this one).

10. Luis Sepúlveda, *The Old Man Who Read Love Stories* (I haven't read it, but I included it for its title; according to a personal survey, male customers often trust male rather than female authors).

· ——— ·

New York, July 17, 2001
BBB, 41 E. 11th St.

Dear Emma,

You never forget the first kiss? True. I documented it in an essay I found in the "Health" section (chock-full) at the Strand, which you wrote me about, the eighteen miles of books on Broadway. I only leafed through the book, ashamed of bringing home a manual that would make anyone suspicious. The author, whose name I didn't write down, is a neurologist at some American university. He maintains that the first kiss remains locked away in a corner of our brain, along with dozens of other unforgettable firsts. You should be able to find it among the cells of your nervous system. According to Dr. whatshisname, you too commit things to memory, because the brain—everyone's, including yours—creates connections between neurons that allow us to remember today what we did yesterday, a week ago, or many years ago. Memories remain engraved there for a lifetime. Noted in my Moleskine: "Remembering an event means reactivating a group of neurons that are associated with the sounds, smells, images of a particular moment." I reactivated mine and found you there, along with the first kiss, or, more precisely, the instant that preceded it, when "the DNA of the neurons in the hippocampus, the area of the brain that records the memorization process, becomes aware that something out of the ordinary is about to happen and instructs its cells to store that memory among the other jewels in the strongbox." The history of every individual, in short, is imprinted in his DNA, an emotional map that is searchable. Here's ours: Late afternoon, drizzling, you were sitting on the low wall in front of the school entrance, your legs dangling. The situation wasn't the most favorable; the rain didn't help, but you didn't care. I had my arms around your waist. My lips drew close to yours. You did not pull back. I don't remember exactly what time it was, but the joy of that silent (and never-ending) Kiss . . . *that* I do remember. How can you have forgotten all this? I don't know if I'll be able to forgive you. I'll have to think about it.

Federico

P.S. Tonight, after supper, Sarah was curled up next to me on the couch as I was reading the paper. I looked at her and asked her point-blank if she had already kissed a boy. She replied with a question: "Dad, are you out of your mind?"

• ——— •

Milan, July 24, 2001
Dreams & Desires

"What did you forget today? A decisive date, that bill payment, an important phone number, a client's name, the pages you studied a few days ago?" Alice printed this ad for me, which she received at her e-mail address (at home). At first I thought she was teasing me; then I realized that it was real. Federico, they actually sell courses that teach you how to remember your wedding anniversary, a friend's birthday, pages from a book you've read. And all for a mere 225 euros. An astronomical sum, the cost of at least fifteen hardcover novels! A trifling figure, you'll say, if the course could really take me back to that day on the wall. I had just been to the post office and picked up your letter about Dr. whatshisname's study, and this absurd ad seemed to be urging me to train my neurons. While waiting for your next letter, I've decided to decorate the display window with novels in which the first kiss comes after extended courtships, insurmountable difficulties, or daring misadventures. The best? Read this: ". . . Then move not, while my prayer's effect I take. Thus from my lips, by yours, my sin is purged." William Shakespeare. Romeo to the young, audacious Juliet. I have to go: Alice has proposed a summer display instead and is looking for clichés, such as sunny nature scenery, pristine beaches, enchanting vistas, lush plants, roses and flower beds, cool breezes, leafy boughs, woods, romantic flirtations rather than loves, and gardens, gardens, gardens. I suggested *The Secret Garden*, by Frances Hodgson Burnett; *Elizabeth and Her German Garden*, by Elizabeth von Arnim; Goethe's *Elective Affinities*; Blixen's *Out of Africa*; and *Four Letters of Love*, by Niall Williams, which arrived yesterday and which I started a couple of hours ago. Unable to put it down. And longing to leave immediately, for Ireland.

A hug from your forgetful Emma

P.S. What about Morgan? Besides making money and acquiring art, did he have time for love?

. ——— .

New York, July 30, 2001
Rapture Café, 200 Avenue A

Dear Emma,
On the night of March 26, 1902, after an unsatisfactory day of business, John Pierpont Morgan was in his study, alone, as often was the case. When suppertime came, he phoned the architect Charles McKim and invited him—or rather, summoned him—to a meeting the following day: "I'll expect you tomorrow at my place, at ten." McKim, who lived on the corner of Thirty-fifth Street, a few blocks from the financier's home, did not wait to be asked twice, and on Thursday, March 27, he showed up at 219 Madison Avenue. Over a cup of tea, J.P.M. informed the architect that he had acquired the property adjacent to him, and he commissioned McKim him to design a house for his daughter Luisa and a building for himself, to be used as a library. He wanted a gem, which could also house the collection now at his London home, he told the architect. McKim proposed building a marble Italianate villa. A few months later, construction was begun under the vigilant eyes of the property owner, who personally checked every detail. J.P.M. ordered a balustrade lowered, blasted the subject of the back cornice, demanded that five stones be removed from the outer edge of the front steps, suggested materials and fabrics, and signed purchase orders without batting an eye. Imagine, he sent McKim to Rome just to buy a pair of sixteenth-century andirons. Reconciling his own architect's vision with the requirements of the man nicknamed "Lorenzo the

Magnificent" must have been an exercise of supreme diplomacy for McKim, yet a strong empathic relationship was forged between the two men. When McKim suffered a nervous breakdown in the summer of 1905 and was prescribed absolute rest, he suggested that his associate Stanford White complete the project. Morgan wouldn't hear of it. He told him to take a vacation and forget about the library: "When you go, work on the library will stop until you return. No one else shall touch it." Great satisfaction, my dear Emma, for an architect to feel indispensable to his client. In November 1906, J.P.M. held his first business meeting in the West Room of the library, surrounded by walls in red damask adorned with the Renaissance crest of the House of Chigi. Rarely, from that moment on, would J.P.M. use the Wall Street office, preferring the one that his colleagues referred to as "the uptown branch." This morning, I was there with Frank. We were received by the director, Charles E. Pierce, Jr., who knows every inch of this jewel. He led us to a safe in the study, opened an armored cabinet, took out a blue cloth box the size of an atlas (the kind you keep in the car to consult the road maps), and left us to ourselves: "It's one of the rare copies of the Bible in Latin, printed by Johannes Gutenberg. Enjoy," he said with a serene smile. By that impressive phrase, he meant one of the rare copies existing in the world. Can you imagine? I was stunned, mesmerized. As I held that parchment monument in my hands (purchased by J.P.M. in 1896 from a British merchant for £2,750 ps sterling, more or less $13,500), I felt as though I had retreated to a monk's cell, in the heart of a special place whose space I was to reconceptualize, breathing in the spirit that had generated it. Yes, but why did that wealthy man have such an exasperated need for beauty? Perhaps the answer lies in his nose. J.P.M. suffered from rosacea, a mysterious, disfiguring condition that plagued him throughout his life, and was famous for his big ugly nose. I'll check into it, but I think I'm on the right track to humanize the myth.

With a hug,

Federico

P.S. As for our man's love life, I'll tell you about that in a subsequent letter, though that amorous aspect is the side of his life that interests me the least.

·———·

Milan, August 4, 2001
Dreams & Desires

Federico,
The large-nosed swordsman secretly loves the beautiful Roxane, who in turn loves the handsome Christian. To win her, however, it is not enough to be handsome; one must also be a poet. Christian is handsome; Cyrano is a poet. There's strength in numbers, and the beautiful Roxane capitulates when Cyrano writes for Christian. But the inconvenient third party, the powerful, lustful villain of the day, who is also infatuated with Roxane, sends his rivals off to a siege, where Christian meets his death. The beautiful Roxane, in the finest tradition, becomes a nun, and only in old age does she learn of Cyrano's love. Though she is willing to reciprocate, it is now too late. I wonder if J.P.M. read Rostand and empathized with the most famous nose in French literature.

Emma

P.S. You're wrong not to be interested in the amorous side of his life. Childhood events and romantic relations are the best cues by which to understand an individual.

P.P.S. I'm leaving for two weeks with Gabriella, Alberto, and some friends. We've rented a country house in Roussillon, in Provence. Mattia is joining us with his new girlfriend—his first!—whom we all hope will be likable, cooperative, and, above all, tidy. I'll have lots of time to write to you.

·———·

New York, August 11, 2001
A park bench on University Place

Dear Emma,

New York is an outdoor oven. Sarah and Anna are in Maine, the land of lobsters and giant clams. I'll join them for a vacation that will take us up to Canada. I've gone off to write to you in the park near the studio, where students can be heard under the sycamores. The thermometer reads 98 degrees Fahrenheit, the humidity makes your shirt stick to your skin like a shroud, it feels like someone ran a vacuum cleaner over the Hudson, and the asphalt is nearly melting, while the air conditioning in the restaurants and supermarkets is murderous. I bought a guidebook to familiarize my girls with the beauty of Mount Desert Island, where our Morgan had one of his villas built in Acadia National Park—the point where you are the first in the entire continent to see the sun rise. Thrilling. I thought of you as I leafed through the guide. Besides Morgan, the Vanderbilts, and the Fords, a writer who is surely present in your bookshop lived in that park for a time (and died there): Marguerite Yourcenar, who wrote the *Memoirs of Hadrian* (haven't read it) in her wooden cottage set among the maples, oaks, and birch trees. It seems the cottage has remained intact: its walls lined with books, and a rocking chair under the arbor. I'm taking Sarah to see the whales; actually I, too, want to see them. Like a novice. Enjoy Provence, my friend,

Federico

P.S. Up until a few months ago I wouldn't have included the home of a writer among my list of places to visit: thanks to you or to the Morgan?

• ———— •

The most cheerful place in this village is the café in the piazza, where I ensconced myself among the wood and wrought-iron tables. Eight old men whose faces seem carved out of tree bark are playing *pétanque*. The morning's silence was suspicious. They avoided me, surely due to excessive sensitivity. Only Mattia burst into my room at half past eight. "I set the alarm clock, Mom. Be grateful for the effort, and happy birthday!" he shouted in my ear, his voice thick with sleep as he rumpled me with the grace of a Great Dane. After breakfast, I was politely thrown out of the house. They got it into their heads to throw a party, and the idea terrifies me. I don't like being the center of attention, I'm too afraid of disappointing their expectations, and I would rather avoid any kind of celebration, but it's impossible to account for feelings on such an important day.

· ——— ·

Roussillon, August 20, 2001
Café du Village

Dear Federico,
Today at ten minutes after midnight, I turned fifty. Mood: I am not depressed or upset, though I thought I would be. I'm surprised. I started the day without a shudder, I did not make any solemn promises; I did not experience any mood swings, not a trace of euphoria or depression, no merciless examinations in front of the mirror, except for the arm. The subject is feminine, very feminine, so I don't know if you will be able to understand, but I'll try anyway. I feel an intimacy with you that can't imagine scorn; besides, you're far away, and although I am absolutely certain that age makes us insecure, I can ignore your reaction. So then, this morning, I put on a pair of jeans and a white blouse. Sleeveless. At the gate, I raised my arm to wave to my captors and, turning my head to the right, I saw the scrawny triceps jiggling like a pudding: an arm that was telling, despite my triweekly workouts! Federico, from this morning on I am officially a middle-aged woman and I was gripped by panic, which I will admit only to you. How can I die without having reread the extravagant catalog of human passions that Marcel Proust wrote by the sweat of his brow, or *War and Peace* (fourteen hundred pages), *The Pickwick Papers, David Copperfield*? How can I overcome my

guilt for never having opened *Zeno's Conscience, Lord Jim*, all of Kipling, or for not having gone back to Balzac's *The Human Comedy* and Manzoni's *The Betrothed*? At school, they made us hate Manzoni's book, yet now I felt uneducated, inattentive, and shallow, with no time left to make up for it. Who knows if there will be a library in the "great beyond," when I'll have all the time I want to read. An eternity of time. I'm drinking a beer; for someone who doesn't drink anything stronger, that's all it takes to lose the contours of reality. Before leaving for her "women only" vacation, Alice left an unmistakably shaped package on my desk, wrapped in sheets of tangerine, yellow, and orange tissue paper, with a maroon grosgrain ribbon. As promised, I unwrapped it today. It is Elizabeth von Arnim's *Mr. Skeffington*. I'll copy the opening words for you, to show you—should proof be needed—how much power the printed page has to merge with real life and act as a pitiless mirror of the female condition: ". . . she was soon going to have a fiftieth birthday, . . . so conspicuous, so sobering a landmark in one's life . . ." *Sobering*, what a foolish word. Sitting at this table like a vacationer from another time, I sip my pale ale as I watch the eight old men bowl, and I can't say that I have much desire for sobriety. It may be because of my birthday or because of these wrinkled clouds, which seem inappropriate for beautiful Provence, but I see the shadow of the rest home looming: a very old Emma, shrewish and angry. I will become so, of course. The idea is unbearable and I don't understand the enthusiasm of those who argue that we should live increasingly longer, longer, longer. Will it really be a good thing? Today, I rightfully enter the geriatric sector and, like a frightened child, I imagine the red-nosed clowns who will devote themselves to brightening my days. And yet, dear Federico, there is the flip side, the positive thought for today: Age brings with it certain advantages. We can no longer have sex wherever we happen to be and we prefer a comfortable bed to a grassy meadow, but it is no longer obligatory, at least for me, to seduce. Today, I have become innocuous. Naturally, I don't keep late hours like my son; I go to bed early. But I'll have to start wearing turtlenecks in the winter and clunky necklaces in the summer, I will no longer stay in hotels rated lower than four stars, and I will avoid camping. It takes time to look presentable; I'll walk with a new, slow bearing, but . . . there's no question about it. Starting today, an array of new opportunities will open up: I feel free not to have to look younger, so when they tell me that I don't look my age, the joy I'll experience will be absolute. I'll just slip my wisteria-colored shawl over my arms now, go and mail this, and return home to my jovial family of friends, free not to take part in the household chores, intoxicated with a diversionary beer.

Thinking of you, with a new sobriety.

Your Emma

P.S. "I can still see the hedge of hazel trees flurried by the wind and the promises with which I fed my beating heart while I stood gazing at the gold mine at my feet: a whole life to live. . . . And yet, turning an incredulous gaze towards that young and credulous girl, I realize with stupor how much I was gypped." When she wrote these lines in *Force of Circumstance*, Simone de Beauvoir, the woman who forged my adolescent years, was fifty-five years old.

. ———— .

New York, August 30, 2001
BBB, 41 E. 11th St.

Dear Emma,
I would like to reassure you about something: The same number of years have passed for me. I exercise with weights every morning; my biceps are still firm, but I know the feeling (the gelatinous arm), which for me is centered on the hips. Recognize that we have an advantage: At age twenty or thirty, we don't have a clear picture of how we will look when we're older. Once past fifty, we do. You and I can already determine, more or less, how we will look in ten years, with no great surprise in store. We have a past behind us, under our skin; our reproductive organs have completed the duty for which they were responsible. You and I are two continents that may risk

colliding, but we are in the midst of a revolution, that of longevity, which prepares us for the demographic tsunami that awaits us. You know I track statistics, which are useful to understand and make sense of phenomena. I offer you some data for reflection, while allowing myself this mail break. Demographers maintain that in advanced countries the average life span will reach ninety by around 2050. While we won't live to see the world populated by fragile creatures on the brink of dependency, this scenario nonetheless urges us to exercise as long as the last neuron is still functioning. The bookstores in Manhattan are full of manuals such as *Sixty Things to Do When You Turn Sixty*, sixty essays by writers and futurists who have their say about our upcoming birthdays. We have plenty of time to prepare, have no fear.

Federico

P.S. To be read in a whisper: Happy birthday, my dear friend.

. ———— .

An unreal silence has descended over Piazza Sant'Alessandro, like the hush at a final match in the world soccer championships. All you hear are metallic sounds and voices filled with anxiety, apprehension, and awe. The world is glued to the TV.

. ———— .

Milan, September 12, 2001
Dreams & Desires

Dear Federico,
The bookshop is as protective as a newborn's incubator: Dreams no longer overwhelmed and beset me, haunting my senses. I no longer suffered from ominous nightmares. But as of yesterday, they've returned. There's talk of nothing else, and I confess to being concerned about you. In this secluded spot, I listen to the radio, dumbfounded: the greatest tragedy for those of us who haven't been touched by war except through our fathers' stories. I'm thinking of you, and resisting

the urge to look up the number for the studio in Paris, if only to ask where you are. Changing the rules midway is wrong and I won't phone, but please, write to me.

Emma

P.S. A thought for you. The poet Marina Cvetaeva wrote to Boris Pasternak that the type of relationship she preferred was otherworldly: envisioning in a dream. Her second preference was correspondence.

• ——— •

New York, September 20, 2001
42 W. 10th St.

Dear Emma,

I'm all right. I am writing from home, where I have remained by myself. Renzo has returned to France, and trying to tell you about these last ten days may help me to keep from shaking. I'll start from Monday, September 10, when I landed at JFK in the late afternoon after a boring, unproductive flight (I was unable to sleep or read or even work). In a bad mood, I made a few calls, then slumped, exhausted, in the backseat of the cab. Oddly, the driver did not take the usual tunnel to bring me home, but headed toward the Queensboro Bridge. Renzo was already in New York for a public appearance with Mayor Giuliani and other city officials regarding Manhattan's new architecture. He was expecting me for a board meeting at the Morgan, scheduled for Wednesday. The agenda: cost cutting. We were prepared to present modifications to the project: Three underground floors instead of five would allow us to address budget issues without radically changing our initial concept. Sarah and Anna were out of town with friends (as you might imagine, they have remained there). I was in the taxi. I remember that the sky was livid (though only afterward did this detail come back to me). I looked out the window and was aware of a strange sense of anticipation, a kind of suspension, and as we crossed the bridge, I was struck by the image of a lightning flash right there, between the two towers.

Selfishly thinking only of myself, I was hoping to get home before it started to rain. I was tired, and I went to bed after making myself a couple of eggs and a salad. The next morning, I was supposed to meet with Renzo in Midtown, not too far from the Morgan. As you know, I live downtown, not far from BBB. Tuesday, that horrific Tuesday, I made a few calls to the studio in Paris, then left the house. At half past eight, I was on my way to have breakfast at my favorite coffee shop just down the street. I didn't see or hear anything. But in a few minutes, the entire world, and mine, changed. Impossible to phone, connect to the Internet, understand what was happening. The sounds, Emma. The sounds of sirens, ambulances, the TV monitor there at the luncheonette counter: I saw what you and millions of people witnessed during those same moments. I couldn't make a call. I couldn't grasp what was happening. I could only stare at that screen. Physically, I was a few blocks away from the inferno. I felt all alone. I remember thinking, I believe for the first time, that—just as you wrote—we had been spared the circumstances of war, what our parents and grandparents had experienced. For two days, I knew nothing but what I saw on television. Anna and Sarah were unreachable. Renzo was a few miles from me and my anguish. I managed to reach him by phone Thursday night. He was badly shaken, despite the fact that he has known war. We agreed to meet in the lobby of his hotel. The subways and buses weren't running, and marching uptown like a soldier without an army eased the anxiety somewhat, though not for a second did it completely release its hold on me.

Friday, September 14, ten o'clock. It was the boss's birthday, which we usually celebrate all together, depending on where we are. Brian Regan and Charles were waiting for us. The agenda had changed. No longer a budget to trim, but a question that required an answer: What to do? Sitting in front of some of the most influential figures in New York, whom we had met earlier when the project was assigned to us, we felt everything was different: their faces, their hands, the shock we could read in one another's eyes. The chairman of the board was brief: "Whatever it is, we go forward," he said. The energy was unchanged; if possible, even stronger. Renzo sketched a few lines—each of his drawings already contains everything there is to know—and the new Morgan was there, in a stroke that reduced the depth of the excavation. The project was approved in its new version, but it was just a detail, you see? We went out under an ashen, cloudless sky, like the Virgin's mantle in Antonello da Messina's *Virgin Annunciate*. We sat on the steps of the John Murray House at 220 Madison Avenue. The spa was closed, the restaurants, the bars; the shutters were rolled down over the windows. Everything was suspended. We kept our eyes down, staring at a rectangle of pavement bounded by thoughts. Two homeless men in the shadow of solid, sumptuous buildings. "Happy birthday," I said to Renzo. He smiled at me with that clear, kind look that has the power to reassure me, and ran his fingers over the trim beard of a modern patriarch. "I hadn't cried in years," he confided to me, "but last night I did, Federico. I saw them collapse in front of me." At that moment, we heard a rumble; it was like a growl of muted thunder. We stood up quickly and headed toward the sound behind us. It was coming from Fifth Avenue. It was incredible. Imagine, Emma, camouflaged armored tanks, like gigantic toys on a Spielberg movie set, were making their way uptown on a four-lane-wide avenue. It was not science fiction. All true, my cherished friend, the dazed feeling and a sense of hopelessness and impotence that I cannot— perhaps don't want to—shake off. Nothing has resumed here. Everything has started over. Being a passive witness of history doesn't cheer me in the least. I haven't learned what war is, and I feel like a fifty-year-old man who is older than he was ten days ago. Sarah and Anna are coming back tonight. Like everyone else, we will have to try to find our own modest semblance of normality. I'm thinking of you, hoping that this reaches you soon,

Federico

P.S. At the post office, I organized your letters, which, stacked in their metal pod, made me feel less alone.

• ——— •

"It's been a year. The bookshop needs a Web site," Alice declares.

"The bookshop is fine just the way it is."

"Oh, Emma. I'd take care of it all; you wouldn't have to worry about a thing."

She's adorable when she decides to try to convince me about something she has been mulling over for some time, pretending the idea popped into her head the moment it came out of her mouth. She thinks I'm not aware of it, but I know her well enough; I can tell by her body language when she has something to confess. She tilts her head sideways, raises her eyebrows like an astonished clown, wrinkles her little nose like the star of *Bewitched*, and speaks in honeyed tones.

It's clear she has rehearsed the conversation.

This idea that you're nobody if you don't have a Web site has become a nightmare. The Internet invades our lives without a shred of decency, boasting the power to offer answers to every possible question, even the most impertinent ones. There we are cataloged and archived; our life is an open book for the curious and prying. The Internet leads to approximation; searching the pages of an encyclopedia is much more instructive. If you know you have all of human knowledge inside your computer box, you inevitably become superficial and lazy. I toiled over dictionaries in order to learn foreign languages, and these guys claim to have simultaneous translators that force terms into strained metamorphoses. Inert, the poor words remain silent, when they should cry out, defend themselves, protect their well-being. An impoverished English dominates the Internet; as a result Mattia and, with him, an entire generation of dunces feel entitled to toss in borrowed Anglicisms and acronyms. A well-turned phrase becomes a spiky, hasty "btw"; the expression "keep your fingers crossed," four little words full of hope, is squeezed into an illiterate "kyfc"; "hugs and kisses," a more conservative closing than "with love," is clumsily cobbled into a tinny "hak." They write that way to everyone, not realizing the challenge they pose to a multitude of people.

It's no use complaining. I am alone here, in my legitimate defense against a world that I can no longer understand and don't even really want to understand. I am a cultural minority now, and I have no intention of posing as a fifty-year-old attuned to other people's eagerness for contemporaneity. "Mom, don't sweat it," my *hak* son keeps telling me; "the world changes and we have to go with it." Mattia uses the expression "go with it" to indicate dozens of different situations, when he could easily alternate it with synonyms such as "adapt to," "be comfortable with," "feel at home in a situation." In the case of a relationship, he has explained to me that "go with" doesn't mean literally going out with someone, but being at ease, feeling loved, finding comfort and contentment in the company of the other person—much more simply put, not having any problems. Mattia doesn't say "woman" or "girl," but "chick." *Chick* seems almost offensive to me. Today he called me "a wicked mom," and I didn't react, unsure whether to consider it a compliment or a reproach. I thought he meant "a bad mom," but I was wrong. *Wicked* refers to a mother who is "cool," spontaneous, unstructured, in dress and demeanor; to my son and his peers, therefore, it is not considered an insult, but rather a badge of merit, a medal of valor.

I'll have to put a stop to my negligence and make Alice happy. While I certainly don't like the idea of the bookshop having a Web site, I don't fancy the thought of being viewed as antiquated. When I accepted her invitation to dinner at the sushi bar that just opened— she has two gift vouchers for a complete meal, presented to her by the owner, an Italian who is married to a Japanese woman—I was hoping she wanted to disclose something about her love life. Alice doesn't have a boyfriend, and I'm afraid it's partly due to the bookshop's hours, which reduce her social life to a minimum. Over tiny portions solidly molded like Lego bricks, she gets to the point.

"Customers could write to the bookshop."

"Why should they do that? Customers come to us to buy books, and if they want to chitchat, they go upstairs. I hate computers and I think it's mutual: They don't like me, either. We happily ignore one another. Behind that screen, you're hiding; you become some-one else, Alice. You're unable to reveal your frame of mind; in short, you pretend. The computer emits alarming sounds and badgers you with its absurd questions: Are you sure you want to delete? Connect? Disconnect? Do you want to save? Saving is an obsession that interrupts the flow of your thoughts."

"As usual, you're being extreme. Think of the advantages, instead: By putting our catalog online, the bookshop can become known throughout Italy and even abroad. A virtual shop that has the same look as the original won't cost much. Even Alberto thinks so."

"Since when did you and Alberto form an alliance against me?"

"We talked about it the other night; he stopped by to say hello while you were at the gym. It's not a conspiracy; he simply agrees with me. We could expand our customer base. They could e-mail us and we would respond with the same courtesy that you like to show them in the shop. It would be a sign of further consideration. . . ."

"Would I look bad if I asked for a fork? These chopsticks are irritating, Alice."

Reading books, much less opening a bookshop, is not the path to "attaining shanti," but it has turned out to be an unparalleled means to not "be here now." And now those two have decided for me which parallel world I should live in.

"I don't know. I'll have to think about it. Do you think I can get drunk drinking sake?"

I've worked through losses, separations, and changes in general by rearranging the furniture, and it's always worked, but I don't like the idea that Dreams & Desires may end up inside a computer monitor. I would feel as though I were laid bare. And my books . . . sold online as those two intend to do, they would be artificial: prostheses in place of limbs. The progeny of genetic manipulation. Ghastly.

. ——— .

New York, October 25, 2001
BBB, 41 E. 11th St.

Dear Emma,

Life is starting to resume, here, though with some effort. Nobody
talks about it in the studio, but Frank and the others can think of
nothing else. It seems that every colleague has a story to tell regarding the Twin Towers: friends and friends of friends who remained
under the rubble, stories of when a father took them there as a child
and when they took their own children there. I never took Sarah
there and I can't seem to feel normal. We work as much as ten hours
a day, as if to restore some meaning to what we're doing. But let's
talk about you. I think that the success of your bookshop has to do
with urban architecture and planning. Don't smile. Consider this:
In the twentieth century, megacities were created—for example,
Tokyo, São Paulo, and Mexico City. Today, 51 percent of the world's
population lives in cities and is concentrated on 2 percent of the
earth's surface. It is the urbanistic equivalent of the excessive growth
of those large bookstore chains that so distress you. Today, instead,
smaller cities are developing around the megalopolises: Suzhou,
near Shanghai, or charming Brighton by the sea. It's indicative of a
need. As if exceeding a certain population level results in discom-
fort, in a worsening of the quality of our lives. Dreams & Desires
should evolve by becoming a refuge against urban misery. Milan,
from the impression I got last time and from what friends have told
me, has become a dismal city, and your bookshop can be an island for
everyone. So continue what you've been doing; you're on the right
track.

   Your favorite sociologist is thinking about you,

Federico

Milan, November 20, 2001
Dreams & Desires

Dear Federico,
We have a Web site: www.dreamsanddesiresbookshop.com. We can't
use the ampersand—don't ask me why, as I have no idea. The site is
actually lovely, full of pictures and information. Just think, a friend of
Mattia, a twenty-year-old man, designed it in just a few weeks. He
certainly doesn't look like an avid fiction reader, yet the site resembles
the bookshop in all respects: There are my bookshelves, and the novels
are arranged by type of love story. All in all, it's as if that young man
was able to interpret my spirit and my aspirations and transfer them
into that box. The site "is" the bookshop, only, as they say, virtual.
Alice manages it; she even started a blog (a kind of pulpit where everyone is free to have a say), and people write to us. They send recommendations, ask for and make suggestions. We sell books via the Internet; I
can ship them anywhere in Italy, and many customers have begun asking us to send them as gifts. Alice had a graphic-artist friend design
cards like the one I'm writing to you on, and I "stipulated an agreement" (it sounds so formal, but that's what they say) with the Italian
post office to ship books in their yellow containers. To you, I can admit
it: I like the idea that the bookshop can become known (and perhaps
loved) outside these walls. Mattia writes to me (he lives at his computer, rooted to it) even just to tell me that he won't be home for dinner or to ask questions about his Latin exercises, e-mails saturated with
abbreviations that offend my respect for spelling, yet flowing with affection even when trampling the most basic grammatical rules. Alice
prints them and leaves them for me, timidly, on the desk. When necessary, I dictate my replies; otherwise, I file them away in a folder labeled
"Mattia." Take a look at the site if you like, but don't you dare write me
an e-mail! Since it's not a letter, it requires its own language, perhaps
some rules of etiquette, but it makes reflection impossible and kills
creativity. I'd never admit this to the young people who come into the
bookshop, Federico my dear, but I've grown fond of the excitement I
experience whenever I go to the post office to check if a letter has ar-

rived, and I feel real disappointment when I don't find a new one. I have a friend, Cinzia, who is having an affair with a manager at her bank, a bank-window romance from one account statement to another. Both are married. Before she goes home, she deletes the text messages and call log from her cell phone and her banker's e-mails from her computer. She gives them up forever, do you see? And if she transfers them to the PC (Mattia says "downloads" them, but I don't like the expression; it makes me think of something a garbage collector does) so she can reread them without being detected, she has to use a password, and if by chance she forgets it . . . the romance vanishes. I could never have an affair with a banker or "download" letters; I'd be afraid I'd never find them again. Our mailbox is an intruder-proof haven.

Let's not lose it,

Emma

. ——— .

"See how nice they look here? They don't take up much space. I'll stand the book next to the DVD. Don't they look great together?"

I gave in. I always give in when Alice insists with her tilted head and that upturned little nose. I have to admit she's right. The shelf is dedicated to films "based on" or "inspired by" romance novels, famous or not; it makes a great display. Initially, I was puzzled. Despite good intentions and the directors' attempts to be faithful to the written page, a film simplifies and demeans complex love stories and magnificent romances. I haven't read *The English Patient,* by Michael Ondaatje, but the novel started selling more than ever after the death of the characters played by Ralph Fiennes and Kristin Scott Thomas and those damp handkerchiefs clutched by the viewers. In the display window, I prop books against the reels given to me by the photographer on via Torino. He's closing. The rent is too high and he can't make ends meet anymore. He also gave me rolls of film and home movies that nobody picked up. How you can leave a memento of a confirmation or a birthday with a stranger is unclear to me, but he had a big boxful headed for the garbage dump.

"I'm going back to my village in Romagna. I leave you this

small legacy, Emma. . . . They're beautiful aesthetically, but no one but you would know how to put them to good use. I'll call you to have you send me books—me and my Rosa will have more time to read now," he told me.

A shop that sells socks will open in the space where the photographer was. Feet and calves instead of eyes. I want Mr. Cremaschi to see the window display before he leaves. It's a dressing room with a mirror framed by lightbulbs, along with photos of actresses, postcards, notes. On the table, there's a bottle of perfume, a red rose, empty jars of cream, some novels, and Alice's DVDs. I stacked more books on the chair and draped a beige silk dress across the back. A vase of flowers stands on a shelf to the side of the dressing table, with a note from an admirer tucked among the leaves. On the right is a metal stand that the dry cleaner lent me, with film costumes dangling from hangers. I pinned the title of the film on each garment and accessory: the little black sheath from *Breakfast at Tiffany's,* long satin gloves, a hat; a colonial jacket à la *Out of Africa,* a tulle skirt, and a powdered wig hanging from a ribbon; I sewed an *A* on the dark velvet dress from *The Scarlet Letter* and placed it near the flower-print apron similar to the one worn by Francesca in *The Bridges of Madison County;* a small hat with a veil for *The Age of Innocence.* I placed shoes on the floor, arranged in a row below the garments: three- and four-inch stiletto heels, taken from my shoe rack, styles I no longer wear but that I can't bear to part with.

I stopped by the post office. Federico's last letter filled me with an anxiety I don't want to feel.

·————·

New York, November 30, 2001
BBB, 41 E. 11th St.

Dear Emma,
I'm dashing this off as if I were talking to you. Beneath my window, the bare trees of a cold, clear morning. The stench of Ground Zero comes from all sides, from the TV screen, from the radio, the street,

Sarah's questions and those of her classmates. Before now, I never heard them talking about their future, only the present, which is natural at their age. Instead . . . Privilege is weighing on my sternum; it's a physical affliction, not just a perception. It's anxiety; it's a latent fit of rage. Rage can actually be useful if it makes the most of the initial convulsive phase; at a certain point, however, it changes: Breathing becomes regular again and leads to solutions, individual or group. I'm waiting for a journalist friend; I have to give him some material for an article about the project. I'm reading Edgar Morin (a gift from Frank). The philosopher writes: "Those who recognize the diversity of cultures tend to minimize or obscure human unity; those who acknowledge human unity tend to consider cultural diversity as secondary. It is on the contrary appropriate to conceive of a unity that ensures and encourages diversity, a diversity that fits into unity." A fine thought. Sober, correct, pacifist, armchair thinking. What's missing are parentheses, an inserted clause that includes human dignity in an ethos of life composed of things as well as borrowed words and creeds. Outside this studio, the world is in constant motion, like nature, the seasons, man himself. I'm a privileged individual. I'm getting to the fundamentals, Emma. My eighteenth year is a sharp memory and it has your face. I've always been an acquiescent type. Enough of that; I'd like to think of changing for other people. A dialogue requires that at least two be good at it. I'd like to try to do that, to be of a little more use. Forgive my venting, but aside from you, I don't know anyone else I could say this to. My drawings. Your novels. And then?

Federico

• ———— •

Milan, December 10, 2001
Dreams & Desires

Dear Federico,
I'll start this letter from this corner, where I can peek at Alice without her taking it wrong. You've seen her. She's delightful; she has

small, perfect breasts and her whole life ahead of her. For some time now, I've found her irritating, and now I know why. It's envy on my part. A more violent feeling than mere anthropological interest in a generation, the thirtysomethings, whom I basically always considered unfortunate, though I wouldn't admit it. I'm aware of our good fortune and I sense an abyss with respect to us; or perhaps every generation tends to absolve and defend itself, in some way glorifying what was perfectly normal at the time. Their misfortune, compared to ours, was to ours, was to have attended high school in the eighties, when the era of grand political passions was over. Individualism blossomed, and has come down to our children. The thirtysomethings have animated cartoons instead of songs; they sing "Lady Oscar," and we sang "Blowin' in the Wind." We shouted slogans in the universities, including a lot of bullshit, to be honest. I was the daughter of an unassuming shopkeeper, you the scion of an industrialist, yet as their offspring, we tried to shuffle the deck, to link our destinies, despite the fact that your father sent you abroad. Every generation has its codes, though I would give anything now to be Alice's age and still be able to choose a future. I'll stop here; otherwise, I'll have to cross out some of the silly things I wrote in this letter—which does not respond to yours, except for the bewilderment and anguish that I understand and share, and from which I try to escape by taking refuge in the pages of a novel. Our young people, at least on this side of the ocean, do not seem shaken by what happened. Why is that?

Emma

. ——— .

Up until yesterday, the only place you could shop on Sundays was at the so-called megastores. Starting today, on two Sundays a month, people in Milan can count on me. A few hours ago, we launched a local traders' market. All sorts of people are wandering among the tables. Some are faithful customers; others are abusers who, according to that cynic Alberto, come in just to get out of the cold. To me, they don't look like freeloaders, just people who love to exchange nice things—a look, a glance, a book, a film, a show, an exhibition they've just seen. They talk among themselves. I observe them from my corner and I enjoy imagining their lives; I think that even just by inventing something, anything, it can become mine a little. At Dreams & Desires' traders' market, you can buy new novels or swap romances brought from home. A story with a happy ending is worth two that end tragically; a novel whose main character is a male villain is exchanged for two with a contemptible female protagonist. The customers have a lot of questions, putting me in serious difficulty at times.

Figure it out for yourselves, I think. Where is it written that a bookseller has to know the plots of all the novels she's selling?

By lunchtime, the swap market has already produced its first results. I had four copies of *Anna Karenina;* two have disappeared from the table (legitimately—I have the receipts), a good average if you think that this text has been around quite a while since it was published (in installments) between 1873 and 1877.

"She's a whiner," I say to Alice.

"Who?"

"Karenina. She threw herself under a train and met the only end she deserved."

"Don't you think that's a little hasty? Besides, why a whiner?"

"From the time she meets poor Vronsky, from the first time they go to bed together, all she does is cry. Sometimes quietly, clutching a damp handkerchief in her pale hands, pressing it to her lips, often sobbing in it like a common shampoo girl."

"Excuse me, but what do you have against shampoo girls?" Alice asks, unusually sensitive toward the category of hairdressers.

"She wants him to feel like a scoundrel every time he looks at her. Karenina doesn't have the stature of a lover. Real lovers know their place from the beginning. She's the one who's married, not him."

"Love doesn't go prying into someone's identity card. It's blind; everyone knows that," Alice says.

"Vronsky is the one who's really in love. And adulteresses in novels always come to a bad end; this, too, is well known," says the voice behind me. It has a fine baritone timbre. I can't resist, so I respond to this comment.

"I think Karenina is simply a romantic woman. She has within her, as the author says, the passion of a poor woman who 'has lost her freshness.' It happens to many women, don't you think, Mr. . . . Mr. . . ."

"Carlo, Carlo Frontini. A pleasure. Don't misunderstand me, Emma. *Anna Karenina* is a masterpiece for its writing, plot, and stylistic modernity. It's she who is unbearable. One can love a book without necessarily admiring its characters, right? I'll take a copy, but not in paperback, please; I prefer hardcovers. I want to give it to the friend who is expecting me for lunch. Vronsky is a saint, believe me. Besides, everybody knows that Tolstoy was a misogynist."

Frontini is a handsome man with salt-and-pepper hair; he's wearing a green loden coat, which is slung over a tan wool sweater. A plaid lumberjack shirt and corduroy slacks complete the control. He's passionate about books and seems to appreciate the bookshop. A fortysomething woman with bee-stung lips and an explosive figure approaches him languidly. She probably thinks that husbands are swapped here, too, and we let her think so.

"This piazza needed a shop like this. Now all we have to do is persuade the tobacconist to stay open on Sundays. This city is so hostile to us smokers. You can't find any tobacco shops open on Sunday, not even in the town center, and those automatic vending machines that take tokens are hideous and complicated to use."

"True," I say, sidestepping the adjective *hideous,* which somehow isn't applicable to a machine. "I can offer you a cup of tea or coffee, if you'd like. As for Tolstoy's misogyny, I read *The Kreutzer Sonata* years ago, Mr. Frontini, but it would be interesting to revisit it in this new light. It's a perfect tale of adultery. Great literature and great music, for a story that ends up with the woman being killed by her jealous husband. If Karenina is a whiner, which human category does Pozdnyshev belong to, in your opinion?"

"Carlo, please call me Carlo. He kills the wife, an innocent woman: a sign of misogyny."

The "Love Triangles" section is very popular, perhaps because Sunday is the bleakest day for covert lovers, a bit like December 25, New Year's Day, and the month of August. Three copies of *Anna Karenina* sold, one of *Madame Bovary,* two of *Portrait of a Lady,* one of *Dona Flor and Her Two Husbands.* Unsold at the same table: *Stories of Misguided Adulterers,* by Juan José Millás, and Michel Butor's *Second Thoughts,* a cruel, painful novel from 1957, whose merits I can't seem to make people appreciate as I should.

"Isabel Archer is one of my favorite adulteresses; she is always poised between making love and dreaming about it, which, in the end, is the same thing," Carlo says, "even though most stories of adultery end badly. Better a solid bourgeois marriage."

"Then I have just the thing for you—Alberto Moravia's *Conjugal Love.* It was recently reprinted."

"I haven't read it, Emma. I trust you, so give me a copy."

"Silvio and Leda: He's an intellectual, but not a very serious one; she's unschooled, though not entirely ignorant. He's struggling with an amateur aesthete's ineptitude; she's very sensual. The country house where Silvio is writing his life's masterpiece is visited daily by a distasteful barber, who seduces the wife. The husband is aware of it but pretends not to know; he loves his wife, and when someone is really in love, he loves that person for what she is."

"You've given me an excellent idea for a 'Marriages' shelf," says Alice. "I'll also include *A Bourgeois Drama,* by Guido Morselli. An unhappy story, his is. Published posthumously, following the author's suicide." At the word *marriages,* her face lit up, her big eyes wide, as she pictured herself in a meringue-colored gown. I move off, leaving them to their conversation. My first customer, Cecilia, is also attracted to Frontini: She dreams of older men, someone to drink a cup of tea with by the fireplace, wrapped in a fleece throw, like in the movies. It wouldn't surprise me to see them all leave here together for brunch, my young assistant's latest idée fixe. I've deferred the matter of food: Too many innovations can disturb even a creative soul like mine. Alberto has arrived, arm in arm with Gabriella, who is holding Mondo on a leash.

"Just for an hour, Emma. We're going to see an exhibition at the Royal Palace, and he's not allowed in." Mondo, who prefers books to paintings, holes up under the counter and starts chewing a paperback catalog that he mistakes for a bone. A big dog like him complements the shop, a frugal adornment. Animals are welcome here, and I have a letter to write.

· ——— ·

Milan, December 12, 2001
Dreams & Desires

Dear Federico,
These days, Milan is decked with dusty strands of lights, miserable displays compared to the ones you see. Dangling wires, power switches clinging to tree trunks, angel heads or whole cherubs flying around with palm fronds in their hands, Santas and psychedelic sheep. I have never liked the superficial aspect of Christmas, and this year Christmas will be even less cheerful. Mattia has decided to go to California, a vacation at the home of friends who have moved there. How can you believe in Santa Claus if you live in a warm climate? It has to be cold to think there is one. Nineteen years minus one day ago, I was so fat that I had trouble walking. Tired of carrying around that mystery, like a kangaroo in its pouch. Nineteen years ago, twenty inches, seven pounds, and two ounces changed my life. Those years are now in the basement, stored in boxes: blue soft leather shoes, plastic Transformers monsters, his first compositions, notebooks from elementary to middle school, bound in Florentine paper, a pony with wheels, dozens of dinosaurs and toy cars. Where were you, Federico, on December 12 nineteen years ago? We were absent during the fundamentals of each other's lives, as you call them. And I don't know if talking about the past is a good idea. I have to go; I'm by my-

self in the shop and a customer has come in. Later on, I'll stop by the post office, where I hope to find a pre-Christmas letter.

Write to me, in any case.

Emma

P.S. Tonight, Mattia is being subjected to the affection of his "extended" family: His grandmother—did I ever tell you that I have a kind, generous mother-in-law?—is already at the stove.

. ——— .

Harbour Island, Bahamas
December 20, 2001

Dear Emma,

I am enjoying a rare moment of solitude during these holidays; the vacation has just started and already I'm bored. Sarah is at the beach with Anna and the friends with whom we rented a large clapboard house that has a patio and direct access to the sea. I had a quick snack and am resuming our correspondence, despite the alligators, a strained finger, and the incorrigible lethargy that has come over me in this oasis, which is too exotic for my taste. This is not your kind of place, nor is it mine. The fact that Sarah is having fun makes even the beach barbecues tolerable. You're right: You can't believe in Santa Claus if you live in a warm region.

Sealed with a kiss. I hope to write to you when my spirits are a little higher than they are today.

Federico

. ——— .

January. The city is deserted. I stop by the post office. There are no new letters. To make up for it, Alice printed me an e-mail from Mattia, sent from California a week ago:

mom i'm here after 31 hours. dead tired. let dad know.

I sincerely hope that he was just too exhausted to compose a more articulate note and that he thought this pathetic message—read a week later moreover, just to confirm the absolute unreliability of the medium—would put our minds at ease if we hadn't phoned him, thirty-one hours later. To console myself, I dedicate the display window to epistolary novels. There's not an inch of space left on their shelf, even though they are almost all books of a certain age—I'm in good company and this makes me feel less idiotic. "A true letter should be as a film of wax pressed close to the graving in the mind" (Virginia Woolf, 1907); "I'm beginning to think that the proper definition of Man is an animal that writes letters," claimed Lewis Carroll. Alice thinks otherwise.

"No one writes letters anymore today!" she shouts from the stockroom as she arranges the books for inventory. "Get over it!"

"Sibilla Aleramo wrote letters that were as long as a hundred and fifty pages, Voltaire's correspondence includes more than twenty thousand letters, and those of Proust fill nineteen volumes. Examples abound, my *dear* Alice."

"Nowadays, lovers copy letters already written; it's quicker that way, my *dear* Emma. Or else they chat online. Read *Norman and Monique: The Secret Story of a Love Affair Born in Cyberspace*. After sizzling e-mails that went on for years, the two meet and . . . have sex, to seal their love. In a word, they're attracted to each other."

"And what if, after writing to each other, it doesn't work? I mean, what happens if two people write each other terrific e-mails and then, when they finally meet, they aren't attracted to each other? It's embarrassing to tell someone 'Sorry, I made a mistake. You're not physically attractive to me. I don't like the way you smell.' Too risky."

"Well, the affair ends and maybe they continue to write without fucking. It's not a tragedy. Let's change the subject. Virtual sex is too complicated for you. Why don't we create a display about 'Mature Romances' instead? We'll include Aleramo, who had affairs with young men, and also Colette. . . . Oh, the bookshop is chock-full of late-blooming writers."

"That's a horrible expression, 'Mature Romances.' Besides, what about George Eliot, who, after losing her lifelong companion, made a man much younger than she, and extremely wealthy to boot, fall in love with her at age sixty?"

"He must have had some defects. I personally don't believe in May–December romances with a significant age difference. It would be like you hooking up with a thirty-year-old. You'd spend all your time wondering how long it could last. Just think of the stress. . . ."

"As that teacher who taught Italian to Italians on television used to say, it's never too late. In any case, I say we drop the idea of mature romances, Alice. It would offend the sensibilities of too many loyal customers."

And also my own. But she mustn't know this.

. ——— .

Milan, February 15, 2002
Dreams & Desires

Dear Federico,
I like book lists, but I'm suspicious of polls. Today I read one that I'll copy for you. When people were asked "What is the most beautiful word in the Italian language?" the word *love* was ranked as the top favorite, followed by *mother*. I'm a mother and I sell love. I'm in sync with the statistics; my conscience is at peace.
A kiss from chilly Milan,

Emma

. ——— .

New York, March 4, 2002
BBB, 41 E. 11th St.

Dear Emma,
Today I'm going to talk about coincidences. By coincidence (or the benevolent faculty of a sympathetic spirit), we met on April 10 last year. These eleven months of letters have reconstructed some of the missing pieces in the blank canvas (your words) of your memory

and have given me—you know how grateful I am—the desire to reveal myself through words rather than the usual drawings of an autistic. April 10 is not just any date. On that same day, a Wednesday in 1912, something happened to my employer that radically changed the course of his life. As a result of trivial glitches (some say), or because of a young woman who detained him in France, on that day Mr. Morgan did not board the *Titanic*, the ship he owned through his shipping company, White Star. The ill-fated transatlantic liner set sail from the port of Southampton, England, at eleven o'clock on a cold spring morning, traveling to Cherbourg, France, and then to Queenstown, Ireland, headed for its final destination, New York. Can you imagine J.P.M.'s relief, four days later, at having remained behind, his feet on terra firma, in the arms of his mistress in Aix-les-Bains? Our destinies are linked to him, and this small, comforting discovery convinced me to venture a proposal that I've been thinking about for weeks: I would like to see you again. Can you get away from the bookshop and join me in Belle-Ile-en-Mer, an enchanting island in Brittany that I've wanted to visit for years? I leave for Paris on the second, I'll be working in the studio there for a few days. I await your response with some trepidation. And, hopefully, five days all to ourselves. Write to me as soon as you receive this,

Federico

·——·

Milan, March 14, 2002
Dreams & Desires

Dear Federico,
History can be reconstructed by following the trail left by books. If you know how to look, every encounter with destiny contains traces. Listen to this. A copy of the *Rubáiyát of Omar Khayyám*, with illustrations by Elihu Vedder, bound in the London atelier of Sangorski & Sutcliffe in 1911, with a leather cover studded with rubies, emeralds, topaz, and turquoise, was purchased at an incredible sum

by a wealthy collector, Mr. Gabriel Wells. The article was shipped to New York, but that ill-fated April of 1912, it sank in the coffer of the *Titanic*. Now it lies in its oaken casket at the bottom of the Atlantic. Books and the two of us. Books, Morgan, and a date that accidentally worked its way into our lives. In these eleven months, you have been a place of respite, my diary, my island. Do we mean anything to each other, or do we write, feeling a need to keep each other informed, simply because it comforts us to have someone in whom we can confide? I'm not sure yet. And so my answer is yes, I'll come to Belle-Ile-en-Mer on April 10 of next month. I read up on it: Gustave Flaubert, Colette, and Jacques Prévert visited there, and Dumas imagined the death of the musketeer Porthos at Pointe de l'Echelle. Colette spent a summer on this island, with her long braids, as the new bride of the infamous Willy.

An island and five days all to ourselves. I'll be there.

Emma

APRIL 10, 2002

"*Ça va?*"

"*Où es-tu?*"

Even while we are seated in the Boeing 737, the first thought is to keep the relatives informed in real time. At every latitude, there's a series of messages: "Where are you?" "We've just landed." "I'm on my way home." "How are you doing?" I've read about cell phone models that provide false alibis: airport background sounds ("I've just arrived" or "I'm about to leave," depending on the need), supermarket noise ("I'll call you back; I'm in line at the checkout"), lapping waves, train whistles, a call that cuts in and out and a tinny voice ("I'm in a tun-n-n-nel; I can't hear you"). Yet everyone goes on asking *that question,* as soon as the airplane touches down, when the train puffs wearily into the station, while standing at the tram stop, after Mass, while waiting for the kids after school, in the park. Everywhere. An amen to check on wives, husbands, lovers, friends, children. "Where are you?" I travel incognito; no one knows whether I've landed, if I'm arriving on time, if I'm airsick, if I'm in a decent mood. There's no one I can tell to start cooking the pasta. I vaguely announced that I was going to Paris. An insignificant bookshop explorer on a reconnaissance mission, scouting for ideas to copy and taking in a glorious spring week. Alice seemed relieved at the thought of not having me underfoot for a few days.

"You'll find everything running smoothly when you return, Emma, don't worry," she said, driving me home in her new Smart

car, a gift from her parents for her thirtieth birthday. I think she's
enjoying the idea of putting herself to the test and having a free
hand in compiling the weekly book list.

The little chorus of *clanks* produced by the seat belts is a prelude
to the passengers' frantic keying. Someone whispers a quick "I love
you" into the microphone and appears to be talking to the air or
thinking to himself. As soon as the little red light gives the go-
ahead, even my neighbor, who had been reading the *Sports Gazette*
for an hour and fifteen minutes, presses the button on his cell
phone—flat as a slice of cheese—and begins his technological reci-
tation: how he feels ("Everything's fine, dear"), departure time,
number of minutes late (baloney, the flight is right on time), weather
conditions. From the small window, I can make out four aspirin-
shaped clouds in a sliver of sky, but it is absolutely impossible to
tell how the weather is. The pilot must have told us, but when the
captain speaks, no one bothers to listen to him, and consequently
the outside temperature remains a mystery until I reach the boarding ramp. So my neighbor is talking through his hat. I look at him
with an air of fake complicity as he starts to elbow his way down
the aisle of the aeroplane (there are old words that I adore, like this
one, for example). He's in a rush; I'm not. I proceed unhurriedly to
the revolving rubber belt that will return my new wheeled suitcase, excited about this trip and fully indulgent even toward him.
I imagine him as a faithful husband, the proud father of three
children, with whom he has spoken in turn, a few words apiece:
"Don't make your mother mad." "Don't forget to study." "Send
Dad a kiss." In the hand that's not holding the cell phone he's
clutching the handle of a dove gray leather overnight bag, so he
shouldn't be away from home too long. Ergo, he must have a mistress in Paris. Therefore, all that reassuring stems from a sense of
guilt. My neighbor cheats. And I tend to interfere unreasonably in
other people's business and misinterpret their behavior; I suspect
schemes and amorous intrigues, even in the most innocent. It's
not right.

In twenty-eight minutes, the RER rapid transit whisks me to the

Montparnasse station. Trains headed for Brittany depart from here. Over my head is a gray-blue pasteboard Paris: It's the scaffolding for the restoration, as the signs politely inform us. This iron and marble sarcophagus—its display windows filled with odds and ends—will be renovated in a few months. In the entrance hall, a billboard urges you to choose Brittany for an *unforgettable* vacation. It's speaking to me, though I have no need to be convinced. With half an hour to kill, I stroll through the shops: newspapers, magazines, souvenirs, but most of all stockings, skimpy dental-floss thongs, late eighteenth-century culottes in colorful Lycra, checkered boxer shorts with penguins printed right there in front. The bookstore offers only bestsellers, along with candy and the Eiffel Tower in glass balls with artificial snow. At track 20, I'm prepared for the ticket-stamping machine. Being insecure, I always stamp, even when it's not strictly necessary. I look around for the machine, and turning to the right, I see it smashed on the ground like a metal doll with its head lopped off. To the left is a twin, which is working perfectly. I can't find my ticket. Immobilized, as usual, by anxiety, I empty the entire contents of my purse on the ground. It's not there. Where can a scatterbrained bookseller have put her ticket? In a book, where else? In fact, that's where I find it, between the pages of a volume of Marguerite Duras's novellas.

Paris-Quiberon, 12:50. Coach 3, seat 56.

I slip it into the metal slot, push it in firmly, then lightly; I try it casually, but the stamping machine doesn't react. The ticket is worn to a frazzle by now; it goes in and out of the slot unstamped, while blond, blue-eyed children smile at me from a plasma TV and mom and dad, attractive and in love, dance around a new pleasure vehicle. I have to get my ticket stamped and I don't feel like standing in front of a television. Calmly I reinsert the ticket. There, done. It worked. All it took was a more relaxed touch. The little plasma family climbs into the new Renault family model and I look for my train. The powder gray TGV bullet train with a red stripe on its side is a grasshopper with lowered wings. It slides along the rail, puffing its *ssssst* like a rubber dinghy being deflated at the end of vacation,

before being stored back in its box. Just time to clean up the mess
that boorish passengers have left behind and it's ready to leave for
the wild coast of Brittany. My suitcase weighs a ton. I have a hard
time choosing, and to avoid going wrong, I carry everything with
me, like a snail. I'm unable to pack a bag decently, and this time it's
no different, despite the fact that I applied myself diligently last
night. I put the moisturizers in small transparent plastic bags so as
not to find expensive dabs on my clothes; I arranged the books on
the sides like protective shields, wrapped the shoes in white cloth
bags and the dresses in sheets of tissue paper. It took me three
hours to achieve a result I could be proud of. I drag it onto the
train. A big guy with disheveled hair helps me place it up on the
metal rack, settling it like an elderly lady next to his youthful backpack plastered with stickers. I think of Mattia and his nomadic life
and how enthusiastic he was about my departure.

"Right, Mom, you can't spend your whole life in that bookshop.
Get some rest, okay?" he told me when he heard "empty house,"
crushing me with generous, self-serving kisses.

"I'll be away for only five days," I objected, pretending to be
worn-out by his euphoria. Actually, I'm happy to be leaving home
and the shop for my getaway with Federico. We're ready. The train
glides out of the station; my neighbor bites into a baguette with
cheese and prosciutto. As he plugs up his ears with his iPod ear buds,
eliminating any possibility of conversation, the wing of a gull peeps
out, tattooed on his wrist.

I am in France. And the future, disguised as the past, awaits me.

After the first suburban homes and factories lined up like tin
cans, supermarkets flashing optimistic signs, and crowded clusters
of hotels with fiberglass swimming pools, the countryside begins
scrolling by, painted in tempera, in candied-fruit colors: The yellow is the intense hue of sunflower petals, the sky is a whirlpool of
blues, and the green of the foliage shields the branches of the trees
like a shiny umbrella. I take off my shoes, rest my feet on the vacant seat in front of me. I didn't ask Federico the reason he chose
this strange destination. I said yes, without asking anything further.

I've never been to Brittany, and I hope I've chosen the right clothing. Even on the train, I am a bookseller, and an irresistible urge makes me get up and stroll down the aisles, peeking at the pages. I observe and classify. Everyone in coach 3 is reading and no one is talking on a cell phone. The little boy with the straw-blond hair has a Tintin comic book on his knees; his little brother is frantically pressing his thumbs on the keyboard of a blue plastic gadget; the mother, pleased at the difference between her sons, is leafing through a magazine; a pimply-faced young man (Canadian or American?) is absorbed in the pages of an essay whose title I can't make out. I light up when, as I go to look for the bar car, I encounter the gaze of a young woman who is holding a worn copy of *Bonjour Tristesse* in her left hand, her right elbow resting against the window.

It was the summer of 1953 when an eighteen-year-old girl at 167 boulevard Malesherbes secretly filled the pages of a notebook. Six weeks and the text was finished. On the cover, Françoise Quoirez noted her address and her date of birth. She had Florence Malraux read it, and her friend thundered at her, "You're a writer!" That was that. That's how Françoise Sagan was born, at least so the legend goes. I recognize that type of reader at a glance: They scan the lines eagerly, absorbed in falling in love anew or caught up in the most bitter amorous disappointment. A woman reading Sagan today might be a language teacher in a girls' high school or she might be having a secret affair and be suffering over her precarious role as lover.

Three hours, thirty-nine minutes, and several chapters later, the train slows down. We enter the small flower-filled station of Auray. My muscles are stiff; my legs have pins and needles. Arms, joints, sinews, tendons (which I always imagined as white elastic bands holding me together)—even my brain—are gripped by twisted cables. And there, where that erratic red fist they call the heart is, I hear an infernal uproar and pray with all my might that those around me are deaf. I look around. Everyone is minding his own business and no one seems to notice my agitation.

You're just going on a jaunt with a former high school friend with

*whom you had a romantic relationship that lasted one year and sixteen
days. You were that young man's age. And that of your son today. So calm
down.*

The tall boy helps me get my suitcase down without taking out
his ear buds. I feel like lowering the window and shouting, "Do
you know how many of us on this earth feel *invincible* at this precise moment?" Like when you read that "at this very instant some
spot on the planet is vanishing from the maps," can anyone calcu-
late, here, now, at this exact moment, how many people are as
happy as I am? I change trains. In twenty minutes, the Tire-Bouchon
(literally, "corkscrew") train is traveling along a narrow finger of
land with a view of the lagoon, water to the right and left, and I'm
in the midst of a sea of fragrances. The train graciously deposits me
two hundred yards from the harbor.

"Welcome, Emma," the friendly fairies of Merlin the Magician
whisper.

The poor things were driven out of the Forest of Brocéliande,
where for millennia, in the moonlight, they danced in their white
tunics, dipping their golden hair in the sacred springs. Their tears
were so copious as to form the Morbihan, or "little sea," and into
these waters, swollen with weeping, they tossed the wreaths of
flowers they wore on their heads; the flowers formed as many islands as days in a year. The blondest, fairest of the fairies, in a final
sob of regret for that enchanting place that she was leaving forever,
threw the flowers from her wreath onto the waters of her tears,
beautiful, fragrant flowers, which, driven by the wind, were set
adrift toward the open sea; the garland drifted with the flow, but
one day the rocks emerged from the sea to protect it. And so the
loveliest of the beautiful islands rose up from the seabed and became Belle-Ile-en-Mer.

At Quiberon, a beach resort for the wealthy, it's the dead season. I have a few minutes to buy my ticket and enjoy the sound of
the sea, which eddies and whirls, caressing the sides of the high-
speed ferry Locmaria 56 with the sound of a promise to be kept. I
have sixty minutes to get used to the idea of spending a few days'

holiday with a near stranger who has a silver-tongued pen. There
are about twenty of us, a few fortunate passengers. The sun is shining serenely and there's not a single cloud in the sky.

What if something kept him from coming?

I don't like adventure trips, which is why I never went on a safari;
I can't tell the stern from the bow, and at this moment I could, un-
questionably, use a cell phone. I settle down on the deck, paralyzed
by the difficult crossing. The boat rocks and sways. Nausea grips
me; my head is spinning. I go belowdecks, where I sit down, hands
folded in my lap. For some reason, I feel the need to maintain my
composure, like those daughters of wealthy families who at one
time—if they stumbled into a romantic disaster that displeased
their parents—were forced to embark on sailing vessels and steamers,
sent to the ends of the earth, timid, pale, and elegant, loaded with
trunks, tears at the ready. Fifty-five minutes later, the lighthouse of
Sauzon appears. Painted white with a green cap on top, the tapered
cylinder with its underwater roots bobs like a champagne cork.
Longères, fishermen's houses painted like bonbons in pale yellow,
candy pink, and silvery blue, embrace the sea, as in a crèche. On the
dock, two men in tomato red jackets, loaded with bags, dodge the
scrawny little legs of two young boys in shorts who are chasing
the skimming flight of a seagull. The sea slaps against the port's low
stone seawall, but this doesn't bother the guys with fishing rods,
who are staring into space while waiting for a nibble.

And then, there he is.

Nothing seems sillier now than all the worries that accompanied me to this island whose existence I was unaware of and which
I am now absolutely certain I have always wanted to get to know.
Nothing seems more idiotic than worrying about having my hair
mussed up, my makeup smeared, my mascara running as the vi-
brato of the waves tosses me up to the port. The Locmaria slows
down as its ungainly bulk approaches the wharf. Federico is bundled
up in a yellow slicker, from under which a blue turtleneck peeps
out. Hands in his pockets, standing on the dock, he is unaware of
the fact that he is my *lampara,* my own personal fishing lamp. My

euphoria—disguised in the more or less lightweight letters—
trickles from my diaphragm like a drop of honey and comes to rest
at the center of my body. I want to walk on water to go and meet
him. I can barely stand up straight. Federico raises his arms, waving his hands like welcoming flags, and smiles; he is smiling, of
course, as only he can, with that special intensity of his lips that
bunches up his cheeks and crinkles his eyes. Irresistible. Chroni-
cally insecure, I pull the sleeves of my sweater down over my
hands, holding on to my forget-me-not-blue cloche with my right
hand, and my heart quiets down, as if someone had given it a provi-
dent cardiac massage.

It's beating regularly now.

Lub-dub, lub-dub, lub-dub. A flesh-and-blood metronome, a com-
pass of emotions and feelings and fears. All my insecurities coalesce
in a single sound. *Lub-dub, lub-dub.* Federico is a few yards away
from me, and I don't know how I should act. *Lub-dub, lub-dub, lub-
dub,* my pulse like a living creature. Living and not at all normal,
Gabriella would say; she would so much have liked to come to Paris
with me if it hadn't been for that "damn high school."

A cormorant spreads its wings like an umbrella and is swallowed up by the sky.

La Touline, a few steps from Sauzon harbor, is an eighteenth-century
house with thick stone walls, converted into an inn. It has two
floors, five rooms, and terraces of well-kept lawn, scattered with
white-and-blue-striped chaise longues, wicker chairs, and wrought-
iron tables. Madame Annick Bertho, the proprietress, with her
rounded *r* and pale, shy eyes, her short brown hair streaked with
blond highlights, stands in the entrance to welcome us. I follow
Federico up wooden steps studded with granules of sand that have
crept into the grain. He has one arm slung around my shoulders;
with the other, he carries my suitcase and his shoulder bag. Again,
he whispers "So glad to see you" in my ear. Our room, number 5, is
on the second floor. It's homey, unpretentious; everything is in

place, as if it had been left in order centuries ago. There's a quilted bedspread, and two large pillows with a blue-and-yellow herring-bone pattern have been hung on the wall in place of a headboard, perfect for reading in bed. A bathroom with tub, white tiles, and a bleached-wood, powder blue plank floor. An empty nest meant for love, or something that resembles it at least a little.

"It's still light. I'll take you on a reconnaissance tour. I rented a Jeep."

Federico the wise, inspired by patent self-confidence, demolishes the awkwardness and shyness.

"Give me five minutes," I say as I slip into the bathroom with the exposed beams; through a tiny cobalt blue window, it offers me a sliver of sea. Activity is a form of protection. We are happy to see each other. Happy and that's enough; there is no need to acknowledge it. In the apple green Méhari, a toy car that seems ready to fly away at the first gust of wind, Billy Swan sings "I Can Help" from the radio.

"I only stopped worrying when I caught sight of your little hat," my favorite architect tells me.

"You're right: It's a real problem not being able to reach each other by phone. I was anxious, too. It's all over, now that you're here," I reply.

"Ditto." He nods succinctly, taking the cloche off my head, unable to go beyond a general admission of relief. "Belle-Ile is your ideal island, Emma: a paradise without network coverage. It resists the lure of progress; in some parts of the island, cell phones don't work. We are unreachable—'The user you are trying to reach is currently unavailable.' Satisfied?"

I can't manage a clever comeback; it's as if an entire army of words has been razed. Having him beside me obliterates the intimacy that permeated our letters.

"I feel like a heroine in a romance novel."

"You thrive on those romance novels, don't you?"

"Don't you dare. I'm touchy, remember?"

The Jeep clambers up the narrow mule track that runs along the coast, climbing to a crest and stopping in front of a blue strip of horizon. The cliffs, softened by greenish veins, are sheer; from up here, you can make out the rock faces. You can sense their height just by listening to the thundering waves that speak of corrosion. The ocean is a furious prairie of foaming crests. Federico brakes without warning.

"Come with me," he says, opening the door with a bow. He holds out his hand and looks at my feet, shaking his head. "Walking shoes would have been better."

"I *always* walk in these," I retort, stretching out my right foot, which is clad in a laced-up Francesina with a rounded toe, certainly more suited to the bookshop's parquet floors.

"Besides, I'm too short. For wearing flats and for dancing slow dances, I mean."

"You're not short, Emma; you're *petite*. You always used to tell me that."

"Really? Just think, to avoid revealing how small she was, Marguerite Duras wore clothes that all looked the same. A kind of uniform, and woe to anyone who made a comment about it."

He takes my hand, pitches a stone toward the white foaming waves. It seems to hang suspended for a moment, then glances off the branches of a shrubby plant, slides into the water, shatters into small fragments, and disappears.

"This is Port Coton. Claude Monet would sit more or less in this spot, open his box of paints, set his canvas on the easel, and not think about his troubles."

"Why? What troubles did Monet have?"

"Oh, Emma, it's just a manner of speaking. We all have troubles, more or less. Monet spent a few weeks at Belle-Ile in the fall of 1886, in a house in Kervilahouen. It rained continually; the sky was dark and the sea angry. Think how furious he must have been. In winter, if you're alone, this place must be terribly depressing. In fact, people get drunk often and gladly, and when alcohol isn't enough . . . there's a high percentage of suicides here."

"How do they do it? Jump into the sea?"

"Poor Monet spent his days wandering the shores of this wild coast, accompanied by a certain Hippolyte Guillaume, known as 'Poly.' He painted thirty-nine canvases from this spot. Thirty-five of them portray these rocky cliffs, as if he turned the easel inland toward the countryside only four times. It was the sea that erupted in his paintings, nothing but the sea and its nuances."

"Who knows, maybe he got over his fury those four times. Iris Murdoch managed to paint dozens of shades of seawater in a single novel. Without ever repeating herself," I say, hanging on to my erudite tour guide's arm.

"Not Conrad?"

"Darling, I haven't read *The Shadow-Line* since high school. He may be a great writer, but after a while, too many adventures get boring."

We get back in the toy car. Around us, fields of mustard are polished by rain that starts falling lightly from a sky split in half: dark gray to the right, milky blue to the left. We are alone, amid low stone dwellings with slate roofs and twin chimney pots. Federico stops the car in front of a miniature beach. The water recedes into puddles and, sucked up by the sand, fades from yellow to golden brown. Seen from below, the cliffs seem like innocuous, lopsided cyclopes.

"If you're not tired, I'll take you to see something."

"Me, tired? Why on earth should I be tired? I only took a taxi, a plane, a subway, a train, another taxi, and a boat. A walk is just what I need to stretch my legs a bit. How come you know this island so well?"

"My mother told me about it. I've imagined it for years and I thought it would be a good idea to discover it with you."

"Do you miss her?"

"Sometimes."

Federico withdraws from intimacy, pulling away abruptly, almost rudely, as if to say, Don't ask me anything more. He steers by chronology, whereas I'm guided by impressions. He is a straight line; I veer off between parentheses and brackets—curly { }, square [ ], and round ( ). Federico has a warm heart, but he's cautious. He's consequential; he starts from the past and proceeds to the present: I did this, I said that, I think that. His letters are narratives; now that he's here, gripping my hand so tightly that I can't move my fingers, he retreats into his shell like a child covering his ears so he won't hear the wind.

"Let's go, then. It will just take a few minutes by car."

We drive along a road that cuts through an expanse of bare fields, which in a few weeks will be covered with golden grain. The white limestone *chaumières* are an embroidery. A few have preserved the charm of the stone originals, one-story farmhouses with thatched roofs of mud and straw, topped by a windowless granary. Federico brings the jeep to a dead stop in front of a tapering stone sentinel. We get out.

"Emma," he begins, in the tone of someone who is introducing you to a childhood friend, "this is Jean."

"It looks like just a stone to me. Megaliths here are like churches in Italy: Even the most godforsaken village has its regulation menhir."

"You're overlooking the emotive significance of these architectural forms, Emma. Every menhir is the stylized image of a man. There were a great many of them on Belle-Ile, but most of these giants were demolished in order to build houses like the ones over there. Architects, Emma, were architects out of necessity. The motivation that drives man to build is the need to remember; it's logical they don't say much to a forgetful person like you. Over there is Jeanne, the woman he loved," he adds, pointing to a slightly stumpier menhir.

"Jean was a bard; he sang about the sea, the legends of the valleys, the triumphs of war. Jeanne tanned the hides that would protect her parents during the winter. She was poor but so beautiful and pure that, as soon as he saw her, Jean fell in love with her."

"Beautiful and pure like Snow White! Nowadays, they're called 'prissy,' an insufferable type of female. With all due respect, it seems to me that only an architect can get excited over a stone. Brittany is a stockpile of rocks with magical powers; there are some for every need: stones that bring wealth, divinatory stones, stones that restore sight and lower a fever, stones to invoke when you want to get married, stones that suck up the sea when church bells sound the stroke of midnight on Christmas Eve."

"Forgetful but well-read! Let me finish, though, oh woman of little faith! The druids decided that the love between Jean and Jeanne was unworthy and impossible, and they ordered the witches to turn the two into stone, but the good fairies allow the two lovers to reunite one night a year. It's a legend that would work well in your bookshop. I'd place it in the section 'Impossible Loves . . . with Possibilities.'"

"If they're impossible, they remain so. The plot wouldn't permit—"

He draws me to him and kisses me, lightly brushing my neck, my cheeks, my eyes, and mouth with a tenderness that was left suspended for eleven months. I cling to his shoulders, and my shyness slips off me like an old, useless skin. The sea, now calm as the one on a globe, stands in the distance, behind a man and a woman kissing each other with kisses left behind for too many years. Kisses that fell off course, voyagers who have now found the island they were seeking.

"What if it's all a crock?" I whisper, rubbing my nose on his slicker. When they feel awkward, shy people say silly things at the most inopportune times.

"What?" he asks, his eyes boring into mine.

"The legend. Jean and Jeanne."

"I like to think of it as true. The menhirs preserve their secret; only those who brought them here could reveal it. It wasn't the Gauls or the Celts, but powerful men of the Neolithic period who came from Mesopotamia. They felled trees, plowed the land, carved these stones from the rock face."

I'm holding Federico and I couldn't care less about the menhir. Between us, there is nothing awkward about the silence. It's entirely normal, and so is his kiss.

. . .

On the stairs in La Touline, we run into Madame Bertho. Federico opens the door to the room with the cobalt blue windows and closes it behind him. I bury my face against his chest, rub my nose on his sea-damp sweater. He goes on kissing me as he unbuttons the cuffs of my blouse, takes off my skirt, lets my hands undress him. I look at the face of the man I've known for a thousand years. I undo his belt buckle, place my cheek against his belly. We can feel our bodies. Full of fear. People think that age makes a person sexually sophisticated. But it doesn't. Not as far as I'm concerned. He smells of salt; the veins of his arm are throbbing. A fading light lends our gestures an absurd sacredness. I sit on the edge of the bed, almost as if not wanting to crumple the perfection of the smoothly stretched covers; Federico is now standing between my legs. He leans down to meet my embrace. I put my arms around his neck, hold my face up toward his. The soft skin behind his ear, yes, that I remember. And the hollow of his neck, his eyelids, those soccer-champion legs. Vulnerability is shattered; shyness disappears; fear is overcome by an urgency that overtakes us. The debris and shrapnel vanish beneath the fingers of confident hands. We've waited eleven months and 271,560 hours for this moment. Our first time. I don't have time to think about it now, but I've thought about it the entire trip: *Federico is a man you've never been to bed with, Emma.* We're unable to smile; everything is terribly serious. Only our caresses loosen muscles and make our hearts less sober. Two stones come to life again, thanks to the pandering fairies. We make love unhurriedly, almost as though to ease the torment involuntarily inflicted by that blameless expanse of sea that for a year separated our lives.

Finistère, finis terrae: Opposite us, on the Continent, lies land's end. Here, on the largest island in the Morbihan Gulf, the end of the quest.

I'd like to lie down on the wet grass and watch the clouds. They, who have seen it all, would be able to give a name to my condition.

I certainly can't describe it as anguish, nor distress, let alone an affliction. I have to find a synonym. *Yearning* is too strong a word, even for this harbor: a vessel entering port with white sail aloft, while the beam of the lighthouse quivers amid fragrant currents of air. I made the wrong prognosis. I feared the awkwardness of waking up in bed with a stranger and spending days with an internal taximeter reminding me that I have only five of them. Federico is not a stranger, nor have I been anxiously measuring time. In this seaside dawn, in the uncertainty that passes from night to day as if even the light isn't really sure where it is, I wait. Shadow and light. Watching him as he sleeps makes me feel in control of the situation. He has strong shoulders and soft hips; his arms are a tapestry of veins swarming beneath the skin. His sex lies limp on the left side of his groin. A dismantled puppet, his head slack against the pillow. The sheet covers those legs that were unanimously voted the best on the team. His face radiates trust and vulnerability amid faint wrinkles surrounding his eyes. The body of a man at the midpoint of his life. Or maybe beyond that point. A scar on his right shoulder. Tenderness. This seems to be urgent now. We talked about ourselves in our letters, failing to see that what filled the unspoken was the youthful love between two people who did not recall how sweet and frustrating and frightening tenderness could be. There is nothing to be afraid of.

You can fall in love with a man who is sleeping.

And with *normality*. With this serenity that lets me be who I am without having to experience shame, vertigo, or the desire to flee anymore. I want to stay here and I don't care about my physical appearance, my exercises, the miracle-promising cream eyeing me from the dresser. I made love with a man without worrying about being good enough, I who never feel good enough for anything and have thrown away relationships because of it. I can't find words for this tenderness; I haven't used such words in many years and I feel somewhat deficient. I would like to object to their disappearance, but it's as if a thief has sabotaged my syntax, leaving me inarticulate and mute.

A kiteboarder's white kite skitters along the small patch of sky. The clouds of Brittany are impetuous and edgy, moody and fickle; they are constantly changing shape, a bit like people you don't know how to take because you have the idea they're trying to fool you. Barefoot, I tiptoe around like a thief afraid of being discovered. I don't feel ridiculous, though there is nothing more ridiculous than a woman who thinks she's in love. Or just infatuated, maybe head over heels. What's the difference, here and now? I don't know which section to assign this romance to. All I know is that I want to stay in this little room forever. Or at least for a while, to enjoy this new feeling of contentedness, the change from a regime of restraint to taking pleasure in the desire that courses through me, weightlessly.

I draw the curtains.

Someone decided to reopen the floodgate. *That thing,* that thing we vaguely call love—unable to define its boundaries with a minimum of precision except through metaphors or examples borrowed from literature—is lying there before me, between crumpled sheets. All we women want is love; it's quite obvious.

The ocean's song is natural and raging; it follows me as I spread moisturizer on my forehead, which is no longer lined. The sun grows as hot as a dish of polenta.

I lie down beside the man who is sleeping.

"Would you like to take a walk to someplace special?"

With him, *anything* is all right with me. I leave my high-heeled shoes at the inn and give in to the memorable All-Stars—burgundy, with a worn rubber toe—that I found in the basement and brought along in the suitcase as a trophy. From the road, I don't notice anything special; low stone walls covered with chips of schist have been preserved in the fields. We go down to Port Skeul, a point where sunken valleys converge among maritime pines surrounded by large, dark ferns. It's low tide. We walk along a dirt road. The cliffs are high but less menacing than those of yesterday evening. Clumps of asphodels, flower symbol of immortality, nip at our ankles. Federico leads the way for me along a mule track.

"Follow me, Emma. The view from here is spectacular."

On either side, the narrow path is protected by a wall of stacked stones, less than two feet high. Federico holds my hand until we reach our destination, which has a sloping, asymmetrical roof and is different from all the other houses on the island. Not an artist's whimsy, but an unearthed gem, a prow with small windows leaning toward the sea. On the facade, facing a carpet of heather that has claimed the right to grow freely, three iron letters are mounted on the wall: MTH. "Marine travaux hydrographiques, Marine Hydrographic Works," he explains.

"It looks abandoned," I say, worried by the signs of a storm crackling in the sky. He seems not to hear it, excited by the architectural revelation.

"It's a semaphore. The island had four of them—at Er-Hastélic, Pointe de Taillefer, Pointe du Talut, and this one at Pointe d'Arzic. The one at Er-Hastélic is in ruins, and the other two have undergone a transformation that has erased all their charm. In the nineteenth and twentieth centuries, they enabled vessels to keep a close watch, sending out signals that indicated changing weather conditions. The caretaker received signals from ships that were in trouble. Truthfully, they might have been warships or scows of a certain size piloted by competent sailors, whereas the fishermen of Belle-Ile did not know the sign language. Their heavy crafts were sturdy enough to withstand the waves' attacks, but their bulky form restricted their movement."

"They sank?"

"A lot of fishermen couldn't swim. Anyone who fell into the water had little chance of surviving."

The sky is blue now, drenched in a light that dazzles the eyes.

We are at the outermost extreme of a barren moor, suspended between water and terra firma.

Barriers. Defenses.

Men by the sea have constructed abject, makeshift walls to counter the ocean's fury. The house—or rather, the semaphore—is practically in ruins, exposed to view without any fencing. To get a peek at what's inside behind the dirty windows, we follow a path that runs along the edge of the drop. The windows have no casings; a battery of cannon carriers indicates various landing attempts. It is a proud, uninhabited house. The bow of a ship, chest thrust out. We go in. On the ground floor, the flooring is half wood, half earthen, and the chimney is intact. The windows are mostly broken, and the few that have remained undamaged are grimy with a mixture of dirt and dried salt spray. Federico seems to be expecting something. I've never had a passion for restorations, if you don't count the bookshop, and this precipice is not reassuring. "*Wuthering Heights,* I'd say."

When he talks about houses, he gets as excited as I do when it comes to books.

"I daresay it's abandoned, Emma. What is *Wuthering Heights* about?" he asks, pretending to be interested in romance novels while holding me in his arms.

The tide inhales and exhales with the cadence of a metronome. The sand, like a glass of draft beer, goes from pale to dark. The blue is more intense now; it's indigo, pink, with touches of orange. The thought that we will fly away in a few hours has made me nervous. Belle-Ile–Quiberon, Quiberon–Auray–Paris. A railway schedule can tell a love story. We will be together on the train, afraid of going back to what was. I hate Milan, and I'm leaving from Orly. They didn't even assign us the same airport, these bastards. The separation has begun. Federico is asleep. I try to decipher his dreams through his long, dark eyelashes, ignoring the crack that widens in my thoughts. "You must always see to it that you don't have anything dangerous within reach," Duras wrote. But she was talking about alcohol, not love. Or maybe both. The left side of the bed is untouched, unused. As soon as I tried to move away from his hold, he became aware of it and drew me back to him. He's waking up. He looks at me and smiles as if he is in a kind of limbo. We talk a bit, yes, those frivolous, banal exchanges that I like so much. Ordinary chitchat. He looks at the clock; it's five minutes before nine.

"Time to go."

The breakfast room is empty. There's the aroma of coffee, and the fragrance of toasted bread. We give the impression of a man and a woman who have nothing new to tell each other. Not even a bad dream. Federico smears cheese and jam on slices of buttered bread. He brings the café au lait to his lips. All I want to do is lick the crumbs stuck to those pursed lips. I'm jealous of them, too. We're incapable of making conversation, of making small talk, even about the weather. Much less how we feel. Madame Bertho has arranged a jug painted with yellow flowers as a centerpiece; the toast basket is of woven straw in a herringbone pattern. Everything is perfect. Except us. Despite the intimate lighting, we are unable to come up with a comment, an opinion, a verdict on how this holiday has been. You always take stock. He drinks his café au lait in small sips; he looks at me and strokes my wrist with his free hand.

"As a child, I gulped down my breakfast in no time just to be able to run off as soon as possible."

"I'd rather not get up; I don't want to go back."

On the lawn, a hotel guest is reclining on a wooden chaise longue. She's holding a book in her hands, nibbling a pencil. I resist the temptation to ask her what she is reading and if she is underlining the sentences; I refrain from meddling and avoid cataloging her in my dictionary of readers, a sign that something in me has changed these last few days. Reality has prevailed over my worthless literary world. Leaving here is like losing "the diffused white light of . . . the skies, those long-haul travellers," as Duras wrote of her Trouville, not very far from here. From the harbor of Sauzon, the pink houses and blue windows grow smaller behind us, until they disappear. The sun is warm, my belly is full of tarte tatin, and I feel bathed in a kind of peace. I start to speak; he silences me with kisses. I feel the sweet flutter of his breath on my neck.

"Can I ask you a dumb question?"

Federico responds without faltering. "You're entitled to ask any kind of question."

"Why did you come back?"

"I think it has to do with destiny, though I never thought I had one."

can't believe it. You kept silent about it for a year. With me! We talk once a day, we consult each other on every crappy little thing, and you don't tell me you have a lover? You're . . . you're really . . . a shit, you know. A great big shit."

"You're right, but it's not true that I have a lover."

I try to make amends by replying contritely, but it doesn't work. Gabriella is truly offended. She's my best friend. A rare friend, with enough imperfections to discourage the practice of envy. Besides being one of the people I care most about, she bears witness. She could write my authorized biography. She knows everything there is to know about me (more or less, at this point)—my moods, my depressions, my euphoria, Michele, the prenatal courses, the rhythm of the labor pains (mine, since she was unable to have children)—and has never envied me Mattia. Our friendship does not require recapping, which is a great convenience. We had the same teachers, the same gynecologists, and the same priests (in high school, we experienced mystical crises galore). We shared mistakes and vacations, doubts and tragedies, births and deaths, nights spent studying, job changes, marital disputes, marital crises, marital reconciliations, endless exercise classes of any kind, and equally endless visits to the hairdresser. We visited museums, took our first trips on our own, and worked as salesgirls during an unforgettable summer in London—I at a luxury leather goods shop in Knightsbridge, she at Galt Toys, a toy store for environmentally correct parents. And in the evening, after putting up with the whims of my Arab customers all day (they had assigned me to the handbags and scarves department; I was efficient and polite and earned a lot of tips for it), we stood in endless winding lines in front of Covent Garden, hoping for discounted gallery tickets for the opera and ballet. We felt like starving bohemians, two young women with a future just ahead of them. In the morning, in Miss Peate's frigid flat, we loaded our toast with salted butter to boost the calories, so we could skip lunch and stick it out till supper. On Sundays, we wore our feet out, walking along the Thames and roaming through museums, where she managed to explain the paintings and statues to me one by one, being the victim of a perennial case of Stendhal syndrome as I was. With her, I saw Paris for the first time from the top of the Eiffel Tower and from Belleville's heights. I always told her everything. She is as controlled as I am impulsive.

We've come to a restaurant, as we've done for decades in delicate situations. Usually after our Wednesday-night movie, we get a pizza, then early to bed, but the news I had to tell her deserved a formal invitation to a very formal restaurant in the city center. It's the same trattoria where I dined with Federico; this gratifies my penchant for self-inflicted pain and triggers memory's emotional refrain: his face, his hands, his voice, and the Eau Sauvage. I enjoy the masochistic pleasure of raking things up; I twist the knife in the wound consciously and efficiently. I am in danger of losing my best friend. And since I can't bear the tortuous strains of abandonment anymore, I've decided to come clean. A corner table, given the subject. Risqué.

"He's not my lover."

"Then what is he?"

"He's not the usual male I have to guard against."

"Well, so that's what love does. Turns you into a gullible sucker."

"Who said anything about love?"

The subtle distinction is an attempt to smooth over the affront caused by a year and ten days of silence.

"You're a fifty-year-old woman infatuated by a fifty-year-old man who is halfway around the world. So what is he like now? He was good-looking back then, a little vain, but very sexy."

"He has thick eyebrows and he writes beautiful letters."

I make an effort to describe him, and it's as if he's appeared here, in a crowded assembly of ghosts. I'm distracted by Federico's body—I want to reach out my arms like a sleepwalker and caress his face—while she stares at me, wounded and betrayed.

"You want details? You want to know what we did? Oh, Gabriella, come on, don't take it that way. I didn't say anything because I thought it would come to nothing. That he would go back where he came from, that he would disappear."

"Don't change the subject. And stop talking about people disappearing. Your divorce with Michele was a consensual one. In the end, you were composed and confident. He always had those thick eyebrows, though."

"Look, it was Federico who ditched me, not the other way around."

"It was you who provoked him, only to then pine away like a sick sheep and cry for months. I don't understand how you can have forgotten all about it."

"It's been years and years, and there's no need to dredge things up. We were kids."

"I repeat: He comes back, married, *very* married, and you fall for him all over again."

"He didn't *come back;* he came into the bookshop by accident. Brittany is magical; you should go there with Alberto. However, if you must know, we talked about everything except his marriage."

"Married men never talk about their wives with a lover. Silence doesn't change his marital status, Emma."

"Since when have you become such a moralist? We have loads of married friends who have boyfriends. The role of the betrayed wife is hackneyed, even in novels."

"Oh come on, forget novels, Emma. You're not the type to have a relationship without falling in love. How did you leave things?"

"We didn't."

"After fucking for five days, you said good-bye at the airport with a nice kiss on the cheek, so long, it's been fun, have a nice life? You'll go on writing to each other, I suppose. Red-hot love letters . . . if that's as far as it goes, it may be okay, but at the first sighs, we'll talk again; better yet, you'll give me his phone number."

"You're cynical and in my opinion you're jealous, but I like that; it means you care about me. And I don't have his phone number in the States."

"I'm not cynical; I'm a realist. What are you having? I'll toast you with a glass of wine. You? The usual?"

"A beer and a glass of sparkling white for my friend, thank you."

She's right. A woman doesn't go to bed with a man unless she's at least a little in love. Federico is far away; the problem of a future doesn't present itself.

"To you, Emma."

We linger and go on chatting. I've drunk three beers. I've salvaged a friendship. Tonight, a new life begins. Federico has become the subject of a narrative. We are no longer a clandestine twosome; we can count on a witness who is sincere, and sanctimonious.

•———•

New York, May 2, 2002
Bistro Lucien
14 First Avenue

Dear Emma,

I am in the East Village, where you can find, side by side with fabric stores, shops selling candy by the pound, dilapidated apartment houses, bohemian lofts, and drugstores that have seen better days, boutiques offering knitted tops and dresses that to me seem like rags and that cost hundreds of dollars. Sarah is, of course, quite up-to-date on the dizzying changes in such fashion trends. Lucien Bahaj is a gray-haired gentleman who wears his long hair shoulder-length, like a nostalgic hippie. He moved here from France, in 1998, and after twenty-five years as a cook, he opened the little slice of

Paris I am now in, where you can eat foie gras and fresh oysters or *frites maison* (not frozen) with excellent steaks, and choose from wines listed on brasserie mirrors. I'm having hallucinations, or I'll have to start believing in synchronicity: I am in New York and a photograph of your beloved Simone de Beauvoir is mounted on the wall in front of me; on top of that, *The New York Review of Books*— hanging from a hook here—decided to publish an article on Sarah Bernhardt in this very issue. Old Lucien seems to have done it on purpose: Everything here speaks of you. He offers me a glass of white wine and asks how I'm doing. Either my face is plainly disconsolate or he can read my mind. I'm waiting for Anna and some friends, while Paolo Conte twists the knife in the wound, singing *"J'ai besoin d'une p'tite tendresse, m'intéresse."* I'm finding it hard to look at this city and at myself objectively, even though the wine is starting to take effect. It's the first time in twenty years of marriage that I've ever touched a woman other than Anna. It's the first time I've ever desired another woman. I think of your eyes gazing at me, bewildered, as you hold me tight; I think of you as soon as I open my eyes in the morning and as I'm brushing my teeth, as I climb on the Vespa to go to the studio. I sound like one of Battisti's songs— without its poetry.

I work and I think of you. I go home and I think of you. I call her and meanwhile I'm thinking of youuuu. *Everything all right?* And I'm thinking of you. *Where are we going?* And I'm thinking of you.

On the street, like in a monochromatic kaleidoscope, I see you; I feel your touch and do nothing to shake it off. I'm irritated by my inability to control what I so definitely wanted. And a fuck is never "just" a fuck. Not even for a man. Or not for me, in any case. With you, it was a promise. I'm not nostalgic by nature and I hate doom and gloom, but I feel like I'm on the edge of a Breton cliff; clinging to these sheets of paper is like a consumptive entering a sanatorium. I miss the intimacy. The kind we shared three weeks ago. You are with me. Every moment.

Federico

P.S. Forgive the tone of this letter. It doesn't begin to express the thoughts that have held my brain in a vise ever since I saw you pass through the metal detector and was left staring at a void.

· ——— ·

Milan, May 2, 2002
Via Londonio 8

Dear Federico,
The dark night is over. I took the time I needed to come around, like after the flu, when your bones resume their calling: that of holding you up. Firmly. During these weeks, your indolent Emma sought distractions, accepted invitations, and wore herself out at the bookshop. The only thing I refused to do was go see a movie that Gabriella wanted to drag me to. *Far from Heaven* is the story of a perfect wife, who always has an apple pie ready in the oven, a husband who never lets her want for anything, and proper, well-behaved children. All her certainties crumble when by chance one evening she sees him flirting with a man. I am intractable. Alice assailed me with questions about Parisian bookstores, and took it amiss when I wasn't more enthusiastic over the sales in my absence; nor did I comment on how orderly things were or notice the new shelf, "Romances in Brief," devoted to short stories. She even included *Here Lies*, by Dorothy Parker. I love her, but these days, if I could, I would just as soon avoid the subject of romance. I am trying to regain possession of my faculties. I was almost relieved to put up with a two-hour tête-à-tête with Alberto, who went over the accounts with me. I came to appreciate the car-repair shop across the street. I resumed my talks with Emily. I did translation exercises with Mattia; I took it upon myself to make the rounds of his teachers. And I enrolled in a Pilates class, a form of exercise that restores your back to its proper place. It's very popular in New York; you can easily find gyms where it is offered. Gabriella sends her regards. Since I told her about us—I HAD to tell her about us—she seems less set against you. We have an ally. I have a question to put to you. I'll go ahead and ask it. I know I

shouldn't; I know there's nothing literary about it and that it's a question a woman would ask, but I'll ask it anyway: Where are we headed?

A kiss from your paper island

P.S. The first weeks are the worst; like with chicken pox, the itching subsides after a few days. Maybe the same thing will happen to us.

. ——— .

New York, May 15, 2002
Central Park running path

Dear Emma,

I am writing to you beneath an apple tree bent under the weight of its flowers; adolescent couples kissing as they lie on the grass in Central Park surround me. A dog-sitter whizzes past me, dragged along by a bloodhound and a basset. Some kids equipped with bats, balls, and baseball gloves are getting ready for a game. The pitcher is small; his eyes are sharp and focused. A few feet away, they're selling ice cream. We could eat it sitting astride the low wall. If only you were here. I'll try to explain the mood I've been drowning in for days, avoiding any self-pity—you demanded that and I am following your instructions. Since I set foot back in New York, I've felt a kind of gulf between my internal energy and my body: I have a "physical" perception of a time that awaits me. Are you the origin and cause, Emma, of the incoherent thoughts that are disturbing an architect's rational world? I'm sitting on the grass, yearning for new experiences. I look at these young people and I feel like I'm too late. Do you think Marcus Tullius Cicero would have written the *De Senectute* the same way he did if he had met the girl of his youth when he was fifty-one years old? I was egotistical and now I feel incapable of giving a reasonable answer to your question—which is not a "woman's" question, because I've asked myself the same thing, swatting it away like you would a fly. You ask me where we are headed. I can't answer that, for the simple reason that since I've been home, I no longer know where I am. The irony is that I don't feel like a traitor, even though I'm being evasive for the first time—with her.

No mushiness, I promised. All the same, I miss you.

Federico

P.S. I'm thinking of you. With each and every line.

• ——— •

Milan, May 27, 2002
Dreams & Desires

Dear Federico,

New jasmine-scented ink found at the stationery shop on Corso Garibaldi: Can you smell the fragrance? I bought a copy of *De Senectute* for the colossal sum of 4.50 euro at the used-book kiosk on Piazza Missori, just steps from the shop. Each time I pass it, I feel like asking the vendor if he gets by, how many books a day he sells, who his customers are, if he's familiar with my bookshop, but then I stop myself because I feel rich and arrogant to have a real roof over my head instead of a bookstall. I read a few pages, skipping here and there in the text, and got terribly bored: lofty prose and tedious scholastic echoes. I didn't find him pessimistic; on the contrary, his invitation to water old age as if it were a plant is amusing, although I don't know which plant I would like to embody. You would be a tulip. Yellow. We are light-years away from him, and I don't know how much—or if—he would have changed had he met the girl of his youth at fifty—or rather, fifty-one. At our age, they were decrepit. We aren't there yet. Then, too, grandmothers look great nowadays, provided they are buffed, witty, go to the gym, stay well informed about the facts. We are two prospective grandparents; get ready.

I miss you, too. But I don't think about it.

Emma

P.S. I haven't heard anything more about Mr. Morgan.

•———•

Michele is a journalist, and a loving father who has been there for us: He's changed tons of diapers, taught Mattia song lyrics, proverbs, magic tricks with cards and matches, and a few sound rules of behavior. He wasn't the worst of all possible husbands. I was madly and hopelessly in love with him. His insurmountable flaw? He was irresistibly attracted to women. Not quite all of them, but way too many, and when I realized that it bothered me to be excluded from the group, I changed the locks on the house. He was almost offended by it. His time was up on the day of Mattia's fourth birthday. I had invited his playmates and their mothers to the house for the usual cake with the spiral candles, and the far-too-complicit glance between Savannah's bleached-blond mother (the child's name itself should have made me suspicious) and my handsome husband made me realize in a flash of hindsight the reason for all that eagerness to accompany Mattia to nursery school. Our marriage continued only long enough to explain to our son that his parents were great friends, like him and Patricia, the little blond girl in the class next door, and would never stop loving him. I'm not sure if we were able to clarify the difference between love and friendship to him, but we kept our promise that "for you, nothing will change." Though Michele and I cannot easily confide in each other regarding more intimate matters, since our irreparable differences toward married life were formalized by the court, every decision concerning our son has been a shared one. Thrashing out Mattia's romantic problems is my job and entails long conversations between the two of us, discussions that I prefer, compared to subjects I find boring: sports, which brand of scooter to buy, vacation destinations, money, and politics. The tough decisions are agreed upon beforehand by Michele and me, the intention being to thwart the kid—unanimously. Mattia calls them "ultimatums."

The ritual has been the same for years: chicken and tuna sandwiches, beer and Coca-Cola, parents sitting on the cream-colored sofa, Mattia sprawled out on the egg-yolk yellow couch opposite. The topic on today's agenda is as vague as it is pressing: his future. It's just a few weeks before his final exam and Mattia is "below" (his barbaric language for *unsatisfactory*) in three subjects, which he thinks he can make up by spending a night or two copying mathematical formulas on microscopic little notes to be rolled up in his shirt cuff. Biology, chemistry, and math. A breeze, he insists. Millstones, in my opinion. He concocts exasperating calculations of pluses and minuses and somehow magically manages to achieve parity between what he owes and what he claims is due him in terms of points. The graduation exam in our day was a nightmare; they could grill you on any number of subjects, but we were spared the supermarket unit pricing, and the criterion for admission to the examination was an adjective, not a number: satisfactory, fair, good, excellent. Though we speak in an a cappella chorus, Michele is less emotional; he doesn't lose his patience and stands his ground with immovable composure. Mattia is on his third sandwich and just stares at us. He has the classic contrite expression of someone with a guilty conscience: He feels accountable for those three subjects, which even his father, oddly enough, glosses over.

"Passing the exam is nonnegotiable. No repeating. Start studying and pass it with at least a seventy. We have a proposal for you before the final rush."

"What proposal?" he asks, widening his eyes and lighting a cigarette under his father's withering gaze: Michele never inhaled tobacco in his life, not even when he inhaled everything else.

"Since you haven't yet decided whether to enroll in college or get a job, and since we don't want a son who is still curled up on the couch at home at age thirty, we are offering you a year of study abroad. At least you can sort out your thoughts in English."

"Study in what sense?" he stammers, suspicious.

Mattia, who was expecting a lecture about the importance of enrolling in college, continues staring at us, not sure if we are persecutors driving him out of the house or democratic benefactors.

We're offering him a one-way ticket to an international education, and a very costly, for us, life experience.

"If you accept," I chime in, "there is only one condition: London and New York are out; we have too many friends there and you'd end up speaking Italian all day. I was thinking of Sydney. It has the sea and skyscrapers, nature and culture. It would be a unique experience for you. And it's always sunny."

I caught them both off guard, but I had been mulling over it for weeks.

"Damn, you guys, it's a fantastic proposal. Give me two days to think about it at least."

Two days. If they had made me a proposal like that thirty years ago, I would have jumped for joy at just the thought of being on my own and far away, with enough money to eat. *He* has to think about it. Which means talking it over with Emanuela, his "steady" girlfriend for some months now, who has already decided to enroll in law school and follow a smooth path between home and university. Being without her for a year means taking a risk, and Mattia, where emotions are concerned, takes after me. He lives in fear of not being loved. Of being forgotten, he says. As if it were possible to forget such a dear, sweet boy. But I'm speaking as a mother and my opinion doesn't count. Having polished off even the tuna sandwiches, the men in my life depart. I take my mind off things with Federico. What would I do without his letters?

· —— ·

New York, May 30, 2002
42 W. 10th St.

Dear Emma,

Close your eyes. Imagine you are listening to my voice and feel my excitement. Imagine being with me inside Charles Follen McKim's marble edifice, a prisoner in his tribute to Renaissance architecture, speechless at the style of a man in whom discipline and opulence combine in a sensual embrace. Climb the steps to the bronze door of this library with me, past the silent consent of sculptor Edward Clark's two lionesses, mute, docile sphinxes who sit on either side of the staircase. Linger with me in Morgan's studio, hold my hand in this paradoxical place, intimate yet congested. We are alone, as they say he often was, playing solitaire to cope with the depression that periodically assailed him. We are violating the room where on October 24, 1907, a man rescued the United States of America from bankruptcy. The stock market was at the point of collapse; depositors were besieging the banks, demanding to withdraw their money. In a nation afflicted with "credit anorexia," one man had nerves of steel: John Pierpont Morgan. Dozens of seekers came knocking, crowding in front of this building, hoping to find a solution. J.P.M. invited them to come in, listened to them, began writing checks to stock exchange brokers and sent a telegram to his partners in London; as a result, the *Lusitania* set sail from England with a precious cargo: gold ingots. America was saved. Some ninety-five years later, you and I, in this room, perceive only the scent of wood and paper, the smell of used books and the dust that desiccates them. The frescoed vaults of the ceilings suggest the private chapel of a wealthy man. On the red damask tapestry, there is an oil portrait of J.P.M.: stocky, buttoned into his tailcoat, bushy eyebrows, eyes like coals, his nose a lumpy potato painted a delicate flesh pink, thanks to the compassion of a corruptible and merciful portraitist. We are in the East Room, one of three rooms that will remain closed during the restoration. Hundreds of volumes are locked away like cloistered nuns behind slender metal gratings. We climb the little wooden staircase to the third landing: It's like standing at the rail of an ocean liner, and our only task is to offer visitors in the new century what that man saw with his cynical child's eyes. A ship or even an eighteenth-century Italian theater, its tiered boxes illuminated by the crystal drops of a magnificent chandelier. I'm thinking of La Scala and Piermarini, of the passion that led to all this, and the durability of the materials that shaped his dream: marble, wood, metal, plaster. And there it is. Before our very eyes, in the center of the room, a corpulent chrysalis of white fabric, wound like gauze around a wound, swathes thousands of books stacked on scaffolding. Dozens of blue cloth boxes cataloged by the Morgan's curators. Mummies. Mummies of manuscripts enclosed in a butterfly's cocoon, which protects the specters like a space wrapped by Christo. The mosaic-style marquetry wood floor has to be able to bear the weight of all this knowledge; the collections cannot be split up to accommodate us architects. They've piled them up here, in front of this marble fireplace in the library of J.P.M.: that powerful man saddened by a nose that was too big. We descend the spiral staircase that Morgan used whenever he felt the urge—not to read (it seems he was interested only in financial newspapers that extolled his exploits), but to touch or even just gaze at these riches. We are in a treasure house of leather and parchment, paper and inks. The cocoon that has never stopped growing is here to be embraced by an architect who never yielded to the fascination of books until he met a book lady.

Can you feel my kiss on your right shoulder?

Federico

P.S. Behind the grating, to the right of the desk, I sneaked a peek at the other volumes that will be packed up. The first name I came across, on the spine of a leather-bound book, was the Emma of a certain Jane Austen.

· ——— ·

On a scrumptious morning, I arrive at the bookshop straight from the post office, the paper booty tucked safely in my purse. I read the letter hastily while wolfing down a croissant, in anticipation of enjoying it in peace later on. I am with him at the Morgan Library; I admire the giant chrysalis protecting the manuscripts and volumes like precious treasures (oh, how I understand old J.P.M.!), not at all shocked by "a certain" Jane Austen: the power of the written word, which shows that the virtual world to which Alice tries to convert me is irrelevant. I sink into the English wing chair, rest my feet on the ottoman, and, among the bills, find the pointy peaks of my name penned in meticulous script on a saffron-colored envelope.

. ——— .

My dear Miss Emma,
I am too old by now to look after my home library. Some days ago, reading an article about your bookshop, I was struck by the elegance of the interiors in the photograph and I thought of you. The writer Liala enabled me to dream for decades. I know that many consider her work to be romantic drivel for silly women, yet I, even now that so many years have passed since those afternoons spent daydreaming among the pages, am grateful to her. It makes me sad to think of her novels piled on the ground in a local street market, so I thought that Dreams & Desires might perhaps be a proper home for them. I would present them to you as a gift, of course, requesting only that you do me the favor of having them picked up. Since I rarely go out, it would not be possible for me to deliver them in person, though it is with reluctance that I will miss the opportunity of visiting your charming bookshop.

Thanking you in advance for your reply,

Angela Donati

. ——— .

"No one buys Liala's novels anymore. And where would we put them? The shop is bursting at the seams."

"We could set up a vintage section, where Mrs. Donati's collection would be a big hit. A book twice chosen is twice loved. How can we say no to such a courteous offer?"

"Sure, and maybe we can put Carolina Invernizio in the old hags' section, as well: two nice old ladies who believed in eternal love."

Who is she calling a nice old lady? The Kiss of a Dead Woman is an anthology of human passions, necrophilia, and cream-puff endearments, a tangle of "scorching" encounters and enough intrigue to make your head spin. They speak because they have a mouth, these young women, and don't know what they're talking about.

"Let's call Mrs. Donati and tell her that her Liala has found a home."

"Let's think about sex instead."

"What do you mean?"

Alice drags her stool over and settles in front of me, batting her mascara blue eyelashes like threatening fans. It must be a subject she's been mulling over for some time. She takes advantage of an irresistibly quiet shop. I don't feel much like talking. For two days now, I've been trying to get into Louise de Vilmorin's *The Letter in a Taxi,* which a kindhearted publisher decided to bring out in translation. My customers were unfamiliar with her, and the twenty copies of *The Earrings of Madame de . . .* that I sold are a great source of pride to me.

"People are saying that the bookshop is too feminine . . . and sexist."

"Well, it's hardly a crime to be feminine. It's a fact that women read more than men; we're consistent with the market. What's wrong with that?"

"We should allow room for erotic literature."

"Right."

"Right? That's all?"

She introduced the idea as though gearing up for a run. Maybe she was afraid of evoking repressed memories in me or thought the subject might somehow disturb me. Now she hesitates. I've pulled the rug out from under her.

"Contemporary erotic fiction is deadly boring and of poor literary quality, Alice. There's obscene and there's obscene. Talking about sex, much less writing about it, is a complicated matter, even for elegant pens. Let's divide up the responsibilities: I'll see to the classics; you take care of the copulations of Almudena Grandes and the like. Pathetic texts and pornographic jargon—that, I happily leave to you. Men are far better able to describe exploits that are, after all, repetitive. They have the simplicity of phallic arrogance, that's why. We women are more complicated."

Stunned by my acquiescence, Alice begins searching the Internet for scurrilous quotes. She indulges me when I try to summarize the plot of Choderlos de Laclos's *Dangerous Liaisons*. Actually, I haven't reread it since high school, when, purely to provoke our French teacher, a fat, frustrated spinster who even forbade us to read *The Princess of Cleves,* I wrote a short paper showing that love affects even the most cynical. And wreaks havoc.

"Fine, let's begin with the window display."

In the center of the window, I place a copy of *Dangerous Liaisons* in its original language and a new edition, just republished in paperback; meanwhile, my usual nagging little internal voice reminds me how unwise it may be to leave letters lying around the house. Gabriella, dragged into the shop by a nervous Mondo champing at the bit, distracts me from the thought of my precious aluminum strongbox. The overgrown pup skids toward me like a giant hare and sinks his teeth into the crimson cover of Schnitzler's *Casanova's Homecoming.*

"What's wrong with him? He's acting strange."

"Never mind, he's very jumpy. He leaps at me, snarls, and, on top of it, he's lost his appetite. He goes over to his bowl, looks at it with a sigh, and walks away. He hasn't eaten since he took a fancy to Smyrna, the neighbor's dachshund; he sniffs her, not realizing that he could wolf her down in one mouthful. He has no sense of proportions, this dog. I'd like to leave him with you for a few hours, if it's no bother."

"Come to Aunt Emma, Mondo. If a little female doggy comes in, I certainly won't hold you back." It's our fate, those of us who are different. Gabriella doesn't understand that once the arrow is released, it doesn't distinguish between breeds or sizes.

"I set aside the new McEwan for you, the one you left on the train a few months ago. You're neglecting your author. . . . *Atonement* is a perfect title for someone like you, who always has something to atone for. I'll look after this poor beast."

"You're right. I'm cheating on McEwan with art history essays; I haven't got time for fiction. But since when has he converted? Usually, he writes about children who have disappeared, marriages that deteriorate, insignificant events that turn quiet lives upside down. *Enduring Love*, though, is actually a love story."

"*Atonement* is a historical novel, but it's also a tragic story about feelings. Trust me, sweetie, there's a sex scene set in a library that is worth the purchase price. Ah, what I wouldn't give to experience something like that here among these stacks. . . . Just joking! I saved an interview that appeared today: 'Extreme cruelty,' the cult author says, 'is a failure of the imagination,' so go run your errands and be back by seven. I'll buy you a drink at Zucca's."

"Are we celebrating something, or have you turned to alcohol?"

"I feel like spending some time with you, and the tomato juice at Zucca's is sublime and the french fries nice and crisp. Go on now, leave us alone."

We haven't talked about Federico in a number of weeks. She caustically accuses me of withholding information. I have to make amends with a summary, though there's not much new I can tell her. She certainly isn't impressed by Mr. Morgan.

"Come, Mondo, say good-bye to your surly mistress. That's a good boy."

•———•

Milan, June 12, 2002
Dreams & Desires

Dear Federico,

Alice must be convinced that sex and I are light-years apart. As she attempted to explain to me which novels or interesting passages about sex entice people her age, my mind's eye was focused on an image of you, naked, lying beside me in the big bed at La Touline. They would all be shocked if they knew. I hope the subject distracts her. For days now she's been depressed; she retreats to the stockroom, her eyes shiny, and I don't know how to comfort her. Her relationship with a certain Maurizio, a stockbroker (Tell me: What can they possibly have to say to each other, a fine, cultured young woman and a man who busies himself on the phone all day, in his shirtsleeves, staring at luminous figures on a monitor?), must have ended before taking on an aura of seriousness. These thirtysome-things seem so liberated, but underneath it all they dream about a trailing white dress, bridesmaids, sobbing mothers and jealous fathers, wide-brimmed hats, and frosted cakes topped with plastic bride and groom figures. "A lady's imagination is very rapid; it jumps from admiration to love, from love to matrimony in a moment," wrote a certain Jane Austen. Alice wouldn't like the quote because it would touch a sore spot. We talk a lot, she and I, but she doesn't welcome intrusions into what Alberto describes as the bookshop's "core business": affairs of the heart. There is something immoral about seeing her so upset over an idiot who cares only about silly NASDAQ numbers. But convincing a woman, any woman, of the insubstantiality of her love object is an essentially impossible feat. Even the most boorish bastard, if we are infatuated with him, has the bearing of a prince. Despite her broken heart, Alice has not lost her creativity: She has named the section of books with erotic over-tones "Così fan tutte."

Thinking of you. I'm sure you can imagine how. . . .

Emma

P.S. I've become aware that novels are brimming with sex: veiled, implied, explicit, imaginary, solitary. I think this discovery has to do with you. But don't get too cocky about it.

• ——— •

New York, June 27, 2002
42 W. 10th St.

Dear Emma,
A few weeks ago, the last girder of a corner of the south tower of the World Trade Center—it had remained standing amid the rubble—was

removed during a solemn ceremony. The job of redesigning the contours of lower Manhattan and its underground transport was
awarded to the architects at BBB, so I went there with the guys
from the studio. In the afternoon, I had a meeting at the Morgan
and I took the opportunity to stroll through J.P.M.'s rooms again. I
had missed one, the central room, around twenty square feet, dark
and austere, gloomy and a bit garish, full of objects, chandeliers,
bronze statues, and a 1914 photograph by Baron Adolf de Meyer,
one of the most celebrated fashion photographers of the twentieth
century. This cultured detail is not my own brainchild; it was Frank
who enlightened me. Mesmerized like a kid in a game arcade, he
took advantage of the occasion to tell me about the occupant of that
office and her amazing (for those times, certainly) story. I'll start at
the beginning and try to summarize it, since I know you'll like your
symbolic forebear, Belle da Costa Greene: Small and slender, with
dark hair and an olive complexion set off by enthralling eyes, she
was, like you, in love with books. But all in good order. Collecting
and storing works of art without assigning any classification scheme
to that patrimony was becoming a problem for the old man. Then
Junius, J.P.M.'s nephew, recalled a clerk at the Princeton University
library and spoke to him about her. Morgan invited her to his office
for an interview. We will never know the details of that conversation, but the mysterious young lady was hired, and in January 1906,
she assumed the post of librarian for the Morgan Library at a
monthly salary of seventy-five dollars. Morgan did not ask for references, proving he was the meritocratic type of man he was said to
be. Naturally, the gossips suspected that she was his mistress, but
when they asked her about it, years later, she supposedly replied,
"We tried." In one of the rare interviews with her, which I found
traces of in Morgan's biography, Belle said, "I knew definitely by the
time I was twelve years old that I wanted to work with rare books. I
loved them even then, the sight of them, the wonderful feel of
them, the romance and thrill of them." (A sign of the times: Sarah,
who turned fifteen yesterday, imagines herself an architect on Monday and by Friday has already decided that her future lies on the

Broadway stage.) The ambitious young woman proved to be a liar, however, and any information she revealed about her life turned out to be . . . false. It was said that she changed her date of birth the way you move a plant around in your apartment. Still, at a time not long after the end of the Civil War, I think she had good reasons to obscure several facts about herself. Her real name was Belle Marion Greener, daughter of Richard Theodore Greener, an attorney, academician, and Republican activist, and Harvard's first black graduate. When the Greeners separated at the close of the century, Mrs. Greener and the children dropped the final *r* of their last name and made up the da Costa pedigree to justify their dark somatic features. In her interview with Morgan, Belle may have told him that her first surname and her exotic appearance came from her maternal grandmother and, out of whole cloth, invented the account that her parents had separated when she was a child, and that her mother, a native of Richmond, Virginia, had moved with her children to Princeton, New Jersey, where she gave music lessons. Ingenious. And untrue. Belle's birth certificate identifies her as the daughter of Genevieve and Richard Theodore; place of birth: Washington, D.C.; date: November 26, 1879; note: colored. Impossible not to think of you, my little Emma, as Frank and I walked around the office of the woman who was the director of the Morgan Library for forty-three years, during which time she did not lack for anything. When her patron sent her to Europe in search of masterpieces, she stayed at the Ritz in Paris and at Claridge's in London, having brought her horse with her so that she could ride him in Hyde Park. She spend millions of dollars to buy rare manuscripts, books, and art, as though she were a court librarian. Over time, she became indispensable. It was as if she were part of the family; Morgan placed his trust blindly in this sensual, intelligent woman who bewitched both men and women, loved pearls, went around wearing scarves wound as turbans, feathered hats, or, alternatively, dressed as a man. When a reporter asked her why she dressed so elegantly, she replied, "Just because I *am* a librarian doesn't mean I have to *dress* like one." I offer you this brilliant response.

Ah, if only I could tell your Alice how fantastic you are in bed.
A kiss from

your cocky Federico

P.S. To answer your questions before you even ask: Belle never married; she had numerous boyfriends and a special lover, a cultured individual known even to us Italians. He was married. It was not a fling. It lasted for decades.

. ——— .

Alice places a ceramic dwarf with a chipped cap on a rung of the step stool: a cross between Grumpy and Sleepy, of dubious origin. I don't see what that pilferage has to do with the bookshop's decor, but it's best not to comment, as my assistant is testy. I can tell this by the way she walks—strutting stiffly, head held high, as if to inform the world "I can make it on my own." I gave her a raise, but money cannot fill the void left by a beau's intellectual deficiency. At times I act like a mother, caring and solicitous, but I'm unable to give her any sound, honest advice. By the time I was thirty-one, I had already produced a son and faced numerous difficulties, but in my day a boyfriend was not such a rare commodity: You could find them at parties, at the university, anywhere. Once, a guy started up a long conversation on the tram, struck, he said, by my eyes, which were "bright as stars." We're still friends, after a brief flirtation that took place from stop number 12 to his house. Why are these thirtysomething graduates, so emancipated and financially independent, doomed to remain spinsters, "single," as they say, which seems less offensive but is actually the same thing? I would inquire into it, but Alice would take offense, so I let it go and trust in destiny—a benevolent one.

A fellow wearing a blue shirt and a tie with horizontal beige and burgundy stripes is standing in front of the shop, his grim face surrounded by a mass of dark curls. He's looking at the books, moving his lips. He steps backs, is silent as he apparently listens to a mysterious voice, then resumes making lip movements like a silent-film actor. Now he's gesturing; he seems agitated. Making faces like a macaque in a cage, he waves a piece of paper, reads it. Maybe he's looking for a specific title or maybe he's just undecided; perhaps he has to buy a gift and is weighing his choices to himself.

"Sweetie, look at that man. He's talking to himself."

"No, Emma, he's talking to someone. On the phone."

"He hasn't got a phone, Alice. He must be a loony. Only crazy people talk to themselves; they don't need to have anyone hear them."

"He's talking into a microphone and listening to the responses through the earpiece. Look closely; it's there in his ear. It's very useful; I use it when I'm driving."

To me, it seems foolish to wear yourself out with all that facial energy, but for Alice this type of conversation is an added bead on her abacus of eccentric modernity. Her patient voice pretends to be indulgent with me, but really she's just like Mattia, thinking I'm out of it. Literally out. Cut off and left clinging to Federico's irreplaceable green felt-tip pen. I don't miss his voice, though for some weeks now, by some strange sorcery, I've been seeing him everywhere I turn. Every novel seems to be talking about us. All I have to do is pick one up, open it to a page at random, and Federico materializes in the features of the protagonist, a fellow lodger, a supporting character, a casual passerby to whom the author devotes a few lines. Enough to recall his body, his voice, a strand of hair tangled in his fingers. What sort of world would this be without novels?

To distract myself from the ambushes lurking among the pages, traces of ink and my heart, I vent my frustration through intense physical activity in the bookshop. It subdues melancholy even better than Pilates, and today I have an especially good reason to apply all my decorating efforts: The weekly magazine *Panorama* is doing an article on Dreams & Desires and the photographer will come by this afternoon to take some photos. The theme of the piece: the disappearance of small shops. For the journalist who hopes to flush me out, I must be a prototype of a survivor; he was cautious on the phone, and I'm sure he thinks he'll be meeting a decrepit old lady. To challenge his meager imagination, I've taken as much care as possible with my appearance: gray cashmere sweater, red skirt embellished with a Pop Art appliqué, and glossy black pumps.

Just because I'm a bookseller doesn't mean I have to dress like one.

I brought two scraped suitcases from home; I think they belonged to my grandmother. I open them and arrange the books like a corolla on the worn sage green cotton lining. Each book is a petal set among the white-veined gray pebbles I found in Mattia's room, a souvenir from some trip to a lighthouse. On the bottom I deal out some black-and-white photographs as though they were playing cards: vacation and holiday destinations faded by time. Couples are constantly traveling, their exploits described in books about them. I start with the foolish Sibilla Aleramo and that other lunatic, Dino Campana, whose letters are entitled *A Journey Called Love*. I never saw such hyperbole. Found in a bookstall, still encased in their cellophane shrink-wrap: Kyra Stromberg's *Zelda and F. Scott Fitzgerald*, Joachim Köhler's *Nietzsche and Wagner*, Christa Maerker's *Marilyn Monroe and Arthur Miller*. In half an hour, the display window is resplendent with love journeys.

Federico would get it. The rest of the world, no.

· ——— ·

Milan, July 5, 2002
Via Londonio 8

Dear Federico,

I've done my research. It was hot that day in 1910, despite the fact that summer was now just a pen mark on the calendar and the leaves of Villa Suardi's chestnut trees had already given way to the ocher that announces fall. The car moved slowly and bumpily on the cobblestone road leading from nearby Bergamo to Val Cavallina. Trescore Balneario was the last stopping place in their journey around Italy, where, two years after their first encounter, they had fallen in love as they went in search of treasure and clandestine privacy. He is Bernard Berenson, forty-five years old, a gallant, eccentric art critic married to Mary. She is Belle da Costa Greene, the librarian. Bernard wrote about art; Belle acquired it, hunting for sculptures, books, and paintings on behalf of her "Boss," as she called Morgan. With the casual insistence of one who is familiar with the treasures and delights of Italian art, Bernard had told her that she absolutely had to see those particular frescoes. And she, whom only a manuscript could excite more than a painting, had accepted, submitting to her lover's passion for "Lorenzo." He spoke of Lotto as though he were a friend, referring to him by his first name. Confessing that a critic always better understands the artist who is closer to him in temperament, he told her that if he were an artist, his work would resemble that of Lorenzo Lotto. Count Gianforte Suardi waited for them at the heavy wooden door, stern and imposing as the cedar that barred their way, proud of the regard that Berenson, the scholar who had discovered Lorenzo Lotto, wished to give the oratory, formerly his family's private chapel: a place of prayer, whose double row of pews had for centuries witnessed masses, weddings, baptisms, and other church services, and which that day was opening its doors to the eyes of "foreigners" from the New World. Roses, cypresses, and chestnuts flanked the couple as they entered. A dim light filtered through the windows inside the chapel, imparting a sense of mystery to that visit. Belle joked, mocking Bernard's pride as he held her hand and led her into the heart and soul of his preeminent painter. She lit up in awe, however, when she saw the gentle colors and the modernity of those little figures painted in fresco in 1524, an autumn, winter, spring, and summer in all, by an artist who was finally free of ecclesiastical patrons dictating the rules. Here, what had to be respected was the vow of the cousins Giovan Battista and Maffeo Suardi: Given the danger of being tainted by the Protestant Reformation, the chapel was to celebrate Christ's victory over evil, foretold by the prophets and sibyls and pledged by the lives of the saints. For the rest, he had a free hand. And so the martyrdom of Saint Barbara, persecuted and killed by her father, is certainly horrific and cruel; the afflicted nudity of the saint who occupies the left wall chills the heart, but a little white dog, always by her side, momentarily brightens the scene; and on the right wall, the miracles of Saint Bridget of Ireland, Saint Catherine, and Saint Mary Magdalene, along with echoes of the sibyls and prophets announcing the coming of Mary, breathe a lighter touch, while on the slanting ceiling, plump, mischievous putti, rather than angels, fly about in the faux pergola, naked and radiant, the way the artist wanted them. So Bernard explained to Belle, at Trescore Balneario, in the province of Bergamo, on a late-summer day, during the last leg of the romantic journey of an early-twentieth-century clandestine couple, blessed by the gaze of Count Gianforte and by the immortal talent of the *pictor celeberrimus*.

Weren't they adorable?

Emma

P.S. Berenson had many amorous assignations outside of his tolerant marriage, but according to his biographer, Ernest Samuels, the one with Belle was unique: "So began the one romance in Berenson's life that would stand apart from all others in depth and intensity." Its transatlantic heat lasted for years. Berenson kept the letters Belle wrote him; she destroyed the hundreds of letters from him. Don't worry, I could never burn yours.

• —— •

Moving novels from one love section to another is permissible and can be cathartic. It's revitalizing, a little like rearranging the furniture in a room, or organizing the objects in a messy drawer: keys grouped according to size, clips sorted by color, erasers by how worn down they are, ballpoints and fountain pens, beauty creams and agendas. Even Alice has been shifting books from one shelf to another; the cause of her thirst for renewal is still the stockbroker, I am almost certain. She's gotten it into her head that novels should not have a fixed abode, and she now emerges from a mysterious new section: "Freestyle." I decline to ask what it means and what type of novels it contains.

"Oh, Emma, I'm sorry. I've been so distracted these days. . . . I forgot about the package. Emily brought it this morning. I didn't know you had ordered books from America."

"I didn't order any books from America. Where is it?"

"I had her put it in the stockroom."

I found a new letter from Federico and now a package arrives from the United States. Talk about starting the day off right. The handwriting on the label of the anonymous package is unmistakable; I know only one person in the world who uses green ink.

Alice follows me, sniffing like a puppy dog. I pretend to be calm, indifferent almost, as if receiving voluminous packages from overseas is a normal occurrence.

"Cute dress, Emma. Did you ransack your mother's closet?"

"God rest her soul—my mother, that is—but no, this belonged to my maternal aunt, who married well. I have many others and I enjoy recycling them; the question of what to wear is legendary for me. It seemed appropriate for tonight's party. Vintage is extreme: Either it fits you to perfection or you can't find your size. But you should go to that shop that has your name, Alice's Boutique. If you search patiently, you can find a Chanel suit for little more than seventy euros."

"Aren't you going to open it?"

"What?"

"The package."

"Let's take it upstairs. Hand me the brass letter opener. They put so much Scotch tape on this that Aunt Linda's whatsit can finally be put to good use."

I have to dissemble; all Alice would have to do is get a look at my face to realize that I know who the sender is. In the package, there's a package—a set of nesting dolls. It smells of Eau Sauvage. White paper with a blue border and the face of an eagle covers the outer package.

"Express Mail, United States Postal Service. Extremely Urgent," it reads. I unwrap it. The second nesting doll is wrapped in olive green paper and has the unmistakable gold logo of Barnes & Noble. Wrapped in tissue paper are twelve white cups with an eloquent exhortation: SHHH . . . I'M READING.

Even deputy booksellers have a private life—that is, a complicated life. Alice's life is complicated, but that does not dim her enthusiasm: She probably thinks that anything is possible in life and that one day she might find a boyfriend in the shop, inside a package.

"Whoever could have been so thoughtful?"

"Maybe a customer visiting New York thought about us. We'll find out. For now, let's leave it here and get a move on; the party is at six. Did you make arrangements with Mrs. Donati to go and pick her up?"

Angela Donati has agreed to sponsor the new vintage section named after a prolific author of edifying sentimentality, Amalia Liana Cambiasi Negretti Odescalchi, pen name Liala. We now possess an original copy of her *Signorsì*, the 1931 novel that brought her fame.

. ——— .

New York, July 17, 2002
Peaceful oasis number 1, Bryant Park

Dear Emma,

I am in the park behind the New York Public Library. A man and a woman are dancing, heedless of the looks their obese bodies are attracting. A beautiful lady our age (I think) is fanning herself, and an old man, sitting next to me, is devouring a slice of cheese pizza. "Makes me feel young," he mumbles as he tries to stem the flow of mozzarella oozing down his finger. "The dance?" I ask. "No, eating pizza like this." It's like an outdoor reading room here. Reams and reams of pages resting on the knees of solitary readers intent on sweet summer idleness. A girl with long shoulder-length hair smiles at me. She smiles like you would expect a nurse to smile, or an elementary school teacher. In her eyes, and in mine as well, I'm an unfortunate single; I give off a feeling of yearning that makes me feel like an indecent, solitary loser. I have difficulty breathing because of the allergies that have been troubling me for days; wistfulness drips from my runny nose and watery eyes. I watch the couple dancing; they are radiant and happy. You're right, Emma: The allergies of love are the same at any age. This can mean one of two things: Either I'm stuck in adolescence or the cold that has lasted beyond spring but won't let go indicates the inevitable. Our age dictates that we master a sense of humor even when there is nothing to laugh about. It requires us to smile even when a loud wail of self-pity would be better. A good long cry, protracted, unstoppable. Like a storm that cleanses the streets. I defer, of course, putting it off. I drown myself in my work so I can return in the evening, postponing the moment when I feel worn to a frazzle and can find no peace. My bench mate has finished his slice of pizza and is wiping his oily fingertips with a white cotton handkerchief, like a lady.

I'm going back to the studio, but first I'll mail this letter written by a taciturn geriatric. Write to me; I need it.

Federico

P.S. I sent you a copy of J.P.M.'s biography. I'm an egocentric because I know that when you read it, you'll think of me.

· ———— ·

Milan, July 30, 2002
Dreams & Desires

Dear Federico,

What I adore about you—besides your mouth and everything else—is your sense of equilibrium, your ability to walk a tightrope with your arms outstretched and your body pivoting on a wire stretched between reason and emotion. You share this with Pierpont. Thank you for the biography; I'm distilling a few pages a day. Reading about him, I can imagine I'm doing it with you. Since the

story of your Morgan is arranged by subject, I gave up the idea of
reading in chronological order and chose the pages that you've neglected to summarize—namely, those that give the reader an account
of his love life. Well, on the basis of information gleaned from them,
I have developed my own theory: J.P.M. became one of the greatest
collectors of beauty as a result of . . . the void left by the death of
his first wife. I can just see the curve of your lips, the ironic expression and your enchanting smile, but it's the first love that leaves
marks we cannot process; we carry them inside and they keep digging away at us even when we think we've safely filed them. Think
about it: J.P.M. is twenty-three years old; he meets the young Ame-
lia Sturges, known as "Memie," belonging—naturally—to one of
New York's richest families. Romantic and impulsive, he falls in
love with her, but a few months later, in the spring of 1861, Memie
is diagnosed with the most dreaded disease: tuberculosis. Morgan
marries her just the same, takes her on a honeymoon to Algiers and
then to the coast of southern France, confident that Nice's climate
will cure her. Four months later, on February 17, 1862, Memie
dies. At age twenty-four, Morgan finds himself a widower, and in-
consolable. Following his father's dictates, he throws himself into
his business affairs; he absorbs that awful pain and transforms it
into wealth and power. He finds Memie waiting for him at night, in
the empty shell of their bed. What could his second wife, after the
war, have been like? Frances Louisa Tracy—"Fanny" to her friends—
the daughter of a wealthy New York lawyer. Tall, robust, rigid,
certainly dreary. Morgan has four children with her (three girls and
a boy, destined to become his business successor), but Fanny is not
Memie; the two lead parallel lives in a "solid and serene" marriage,
adjectives that indicate a union of appearance, useful for procreation. Passion lies outside the doors of the Murray Hill mansion.
There is a photograph in the center pages of the book: Fanny poses
impassively before the camera, corpulent and reserved. Morgan dis-
sipates the rest of his life among more or less passionate lovers,
young intellectuals, high-class prostitutes, and simple servant girls,
but he continues to love only Memie and his business, pouring his

consuming need for beauty into his library. For him, art is a gift
from the past. And the past bears the face of Memie, his first and
only great love. Why does he favor antiquity over contemporary art?
Because he's living in "his own" past. I know, you think I turn the
lives I meet into narratives, yet I'm convinced that the early years of
life are the tracks that lead to all the rest. I'm in the bookshop, by
myself. Alice took a day off, from me, from books, from the accounts. The summer is scorching; the ceiling fan's blades cool pages
that would otherwise be sweating. Milan's sun, pallid and sultry, is
fading here in my rooms.

I'm thinking of you, you know that,

Emma

P.S. The cups express the wistfulness you write about. Would you
ever say "Shhh . . . I'm reading" in an angry tone? Those words are a
polite plea: Let me read in peace, please.

• ——— •

Rather than returning them and before the Faithful Enemy's ax
can fall upon the former trees that have now become "my" books,
I thwart his plans with a new window display. Alice considers summer sales a Paleolithic tool, gerontocratic marketing. I cannot accept the fact that a book is worth half its value after only a few
months of life. If it were up to *them*, the publishers, books would
have an exceedingly short life. Strangled in the cradle, poor dears.
Forty days on the new book tables, then off they go, quick, to make
room for the newborns, miles of titles that devour their older brothers in a massive, irreversible act of cannibalism. And after the return, the shredder: turned to pulp. Words in a landfill, a common
grave. Like the bones of Wolfgang Amadeus Mozart. The only ones
who gain from it are the haulers: those who deliver the books and
those who come to take them back. There are thousands of books
that end up going out of print each year, vanishing into thin air.
Each day, 150 new titles are published. And what if my customer
has an urgent need, the kind that won't keep, to read a book after

the poor thing is already in its grave? Missing? Gone? Not at all: In two days' time, I'll find it for him.

I arrange "Love on Sale" on a raised area above a bottle green linoleum floor, where I have re-created a small supermarket with items that I used as a child. On the sides, Ikea metal shelves with small boxes of cereal, canned goods, and containers of detergent. In the corner, on the right, three wicker baskets: in the first, red plastic peppers; in the second, red plastic strawberries; and in the third, red plastic hearts. Small blackboards list the prices, written in chalk. The sale books stand on the shelves, along with the artificial products, and in the center of the scene I place a real supermarket cart (stolen property found in the basement) filled with boxes, bottles, cans, plastic fruits and vegetables, and, naturally, books. A story with a happy ending is worth two that end tragically; a novel whose main character is a male villain is exchanged for two with a contemptible female protagonist. Just like at the Sunday traders' market.

"It's only fair," Alice says. "Stories with happy endings are less probable than those that involve a tragedy; between adversity and a stroke of luck, the first always wins. We should sell unhappy plots with a symbolic discount. It would indicate a kind of solidarity with the victims, being on the side of the losers." We end up having a good time mixing centuries and genres, women and men, pin-stripes and jeans, flounces and miniskirts, corsets and push-up bras.

The multiethnic window is a challenge: Alice is convinced that some titles will never sell. I'm willing to try, so I tell her about some stories she doesn't know, while she describes her new heroines, such as Carrie Bradshaw, Miranda Hobbes, Charlotte York, and Samantha Jones: New Yorkers who are her contemporaries and the protagonists of devastating romances with improbable dialogues—funny, of course, but focused on the topic of sex. The four women talk about clothes, shoes, boyfriends, and . . . vaginas. I have never spoken to Gabriella about my vagina or about my sex life. I can scarcely even imagine my Faithful Enemy accountant excitedly possessing my best friend. For these thirty-year-olds, it's normal. *Sex and the City* is in the basket of plastic hearts; Alice has copied epic phrases on the price tag, such as "If you're never someone's girlfriend, you can never be someone's ex-girlfriend" and "If they're not married, they're gay or going through a divorce or aliens from the planet Don't Date Me"—her personal vendetta against one of Cecilia's coworkers who, after having turned up in the shop four times, invited her out to dinner without even buying a novel and, above all, without deigning to call her again. She liked him; in fact, she was upset about it and spent a week glued to the computer screen, waiting for an e-mail to pop up. Goethe's eighteenth-century *The Sorrows of Young Werther* and Stendhal's nineteenth-century *The Red and the Black* fit in well among the cans of peeled tomatoes. Along with Sibyl Vane, who has not yet known love and experiences it through the roles she plays. Oscar Wilde's *Picture of Dorian Gray* is not exactly what you'd call a romance novel, but I have three copies of it and I'd like to sell them before the vacation break. I add a touch of Spain to the cart with *The Lovers of Teruel,* a legend comparable to those of Romeo and Juliet and Abelard and Héloïse.

In the thirteenth century, two young people named Diego de Marcilla and Isabella de Segura, who had known each other since childhood, lived in Teruel. They fell in love, but when Diego asked Isabella's father for her hand, the man refused him. Being the second-born son, Diego would not have an inheritance; therefore he first had to make his fortune in life. The young man chose a military career and made a pact with Isabella's father that he would become rich in five years' time. When the five years were up, he returned a very prosperous man, on the very day when Isabella was being unjustly married, at her father's behest, to another gentleman, who had long been wealthy. Diego asked Isabella for one kiss, promising that he would go away forever. When she said no, his sorrow caused Diego to die of a broken heart. The following day, everything was in readiness for the funeral. It was then that a veiled lady was seen approaching the corpse and kissing him on the lips. Sweet Isabella slumped to the ground in turn, to the supreme joy of the undertaker, who saw his proceeds double so unexpectedly.

Other love reading on sale: *Days of Love Almanac: 365 Days of Reading and Passion,* an anthology by Guido Davico Bonino, perfect for vacation; Susan Minot's *Lust and Other Stories,* delicious, though her stories don't sell in Italy; *My Immortal Beloved. The Greatest Love Letters of All Time* and *Four Letters of Love,* by my Irishman, Niall Williams. Alice chooses *The Amorous Conversation,* by Alice Ferney, a contemporary story of adultery; as she sprinkles it with plastic strawberries, a sneaking suspicion dawns on me: She wouldn't be falling in love with a married man? A dash of sex in the red peppers basket, the remainders from the *"Così fan tutte"* shelf, literary mixtures, and that's not all: Henry Miller and the writer Anaïs Nin, who wrote numerous erotic stories without being considered "minor" as a result of it. I mingle *The Delta of Venus* with *Tropic,* a tribute to Anaïs's relationship with Miller (and with his wife), then add two copies of *Lady Chatterley's Lover,* which everyone claims to have read (including me), though it isn't true. Ten days of sales and then I'm off to Provence for vacation. Sun, great food, books, and Federico's letters. I went to the post office to pick them up. Instead of the young lady, a young man with a wrinkly little face and slits for eyes sat huddled behind the window. I wonder if he likes to read.

· ——— ·

Milan, September 1, 2002
Via Londonio 8

Dear Federico,

Thank you for ignoring my birthday; thanks for not sending me a card, for not clogging my mailbox with gifts. Thank you for the two summer letters. Back at home base, the only sure feeling I have is one of regret that the vacation was too short. It's as though a sluice gate descended in the river, reminding me of a trip to Alsace, when Mattia was a child. We rented a barge to navigate along the canals. The moment I awaited with the greatest excitement was when we stopped in front of the locks, devices that are raised and lowered to soak up the water like a sponge. At age fifty-one, I feel entitled to a sense of loss and I don't feel the least bit guilty. I have reached a stage that calls for wisdom. The problem is, I don't know what wisdom is. And you, my darling? What's happening on Madison Avenue?

Emma

P.S. The usual gang organized a party in the piazza at Roussillon. Everyone danced, vacationers and locals. The waltz Mattia invited me to dance had something incestuous about it, but I was happy to hold him in my arms. I didn't miss you: At times, the mother-son relationship is truly all-absorbing.

• ——— •

New York, September 20, 2002
470 Café, Broome St.

Dear Emma,
A cappuccino break in SoHo. I'm waiting for Sarah, having recklessly (for my wallet) promised her a visit to the new Apple store. In every town, every city in Europe there is *the* café": the Florian in Venice, the Caffè Greco in Rome, the Sacher in Vienna, Café Angelina or the Café de Flore in Paris, the Giubbe Rosse in Florence. Well-known, typical cafés are found in Eastern Europe (virtually in all of the former capitals of the Austro-Hungarian Empire), in northern Europe, and in Russia. In these cafés, people talk about daily life, sports, politics, literature, and art; they conduct business, scheme and plan, fall in love. They write love letters. There, I've written what occupies my thoughts each day. Sarah is crossing the street to join her favorite dad. I'll have to seal the envelope, before I'm discovered. I don't know how she would take it. Or rather, I do know: She'd be angry. Oh, not because of her mother, whom she argues with over every little thing, but because of me. She won't allow any attachment in my life unless it's to her.
 I miss you,

Federico

P.S. Too brief, I know. A longer letter will follow very soon, full of—better yet, bursting with—affection.

·———·

I'm with Michele at the airport. Mattia is leaving. The only thing needed to make it official is a camera, which I have in my handbag. If I dared stop someone and ask, "Excuse me, can you take our picture?" our son would die of shame, like at the nursery school recitals when I took pictures of his performances with a small video camera. I resist the urge and shoot the moment through the lens in my heart. I chose the wrong husband, but not as far as height is concerned: Mattia now measures a little over six feet of maternal pride. At the Qantas check-in, there's hardly any line; I was hoping for a long, snaking queue to absorb the leave-taking in installments.

"Did you bring a book? And some spare socks in your backpack? Your feet will get cold, and it's a long flight."

"Don't worry, Mom, I have everything, even a book. *The Catcher in the Rye*. You gave it to me two Christmases ago."

He'll be in Sydney for eight months and who knows if we'll be able to go and see him.

"It's always sunny there, Mom. You have an obsession about pale skin; that place isn't for you."

A twenty-four-hour flight, three airports, and thousands of miles away from me.

"Well, so long, you two," he whispers, as though he is embarrassed. He stoops for a final kiss on the cheek. I sense his impatience and fear and I don't dare return the kiss. Michele is silent, but it's clear that if he opened his mouth, he'd reveal a lump in his throat.

"I'll write to you, guys. That way, Mom will have to open an e-mail account."

"Write to the bookshop, as usual. Alice will print out your e-mails for me."

He's dragging behind him a big red suitcase that he bought in Chinatown for seventeen euros. He gets in line behind a pencil-slim girl in skintight jeans and a T-shirt that comes just above her navel; she has a pullover tied around her hips and a tortoiseshell headband clasping curly red hair that falls to her buttocks. Mattia's head is lowered; he steals a sidelong glance at us. He seems so hand-some to me in his sweatshirt, wearing his untied sneakers like slippers. With no socks. "If she's Australian, it's a good start," I say, trying to make a joke, while a tear slips out of my left eye. I can't imagine a more stupid remark. Michele makes an effort to divert me. We walk slowly back to the car. Mattia's going away will not mean a distance between Michele and me. Now that he, too, is past fifty, he's calmed down; he has a thirty-seven-year-old com-panion who loves him. It's October, but there is still no real sign of autumn on the trees, those gorgeous orangey colors, undecided and poignant, the leaves clinging by a thread, ready to drop. The road, trees, and sky are kangaroo gray. He drops me off at the front door.

"Now don't shut yourself up in the house like a monk," he tells me.

"I'm wondering if he'll be able to get by."

"He has more than enough money to live decently. If he spends it all too soon, he'll have to make do somehow. The Australians don't allow students to work off the books. Don't start acting like an Italian mama now. We should be proud of him. Think about people whose kids pretend to agonize over the choice of a major while meanwhile they're glued to their PlayStation. We did the right thing; maybe he'll find his calling."

What will my life be like now, without T-shirts and boxer shorts scattered around the house like Hansel and Gretel's bread crumbs? With no one to keep reminding that there's "a laundry basket you might deign to use every so often"? How will I live without beer bottles littering the floor of his room? Without frozen pizzas in the freezer? And without being surprised, at noontime on Sunday, by the shout of "Mom, what's for dinner?" I don't know what I'll do and I don't want to start acting like an Italian mama.

I begin *The Blind Assassin,* by Margaret Atwood: "Ten days after the war ended, my sister Laura drove a car off a bridge." The narrator, at eighty-two years of age, has decided to recount the tormented affairs of her family over the span of nearly a century, along with a scabrous love story, a novel within a novel, written by her sister and published posthumously to enormous success following her sister's tragic death. The bookmark is Federico's most recent letter; my body, curled up on the sofa, misses him like a feather cushion.

· ——— ·

New York, October 12, 2002
Peaceful oasis number 2, Paley Park

Dear Emma,
I've just come from Sarah's school; she has forbidden Anna to talk with her teachers. She is in a phase of rebellion against her mother; she insists that her mother embarrasses her, when, in fact, Anna is merely very attentive to the curriculum and had a discussion with her art teacher, a subject about which she has something to say. I happily assumed the role of peacemaker, and even managed to charm the math teacher, who seems to have stepped out of a Tim Burton movie: a cadaverous face, a Cupid's bow mouth, purplish lipstick, no aesthetic sense whatsoever, and not very cheerful. The search for peaceful oases is my new passion. Paley Park, a "vest pocket" park, is a small urban canyon, with little tables for the hasty lunches of those who work in midtown and have neither the time nor the money, not to mention the desire, for a sit-down meal in a restaurant. Surrounded by skyscrapers, it has a waterfall, which is a paradox amid the noise of the traffic. I'm sitting on the stone terrace under the waterfall, having a lunch of chicken soup (don't be appalled; it's very tasty) and Coca-Cola and writing to you. To get here, I walked up Madison Avenue and discovered a hotel, which I dedicate to you. I'd like to take you there right now, for reasons other than books, but it deserves a story. The Library Hotel is located inside a twentieth-century building, between the New York Public Library and the Morgan, and is furnished as an actual library: ten floors devoted to books, classified by subject category. I introduced myself as the architect of the Morgan Library (true) and persuaded them to give me a guided tour through the solid-

wood shelves full of new and old books, the Poetry Garden, the Reading Room, and a magnificent terrace. Outside the door of each room, where I would hang the classic DO NOT DISTURB sign, here a more prosaic LET ME READ sign hangs. You would choose romantic fiction, while I would go for fantasy, but I must point out that the Classic Fiction Room, which you would like, has a single bed, while in the Technology Room, which you would rule out, there is a very comfortable king-size. Something to think about. The numbering of the rooms is also curious: They explained to me that it follows the Dewey decimal classification, one of the most recognized library cataloging systems. A hotel-utopia à la Borges, who would have appreciated it.

This afternoon, there's a reception for the opening of a public exhibition of the project; it will be on view until May. No doubt the boss will look serene. He's one of the few people in the world who makes me feel protected even when I do something to mess up. The same thing happens with you: Your distant presence (though by no means *distant*) makes me feel secure. Funny how this rare feeling comes through to me in a letter, but it's true: Every time I stop at the post office and find that pale blue envelope, I feel like a confident man. It thrills me to know that there is someone waiting to hear from me just as I wait for her. It's childish, I know, but with you, not even this embarrasses me; there are no shadows, only episodes that we haven't had the time or inclination to tell each other about. Oftentimes I think that not calling each other is ridiculous, an obtuse form of protection. All I'd have to do is press a button (your number is stored; did you know that?) and I'd hear your voice and we'd tell each other what we're doing. I won't phone; the pact between us is ironclad, superstitious, as though hearing our voices through a cable would increase the distance between us. The words I write don't do that. They have weight; they stay with me. Always.

Your Federico

P.S. It's October 12. Is it okay to wish a bookshop happy birthday?

• ——— •

When a relationship ends, people react in various ways. Some ask for novels that will comfort and console them; others turn to horror, detective fiction, fantasy, or thrillers dripping with blood. Camillo belongs to the first category. He walks into the shop and asks, "Where have the 'Broken Hearts' disappeared to?" Three ladies sitting in the coffee nook lean over the railing, visibly worried by the cry of pain expressed by the man in the camel's hair jacket, a pale yellow scarf knotted around his neck like a morbid noose.

"I moved them upstairs, in the bookcase on the right. What are you doing here at this hour?"

Camillo is fifty-two years old but looks five years younger; he is the father of two teenagers with shoulder-length blond hair, and until a few weeks ago he had had a wife for twenty-seven years. Last month, after completing a round of psychoanalysis, Laura went home, prepared dinner, and informed him that their marriage "ends here." A minimalist. He was struck dumb, as they say (though I don't know the origin of the expression). A world of certainties and routines shattered at his feet and a bite of Sacher torte went down the wrong way. Being a distracted type of man, he was totally unprepared for such a weighty announcement, a bit like when you get a sky-high phone bill because you haven't been aware that your son likes to fool around idiotically on those erotic call centers. Laura was an assured certainty, like grandma's bureau that's been standing in the hallway for years without it ever occurring to anyone to move it or look inside.

Camillo has been my friend since college and he comes to the shop in search of books and consolation. Misunderstanding my job as a purveyor of love stories, he attributes to me the skills of a romance expert; at most, I feel like Lucy in *Peanuts,* offering her dubious "psychiatric help" for five cents, and I doubt there's anything I can teach him about traumatic marital separations.

"Give me something to read, Emma. I finished *The Embers,* by Sándor Márai. I have to talk things over with you because my regular psychoanalyst won't be back for about ten days. Fifty milligrams of Zoloft a day are helping me get through. You were sadistic to recommend a book about a betrayal, but the topic has made me more sensitive. That novel is a gem."

"It doesn't necessarily mean that Laura is betraying you; maybe she just got fed up with marriage."

"Could you be less blunt? Every sentence is a blow to me. Now get a move on, please. I've spent ten hours at the hospital and the antidepressant makes me hungry. I'll take you and Margherita to El Tumbon de San Marc. It's become a trendy place; with its wood paneling, it looks like an English pub, if you use your imagination, but we can talk in peace there."

Margherita is tall, with short boyish hair, and is fastidious to the point of being pedantic. She would have made an excellent surgeon, but the specialization course was packed with men; she couldn't stand the competition and switched to dermatology. To make up for it, a few years and several confirmations later, she graduated in pharmacology and for the last few years has been testing low-cost liniments. She, too, is someone I've known since our college days, and today she is an established dermatologist whose schedule is booked solid. A consistent example with her delicate rosy complexion, she convinced me a decade ago to give up suntanning.

The same thing that happened to Camillo happened to Margherita during that same time, minus the psychotherapy: Margherita and Giovanni have no children; she is eleven years older than he is. Having just turned forty-one, he tersely explained that he felt "pressured." *Pressured*—a humiliating adjective, as well as a distasteful word.

Margherita and Camillo are colleagues at San Carlo Hospital. He is the most charming pediatrician in Milan, and has looked after Mattia and all of my girlfriends' children from the day they were born. He is a generous idealist: In addition to working at the hospital, he treats the children of illegal immigrants, dispensing hugs and medicines, smiles and prescriptions without charging them a penny.

I go to dinner with these two shattered little-more-than-fifty-year-olds and I have to take their problems seriously. With a veal chop and potatoes in front of us, the litany begins with sinister foreboding: "The point is the house, Emma. Laura is sleeping elsewhere, but it's a temporary arrangement. Children are entitled to their rooms; we can't turn their lives upside down just because their mother is experiencing hormonal squalls. I can already see myself in a squalid studio apartment with Formica furniture, an empty fridge, and bare walls. I can't get used to the idea, and what makes me angry is that as soon as she decided to separate, she went around trumpeting it as if she had won the lottery. What need is there to tell the doorkeeper, the baker, or the policeman who's writing you a ticket?"

"She's repeating it to herself; she wants to convince herself she's made the right decision."

"Or maybe she has someone else," Margherita suggests sadistically, and Camillo gags on the potato.

"Just thinking about someone else penetrating her drives me ballistic. I've poked through everything. I found no traces of a man."

"Do you hear yourself, Camillo? You're embarrassingly crude. You should be worried that she *may have fallen in love* with someone else instead. For you men, ownership is what counts. It's love—for another man—that changes a woman's perspective, not the fact that reaching fifty she may get some satisfaction. Still, a woman leaves a man even if she doesn't have a replacement; you men never do," I say.

"I sleep in our marriage bed, but the empty-nest syndrome is unbearable."

"The first thing I asked Giovanni was whether the 'pressure' had a face. He told me it didn't. Simply put, he doesn't love me anymore. You have no defense against someone who doesn't love you anymore."

"Well, tell him to get out, Margherita. Let him go sleep outdoors and freeze to death under a bridge. Shove all his pretty suits in a garbage bag and change the locks. It's over, Marghe, understand?"

"The minute you feel sure about something, bam, everything

changes. Christmas will be here soon; I'll get depressed. I need to have a well-defined horizon. . . . Let's plan a vacation. We could all go to Caterina's at Saint Moritz; a group of fifty-year-old singles on the ski slopes will make quite an impression. Just don't leave me alone, please. Laura has already announced she's going to Kenya. For twenty-seven years, she's insisted that the idea of hunting terrifies her, and now she's going on a safari. Can you imagine? How silly."

"When people decide to change their lives, and maybe shed a spouse, they start by confronting the demons of the past. They do things they've never done before, even when it comes to vacations."

"She's taking the kids with her, so what are you worried about?"

"Do you have any idea, my dear book lady, what a safari for three in the African savanna costs?"

"Take it easy, you two. We have plenty of time to plan a defensive strategy. Friendship is a bond. And you, don't start hitting the bottle. Beer is fattening and the women on the slopes are all slim."

"Easy for you to say, Emma. You separated without any trauma. Now you're enjoying life, you have your bookshop, and you're all settled. What I don't understand is how you can do without sex."

"Making love is not something purely physical. If I'm not in love, I don't miss sex. I can do without it, and I don't need hormone-replacement therapy. I'm sexually neutral, and I feel just fine. Elizabeth the First proclaimed that she remained a virgin so as not to have masters. Chastity has its advantages."

"Just wait till the first desperate hunk of a customer comes along; he'll attach himself to you like a mussel, Emma. Sooner or later it will happen. Booksellers are hot. Listen to your Camillo."

"Don't go on and on. You're hardly the first man who separated from his wife. Edith Wharton divorced in 1902, and she didn't get worked up about it."

"Edith who?"

"One of the greatest writers of the last century, you ignoramus. You should see to your sentimental development. How do you manage to understand all the little mothers who revel around you, entrusting their little dears to you? The problem is education. You don't know women; that's the point."

"We aren't the utmost in competence when it comes to men, though." Margherita laughs, pouring me another beer.

I listen to these two, whom I adore. I think about Federico and, like a coward, I underestimate—or rather, deny—reality: his marriage.

. ——— .

New York, November 9, 2002
Peaceful oasis number 3, Barnes & Noble, Union Square

Dear Emma,

It's Saturday afternoon. I left Sarah at the door of her tap-dancing school, where she forbids me to enter. Before holing up in our book-shop, a short distance from the school, I looked up at the window. Behind the glass, a group of kids were swaying, whirling, kicking their legs to the sound of drums and an insistent whistle. They were beautiful, and it occurred to me that we have never danced together. As adults, I mean. We'll ask Madame Bertho for some records and do a slow dance at La Touline. A promise. From this window, under an ocher and burnt umber mantle of a New York autumn, I can see the tops of the stalls of the farmers' market, where Anna does the shop-ping, ignoring the traditional supermarkets. She has converted us to the delicacies—quite expensive—grown on farms near Manhattan, products that come "directly from the soil": tomatoes that actually taste like tomatoes and Hudson Valley goat cheeses that foul the refrig-erator for days. I know I don't say much about my marriage. I describe fragments of everyday life, but I never get to the "point." It's nothing new. But you don't seem to care, dear Emma. Our letters remain impervious to the reality that we don't want to see.

Am I wrong?

Federico

P.S. I'm going to pop over to the post office, hoping to find new words from you. Feel guilty if I don't find any.

. ———— .

Milan, November 17, 2002
Dreams & Desires

Dear Federico,
Mattia writes via e-mail from Sydney, a city that, according to his emphatic declarations, "will open the door to adulthood" to him. Actually, I have less ambitious plans for him: that he learn to get along on his own, speak a less scholastic English, and appreciate nature in a country less crowded than ours. He is experiencing an opportunity that I never had, except for the year spent in Freiburg, my post–high school and post-us nightmare, which I'll tell you about sooner or later. For now, I'm not bothered by his absence; it's like having another vacation. Michele is convinced that without Mattia I'll feel lonely, but he's a conventional thinker; he doesn't know that a person can feel very lonely even in a marriage.

I'll have more time to write to you, as I rarely go out in the evening.

Emma

P.S. Any reference to actual persons or things is purely coincidental.

. ———— .

New York, November 23, 2002
11th Street and 6th Avenue

Dear Emma,
Due to an uncontrollable desire for France, I'm having a bite to eat at French Roast, in a French-like atmosphere: a mushroom and spinach omelette, a glass of wine, and a brochure from the Maison de France advertising Brittany and our island. It's not really a bistro, but it smells like one and it's next door to my favorite magazine shop, a long, narrow passageway, like a corridor, where Mr. Smith perches on a high stool in a space no bigger than a shower

stall. Look for a magazine from any country, and you'll find it there.

I must confess a new syndrome: I see hearts everywhere. In the past week, I counted five of them: a rain slick on the pavement, the rusty lock of a gate on Broadway, a cloud, the rice-paper lanterns in the Chinese restaurant on Fourteenth Street, a cactus leaf in the studio. I started noting them in the Moleskine that I always carry in my pocket. The beauty of it is that I don't go looking for them; they find me. I thought I was losing it mentally, but now I like the idea of being a heart collector. The last, in chronological order—and order of importance—was a ray of sun that last week, during the presentation of project drawings and a wooden scale model, mischievously slanted through the Morgan's windows and formed a heart of light on the parquet floor.

We continue to meet with the landmark associations and historic districts superintendent, explaining our work to them. I am certain that J.P.M. would love the cubical structure in the space between the original library and the main building, as well as the expanded display space, the new auditorium, reading room, and underground vaults.

I embrace you, with an open heart,

Federico

P.S. I am deferring the subject of marriage until my next letter. I am positive that it—my marriage, I mean—has nothing to do with us.

· ——— ·

Sunday is a big day at Dreams & Desires. And on top of it, today is a Sunday marked by media success: The insert of the *Corriere della Sera* published Dreams & Desires's weekly book list in the column "Bookseller's Word," and many of those who've come to swap books at the traders' market are holding the clipping in their hands. Alice haunted the editorial staff for months: Each week, she sent a polite little note with the list of best-selling romances, and eventually reaped the fruit of her persistence. Here is bookseller Emma Valentini (a photo, decent, of the aforementioned) and, beside it, two small columns: "What She Sells," "What She Recommends." At the center of the page are the history of the bookshop and a picture of the display window. The new theme, "Hearts," criticized by Alice as "something more fitting for Perugina's Baci chocolates," was greatly admired. I discovered that Federico is not the only one suffering from the syndrome. Photographer Fabrizio Ferri, husband of the famous ballerina Alessandra, has suffered from it since he fell in love with her. He produced a little book of photographs on the subject, which I keep on the counter, and he lent me five colored blowups of hearts that he came upon during his travels. He stopped by yesterday to put them up and went into raptures about Dreams & Desires. The result: two blowups presented as gifts and four novels purchased. Am I a fortunate bookseller or what? The window display "The Custard Heart" is a tribute to Dorothy Parker and her story of the same name, which I place in the center, surrounded by images: a tuff rock, the lips of a reclining model, a waterfall in Patagonia whose water forms a frothy heart, the sting of a mosquito in love with its prey, a little pile of garbage in the kitchen. And all around them are heartish books, including the bestseller by Tamaro, which, years later, continues to touch readers of all ages.

· ——— ·

New York, November 30, 2002
42 W. 10th St.

Dear Emma,

On Thanksgiving Day, we went to the Macy's Thanksgiving Day Parade in midtown with two friends who have young children whom Sarah baby-sits for, proud of earning a few dollars. Inflatable cartoon characters paraded by. I was excited to see the Peanuts float, but utterly indifferent to a giant Spider-Man, who was loudly applauded by the children, however. Every generation has its cultural references. Today's kids aren't familiar with Charlie Brown and his predicaments; do you realize that? For dinner, stuffed turkey, sweet potatoes, pumpkin pie, and a bout of uncontrollable longing.

Your masochistic, perhaps romantic,

Federico

P.S. I can't think about the past. I don't think about the future. Am I one-dimensional?

. ——— .

"I'm taking you to lunch. I have to talk to you. Alice, I'm taking your boss off your hands for a couple of hours," Camillo announces impetuously.

"Go right ahead, Doctor. She's all yours."

On via San Maurilio, there's a family-run trattoria. Camillo orders pasta and chickpeas and gives me an update. He's better; he is effectively shored up by fifty milligrams of antidepressant daily and sees his psychoanalyst twice a week.

"Like in Tarantino's best films, though with less blood, my dear coach, we've come to part two. Laura is less aggressive. I won the first round: We'll live separately 'in-house.' A less painful compromise than living separately in different houses."

"And technically, what's the difference?"

"She sleeps at the studio—remember the one-room apartment she used to paint in?—and in the morning she comes home to have breakfast with the kids before they go to school. Better than nothing. I can't stand the thought of her disappearing completely from my life. Not having sex is a nightmare, I haven't fucked in six months; not even an octogenarian could tolerate such abstinence. My self-esteem is at zero."

"You men measure everything in inches and quantity of sex. Have you finished the book?"

"Emma, sex is a necessity; masturbating at my age is a sorry disgrace. I'll end up like that guy over there. Look at him, eating alone and reading the newspaper. The Márai therapy is for masochists.

The Right Woman is depressing, but I admit that the man writes well. He must have had a shitty life."

"He killed himself. Anyway, I brought you these."

"Calvino? Never read him."

"*Difficult Loves*: There's one that suits your situation."

"Charming pediatrician in search of security and someone to have some good clean sex with?"

"Not exactly, but in one of the stories, 'The Adventure of a Reader,' the protagonist is at the shore, lying on the beach, reading. He is seduced by a woman who interrupts his reading, and he ends up making love with her, trying not to lose his place."

"Sorry to offend you, my friend, but given a choice between a book and a fuck, I wouldn't hesitate. Have you heard anything from Margherita? I ran into her in the lunchroom, but I didn't want to ask."

"She's picking me up to go to a movie tonight. Giovanni came back home, sat down on the couch, looked at her, and burst into tears."

"Wow, how come?"

"He had someone else, sweetie."

" 'Had'?"

"Right. After their first time together, the woman realized she had made a mistake and told him so. She just wasn't interested."

"He's crying over another woman and expects his wife to console him? He's a selfish ass, a real bastard. Poor Marghe . . ."

"Giovanni wants to go back home, Camillo. And she loves him, so we have to respect her. . . . Thanks for lunch. Are you coming back to the bookshop? I have to relieve Alice."

"I'll walk you back. I'm not on duty until tonight. Anyway, you're right: We're better off forgetting about romance at our age. We have friendships and our kids. What more do we need?"

What I need is Federico. Who writes to me and doesn't seem bothered by uncertainties. I should ask him about sex with his wife, but I don't dare. I couldn't bear it, so I act calm and discreet.

• ———— •

New York, December 8, 2002
Peaceful oasis number 4, Greenacre Park

Dear Emma,
A pocket park, this little corner found in the heart of east midtown.
The sky is leaden and soon it will rain, that insistent, fine New York
drizzle, which makes this place seem even more lonely and empty.
A waterfall flows from granite blocks and ends up in stone basins
where leaves float. I feel you close to me; I'm exhausted and drained.
Whatever you may say, time does not distance memories. On the
contrary, it intensifies them. I minister to the longing by going to a
bookstore. I dropped by your Strand—eighteen miles of books. The
books there are arranged by subject category. People sit on the floor,
among the used books autographed by their authors. What I find brilliant is the "Books by the Foot" service. Just think, Emma, a decorator is available to architects and interior designers to recommend
volumes for home libraries of people who don't read, or books to
use on a film set. The books offered by the foot are often those that
would otherwise no longer sell; this solution clears out the store-
rooms. You could copy the idea, although from what you tell me,
for you customers and novels are untouchable, and you would find it
immoral to sell discounted books to fill the blank spaces on the walls
of ignorant people.
   A kiss from

                                                              Federico

P.S. The middle finger of my right hand is stained—my fountain
pen is leaking. I leave you the ink mark as a personal revenge against
the nerds.

                           •———•

A workday in the city center. The sky is misty moisty, like in the
nursery rhyme we used to recite in school. The shops don't seem
crowded. The salesclerks look dejected; customers are scarce.
The bars, by contrast, are teeming. People are standing around the

counters, where the irritable waiters work more and more quickly, appropriately so for this metropolis, the city of the three *e*'s: efficiency, excess, and exasperation. We sit at the sumptuous bar in the wing of the Galleria overlooking Piazza del Duomo, where they've installed a glass and iron patio with chrome "mushrooms" that provide heat. A young man and woman stare into each other's eyes while slowly nibbling at a tuna sandwich with tomato and lettuce: a clandestine lunch together, lucky them.

I haven't seen Gabriella in two weeks; our conversation feels its way along, with no specific agenda: "any news of Mattia?" "How is work going?" "Lucky you, a teacher with three weeks' vacation." "Your American friend, does he write?" One thing leads to another, like the bocconcini in my salad, the little balls of cheese sitting side by side with pale tomatoes and corn niblets scattered about the plate. Gabriella has chosen a "small plate" (that's just what it's called, *small plate*) of sepia-colored carrots with boiled cauliflower florets that look beaten. The waiter, strangled in a bow tie, looks composed, despite the pressing crowd in loden green military coats and gray suits, carrying attaché cases. I can picture the courts and offices waiting for heaps of paperwork—*dossiers*, to be precise—and maybe stock trades for brokers always on the lookout for the deal of a lifetime. Christmas will soon be here; spirits are up. Not much snow, but the weatherman has promised some. I reconnect with a friend and develop patience for the corn. It's already been half an hour; the "small plate" provides the calories but not the minutes we're allowed to sit. We order an espresso, sip it. What matters is that we've found each other again. Mr. Bow Tie brings us the check. No time to even decide who's paying and he's already back, giving us a dirty look, drumming on his pad. "Keep the change," we tell him, flashing a smile. No reaction from him. He stares at us. And it's not to seduce us. He wants, *very clearly* wants, us to get up and leave, freeing up a space. She's my best friend; I'm lost without her. I have to talk to her about Federico; I try to tell her with my eyes. Bow Tie pays no attention and clears the counter while we speak. The important thing is to consume.

Tasteless mozzarella balls and brownish carrots, stale *piadine* pockets and cold cappuccinos. Time, though—that's counted. Bow Tie is getting furious; his indignation sweeps over us, plainly menacing by now. His eyes leave no doubt about it: We have to clear out. No allowances made, no time to chat. In Milan, you go to a café with the meter running. I long for Federico's New York, for the peaceful oases from which he writes to me, for those book readers in Central Park. We café orators are legion, yet they treat us like intruders.

. ——— .

New York, December 15, 2002
42 W. 10th St.

Dear Emma,
It's Sunday morning. The light entering the living room window is milky pure, a sign that it's going to snow. The house is very cozy; I feel at home in this dark stone prewar building. New York has that Christmasy feel, and if it weren't for Sarah, flitting around from one party to another, I would sink into depression. I'm working like crazy, and when I'm not at the studio, I like to wander around all by myself, while everyone around me seems to be having fun in a city that is never quiet. Manhattan is overrun with tourists, especially in the "Bermuda Triangle." That's what they call the area between the big department store, Saks Fifth Avenue, the legendary Tiffany, and Rockefeller Center: Christmas carols, display lights, and rampant consumerism. We usually avoid places with mile-long lines and search out alternative oases. Wisdom recommends staying away from the area between Thirtieth and Seventieth Streets, but Sarah insisted, and so, my dear Emma, you won't believe it, but your favorite little-more-than-fifty-year-old went ice-skating, with a tightrope walker's balancing act, right on the rink at Rockefeller Plaza.

This morning, at dawn, I read an online newspaper reporting the results of a survey of approximately one thousand Italians, men and women—you know those idiotic statistics intended to make you feel you're in good company (though not in my case)? I printed it out and will copy some numbers for you: One out of three adulteries takes place during the lunch break, between 12:30 and 2:30. Two hours aren't enough to go home or find a nearby hotel; it takes me half an hour just to write you a letter. Therefore, according to the researchers' rough data—mind you, Emma, they are essentially speaking about sex—adulteries are no more than "quickies," performed in a car or in an empty office. Betrayal still provokes fear; those who forgo it end up regretting not having seized the opportunity. Only one in ten feels guilty. Temptations: Practically everyone is a victim of them. Some often (29 percent), some fairly often (43 percent), some occasionally (17 percent) or rarely (9 percent). It happens every time you meet someone attractive (32 percent), after an argument with your partner (24 percent), whenever you feel particularly fit (17 percent), or when you are away from home for business or vacation (8 percent). The individuals who are most apt to lead us into temptation are, in numerical order, colleagues at work (29 percent), strangers (26 percent), or the classic: the partner's best friend (18 percent). Nevertheless, betrayal is still frightening to almost half of Italians (48 percent). The reasons? The consequences to everyday life (28 percent), a sense of guilt (24 percent), fear of committing to a new relationship (15 percent), even greater than that of being discovered (13 percent). Only 6 percent resist and remain faithful. My sweet Emma, since you sell romances, the survey—idiotic, as I said—impulsively made me think of us. Who are excluded from the statistics, since no reference is made to either booksellers or architects.

A kiss, which is not covered in the book lists.

Federico

. ——— .

Alice stares at the computer screen with dazed eyes. One hour a day, at most, I had warned her. Instead, it's the first thing she does in the morning. Like a robot, she presses the On button, checks her e-mail, and spends her time in the virtual bookshop, dealing with orders. She wraps the packages and I take them to the post office. I'm the person in charge of shipments. Alice reluctantly abandons her station at the sound of the bell that announces the arrival of an actual human being in the shop. If anyone dared keep me from my cup of coffee and newspaper in the morning, I would become very crabby, so to some extent I can understand her. Alice doesn't stain her fingers with ink and performs her rituals in front of the screen. She even cleans it, spraying compressed air on the keys. She has her own forum with faceless customers and friends who, like her, live attached to their computer: They order books, more often they chat with one another, arrange appointments, review novels, seek opinions. Alice prints out for me any requests for titles not found in the bookshop, along with the more bizarre letters and the e-mails Mattia writes from Sydney with some regularity. If you look at her closely, however, she seems to be living in the shadows. She can't seem to find a man who understands her; by the third date, her hopes collapse: Either they vanish (she's too taxing for their tiny brains) or she dumps them. Demanding as she is, she can't stand guys who are ignorant or lack imagination. The icon pops up; an e-mail has arrived.

> Alice,
>
> Do you have Daphne du Maurier's *Rebecca* in stock? A wealthy widower marries another woman, but both he and the housekeeper live for the memory of the first wife, Rebecca, whose dead body emerges from the sea at a certain point; the widower says he killed her because she was pregnant with another man's child, but it later turns out that it isn't true; she committed suicide; she had cancer. But the housekeeper sets fire to the house . . . and so the rich man and his second wife live happily ever. Thanks for your reply,
> Manuele

"Emma, who is this Daphne du Maurier? *Rebecca* reminds me of the name of a movie. . . . There's a customer asking for it."

"Daphne had the way paved for her career. She was the daughter of the actor Sir Gerald du Maurier and granddaughter of the writer George du Maurier, a close friend of Henry James. Well connected."

The detailed reply comes from the fluty voice of an ageless fairy, Mrs. Lucilla, who has just entered the store. An English teacher in the city's poshest high school, an avid follower of the *Times'* obituaries, which, she maintains, "teach the language better than any other text," she is a faithful devotee of Dreams & Desires and of jasmine tea. Lucilla rests her bag on my counter, takes off her coat, and leans close to my ear to confide an impromptu, urgent secret: "I'm terrified, Emma."

"For Rebecca?"

"For my husband, Ernesto."

"Alice, look in the 'From Here to Eternity' section. Actually, it's a mystery. Hitchcock based that film . . . *The Birds,* on another of Daphne's stories. Remember the scene where the protagonist is surrounded by seagulls in a phone booth? I couldn't sleep afterward. The summary your Manuele gives of *Rebecca* is sketchy. . . . A cup of tea, Lucilla?"

"A chamomile tea, please."

"What's going on with your husband that has you so terrified?"

"He's retiring in a month."

"Great, you can do a lot of things when you're retired: take walks, read, visit friends you haven't seen in a while, volunteer, sleep late in the morning. . . . It's fantastic, retirement is."

"Can you imagine him? In pajamas, watching TV all day. Or sitting in the park, depressed. Ernesto has never gone shopping, never paid a bill. I even buy his shirts and socks. His life has revolved around physics and his students."

Retirement. Twilight.

"What do you mean, *my* Manuele? Hello, Lucilla," Alice says, interrupting us. She crouches down to pick up the anxious lady's glove, which has slipped under the counter.

"Manuele the scribbler, who is probably unemployed and bombards the shop with e-mail. Now he writes only to you. At one time, he addressed his letters 'Dear Emma.' Clearly, he's realized that I'm not a desirable quarry. *Rebecca* might even be on the 'Triangles' shelf; otherwise, order it. In fact, order at least a couple of extra copies."

Coincidences. How come that unemployed good-for-nothing happened to think of just *that* book, a novel that has been languishing for decades? Never mind, nothing will make me lose my hard-won composure.

"This Manuele likes to suggest novels. Read this."

Dear Alice,
I would like to mention to you the *Metamorphoses* (or *The Golden Ass*) by Apuleius, which, besides being one of only two extant Latin novels that have come down to us (the other being Petronius's *Satyricon*), contains the famous legend of Cupid and Psyche. God only knows how much art it has inspired—sculpture, painting, and so on. Do you know it? The girl, Psyche, is so beautiful that she arouses the jealousy of . . . Venus herself! Who dispatches her son (Eros, Amor, or Cupid, whatever you want to call him) with orders to shoot the fatal arrow that will make Psyche fall in love with the ugliest man on earth. But . . . Cupid falls in love with Psyche instead, and goes to her at night, making her promise that she will never try to look at his face; this is promptly disregarded, with consequent punishment. In the end, all's well that ends well, and Psyche herself will become a goddess and marry Eros. Which is to say that Eros (physical love) is joined to Psyche (the spirit) in a perfect union. This is the myth's allegory in its brief essentials. Unthinkable for a bookshop specializing in love to be without this book. Forgive me for taking the liberty.
Manuele

Who does this guy think he is?

"Come along, Lucilla. I'll make you some huckleberry tea; it's very soothing. Take my word for it—Ernesto will be just fine when he retires."

. . .

There's a crowd at the post office. There are the year-end bonus checks to be picked up, of course, but it's as if people write to one another continuously at this time of year, and the clerks behind the counter stamp the mail with greater energy. I like the physicality behind that little act: the stamp, the validation as if to say, There, done. In the lobby of my local post office, people spend a lot of time on cell phones. Two boys are shouting and talking about their personal affairs. They're frowning; their lips are moving and curling, gobbling up words. Cell phones cause wrinkles, I've decided. A grandfather is holding a little girl in his arms, pressing her to him as if to protect her. The young woman on line at window 19 must be his daughter. Both grandfather and child are beautiful; he is almost awkward as he hugs her. I'm partial to elderly men because I never knew my grandfathers. They're giving me some competition in here: They've opened a store right inside the post office. They sell everything—discounted books and domestic appliances, as if someone might decide to buy a vacuum cleaner while fuming impatiently in line, waiting to pay the property-tax bill. The only place I don't run into a living soul is in the secret circle for lost souls, the corridor with the mailboxes. I've brought along a novel to give to the righteous young lady behind the window. By now she knows me and must certainly be curious. She must wonder who writes to me, and why on earth I keep the letters in one of her numbered boxes. Or maybe I'm the one making up stories in my head, while she's used to it all. She told me that she lives in Garbagnate, in the province of Milan, and that it takes her an hour to get here by train. "What could be better than reading on the train?" I said, inviting her to the bookshop. And so she became friendly and opened up a little. Franca has a boyfriend who lives in Brescia and can't make up his mind. She endures her garage mechanic's inaction, and I don't have the heart to list the advantages of being free. She wants a veil and a ring, and nothing can convince her otherwise. I've brought her a present.

"Merry Christmas, Franca."

"Thank you, Emma. Did you know that you're my lucky charm?"

"No, I didn't. How come?"

"Remember the novel you recommended I read? *A Venetian Affair*, by Andrea di Robilant. I didn't understand much, but you won't believe it: Two days after I finished it, and after years of waiting, Guglielmo made up his mind. He knelt down in front of me, clasped his hands like when you're praying, and asked me to be his wife. Don't you think it's a fantastic coincidence? Meanwhile, make note of the date: September six at noon."

"What wonderful news, Franca. But how come you're waiting so long?"

"I still have all the arrangements to make—the invitations, the dress, the wedding favors, and then, too, the church. There's a waiting list; it's already all booked up in the spring."

Imagine the scene: Franca dressed like a meringue, Guglielmo, his hair slick with pomade, the aunts, girlfriends, cousins, sisters-in-law. And a rotund priest, stern-looking despite his plumpness. And the promise of eternity, which is almost never kept. It's Christmas and I have a horror-film vision of marriage. It's the *forever* I don't buy. Forever is an impossible commitment to keep.

"It's sure to be a lovely ceremony. I won't miss it; I love weddings. Give my regards to William the Conqueror. See you in a few days, after the holidays. You'll be open, right?"

"Of course, Emma, they'll deliver the mail to us on the twenty-seventh. One of these days, I'll introduce Guglielmo to you. I'm always telling him about the book lady with the mailbox."

I slip Federico's letters in my bag, alongside an e-mail from Mattia that Alice left on my desk. I got it into my head to reread all eighty-nine letters during the holidays. They make quite a nice little pile. My own private epistolary novel. Forget Sibilla Aleramo! I go out. I get on my bike and pedal. Proud of my new role as marriage dispenser. And as a mother who pays no attention to spelling.

From: Mattia Gentili
Date: Sun. 12/22/2002 11:27
To: Mom
Subject: Departure

hi mom this will probably be the last e-mail for 12 days . . . i
arranged to go with 2 of my friends on a car trip to the australian
desert for 10 days . . . tent, campfires and wildlife . . . in the desert
there's nothing so i can't write . . . so don't be upset if i don't write
or call . . . i'm fine . . . i like the house and my housemates sing
my praises . . . they are friendly and helpful . . . we've become
friends after only 5 days and have already had some good times
together . . . i'm doing the laundry, cooking and am like the man of
the house because these girls, angela and jade (a third one, kaia, is
arriving on december 27) are incredibly disorganized and i enjoy
cleaning the house for pleasure . . . some music and off i go . . . as
far as a job, well . . . i asked around and all the places when i asked
to work at christmas told me that they couldn't take me because
they'll all be crowded and for a novice like me just starting out
working in a full restaurant with so many orders isn't possible . . .
i have to gain some experience so i'm taking this trip to get away a
bit and see places that i'll probably never see again . . . school
ended yesterday, and frankly i'm a little sorry . . . i won't see many
of my friends . . . i'm in good spirits . . . i'm sending you my new
address in case you want to send me something . . . gifts and
packages are welcome. 27 Ridge Street, Surry Hills, Sydney NSW
zipcode 2010.
Mattia

Don't they teach punctuation in high school anymore?

Tradition calls for the year to begin with something new. The in-
novation for 2003 is gloomy: The building manager, an owl with

round metal-rimmed glasses on a big round face with bulging, expressionless eyes, informed us by registered mail that the porter's booth will be closed. Brass intercoms instead of Emily's almond-shaped eyes. She is already packing up her knickknacks, her magic lanterns, and the Bialetti coffeemaker that I gave her, allowing her to discover the only coffee worthy of the name. She says she isn't sad. The generous building manager found her a job, attending to the widow of attorney Oldrini on via Nirone, not far from here.

"I'll come see you at the bookshop, Emma," she says, comforting me as I try to find the right words to comfort her. It all comes down to money. According to the owl who rules our lives like a Stasi police officer, having a porter has become a luxury that we cannot afford. As if Emily's wages are any of his business.

I called Alberto to the shop and invited him to dinner. I have to convince him. I couldn't stand it if he were to say no. In short, the porter's booth, 485 square feet, overlooks the courtyard and shares an adjoining wall with Dreams & Desires. There is a fireplace that doesn't work, but painted white and filled with books and accessories, it would be worthy of a photo feature in *Elle Maison*. I spent the last few nights combing through glossy decorator magazines and reading articles with exciting titles, such as "All in 215 Square Feet," "Small Is Beautiful," "Heaven in One Room," and "How to Decorate a Studio Apartment on a Limited Budget." According to the experts, 485 square feet is a huge space for a couple with a child, not to mention me. I dashed off some sketches (little more than scribbles on graph paper) and hatched my plan without saying a word to anyone, a painful restraint for someone like me, who—if you don't count Federico's existence—can't keep her mouth shut about anything. Milan doesn't offer anything by way of cafés for readers, and I want to provide that. Countries in northern Europe have cafés with display windows, where people can eat and read books and newspapers; those in the south have courtyards and outdoor areas with straw chairs and little tables, where young people can study their notes and sip a beer and where managers draft their business plans on laptops.

Now I'm living in fear. When a dream slowly forms out of the blue, I'm sure someone will be ready to dismantle it piece by piece with the irritating clarity of logic. Dreams remain dreams until someone comes along and ruins them for you. It makes no sense to leave that space empty. It's half past three, winter darkness is about to descend outside, and this is my dream: to rent Emily's porter's booth. Tear down the wall that separated our physical presences, though not our hearts, and create a real tearoom with a bay window overlooking the peaceful courtyard. Amid the neurons of my bookseller's brain, my personal Morgan Library is ready and waiting to make its public debut. I can satisfy a need, is what I'm thinking. "A niche market," Alberto would say. He's the obstacle: the Faithful Enemy. I invited Gabriella to the restaurant as well, since she is unsurpassed when it comes to the ability to counter her husband.

Camillo suddenly pushes the door open and stands in front of the counter, wearing the expression of an actor who is mentally trying out his lines.

"Good afternoon, Camillo. What are we doing here at this hour?"

"I have the day off. I have to talk to you. Shall we go out for coffee?"

"Let's go upstairs. I have four kinds of coffee, including decaf. They're the best in the neighborhood and they're free. What's going on? Is it the cold or just my impression? Your skin is glowing. You haven't had a facial, have you?"

"A facial? Don't be silly. I haven't become a faggot yet. On the contrary . . ."

"Lots of men have facials, you know. Heterosexuals. And don't say *faggot*; *gay* is better, or *homosexual*."

"Emma, please, don't start an ideological debate. I'm too cheerful."

"I'm just being precise, Camillo. Clichés are defeated with precision."

He settles himself in the armchair, crosses his legs, and waits while I make him a decaf in a SHHH . . . I'M READING cup.

"I met a woman. A doctor. At the hospital."

"Her specialization?"

"What does her specialization have to do with it?"

"Falling in love with a cardiologist is different from falling in love with a dentist. Her specialization counts, and how."

"She's the new infectious diseases specialist at the analysis lab."

"An infectious diseases specialist can be useful these days, what with all the mysterious viruses going around, pollution, you know, that kind of thing. . . ."

"She writes me the wildest text messages."

"Once we used to flirt on the phone. Now it's aphasic text messages, little more than a string of catchphrases, all the same and addressable to anyone. Still, I think the doctor is great news."

"There's a problem."

"What kind of problem?"

"She's married, quite well-off, and has had lovers in the past."

"Experienced, then. Camillo, don't start in with a case history. Listen to yourself, observe yourself, consider how you feel when you see her, after you've seen her, before you see her. Analyze the symptoms: Do you miss her? Do you want to see her again? After you've seen her, how do you feel? Things like that."

"It's the first time this has happened to me. I reached the age of fifty-two without ever having had a lover. I'm an amateur."

"You shouldn't think as if you were counting on an abacus: first yellow, then blue, then green. You're likable, attractive, fairly well-read; in short, you're not a remainder. You're still crushed from Laura's blow. You love your wife and hope that everything will go back to how it was before. In the meantime, the doctor may be helpful to increase your self-esteem. She's the married one, not you. You've been released."

"I'm apprehensive."

"You underestimate the bends and turns of the spirit, never mind your anxieties. The meanderings of our psyche—mind and soul—are much more complex than you tell yourself. You can't be apprehensive just because you like someone. Also, you're better off if she's rich; there's no economic blackmail. Love in a pure state."

"I never once fell for a nurse, maybe someone poor and needy. I know why I like Valeria. A lovely name, isn't it?"

"Usually, we never understand why we like somebody. I see no reason to be apprehensive about all this."

"Damn it, Emma, you don't give a shit about men. You've distanced yourself from amorous muddles. With her, I gain access to the queen's room, the queen's bedroom, you see?"

"She's royalty? A blue-blooded infectious diseases specialist, the pinnacle of snobbishness."

"Don't make fun, Emma, not you, of all people."

"Okay, I'll be serious. The high-caste doctor is the unattainable queen of the ball and you feel like a loser. It's normal. In high school, someone dropped me, saying, 'I can't be with a girl who uses bad words and doesn't believe in God.' You think I don't understand?"

"Who was that xenophobe?"

"Someone just like you, more or less. Put it this way: If you know the plot of a film or a book in the first twenty minutes and don't feel the somewhat obsessive need to find out how it's going to end, the story doesn't work. We've passed the procreation phase, we're ready to spend a part of our life with someone else. Your marriage is too important and has lasted too long for you actually to be in a real search phase. You're not the type to fool around; you're simply practicing. You're at the first few pages, the first fifteen minutes; let yourself continue along, but don't read into it something that's not there. Don't worry and don't act like an idiot. Now finish your coffee in peace. I have to go down."

"It's wonderful to have a friend like you who wastes her time acting as my coach. I'll buy something; I have to contribute to the day's proceeds. You choose; I'm a mess."

Camillo adores being cared for more than anything in the world. His imaginary erotic-affective world is made up of women doctors in white coats, stethoscopes around their neck, nannies, baby-sitters, and female psychologists. After twenty-seven years of monogamy and some faded memories of youthful adventures, he's discovered that under the doctor's white coat there is a body that is in no way inferior to that of his wife. He has not put Laura behind him and would like to get back together with her. But meanwhile, reading text messages like "I miss you to death" or "You're divine" can gratify his narcissism, frustrated by months of communiqués of a different tenor. He's not capable of being a lover by the hour; he's better at being truly, committedly in love. I have supplied him with over one hundred fifty euros' worth of novels, hoping in my heart that Federico doesn't go to his female friends to tell them about the lure of booksellers.

"Reread Barthes's *A Lover's Discourse: Fragments;* his words are ideal for your practice of texting: 'The necessity for this book is to be found in the following consideration: that the lover's discourse is today *of an extreme solitude.*' We used to use it to figure out what we had gotten ourselves into with some Tom, Dick, or Harry. It acted as a mirror, remember?"

"Never read it; seems to me it was popular with you girls. This is why we men are ignorant in matters of love: We haven't read the right books."

"Later, I'll give you Elena Ferrante's *The Days of Abandonment.* Here, the husband leaves his wife to be with a younger woman. It's a profound abyss, the story of a withdrawal and rebirth. You'll learn a lot about women."

"Come on, Emma, don't punish me just because I've met a woman. Give me something cheerful, a story that ends well, that will console me and give me some clues."

I'll look for something along those lines, but off the top of my head I can't think of anything. And *The Diary of Bridget Jones,* which Alice sells in dizzying numbers, is certainly not the right novel for a little-more-than-fifty-year-old who is emotionally confused.

Alberto bites into the end of the sausage like a Texas cowboy and swigs his beer straight from the bottle. He has listened to me without objecting. Age is changing him. He's decided not to hide his humanity behind the efficiency of a heartless accountant anymore, or maybe this time I have a commercially viable idea.

"It could be a multipurpose space, where you could sell your books, but also other items, Emma. We'll have to study the market a bit to figure out the potentials. You think like a librarian, you know, not like a bookseller."

"There are librarians who have made a fortune for their bosses. Belle da Costa Greene, for example, a legendary figure of the twentieth century."

"Never heard of her. Who is she?"

"Never mind, it's a long story. I don't need to read market-research studies to know what my customers want, but my idea is different: I don't want more space for books; I want to open a café."

"You have a coffee bar; they drink for free and sponge off you. So why should they want to pay just because you expand the bookshop?"

"I want a real café, a place furnished like a living room in a home, where you can sip coffee, eat a slice of cake, meet a friend, have a business meeting, read in peace. Nowadays, no one goes home for lunch anymore; they gobble down cardboard *piadine* pockets and colorless salads, have a quick espresso, and then off they go, quickly back to work. I was thinking of the Sweet Dreams Locanda. What do you think?"

"A *locanda* is synonymous with a tavern with lodging. Why not the Sweet Dreams Cafeteria? Better yet, Sweet Dreams Tearoom; it has an international flavor."

"I will offer lodging to weary spirits and tired feet. *Locanda,* in Italian, is perfect."

"I like the word *locanda,* Alberto; it suggests a welcoming place," Gabriella says, coming to my rescue.

"I think it's time we registered the trade name Dreams & Desires. You never know, someone could copy your idea. I'll call to negotiate the deal."

"The building manager is expecting you tomorrow. At four."

"Slow down, Emma. We have to look at the numbers, see how much it would cost. A minimum of renovation will be necessary. Still, biscotti, pastries, and fruit juices pay off. Unlike books, they represent reliable revenue."

"Will we need a special license?"

"I think the city has to give its authorization."

"*Less is more,* Emma. Your space should acclaim the value of simplicity, meaning very few knickknacks, only essential items of decor, and simple menus. I'll help you," Gabriella adds, raising her glass for a toast.

"You wouldn't buy the furniture at Ikea?" Alberto asks.

"No, I'd aim for a more vintage look," I say. "Used, refinished furniture, and then for ambience and mood, candles, gauzy fabrics. . . . The *locanda* will be a place that's romantic, but not mawkish, and its dominant color will be white."

"White, for virginity, fine. We'll rethink the concept of purity," Alberto says sarcastically.

"Do you have any idea how many shades of white there are?" Gabriella puts in.

"No, how many?"

"Over twenty."

Gabriella is my savior. Her art history degree can finally be of use to me.

Snow white, ivory, pearl, arctic white . . . I fall asleep in a polar landscape, thrilled about my new endeavor.

. ——— .

Milan, February 25, 2003
Via Londonio 8

Dear Federico,

It's late at night. I'm exhausted but too excited not to write to you in bed, in Mattia's hand-me-down pajamas and wearing terry socks on my feet. A positive feature of living alone: I can slide under the covers with a sixty-euro moisturizing mask on my face without anyone saying a thing. I'm unpresentable, but content: As of this evening, I am the owner of the Sweet Dreams Locanda, a literary café, or a bookshop-brasserie, whichever you prefer. We had a grand opening, packed with "lifestyle" columnists and curious passersby who saw the lights on and came in to have a look around. And, of course, there were the old faithfuls. Cecilia arrived with a young man around thirty, in loden blue with regimental tie. I didn't have time to ask her if this was a new boyfriend. Mr. Frontini turned up at eight with a group of friends and a bouquet of pale yellow roses, Gabriella brought her colleagues, Alberto was beaming—you could read the dollar signs in his eyes—and Camillo was there, too, with the doctor, who has raised his spirits (and unbuttoned her white coat), a petite, well-preserved brunette who—great news!—is an avid reader. A large haul of compliments, my darling, on the sweet and savory buffet—we offered the same delicacies that will make up the daytime menu: a compendium of literary fantasies, delicious little tea sandwiches and canapés, with redemptive names. In the evening, on the other hand, we want to transform the Locanda into a bar-lounge serving nonalcoholic aperitifs. During good weather, people can enjoy the courtyard, where vines and flowers grow. I'm rambling on, but you know that my imagination, especially on days like these, has no walls (as the famous song says). Alice put up a new sign alongside the warning meant for thieves. Its inspiration I owe to you: TAKE A BREAK. TURN OFF YOUR CELL PHONE. Not a single ring could be heard, just a confusion of human voices.

A kiss as I go to sleep, happy,

Emma

. ——— .

A morning in late winter of 2003, destined to become *the* morning. A young man around thirty, though he could be thirty-five and not look it, with a corduroy jacket and velvet jeans, is tiptoeing through the bookstacks as though they are trees in a forest where he is playing hide-and-seek. Tall, with a lithe body, he has curly brown hair, a bare hint of a beard, and a direct gaze; the cuffs of his shirt are worn, and he's wearing a Shetland sweater and an orangey yak-wool scarf. He stops in front of the table with the "Irrecoverables" and scans the flap of *The Group,* by Mary McCarthy. He has long fingers and rounded nails with reddened cuticles. His black plastic wristwatch is in keeping with the rest. I don't usually disturb customers; I encourage them with a nod—*Welcome; make yourself at home; call me if you need anything*—and in return I get a smile (though not always). The young man has a disarming smile, naïve, gentle, yet somehow cunning. I'm sure I've never seen him before, yet there's something familiar about him. I could buttonhole him, tell him that that's a women's novel, from the sixties moreover, and censored, at a time when he had certainly not yet been born, and that I don't remember the ending. He would think I'm pedantic, and then, too, there's no such thing as women's novels and men's novels and I should stop minding other people's business. He leans against the wall, thoughtful, and looks up. From the way he moves, he seems to be familiar with the arrangement of the titles. He roams through the stacks with the keen eye of someone searching for mushrooms. He looks at the sign that reads ANIMALS PERMITTED HERE and gives another broad smile. He is the customer-accomplice type, the customer-brother, the "heavy reader" who raises the average in the daunting rankings of Italians, seemingly more plodding compared with other Europeans, so when he approaches me, I don't have to wait long before he speaks.

"Hello, Emma, how are you?" he says, extending a hand.

"Do we know each other?"

I return the handshake and look at him with the absolute certainty that I have made the usual forgetful fool of myself. Maybe he's the son of a friend and I don't recognize him.

"Well, everyone knows Dreams & Desires. I'm Manuele. A pleasure to meet you. I came by to pick up the book I ordered a week ago."

"Oh, Manuele, of course. I'm sure it must have come. Usually the publishers deliver within three days. . . . A-a-a-a-lice, you have a visitor."

The door of the stockroom opens like a sudden gust of fresh air.

She walks through the stacks in slow motion. He moves toward her. One last flurry and it's like watching a film, when at a certain point in the projection, at a place that is meant to go unnoticed, a character enters the scene, *that* character, and you, sitting in the dark movie theater, know perfectly well that from that moment on, the plot is destined to veer inexorably. And you sit quietly and wait for the rest of it to unfold. A few steps before reaching her, Manuele waves to Alice with his big hand. I primly walk away, scuttling sideways like a crab, as though in the presence of the queen of England. The scene calls for eyes to meet. The scene calls for them to be alone and requires that no one enter to spoil the magic, if you please.

"Hello, Alice. Has my Hesse arrived?" he says.

My Hesse? Don't tell me he's fixed on Siddhartha?

" 'He had read, turned the pages, devoured the folios and there behind them, behind the infamous wall of books, there had been life, hearts had been scorched, passions unleashed, blood and wine had flowed, amours and crimes had occurred.' *The Man with Many Books*. I'll take it." He has recited this passage in the inspired tone of a film diva, as if that quotation—lengthy, to tell the truth—has always been there and has only been waiting for the right occasion; as if that burst of culture has the power to change the day's agenda. Something is happening. And I'm enjoying it as though I were at the cinema. *Haven't they addressed each other familiarly, those two, in the e-mails that they've exchanged voraciously over the past few months?* Now the young man is here in person, ready to be gently torn to shreds by that impertinent, somewhat nerdy girl. The first in her class. I mentally cross my fingers. I have a hunch her evenings are about to take an abrupt, imminent turn away from the shop.

The couple that enter the bookshop save me from the sin of eavesdropping. He looks like an actor, an impeccably tailored jacket thrown over his slightly sagging shoulders, his thick white hair combed back; she, a minute woman with drooping eyelids, is hanging on to his arm, clutching her purse tightly to her chest. A blown-glass couple, perfect for a wedding cake. The husband and wife who have been together for a lifetime and love their routines head for the table displaying "Today's New Romances," where I stack the latest books awaiting a home. They're looking for a gift and find it in a sixty-five-euro illustrated volume. I wrap it nicely, and from this vantage point I can peek without appearing to spy an Alice and Manuele, who are talking tête-à-tête, at ease it seems. Anyone passing by would be led to think they've know each other since childhood: two confidants. His shoulder is leaning against the bookshelf, while her body is swaying like a metronome as she moves from one foot to the other. She toys with the volume, comments on the cover, smiles, laughs; in fact, now they're both laughing. She looks directly at him, and I'm sure that all she can see are his eyes and that she finds everything he's telling her to be interesting, audacious, intelligent, and original. Over time, this state of grace passes; yet the wonder remains etched in the memory of the first encounter. The porcelain couple leaves; the miniature woman holds the package gingerly like a tray of Sunday pastries. Alice walks to the door with Manuele Scartabelli, a philosophy teacher at a high school in Monza three days a week, essay reader, and e-mail consultant. She is meeting her future without knowing it, because while Alice is always attentive to customers, she never accompanies them to the door. She shakes his hand and wishes him "Good day."

I have a strong suspicion that for her it already is.

·——·

New York, March 2, 2003

Dear Emma,
I'm having a cappuccino, double cream, to celebrate the 101st anniversary of the Flatiron Building, twenty-two floors designed by the architect Daniel Burnham. I'm sending you this postcard. Isn't the building original?

Federico

·——·

Milan, March 8, 2003
Via Londonio 8

Dear Federico,
I just had breakfast—coffee, toast with butter and jam, fresh orange
juice—and smoked a transgressive early-morning cigarette. Today is
March 8 and you are my first thought of the day. I won't buy a sprig
of mimosa to wear in my hair and I hope that no one will think of
offering me one. Actually, I love receiving flowers, but the skimpy
little ready-made bouquet that some sensitive office manager leaves
on his female employee's desk in a company where males are statistically in charge is irreverent. In fact, it's adding insult to injury. I
don't want to see demonstrators marching on International Women's
Day; all I want is for them to clean the streets and put more trams
in service. Swarms of women are jam-packed on the tram: white,
Asian, black, Chinese, Moroccan, Egyptian, and Milanese. Clerical
workers, shop assistants, booksellers, laborers, bank tellers, postal
clerks, tax office employees, beauticians, hairdressers, manicurists,
accountants, press aides, students, unemployed women, doctors, den-
tists, housewives, journalists, nurses, attendants, traffic wardens, po-
licewomen, cashiers, bartenders, bookkeepers, advertising agents,
assistant directors, copywriters, professors, schoolteachers. Mothers,
daughters, grandmothers, sisters, mothers-in-law, sisters-in-law. All I
want today is for the (male) dog poop to be shoveled out of the
flower beds so we can walk in the park in peace, amid the timidly
flowering trees, with no danger of slipping perilously on the smelly
turds. I'd like them to fill in the holes on the uneven sidewalks; I'd
like the (guys') motorbikes lined up like soldiers—forcing our (ladies') bicycles to retreat, helpless and frustrated—to disappear. I'd like
them to censor the headlines and news about crimes against women
and, for one day, leave us out of the city's violence, inside the walls of
our homes. I want smiles and kind gestures that are not mawkish. As
for me, I'll give my female customers a discount and decorate the display window in their honor—there are books galore about women.

Women who read sitting, reclining, decorous or sprawling, distracted and sheltered in the pages of a book. Women engaged in reading and therefore dangerous.

I adore you, even though you're a male,

Emma

• —— •

New York, March 8, 2003

Dear Emma,
Here is a glimpse of early-twentieth-century New York. And a woman.

In 1911 textile workers at the New York Cotton Factory went on strike to protest the terrible conditions under which they were forced to work. The strike went on for several days, until March 8, when the owner, Mr. Johnson, locked the factory doors to prevent the workers from leaving. A fire started in the building and the 129 women held captive there burned to death. Rosa Luxemburg subsequently proposed that March 8 be declared an international day in support of women's struggles.

There are twenty-two women in the studio. I bought them bunches of violets, and they looked at me, surprised—March 8 isn't celebrated here.

F.

• —— •

Alice has changed. Something must have happened. Or rather, *he* must have happened. The clues are obvious. She comes to the shop wearing a loose dress that falls above the knee, dark blue stockings, and pumps with hourglass heels. Such a drastic change is not like her. Alice is a sensible reformer; she's never been a revolutionary. What does the cropped hair with bangs mean? Audrey Hepburn. Her, too. I prepare myself. She approaches bearing a cup of green apple tea and coquettishly announces, "I had an idea."

"Thanks for the tea. The idea has to be low-cost; you know Alberto. What did you do to your hair?"

"I made a vow."

"You make those in church."

"You know when you think, *If this happens, I'll do that; I swear I will*? Well, it happened. The wager was the hair, so yesterday I had it cut. Snip, I feel like a new woman. Anyway, it will grow back."

"You look fine, sweetie. You had an idea."

"We could do with some help, at least in the afternoon. With the Locanda, I can't keep up with everything. I was thinking that we could use a salesman here."

Salesman, she says, not salesgirl. It doesn't take divinatory faculties to connect the fifty-euro haircut to her ideal salesclerk.

"The important thing is that he be young and on the ball, stylish but not affected, an efficient intellectual. Excellent idea, Alice, a male is just what we need in here. However, I'm afraid we'll have to square it with Alberto."

I allow myself half a day off today; hairdresser, waxing, a facial, a new dress, and a pair of shoes. I say good-bye to Alice without making any specific recommendations on the newly arrived books; I have to hide my excitement over the brief vacation that awaits me. She seems happier than I am to have the place all to herself for a few days.

"You deserve heaps of pampering in Normandy. With all the spas there are in Italy, this trip for thalassotherapy seems a bit excessive, but you'll be in a Proustian setting. Have fun, rest up, and bring me back some madeleines."

Proust is the last thing on my mind, but the destination lends credence to the lie. I can't keep saying that I'm going to Paris to check out bookshops every year. Health is an unassailable argument.

• —— •

New York, March 31, 2003
42 W. 10th St.

Dear Emma,

In 1913, J.P.M. went to Egypt with members of an expedition from
the Metropolitan Museum of Art, a trip he financed, to the tune of
millions of dollars. There, in the presence of those ruins, he became
ill. He returned to Rome, to the Grand Hotel; when his doctor arrived, he advised the family not to bring him back to New York.
There was no hope; J.P.M. was delirious and the fever was playing
funny tricks on his mind. Pointing to the ceiling in his suite, he kept
saying that he had to climb the hill. He lost consciousness on March
29 and died at 12:30, on the thirty-first. They waited for the U.S.
Stock Exchange to close before announcing his death; then the flag
was hoisted at half-mast on Wall Street. The family received tele-
grams signed by Pope Pius, by emperors, kings, bankers, industrial-
ists, traders, and art curators, who, moved, bowed before that "great
and good man." Belle da Costa Greene, disconsolate, sent a telegram to Berenson: "My heart and life are broken." The *France* would
arrive in New York on April 11, bearing the casket of its commo-
dore. Belle, who had lost the man who had created the Morgan,
flooded the library with red and white roses and African daisies,
and arranged a funeral chamber in the West Room, where she kept
vigil as though she were one of the family. Morgan rewarded her
with fifty thousand dollars in his will, to serve as a living annuity,
but it was the library's future that concerned her. The collection
now numbered more than six hundred volumes and was the most
valuable assemblage of medieval and Renaissance manuscripts in
the world; its future depended on Jack, to whom the father had left
it, specifying that it was to remain "always available for the instruction and pleasure of the American people." The son had to sell part
of it to pay taxes. The following year, he put it on display at the
Metropolitan, and that was the only time when the collection could
be viewed in its entirety. Belle remained at her job as librarian for
another thirty-five years. Ninety years have now passed and we are

here to work on the innocent obsession of a man whom all the news-papers of America today commemorate with lengthy articles, refer-ring to Renzo and the studio, as well. I thought it would be nice to tell you about it, with nine days remaining until we see each other again.

Your excited Federico

P.S. Today I feel truly happy.

APRIL 10, 2003

Dusk was falling yesterday when I left the hairdresser's interminable torture routine. Snowflakes fluttered harmlessly. They drifted down my coat, glided onto car windshields, trimmed the curbs of the sidewalks like a silvery deckle edge. Then they dissolved into rain. After hours and hours, my hair falls perfectly straight over the chilly back of my neck.

I make coffee and apply a double layer of an aloe-oil hydrating mask on my face. It stings. I open the curtains, wrap my hands around the cup to warm my fingers. The framed shot is charming; my gaze roams from top to bottom. The buildings of via Londonio are like the miniature lopsided plastic houses in a snow globe whose particles simulate a storm. The roofs are cupolas dusted with white. My personal enemy, the snow, slowly whirls and eddies, trampling my plans without a jot of sensitivity, challenging them to an unfair duel, like the one between Pierre and Dolokhof in the Sokolniki forest. The duelists' seconds measure off the distance, leaving their footprints stamped in the snow from the starting point to the swords stuck upright to mark the bounds. At forty paces, you can't see a thing and everyone is silent. Until there's a shout from Pierre, the calm one, the prudent man in the story, less vain than Prince Andrei, the trifling paramour of the impressionable Natasha. My impatience is irreconcilable with these snowflakes. They touch the ground; some sensibly dissolve; others, more infuriating, settle in a cradling mantle, and I, who had always considered them a blindfold obscuring a lonely childhood in the building's courtyard, now detest them.

The radio crackles bulletins such as "The snow emergency plan was already in motion at dawn, with more than three hundred vehicles spreading salt and providing needed assistance." I booked a taxi for nine. There are still 178 minutes to go. My driver is still sleeping or has just started his shift. Will he be here? The news announcer's voice dashes my hopes: "Milan is being lashed by an exceptional snowstorm. You'd have to go back some twenty years to find a similar situation. Code red for road conditions; the use of chains is required. The highway authority advises against traveling unless necessary." Going to Belle-Ile may be considered a necessity, and I'm not driving. The speaker has a short memory. Be more precise, please. Oh, how wonderful the snowfall of '85 was, that January eighteen years ago. Doesn't he remember how many snow children were born in Milan that year?

"The city has come to a halt. The switchboards of the various taxi companies are swamped."

No mention of air traffic.

"All of Europe is gripped by freezing temperatures. The blizzard of April 10, 2003, is being viewed as exceptional throughout the nation."

And in the life of a bookseller. I stare at the suitcase—or rather, it's staring at me as it waits quietly in the corner by the front door. It's asking, Now what do we do? I change the channel. Now it's a female newscaster talking, and for some reason she's all excited, listing the records with inexplicable enthusiasm: Genoa hasn't awakened to this much snow since 1986 and now, the talking head advises us (you can't see her rubber boots, but they are definitely there, strawberry red), warnings are being issued for the south-central region. The phone rings; the voice is that of an optimistic, friendly person: "Milan is at a standstill, ma'am. Cancel?"

"No, no, I'm not canceling anything. I simply *must* get to the airport, if you would be so kind as to take me." My honeyed voice is my only tool.

"Linate or Malpensa?"

"Linate, Linate. It's not far."

"It's not a good time, ma'am. Call it off. Take my word for it."

I explain to the voice that I have to leave. For a very important meeting. An absolute must.

"Whatever you say, ma'am. I like snow."

Sitting in the backseat of an optimistic, friendly driver's Audi, I pass through a velvety-soft Milan. I try burying my head in a book, but there's no way. He likes talking about the weather. In fact, it's the highlight of the day, and if I weren't here, I would finally be able to alphabetize the titles on the "Women Who Read" shelf, a project that I've been meaning to get to for months. Novels are full of libraries, female readers, and bookshops. I'll dedicate a section to the snow—when I get back.

Here we are, Linate. It isn't even so cold. My suede ankle boots are wet, but choosing to wear them was an indulgence. The snow falls on the pavement in tens, hundreds, thousands of flakes, depleted after their brief run. At the entrance to the international terminal, a few passengers appear calm; all the others—a bedlam of snow-dusted suitcases, feet, coats, and hats—crowd around the check-in counter for information and some hope. In my prior life, I landed in Goose Bay, Canada, in Lapland, in Samara, Russia, in Kushiro, a town in Hokkaido, where they paid me a fortune at a conference on biotechnology. The planes skidded happily on icy runways, the passengers utterly indifferent. Not so in Milan. A few flakes is all it takes for the system to come grinding to a halt: The fluffy white stuff immobilizes the wings of the huge, helpless insects. Light orchestral music filters into the departure area. I'd like to know who chooses the Muzak piped into airports and elevators. Spring started twenty days ago, and my heart is fervent with obstinate hope. From the muted screens, meteorologists mime the possibility of a "marked improvement" starting as early as tomorrow. I'll wait for it. The young lady at the check-in counter shakes her head: "All flights to Paris have been canceled, ma'am. The storm's duration and intensity make it an extreme and certainly unusual phenomenon," she adds, as prepared as a textbook. A core of frigid air has struck Europe. Moscow is showing minimum temperatures of minus thirty-one degrees Celsius and the Scandinavian peninsula will not escape the icy weather on its way from Siberia, with temperatures as low as minus twenty-four degrees in Helsinki, and a horde of minus somethings is forecast for Warsaw, Berlin, and Hamburg. They don't mention Paris, and Federico is waiting for me on the dock in Belle-Ile. Which, with a mantle of white, must be quite beautiful. I make myself comfortable, so to speak, in one of the cramped, rigid chairs that the airline provides and wait as though nothing has happened and nothing is going to happen. The runway looks beautiful from here. Blanketed with ice, it maternally cradles the aircraft at rest in the arctic whiteness of Milan's eastern suburb. There they stand, wings outstretched like the arms of a team of gymnasts. Their engines are silent. I could pray, but I don't remember the words of the prayers that Maria made me recite at night before going to bed. It serves me right. I should have listened to Don Maurizio when he invited me to Mass, but I explained to him that I like churches when they're deserted, because it makes me feel like He is there listening to me. Phone book in hand, I can count on a psychiatrist, a dermatologist, a pediatrician, an aesthetician, a cardiologist, an osteopath, a hairdresser, a dentist, a plumber. I even noted the number of the locksmith, after the time I was locked out of the house, waiting for Mattia, who had *inadvertently* left a piece of a key in the lock: my life is a directory of specialists. No meteorologist, however, and only now do I realize why there are TV channels dedicated to weather forecasting. They allay anxieties and respond to urgent questions at a time like this, when the weather dictates a person's agenda. Alongside the names MILAN and PARIS they've drawn a snowflake. "You don't need a weatherman to know which way the wind blows," as Bob Dylan sings; all I know is how much I could use one right now, someone to reassure me. I'm not resigned; I'm keeping a positive outlook: I'm certain that concentrating will overcome the obstacle that has come between me and my plans. Meanwhile, I have things to read. I always carry a novel with me, but after seventy-two minutes of *The Rotters' Club*, I give up. My heart is an icicle as I look at the departures board, which spins up the verdict: CANCELED. Coe's pages fly by indifferently, while the author wonders "if there are some moments in life not only 'worth purchasing with worlds,' but so replete with emotion that they become stretched, timeless. . . ." This is a moment in life that would be worth cutting short. Do away with all this hyperbole, jump on a plane, and go. What's the problem? Don't they train these pilots to cope with adversity?

I go out to the square and find a taxi. There's a lineup of them, their engines running, ready to welcome the valiant utopians, the mature dreamers with shadows, like dark bruises, already showing under their sad, desperate eyes. I don't usually take a taxi from the airport: the 73 bus takes exactly the same time, follows the same route, and only costs 1.50 euros. But the cabdriver has already opened the door, as if he has been waiting especially for me and my decision to return home through the blasts of sleet, bowed but not broken. Somehow, I think of Anna Karenina and I can picture Mr. Frontini's face: He would be laughing if he could see his favorite bookseller now, in such pathetic conditions. Can there be a more poignant scene than this muffled, dazed Milan, its cars slipping and sliding along at a crawl with a newfound gentleness? No one has thought to spread salt. The driver deposits me at Stazione Centrale, where shovelers in fluorescent jackets smile at the kids sloshing around in their rubber boots.

"Leave me off here, thanks. I'm going to see if the trains are running."

The Eurostars, for the north and even for the south, are halted, called off, canceled. It will end, I think, punishing myself with a cappuccino in a plastic cup at the station bar. It's five in the afternoon. I give it up. I go home. I set aside my pride and call Alice.

"Don't make any remarks; just look on the Internet and see if you can find something besides the conflicting bulletins on the TV news."

"Oh, Emma, I'm so sorry. There's not a soul in the shop. Should I call you back, or do you want to wait?"

"I'll hold on, thanks."

"Air France's site says arrivals and departures are not expected to resume until six tomorrow. Some flights may take off, weather conditions permitting, starting at seven, though with possible delays. Do you want me to look for a spa near Milan?"

"No thanks. Maybe I'll call Elettra at Montegrotto Terme. The spas in the Colli Eugeni are outstanding even when it snows. I have the number."

I'll go no matter what. I want to be on the first plane that leaves for Paris. At six, she said. I'll be there. The radio crackles with news I've already heard.

"For passengers traveling on the Eurostar, the journey from Paris to Milan was a veritable odyssey, lasting twenty-six hours. The unfortunate travelers were due to arrive in Milan yesterday evening at eight P.M., but did not reach Stazione Centrale until 3:10 A.M."

Isn't there anything else going on in the world? What have they done with the usual robberies, trials, quarrels between neighbors, and disputes among politicians?

"Berlin's main railway station was evacuated after a steel beam collapsed as a result of strong winds. A customer in a bar was buried under a wall that gave way. A woman in a car braked in time when a tree fell in front of her; she then tried to back up but was struck by a second tree." This is what they call bad luck. Or destiny. On the live broadcasts, the TV journalists struggle to remain on their feet as gusts of wind batter them. That way, they get to be heroes. News arrives from the rest of Europe: At the entrance to the Channel, a British container ship is in trouble; the twenty-six crewmen on board the lifeboats were rescued by two helicopters. The London-Paris-Brussels high-speed TGV has been suspended. In Paris, the city council decided to prohibit people from entering parks, public gardens, and cemeteries—the risk of falling trees is too high. In the Birmingham area and in northern Great Britain, wind speeds have exceeded ninety-three miles an hour. On the few planes still flying, the flights have been dramatic, the landings eventful: people fainting, screams of panic, crying, vomiting. At Charles de Gaulle Airport, 110 flights were canceled.

And Federico?

"The French railways have canceled all long-distance trains and most of the regionals. Traffic has been at a complete standstill since five in the afternoon; many lines are disrupted due to fallen trees on the tracks. Thousands of passengers have been rerouted on buses."

Thanks. They read my mind. Has anyone ever thought of writing a novel whose plot is determined by the weather? I swallow a pill and to hell with the herbalist; I sink into the bathtub's frothy foam, surrounded by lighted candles. I am reminded of Meryl Streep in *The Bridges of Madison County,* when Clint Eastwood is waiting for her downstairs in the kitchen and she, there in the tub, sipping beer in a champagne flute, looks up and remembers that "he had been here just a few minutes before; she was lying where the water had run down his body, and she found that intensely erotic." I drink from the bottle of Ceres and yearn for the same sensation from the author of the Post-it note that now lies in the desk drawer, in a folder marked "Miscellaneous." It's a hiding place that I have always considered safe and that only now is worthy of the name. An irresponsible act. I set the alarm. I slip under the covers and imagine Federico sleeping as he flies over the Atlantic.

· ——— ·

Dreams & Desires, Dreams & Desires, Dreams & Desires, Dreams & Desires, Dreams & Desires, Dreams & Desires, Dreams & Desires, Dreams & Desires, Dreams & Desires, Dreams & Desires, Dreams & Desires, Dreams & Desires, Dreams & Desires, Dreams & Desires, Dreams & Desires. Usually, my mantra works as I'm brushing my teeth, or when the tram pulls away from my stop and the sadistic driver waves byebye, but then the light turns red and he's forced to open the door again. The mantra works when I have to count to ten before asking Mattia in a neutral voice what reasonable explanation there is for the litter that accumulates in his room. The heroic cabbie drops me off at Linate. The runway is anxiously awaiting me.

I can feel it.

I will it.

I know it.

Radio on, in the darkness of the morning of April 11: "Almost all flights arriving and departing from Milan's airports have been canceled due to snow-covered runways and strong winds." *Almost* all. A sign lights up; the neon flashes hope. But no. There are no planes warming up their engines once the 7:00, 8:00, and 11:50 flights have been scrapped. I'll wait until afternoon. My reluctant suitcase and I walk toward the Air France lounge, a kind of private sitting room with free coffee and publications to read: *Madame Figaro, Elle, Libération,* a little like being already there. I phone Alice. There are no phone booths like they used to have, but silver-plated devices with a keyboard, mounted on the wall. "I took your advice: I found a spa on Lake Garda. I made a reservation. I'm badly in need of a vacation," I say, lying easily.

"Great idea, Emma. I'm planning a surprise for you. Don't worry, just go. I didn't sell much yesterday, but Milan is terribly enchanting."

Terribly enchanting. To me it just seems terrible. I hand my Flying Blue card to the hostess, starched and prim in her dark blue suit, white shirt, and tricolor bow, who obstructs my incursion.

"Silver isn't eligible for entry to the lounge, madame. Gold or platinum is required, *je suis desolée.*"

Displaying a French equal to Balzac, I point out that we've been waiting to depart for two days and that there are no passengers in the lounge, but she is unyielding. If you don't have a gold card, you're nobody; as if I were to treat a customer according to the number of books he buys or make caste distinctions between those who buy hardbacks and those who prefer paperbacks. An Indian couple enters; they have the docile look of those who have seen worse and know all about caste, and it reminds me that I've never been to India and that—damn Morgan, the *Titanic,* and April 10—if Federico had come into the bookshop on any June day rather than on April 10, I would now be wearing a floral dress and high-heeled sandals, and would already be in his arms. I go back to the molded chair. I start making lists; they always work. As a little girl, I was one perennial list—of premonitions, renunciations, plans, desires, and dreams.

Today's list, April 11, 2003.

Title: What Are You Willing to Do to See a Plane Take Off?

More or less: anything.

More realistically, as otherwise it doesn't work:

- Stop smoking (this is a constant). I already managed to, twice. The first attempt lasted nine months, the second eight. I don't know why I started again. But it won't happen the next time.
- Stop smoking FOR GOOD.
- Read science fiction novels.
- Write a letter each day to someone you haven't seen in years.
- Begin studying any Oriental language.
- Give up tea, coffee, beer, fresh-squeezed orange juice.
- Speak kindly to at least ten strangers you meet along the street each day.
- Learn to drink hard liquor.
- Get a driver's license.
- Don't buy clothes, shoes, or handbags when they're on sale.
- Pray, believing that someone is listening.
- Stop neglecting my mother's grave, pretending she isn't dead.
- Admit you love her, for once.

The snow has let up *slightly*. The list has produced its first results. The young lady at the check-in desk, her hair twisted into a chignon, raises her big eyes. They are the commanding, indifferent eyes of a woman who has never been under a spell. In fact, she shakes her head, tossing the blond ringlet cunningly draped over her ear, marring the geometry of her collegiate hairdo. Soon she'll go off duty and her replacement won't understand why I'm so insistent. A group of young people are camped out, playing Monopoly. They may well be slaves of the computer, but there's still something exciting about buying plastic houses and hotels, Park Place and Boardwalk, about probabilities and unforeseen events. The unforeseen event is the snow. The probability that I will depart is near zero. Mademoiselle Air France nods her head up and down. She's the new one on duty, but she must have spoken to her colleague because she seems to understand, or maybe she has a tic. It's seven o'clock. It's dark outside.

"Madame, there's no sense in your waiting; for tonight, we're closing."

"I think I'm in love with him."

"Excuse me?"

"I must, *must* get to Paris, mademoiselle, to tell a man that yes, the fact is, I really think I'm in love with him."

"I see." She sighs. Liar.

"So I'll take the first flight that leaves, any time on any day."

"The situation should improve tomorrow; there's a plane leaving Charles de Gaulle."

"Will you change my ticket, please? That way, I'll be sure I won't lose my seat. My loyalty to your airline should be rewarded, don't you think?"

"*Ça va,* madame, I'll issue you a boarding pass. . . . It isn't allowed, but . . ."

I drank a beer on an empty stomach; I have the courage of a lioness and maybe, starting tomorrow, I'll stop smoking.

AF flight 1913 lands on time, Saturday, April 12, 2003, at the Paris–Charles de Gaulle Airport. Here I am in a double-breasted coat with an organza collar, a blended wool sheath dress with a moss green embroidered bodice, black wool tights, high-heeled lace-up shoes, and a cloche hat, our good luck charm. I'd like to be as light as the organza, to feel the requisite superficiality called for by a romance composed of words, which the unreal absurdity of coincidences must triumph over, in my head.

Is a romance novel still possible?

I'm convinced it's possible, provided we're talking about the impossible. Or about secular miracles. The black hole spits out one wheeled bag after another, lined up like the toy soldiers of a defeated army after surrender. I go out. Carrying chocolates in a gold box, the Parisian lady in front of me, in stiletto heels, runs toward a little blond boy, who says, "*Maman, Maman.*"

My personal miracle is here. I have always thought that if you want something very badly, when you choose one and only one of several options, when you stand firm and your determination is stronger than any logic, than any ominous prediction, when you believe that the past is not a threat and you don't let the future scare you, miracles, or whatever you want to call them, *do happen.* Robert Musil wrote that the language of love is a secret language and its highest expression is a silent embrace. When the written word corresponds to what actually happens, the magic of a novel is complete. And words, as we know, have tons of patience and are able to wait. Federico is a few yards away from me, freshly shaven and therefore immediately kissable. He doesn't look like the last stop, but like the starting line of something that has to do with the word *love.* His eyes are deep pools beneath his thick eyebrows. He strolls along, sure of himself; from his six-foot-something height, he studies the smaller figures with wheeled suitcases as they rush past him. *Maman* is leaving; the little boy skips along with his grandfather toward the apartment in the Seventh Arrondissement. The smile of the man who is waiting is warm, radiant, impudent. A de-icer. "*So* good to see you," he says, cradling me against his sweater. No display of unattractive passion, but the calm of a man who knows and has always known that it would take more than a record-breaking snowstorm to keep us apart. I don't even have to be grateful to him for having spared me a five-hour train ride. I'm about to start crying. But I should have known that he can read my mind. We walk through the airport; travelers are lined up at the counters. He moves with long strides, like all men with long legs. I forgive him. The staff at the reception desk in the Radisson

Hotel seem to be expecting us, just like in the commercial when the receptionist hands you the plastic key card as if awaiting no one but you; when the elevator operator is like the handsome supporting actor in a TV soap who you know will become one of the leading men in the next series; when the deep pile carpet is brushed like a Cheshire cat and everyone smiles happily amid a profusion of fresh flowers. Federico is holding the key to a room in this bustling hive. I've never been good at maneuvers and I don't need them. With him, it's a matter of trust instead. When you know, when you know perfectly well in your heart, that this could not have happened any differently.

The antiques dealer is on my side. Filippo Borghetti is a refined homosexual, at peace with himself after marrying at twenty and divorcing at twenty-five; he now forms a happy couple with Gaston, a forty-year-old whose name has a Disney ring to it. Gaston says his mode of dress is "inspired by Marcel Proust," who actually loved haute couture, while Filippo wears crumpled, unmatched jackets and trousers that he inherited from his father, and boasts a collection of bow ties and foulards to wind around his neck. Each day a different bow tie, depending on his mood or the season. Filippo and Gaston are at ease among things from the past. One is an intuitive type who is perceptive about feelings; the other is familiar with rage and reverence, so when I explained my concern, they understood me.

"We deal only with small pieces, Emma. We don't use trucks and vans, but we agree with you. Let's meet this evening. A neighborhood gathering over an aperitif sounds exciting."

It's evening. I prepare a stimulating pitcher of tomato juice seasoned with lemon, salt, Tabasco sauce, and peppercorns; I lower the shutters, while Alice and Manuele rush off. Young people, you know, think only of themselves, and those two are still in the infatuation phase. Plus, they were born and raised around car traffic and don't understand that heels are an issue.

"You'd be better off switching to sneakers, or maybe you can pull your Supergas out of your shoe closet," Alice pronounced this morning when I invited her to the secret "Carbonaro" meeting. The problem is that you can't walk in Piazza Sant'Alessandro anymore, in front of Dreams & Desires. You toddle along, forced to zigzag and stagger in frustration. I, who would rather die than take off my heels, have a height complex, but I'm not the only one, and my customers are no exception. To get to the bookshop, they have to navigate through a tricky obstacle course. The sidewalk is narrow, you have to say "excuse me" to get by, and if you lose your footing, your heel gets wedged. Scooters and cars, parked in the middle of this out-of-the-way piazza, are an open sore: painted tin relics left to languish at a forty-five-degree angle, head-to-head in a double row, which indulgently also includes a bike or two. This morning, in what should be a small island devoted to pedestrians, I counted ninety-seven motorcycles and six cars.

It's time to put a stop to it.

The battle against motorized vehicles can no longer be put off.

The harm lies in ignoring it, in itself is a general sign of indifference, but taking a stand against cars and motorcycles isn't enough. You have to use your imagination. Without succumbing to postcard picturesqueness and the hopeless search for bygone times, it's possible to envision the square empty: the two small cafés with their mauve-red awnings (which pose no competition to me), the tobacconist, Piero's butcher shop, and Borghetti's lighted windows.

Maria, a third-generation dry cleaner, comes into the Locanda with a tray of pastries; Bruno, the tobacconist, is accompanied by his daughter, in a wool dress with puffy sleeves; Don Maurizio, the neighborhood's shepherd of souls, was quickly persuaded to come. He lives here, right above the Lord, and he cares about the faithful, whom he has looked after for thirty years. He has kind words for everyone.

"If I understand correctly, Emma, you want to request that parking be prohibited," he says, looking up in surprise.

"More or less. The point is, I have no idea how to go about it and I can't launch an antitraffic crusade on my own." The others chime in.

"We have to set a good example."

"I, for one, don't park in the piazza; I park my bicycle in the bike rack."

"If each of us agrees to keep the space in front of his shop clear, appearances would improve immediately. An indication of virtuous civic feeling."

"Sure, but what about the motorcycles? The young people who come to the Locanda for an aperitif leave their scooters everywhere. Do you want to lose business?"

"Most of those on motorbikes come alone. There are more males than females. They drop their bikes off in the morning and come back at seven in the evening. They work in the insurance building, the advertising agency; none of them lives here. By nine, the piazza empties out."

"Spying on your neighbor is an offense, and you're not a traffic official or the urban planning commissioner. I don't see a viable solution."

"Personal commitment on the part of the shopkeepers might move some councilman."

"I've never known a politician to be moved except for expediency or during an election campaign. You're delirious, Emma."

And to think that I opened the bookshop to lead a quiet life!

Don Maurizio, after two glasses of tomato juice, flashes a smile. Gaston and the impediment of a gay relationship do not make him uncomfortable, and the smile is not due to the tomato juice or the appeal I've made. He always has a smile on his face. He offers to talk about the motorbikes during Saturday's homily, the one that draws the most people. Maria promises that she will try to persuade her dry-cleaning customers, even though "the maids of the neighborhood's ladies go about on foot." Borghetti stresses the international makeup of his customers and lays the blame on the managers of the buildings across the way. I feel alone. In reconceptualizing a space, Federico would say. I say good night to them at the door and I'm certain that what I read in their eyes is a look of kindly indulgence. I clear the table, wash the glasses and wipe them slowly by hand because this is the only way I can hold back a sense of helpless frustration and, like a simplistic woman bucking the current, envision a scene without motorized vehicles. A homeless man, young, is arranging his sheet of cardboard on the ground, preparing for the night. He smiles at me, when I should be the one smiling at him before taking refuge in my bookseller's bed, with all those silly notions in my head. "There is no safety for the tender, no matter how straight their route, how innocent their destination," Dorothy Parker wrote in a weary moment of a complicated life.

· ——— ·

New York, April 22, 2003
42 W. 10th St.

Dear Emma,
I'm starting to hate the returns, the separations, and my own twisted character. Your laughter, the chaos at the foot of the bed, your body: You're in sharp focus. I never get tired of watching you, Emma. My tiny wren of a woman, we made love in that hotel designed by a tasteless architect as if we had been fasting for decades. I have to recover. Forgive the gastronomic comparison, but it's the only one that comes to mind at the moment. I feel like a shit. New paragraph.

I can't turn my life upside down. I feel Anna becoming increasingly distant while you, far off, are closer to me. I'd like to be sincere; talking to her would be simple. Would be. I'm in love with someone else; we write to each other; I've only been with her three times. She wouldn't believe me. Anna is able to distance herself from pain, wash away the stench with grace and determination; she has a natural calling for formal beauty. I don't remember ever seeing her in a wrinkled dress and, being the arrogant egotist that I am, I always considered her search for perfection to be a sign of regard toward me. Her talcum powder scent is a cage. My turmoil is locked up in there. I have no reasons to question a fortunate life, or I have all too many, but they are broken pencils in a new pencil case. Anna doesn't interfere with my career and my ambitions. She stands aside, she resolves the most complex matters on her own, and she doesn't impede my progress. Anna and I have lived peaceably since our wedding day: on the lake, two hundred guests—I didn't even know all of them—my father casually handing his only son into the arms of a friend's daughter. Tastes and income equal to his own, so as far as he was concerned, it was all right. I'm not pitying myself. It's just that I can no longer tell what I feel for her, because I've always taken for granted the things that bind me to her. Anna trusts me with her happiness, and I always viewed this sort of equilibrium between us as a perfect glue. I can't ruin the film for her and explain the letters and the mailbox to her. She seems happy here, despite the fact that she complains about missing her girlfriends and their afternoons together. Their exclamations "New York? Fantastic! Now we too have a home in New York"—have turned into e-mails and very few visits. She spent the first months adding personal touches to the apartment. She adapted rigorously to the community of artists, architects, and Italian journalists who accepted us as friends. She goes to the ballet at the Met with Sarah's classmates' mothers. She hunts for outlets. She's regained her enthusiasm for art history, which she had abandoned after graduation. And she looks after me, convinced that I need someone to see to my wardrobe and my social life. Anna is a wife. And that seems to be enough for her, though it's probable, even certain, that I have a superficial view of her. It's four in the morning. I'm writing to you seated at the living room table; the bedroom door is partly open. I've been sitting here looking at her for I don't know how long. She's still beautiful, vulnerable with no makeup. I have loved this woman. New paragraph.

I don't want all this to end and I don't have the courage to offend her by telling her about you and the joy the four letters of your name bring me. I didn't steal them from her, those days at Belle-Ile or the hours spent in certainty at the airport, because it was logical and normal to wait for hours at that airport. Finding you again was a chance occurrence, but chance now has a body, the pieces fit together, and I've found a name for them: Emma. This is the first time I'm writing to you about her and seeing her through the eyes of an unfaithful husband. I am betraying the certainties and successes of twenty-five years of dedication to architecture and to my career. You don't ask and I remain silent. Now that you're far away, I am trying to bare myself, knowing that I'm doing it for me and not out of a spurt of honesty. I am married to the woman sleeping in the bedroom. Unaware, I think, that her husband—or rather, the image she has of her husband—is becoming someone else. I am surrounded by friends who lose their heads over twenty-five-year-olds, feeling further away from death when and if they manage to fuck them. I've found that I'm not interested in feeling young, and I don't think about death. I'm sitting comfortably, watching the miracle of Sarah growing up. I went through it all, from the red spots of her measles to her teenage anxieties, like an attentive father; I hurdled every obstacle of her upbringing, feeling myself adored. I viewed my women like something rightfully mine and deserved, without ever really seeing them. The structure of certainties designed by a distracted architect is chipping away. The building is collapsing, and I don't want this to happen. I thought I lived for my work, for Sarah and for architecture; the Morgan is the most important project of my career. I miss you desperately. Someone who is like me.

And I feel awful.

Federico

· ——— ·

Simone de Beauvoir to Nelson Algren: "It is stupid to write love letters, love is not something you can put in letters, but what is to be done when there is this dreadful Atlantic Ocean between you and the man you love?" I have to find a way out, something along the lines of "It's not good to lie. I can't disrupt the course of your life. Take care of yourself, but we really can't continue the triangle. The least said the better; nothing happened." We're a reproduction, a fake, an artifice, a middle-age regurgitation. I should have SdB's wisdom. Things shouldn't have gone this way; it was an encounter between old schoolmates. It's becoming an exile. I don't want to come between him and her. We're covered with scars and we ignored them, reckless and foolhardy, pretending they were invisible. Now we're paying for it. You can adapt to a "relationship" while far apart. But this is a love story, not a relationship, and should be treated as such: Continuing on is impossible. A long-distance breakup is simple. Yet I find nothing, absolutely nothing, wrong with this arrangement. Nor does the word *relationship* bother me. Over the years, you become less rigid; you take what comes, as if you were unworthy of something whole. As the years go by, the word *scraps* loses its negative meaning. An odd moment is a gift from destiny. Simone wrote to Algren every day. She called him "my beloved husband," "my dearest husband," "my sweet crocodile man." Husband, not lover. The words we choose always imply something. Or something else. The champion of feminism signed her letters "your wife forever" or "your frog wife" (*"bercez-moi dans vos bras mon amour, je suis votre petite grenouille aimante, votre Simone"*). It was the word *marriage* that sanctioned the seriousness of a union. Between them, there was sexual attraction, an incandescent, unfathomable substance, more complex than feeling. Sartre had been her first lover, "but it was rather a deep friendship than love; love was not very successful. Chiefly because he does not care much for sexual life." With her.

There are no customers. I can't seem to distract myself and I don't feel like looking for answers in a book. With a man you see only once a year, it can't be a matter of sex, which would require spontaneity or continuity. And the age of innocence is long since over. I'll write to him after consulting the voice of my (albeit unconscious) conscience, who accepts my invitation to dinner with extraordinary eagerness.

"Is something the matter, Emma? Because you're acting as if something has happened."

Bless Gabriella. Bless her intuition and the tact she shows when she knows I need her while at the same time fearing her conventional judgment. We meet at Trattoria Toscana, in the Ticinese district, a cozy refuge for secrets and confessions. I walk there. It may be that I am particularly receptive these days, but the

Colonne di San Lorenzo, sixteen magnificent sentries, have never seemed more beautiful to me. When your emotions are in turmoil, you are prone to implausible delirium, as everyone knows, yet the moonlight glancing off the bronze thighs of the emperor Constantine seems new somehow. The beauty of the basilica is marred by green glass: shards of bottles abandoned on the steps, jugs of oblivion and enjoyment, boredom and pleasure, in this spot that Milan's tour guides, shouting into their megaphones, call *"un coup de coeur,"* love at first sight. I find one jug still half-full, placed underneath the Christ, as if to keep Him company. Also green are the cans bought for a few euros from the minibars of the unlicensed street vendors, and the jackets of the young people chatting in bunches over their drinks. The two who are kissing, having climbed over the cement flower boxes set out to protect the columns, would have appealed to Doisneau, the photographer known for his lovers at the station. The tram clangs a few yards away. It's the number 3, the same one that Federico took the day two years ago when he found me among the pages of my books. Gabriella is waiting for me at the table.

"I knew it. Something's happened. You look upset."

"Something always happens, good thing, too. Otherwise, can you imagine how boring it would be? Nothing special happened."

"But?"

"He spoke about his wife. Rather, he wrote to me about his wife. I have to make a decision."

"Does he want to leave her?"

"No, it's more subtle than that, more elusive. The fact is, Federico feels terrible."

"Oh, I see. He's the one who's married and he feels terrible. And what about you, then?"

"Gabriella, please. What good is it to establish who has the right to feel how and whether I'm in love? Better not to know. I know that when I'm with him, I feel content."

"When you talk about him, it's like you're . . . ecstatic. You're getting yourselves into the usual mess. Meeting once a year is only romantic in books. In reality, the situation is getting out of hand for both of you. A part-time romance isn't right for you; you deserve a full-time relationship."

"To tell the truth, it doesn't work even in books, aside from some exceptions. But usually men who are right for me, if there are any, die. I don't want any old man just so I won't be alone; I want *him*. Still, maybe it's time for me to step aside. If I leave him now . . ."

"The world is full of eligible fifty-year-olds. If only you didn't push them away. Look at Camillo. Things are working out with the infectious disease specialist; she told her husband everything, and I haven't heard anything about the guy jumping from an overpass. On the contrary, he confessed that he has been having an affair for twelve years. Just think, what a bastard . . . Camillo and Valeria are giving it a try; it may be a new life for them. That's what you could use, if only you weren't going after a man who's unavailable."

"I really don't understand those women of our age who take up with thirty-year-olds. A mature body is more comfortable. I just want to stay out of his family life, to be autonomous. It was supposed to be a relationship independent of all the rest."

"The rest exists. Put the brakes on, Emma, and get this story back on the track of a . . . let's say . . . mature friendship. I had a feeling it would end badly."

"It hasn't ended. The fact that he's far away helps. I never expected much from sex, much less now. I'm fine even if things remain the way they are. Do you think this means I'm hopelessly old? By the way, how is Alberto? I haven't heard from him in days."

"He comes home tense, but he's all right. I'm so glad I still love him. Don't be offended, but I can't see myself starting over again at my age with another man."

"I don't really long for Federico, I'm not hurting. He's the one who torments himself. I miss him only during the first fifteen days—say from mid-April to end of the month. I persist in seeing everything as if time did not exist. I deny time, that's what. Incidentally, have you seen the pitiful condition the Colonne di San Lorenzo are in?"

"You have to make a decision, Emma."

"Maybe . . . We'll see. . . . The decision will present itself, Gabri.
For now, let's decide to eat instead. Love makes you hungry; don't
you remember?"

.———.

Milan, April 30, 2003
Dreams & Desires

Dear Federico,

I've never been someone who cared much for memories—as you
know, they don't move me—so over time I began to systematically
forget. My life is a serial, rather than a film, and the episode of your
letter ends the series. I have no desire to become a third female
problem in your life. Being presumptuous, I nominate myself instead to the role of anchor, refuge, drawer, trunk, jewelry box, safe,
seashell, vault, park bench. It is possible to protect, cherish, and
preserve, without breaking anything. The beauty of our postal exchanges is this: no obligations, no schedule, no promises, no final
exam. No routine, but fluidity. A liquid society—this definition
stamps us: We live in a liquid society. The newspapers write about
it and the sociologists debate it, and even though I haven't exactly
understood what they're talking about, I like the term. Liquid is opposed to solid, which has an unyielding sound, bound by rules. Your
letter made me think about this. I felt you "struggling for breath," a
little like in the game of Sorry when someone's pawn is sent back to
Start. In your letter, you appear rigid, a captive of a life of ease and
beautiful sunsets, but it's as if you are seeing those sunsets through
the window, and . . . always hastily, forced to lease rather than own.
If you think about it, distance is an advantage: It allows us to watch
our sunsets without giving up the belief that they are real. Then,
once a year, the setting is the one you've known with me and I with
you. You have your studio, the Morgan, New York, and Sarah. I have
the bookshop and Mattia, Gabriella, Alice, things to do and passions
to pursue. You have a wife, while I claim a collection of friends and
customers who are my emotional universe. We are basically even.

What's keeping us from continuing this way without burdening our encounter with symbols, losses, and new wounds? Nothing except our own foolhardiness. Fifty-two years are a lifetime, but not the measure of a destiny. We are giving each other "something" of importance that is not disturbing anyone. For this reason, here is my response to your matrimonial letter: You and I are like the Morgan Library, and hopefully the comparison won't sound absurd. Eleven years after J.P.M.'s death, Jack donated his father's collection to the United States and the entire world. You and your associates will make it grander and more accessible, without destroying what was there. You are restoring it, expanding it, allowing the stones and the parchments to breathe again. Look at it this way: This is what you and I are about. We have no right to demolish the original architecture. Anna will not know, if you don't want her to know. She will not be hurt, and I can adore you and be adored in peace. And breathe.

Emma

P.S. See how reasonable I've become?

. ——— .

It's a bell ringer of a day. Mattia's e-mail is quivering on the desk and in my pocket is a letter from Federico that arrived today.

From: Mattia Gentili
Date: Tues. 5/14/2003 12:32
To: Mom
Subject: Party

dear mom, what a nice letter . . . i really liked it . . . it made me long for home . . . my room . . . the year of study and work ahead of me . . . and my whole future . . . yeah, I'm really happy . . . I'm coming home, back to the university, some odd jobs, a new room, tv, studying . . . i like the plan for the new room . . . yessiree bob . . . tomorrow I'm going to Subway, a fast-food place, to ask about any openings . . . and however it turns out my friend who works at a

jazz club told me he talked to his boss and that maybe he'll hire me,
if I can convince him to I'll be washing dishes in a week . . . we'll
see . . . whatever happens I'm feeling good . . . yesterday my flat
mates and I threw a party at the house . . . pervy . . . 100 people . . .
just imagine! . . . now I have to go mom . . . I'm looking forward to
dad's visit . . . i'm really glad he's coming to see me . . . love you
much . . . mattia

"Alice, can you tell me what *pervy* means?"

• ——— •

New York, May 7, 2003
Peaceful oasis number 5, Strawberry Fields

Dear Emma,

RENOVATION QUESTION: STAY OPEN OR CLOSE? ran yesterday's headline
in the *New York Times* regarding our library. New Yorkers are exact-
ing, not only in their sacrosanct compliance with regulations but also
in their affection for their buildings. One of the concerns that Simeon
Bankoff, executive director of the Historic Districts Council, expressed about the project is that the new entrance on Madison Avenue
could detract from the intimacy to which the public is accustomed.
He felt that at present entering the library is like being admitted to
the entry of a private home, and that having to give up that experience would be regrettable. But since the principal objective of the
project is to improve accessibility, Glory Jones, spokesman for the library, replied that the new Morgan is designed to allow people to
move through the buildings more easily, which will improve services
for visitors, researchers, and academics, without depriving citizens of
the privilege of entering a unique private space.

A unique private space, our mailboxes and Belle-Ile. Today, during the final design presentation, your words were safely in my
pocket. To celebrate the closure to the public, Charles E. Pierce, Jr.,
hosted a party for the employees. Starting tomorrow, everything
will change for them: They won't see their offices for two years.

Mingling with them, we wore a little crown depicting the project's design. Renzo was amused at being the theme of a halo cut out of cardboard. People drank, ate, talked, and hugged one another in a situation midway between a baptism and a funeral, a benediction and a burial. John Pierpont Morgan, looking down from his portrait, seemed to approve. We have two years' time to integrate the design of a new building into our lives, without destroying what others have built. Thank you, Emma, for having understood that I was capitulating, overcome by my weakness; thank you for having eliminated the scaffolding that I was constructing around us, and around our relationship. Which is not an extramarital affair, given the depth of the excavation that began when I began delving into myself. Mattia is a lucky boy. I've read and reread your letter dozens, hundreds, thousands of times. It's as if the gift has doubled in value, made precious by your decision to be there despite my sleepless nights, my delirious ravings, and my egotism. My "rants," as our kids would call them. I stopped by the post office every day for the past several days. I was sure you would disappear, scared away by my spinelessness, by the damper I had imposed on our voice. Instead, there you were, not at all frightened. I adore you, too, and I know that I will adore you forever. Your letter has lightened my spirit with a masterly stroke.

I'm off to mail this, my small, precious gift.

Your Federico

P.S. Another sign of your power: My allergy has disappeared. My nose inhales and exhales like a piston. New York is in bloom. All thanks to your words.

·———·

The rain begins falling on the meadow and he, fearless as a gladiator, comes onstage, drinking the tears coming down from the sky. Nobody moves. It's an absurd privilege to be in the stands along-

side Michele and Mattia, soaking up those tears, swaying and pul-
sating along with the seventy thousand wet bodies in the stadium.
"Born in the USA," sings the dark little figure down below, magnetic, overpowering, exciting. The *same* Springsteen sings our
story, tonight, just as he did eighteen years ago. The same stage, the
same trio, songs that are poems, and him, a small garden statue
who touches even those who back then couldn't tell the difference
between real people and cartoon characters. Kids who are now
adults, children and fathers and mothers united by the beautiful
rhetoric of music. I wish Federico were here. We'd sit on the grass,
Sarah and Mattia newfound friends, and then maybe I'd squeeze
his hand and understand *what I'm doing here.* Imagining that a different outcome is possible. I would sing off-key with him, like all
of us have been doing for two hours, fifty- and twenty-year-olds
gathered together in a single wet embrace. These are the times when
missing him makes me miserable; my stomach moves to the rhythm
of "The River," and it's wrenching to think that at matchless moments like these, there he is on the other side of the globe. So then I
close my eyes and it's as though he is here, as I drag remnants of
youth under the a sky lit up like day. I cling to Mattia, hesitantly,
though. I hope he won't notice the tears that are making my mascara run down my cheeks, that he doesn't realize how much I'm using him as a simulacrum for the lover who isn't here, while the
splendid middle-aged man, buffed in his black T-shirt, works up a
sweat with an energy that sets him apart from the human race.
Bruce Frederick Joseph Springsteen, "the Boss," born in 1949, is en-
thusiastically active in his older years, proof that in order to go on
singing about love, all you have to do is keep in shape and have firm
biceps and dark, curly hair. Mattia has been home for a few days and
it's nice to have him back on this hot June night, in the dreamy atmosphere of the stadium. An antidote to the horror of a distant war.

·———·

New York, July 1, 2003
Peaceful oasis number 6, Grumpy Café, 224 W. 20th St.

Dear Emma,

A sunny Tuesday with a light wind, a solitary stroll after visiting the work site. I walk by 222 West 23rd Street, the Chelsea Hotel, a peeling door, twelve floors, a dark lobby. To the right and left are inscriptions that tell of artists who have stayed here for the time it took to write a song or for an entire lifetime. A woman enters, plump and colorful, a grandmotherly hippie, purple scarf around her neck, exaggerated hoop earrings, her skin a web of wrinkles. She smiles at me. Who knows how many strains she's heard in these carpeted corridors leading to apartments that rent for two thousand dollars a month, or maybe the argument between Sid Vicious and Nancy the night she was stabbed to death. Bob Dylan's notes from suite 2011; I was a child when he was playing his gentle ballads on the guitar. The wall-to-wall carpet marks an era, the sixties and seventies, when even the finest wood floors were covered. Here people still live in apartments that tenants may furnish however they like; people sing here, make love, cook. Myths live on here. And Mark Twain's mustache, though I can't remember a story of his, much less a quote. I doubt he is one of your favorites; adventure isn't your cup of tea, and neither is the languid flow of the Mississippi, but you might like to know that in 1909 (Frank told me this), when J.P.M. asked to buy the manuscript of *Pudd'nhead Wilson*, Mark Twain replied that "one of my highest ambitions is gratified." I go into the shop next door to the Chelsea. Dan's Chelsea Guitars seems to have stopped with our youthful dreams; the sign is Pop Art, a colorful yellow and purple. It reads: "The value of a guitar is rarely indicated by its price." I can't resist and give in to a crimson Fernandes autographed by Springsteen that goes for $5,250, with an amplifier. Back home, I lock myself in my study and play it, feeling thirty years younger all at once. I have a high old time; it has been at least ten years since I touched a guitar. My favorite repertory? Ours: the Beatles, the New Trolls, Battisti with some echoes of my jazz period, a nod to Pink Floyd and Genesis, Cat Stevens. I've lost my edge, but who cares; it will come back. I apply myself to the guitar. I'm playing this for you. Close your eyes and listen to your guy. Paul Simon sang it for the first time at Carnegie Hall in 1967: "And the leaves that are green turn to brown."

My landlord has a sensational collection of vinyls, diaries dusted with notes, longtime friends, never mind Sarah's and your Mattia's iPods!

Federico

P.S. Why can't I be with you right now?

• ———— •

Fabrizio Lucchini, roughly thirty years old, enters the bookshop, strangled by a deplorable polka-dot necktie, wearing a white shirt, a navy blue jacket, and jeans with a pressed crease. This young man must have an old-school mother. He accepts a cup of "American" coffee and wolfs down a croissant with raspberry jam, warm from the oven.

"When I found that sheet of paper folded in four inside the envelope, well, ma'am, I thought it was a new type of traffic ticket. I read your appeal, and frankly I had to laugh, but then I quickly felt like a lout. Many people in the office had a similar one, so we talked about it. No offense, but they called you all sorts of names. A colleague says you have no right to judge, sitting nice and comfortable in the bookshop all day while we slave away, but in the end, we were swayed. I don't know what book to pick; it's for my girlfriend."

"What type of girl is she, Mr. Lucchini?"

"Call me Fabrizio, please. My girlfriend is very pretty. She bugs me because I work too much, but she's still in college; she doesn't know what it means to have somebody on your back, reminding you at least once a day, every day, that there is only one goal: to step up our billing."

"Poor boy, my accountant is always talking about money, too. What kind of work do you do in those offices?"

"Public relations, communications, strategic marketing, events for various companies. Procter & Gamble, the detergent company, you know, Fiat, and other multinationals. I'm in the business office. I have them in my power where money is concerned. . . . Oh, yum. Excellent croissants. Consider me adopted. I'll bring Angelica."

"How did you manage to win them over?"

"I read the appeal aloud; then Maurizio pulled his out. Those asshole colleagues of mine—pardon the expression—were laughing, making fun of me. We talked it over; we put our heads together to decide how we should react. You became the topic of the day. Motorcycle parking is still a problem, don't kid yourself. This is a comfortable place. How come I didn't notice this peaceful café sooner? Do you have a happy hour?"

Of course, to him, I must seem not only bizarre but very old, since he apologizes for using bad language and keeps saying "ma'am" so naturally. If I were now to explain to him what I think of the term *happy hour*, I would jeopardize an ally, won over by a sheet of paper. All in all, he's pleasant enough, and behind the sardonic appearances of anglicisms and "elements of communication," he might even be simpatico. I contain my triumphal pride at having managed to persuade that group of idiots with motorbikes to park their metal carcasses in the adjacent streets.

"Your communication strategy is what convinced them, ma'am. They said that the idea of communicating directly with the end user—namely, us—is brilliant. Without a middleman, you know? You presented your requests graciously and politely, a bit quaintly of course, but with some fine tuning, your words could be reused for a client in need of ideas."

"Are you serious? Please, call me Emma."

"*Brevity, alacrity, facility*—these are watchwords, for us. You spoke of unhurriedness, beauty, space. It was that which gave rise to the discussion. You touched a nerve. In the end, we started talking about ourselves and the shitty lives we lead. The pace is stressful, rushed. I don't read much, but I explained to my colleagues that you don't just sell books and that your proposal was an appeal

for tranquillity, not the hustling of a shopkeeper. If we park the
scooters and bikes in the courtyard, the piazza is all ours. I floated
the concept of a privileged island. Your coupon for a lunch is a start.
We'll all be here at one o'clock, when they open the cage doors and
let us out. One last thing: Do you accept meal vouchers? They give
us those, you know."

"Of course I take meal vouchers; I have a contractual agreement. I'll expect you then."

.———.

Milan, July 7, 2003
Sweet Dreams Locanda

Dear Federico,
It worked. I don't know if it was thanks to an alignment of the plan-
ets or Don Maurizio's prayers, but it worked! Some of the more
sensitive ones even apologized. Piazza Sant'Alessandro has been
cleared of scooters, and the bikes, unchained from the poles, have
found shelter in the courtyard. They've persuaded the building
manager to allocate a fenced-in area for parking and . . . the bikes
have disappeared from the piazza! All it took was a letter to the
bike owners, a coupon for a novel, and an invitation to lunch at the
Locanda to convince them to clear out. And nobody called me a
bitch. I made a deal with those poor junior project and account
managers who spend their days glued to their computers or sitting
in boring meetings dreaming about becoming senior communications, press office, and marketing managers. I took some words from
an Adelphi volume that I had never read and added a polite invitation to come and enjoy quiche and dessert and discuss an alternative
to parking in the piazza. I convinced the porters to sweep the area
in front of their doors, and even Borghetti, the antiques dealer, set
about cleaning the little stone strip in front of his shop. In our day, we
called it "self-management," remember? Well, we're self-managing
the piazza; we reconceptualized it—as you would say—on a human
scale. You should see them. They've become very strict with anyone

who dares to challenge our personal urban policy. Some of the guys from the agency and the insurance company have now become regulars at the Locanda, subscribing to a monthly plan: They eat lunch here and Manuele prepares aperitifs for happy hour, when they swarm out of their electronic cubbyholes and crowd around our tables, drinking nonalcoholic cocktails with nary a complaint. I couldn't believe my eyes this morning (it's my shift on Monday), when it seemed as though the fine dust had been kept outside the boundaries of our piazza. Those young men—thirty years old, on average—are much more sensitive than people give them credit for. What did I write in the notes? Quotations from *Zen and the Art of Motorcycle Maintenance*, by Robert M. Pirsig, platitudes such as "I can see by my watch, without taking my hand from the left grip of the cycle, that it is eight-thirty in the morning. The wind, even at sixty miles an hour, is warm and humid. When it's this hot and muggy at eight-thirty, I'm wondering what it's going to be like in the afternoon," but I got the effect I wanted: surprise.

P.S.: For the past several days, feeling happily foolish and a tad presumptuous, I warily give in to summer fantasies. I think about you very, very, very much.

P.P.S.: Your rendition of "Leaves That Are Green" was sensational . . . Thank you, my sound track!

Emma

• ——— •

New York, July 15, 2003
225 Madison Avenue

Dear Emma,
Life at the work site has begun in earnest and I am very, very, very content. I like construction sites. The site is the place where an architect comes to life, it's the material. The site has a smell; it mingles with New York's unmistakable one. You don't know if it's

the hot dogs or the Hudson, the gas fumes or the perfumes of Midtown's women, but there's this particular odor that I wish I could make you smell from here. The construction site is important because it establishes the hierarchy (the boss's words), and gives a sense of physicality (you can tell from the pickaxes, the shovels leaning against the walls, the boots and overalls, and the friendly grin of Antonio, the site foreman, a huge fat man of Italian origin, whom we've nicknamed the "orchestra conductor" because he moves the workers around and keeps everything under control with such grace). His orchestra is composed of masons, metalsmiths, carpenters, engineers, surveyors, and . . . architects. The site entails a white hard hat with RPBW in blue letters and my name hot-stamped on it. The diggers and pneumatic drills penetrate the schist as if it were butter; think of it as an open book on geology, with bloodred walls. Sarah, who came by to pick me up, compared the yellow monsters to *Tyrannosaurus rex*, a great film-culture image that reminded me of when she was a child and collected little rubber dinosaurs. The studio that we set up in Jack Morgan's brownstone is full of drawings and models. I like to decorate the place where I'm working with elements reminiscent of our studios in Genoa and Paris—kind of like when you're traveling and you take along framed photographs and touches of home so you won't feel like a stranger in a foreign land. To the existing 75,000 square feet, we will add 43,000 square feet underground, excavating a hole fifty feet deep and bolstering the perimeter of the existing buildings. Imagine digging into a Parmesan cheese with a very sharp knife, or think back to the sand castles we used to build on the beach when we were kids. And think of me, supercool in my protective helmet and so excited and happy, today more than ever. I'm not intoxicated; it's just one of those positive, sunny days where everything seems beautiful and possible. Plus receiving two letters from you on the same day.

Federico

P.S. The schist that supports Manhattan's weight is the same rock as that of Jean and Jeanne, our Brittany friends. It's an ideal rock for

the foundations of structures as soaring as our . . . love. I said it. Or
rather, wrote it.

. ——— .

Milan, August 2, 2003
Sweet Dreams Locanda

Dear Federico,
The shop's last day open before vacation. It's a strange August here
in Milan. It's eight in the morning (it's so hot that I wake up at
dawn and I'm here by seven) and I'm sitting in the Locanda. I made
myself a cappuccino and I'm sipping it slowly, since there's no line
yet, no one waiting for the fresh fruit juices and oven-warmed pastries that are Manuele's pride. He now works full-time in the shop
(he's no longer teaching school) and exhausts us with his theories
of marketing the café, insisting on the need to "diversify" our offer-
ings. The result: You can choose from espresso, an espresso *lungo*, a
ristretto, a *corretto* with brandy, shaken iced espresso, espresso "slush,"
classic mocha, Neapolitan, American, cold *macchiato*, hot *macchiato*,
and other variations. My two gurus have not yet arrived and I'm
writing to you because I, too, am happy, like you in your letter
from the construction site. And I have to tell you about it. So then.
I was eating a slice of carrot cake and leafing through the newspaper when an unusual sound was all it took to change my day. A
chirping, *tweet-tweet-tweet*. I swear. My guest glided down with his
entire family and is looking at me as I write. His feathers are
streaked with brown, his little eyes are shiny as marbles, and he
doesn't seem fearful. The little Milanese sparrow hops onto my
sugary palm to have some breakfast: For him, my crumbs are a
meal. Strange, this August in Milan; people go on vacation and the
sparrows take over the city. Yesterday evening in Sant'Ambrogio, a
lady in a flowered dress and carrying a wicker basket, a bucolic version and substitute—due to summer vacation?—for the winter "cat
lady," was distributing fish bones and bits of pasta with tomato

sauce to the felines. Not exactly your Central Park squirrels, but
there is at least some resemblance.

A summery kiss from your Emma, who is going on vacation.

P.S. Take care of yourself. Don't you think that's a lovely expression
and one that is rarely used?

· ———— ·

New York, August 8, 2003
225 Madison Avenue

Dear Emma,

Today, passing by the construction site, I ran into an elderly man.
He smelled of beer and was wearing a heavy coat. The man stopped
me and amiably and politely inquired, "What's going on there?" I
had the feeling he was there waiting for me, which is impossible,
but I got two coffees, gave him one, and we sat down in front of the
brownstone. The forty-five rooms, twelve bathrooms, twenty-two
fireplaces, and the Morgans' ballroom, which will become the bookshop, are falling apart, the layers of stucco deteriorating, Frank's bai-
liwick . . . and Morgan and Piano. . . . This will be the entrance; there
will be a café inside. . . . I explained what was happening and the old
man lit up; he became excited (or so he led me to believe). Maybe he
was lonely and just felt like talking to someone. . . . Actually, I was
the one feeling lonely and it was he who was keeping me company.
I would be ready, now, to speak with my father man-to-man, as they
say; I have so many questions to ask him. It's different for our children; we got them used to confiding in us in a society where the
most commonly used word is *I* (though you force me to think *we*).
Well, I realized, despite the awful coffee ("dishwater," your Manuele would say) and thanks to a conversation with a stranger (his
name is Steve and he was a taxi driver all his life; he's a widower,
has no children, lives in Brooklyn, but he likes to come up here to
walk), I still have something to learn and a few things to tell. I'm not

the type to get familiar with a stranger, but I was pleased with my cordiality. I didn't feel ridiculous. Your influence (your geniality) can be felt even in the impromptu relations I have with people. Unusual for a bear like me. You are unwittingly transforming me into a nearly "normal" person.

Ciao, my antidote to the present,

Federico

P.S. I'm taking care of myself and us. The risk, I know, is that you might drift away, but I would notice it. So be careful! Don't stop writing.

. ——— .

Third Saturday of September. White Night, La Notte Bianca, a time-out lasting a day and a night: an idea imported from Paris. We provincial Milanesi don't have the banks of the Seine, and for someone who collapses at midnight like a punching bag, wandering aimlessly is a challenge. Ah, Cinderella, how well I understand you. The ever-wakefuls have planned a reading marathon from 5:00 P.M. to 5:00 A.M.; that's all they've talked about for a week, while I continue to express my bafflement, to no avail.

"Who would come to the shop for twelve hours in a row?" I ask in a neutral tone, not to hurt their feelings.

"We're a creative team, Emma; trust us," they reply in a duet that sounds like someone patting a foolish friend on the back. They're on a merciless path; yesterday, I heard them uttering dangerous words, such as a book's *target market*. Enough to make you shudder. Creative team . . . I suggested a title; they didn't get it, unaware of the film that it inspired.

"They Shoot Horses, Don't They? is macabre, Emma. It's off-putting. We were thinking of Nonstop Reading, something like that."

It was the dance that kept the protagonists on their feet, couples dancing as an allegory of the human condition.

"*They Shoot Horses, Don't They?* received six Oscar nominations, and a statuette for Best Supporting Actor was awarded to someone whose name escapes me now. I, for one, have a yoga class this evening."

"We'll see to everything; all you have to do is be a spectator. Better yet, you stay at the cashier's counter, and when you go to yoga, we'll find a replacement. Even Mattia agreed."

"Agreed to what?"

"To help out in the Locanda, with Carlotta and some friends. . . . We'll pay them a flat rate."

"I see. Have them sign a hiring contract; I don't want people working off the books in here. And focus on dead authors, please. I wouldn't want a living one to happen to come into the shop and not appreciate the rendition. They're narcissists, those writers."

"If you agree, we recruited customers to do the readings. . . ."

"Why pretend to ask permission for something you two have already decided on behind my back?"

"We didn't decide behind your back, and the customers will get to have their fifteen minutes of fame. Everyone chose a passage and a title. They're doing it gratis."

"Five minutes might be enough. Of fame, I mean."

I feel irritable, in a sour mood, and I'd give anything to be sitting next to him in a Barnes & Noble in Oklahoma or Pennsylvania or Ohio, in a bookstore in any American city, listening to someone reading. Any kind of novel. Alice skips up and down through the shop in a pair of tights (as I call them), or leggings (as she calls them), a black cotton cardigan, and pink ballerina flats, convinced that their marathon will be a success. I offer my contribution to this nonsense for insomniacs with a window display, "Pocket Romances." Paperbacks, glue, and a lot of pretty paper slipped into the pockets of jackets and coats found in the closet. On the ground, shoes are strewn about like candy. I never throw them out; I even have the ones from my wedding, hideous dirty white pumps worn for that reckless sprint. I go home. I'm depressed, time for a salad in front of the TV.

"See you later, guys."

No one bothers to answer. They're too busy and their friend the pastry chef is arriving with his imitations of seashell-shaped chocolate madeleines, which Marcel ate at his aunt Léonie's. But by four in the afternoon, when I climb on my bike after having had some coffee, reading the newspapers, and taking a little rest, I change my mind.

It's a stream—flowing out the doors, surging from the depths of the subway, swarming from the trams, feet in sneakers or platform sandals. A colorful urban river that spills through Milan's maze of streets and courtyards. No sleeping pills or wandering sleepless through the house tonight, but an excuse for everyone to go out together, the indolent and apathetic, Casanovas and their girls holding hands. White Night is daytime at night; it flows in waves, in a Milan that's wide open for all to see, an immense supermarket through which to steer your cart of dreams. I park in the courtyard. At the Locanda, there's a little group of ladies sitting at the tables. They're chatting and seem happy. Amid the aroma of hazelnut, chocolate, and wild roses is that of Lucilla's specialties, her almond and chocolate tarts and puff-pastry kiffels with a raspberry preserve filling. It's for Ernesto's debut, the retiree whom we are all looking forward to meeting. His turn as a marathon reader is scheduled for five o'clock. "He has a beautiful voice, you know?" his eager wife said, and Alice jumped in: "Why don't you bring him here to read?" And here he is. Hearing her talk and talk about him, I pictured him as old and dreary, and instead—surprise!—Signor Ernesto is as handsome as Clint Eastwood and only slightly curved, and has periwinkle blue eyes that have nothing to do with the laws of physics: a gentleman reader who emits a bouquet of aftershave. He paces up and down in the shop, like an actor who is mentally going over his lines; he's restless, as though the dais awaiting him were the stage of La Scala. He approaches the lectern, taps his middle finger on the microphone. "Testing, one, two, three," he whispers. He sits in the small armchair, then stands up again and looks toward the counter, as if waiting for me to present him. He holds the pages in his hands as if they were a breviary. Manuele introduces him to the customers and, with a brief cough, moves away.

"I have chosen for you *The Phantom of the Opera*, by Gaston

Leroux, the story of the monstrously disfigured Erik, a man more hideous than Dracula and more grotesque than Frankenstein"— they laugh; the ice is broken—"and his love for the young soprano Christine. The monster manages to seduce her, thanks to his voice. And also, let's be honest, thanks to the fact that women never settle for half measures. A man has to be either strikingly handsome or gruesomely ugly. Don't you think?"

He seems to be speaking personally to each and every one of them. He winks seductively, toys with the corners of the pages, and they hang upon his balladeer's lips. Lucilla is visibly pleased; she looks at him with the pride of a lucky wife, feet together in her square-heeled, square-toed shoes, a flash of jealousy in her eyes for the widow Cantoni in her white-button blouse, her hair freshly coiffed, her neck and earlobes adorned like a lamp shade. Ernesto doesn't so much as look at her. I stand in my sentry box and conceitedly imagine that Dreams & Desires is a raft on the river, an independent republic dedicated to Gutenberg, where my navigators can relax and gobble down kiffel while the minstrel moves on to John Fowles. Alice hands him the copy of *The French Lieutenant's Woman* from the "Untouchables" shelf; everyone (truly everyone) is sipping something, while Sarah Woodruff stands at the edge of a storm-tossed seawall, staring at the waters in which the lieutenant has disappeared. Into this senior citizens' fan club comes Emily, a new gleam in her eyes, her cheeks dusted with scented powder. She is arm in arm with Mrs. Oldrini, whose facial skin is as transparent as a pirate's threadbare map; the old woman has a witchy nose and walks with mincing steps, which are at odds with her imposing, authoritative figure. My gentle friend wanders around her former porter's lodge. Perhaps she misses it, and she is not alone. I read that in Paris they evicted ten thousand porters in ten years. Unmindful ingrates, they forget that it was Voltaire who gave caretakers the role they deserved and that even the engineer Gadda kowtowed to them, terrified of the rumors that spread through the building from their cubbyholes. Ernesto concludes his reading and strolls among the book tables like a proud peacock.

It's six o'clock: Cecilia's turn. She's about to moderate the game "What's the most beautiful romantic love story that you have read?" A buzzing in the room; no one seems shy. On the contrary. Hands go up in the audience, like in school. *"The Lady of the Camellias,"* says one. I recognize the angelic voice of Mrs. Donati, for whom we reserved a comfortable place, where she sits with her Croatian caretaker (though she understands little, the caretaker seems to be enjoying herself). What, no Liala? The game triggers altercations, and I'd like to see the expression of any incompetent fool who might persist in relegating a certain type of literature to the less visible corners of bookstores, branding them with the stigma of romance fiction.

"Forster's *Maurice*," a young man suggests, and Gaston, sitting with Borghetti while awaiting his turn, nods hopefully.

"You wouldn't want to leave out *Elective Affinities*, would you? A benchmark," Mr. Frontini says, holding his Goethe, recently reissued in a new edition with parallel text.

"It sometimes happens that the obvious escapes us when we look for the extraordinary. So I would remind you of Quasimodo and Esmeralda, the Gypsy girl with the pet goat. *The Hunchback of Notre Dame* is such an obvious choice that you might overlook it," Ernesto proclaims, and all the women turn to gaze at him. Who wouldn't have studied physics with such a man? "Genuinely great love is medieval," he pontificates. He, too, is bursting with excitement by now. "Romanticism was nothing more than the rediscovery of chivalric passion for the damsel, the queen, the Lady, with a capital *L*. Woman is uppermost in our thoughts; our every action is for her and inspired by her. A woman can never be cruel and unfathomable enough for us. No matter what hardships she may subject us to, we will not shirk them. Because there is nothing sweeter than a Lady's balm."

"Balm?" Cecilia asks.

"The balm of my life is her, my wife. I can't speak for the others. . . . You'd have to ask them. Manuele, what is Alice for you?"

"Alice is the most competent, prettiest, and cleverest girl in all of Milan," he replies, shamelessly brazen. Raucous applause breaks out, like in a tavern. Is it literature that's making them act this way, or have they all been drinking, despite my rule about no alcoholic beverages? I feel excluded from a well-planned script and my uneasiness shows no sign of passing. I can feel the plasterboard again, like an elastic band squeezing my sternum.

"What about *Love in the Time of Cholera,* by Garcia Márquez? They fall in love when they are young; he waits for her until he's seventy," interjects a girl about twenty years old, attracting the immediate interest of Mattia, who stops making fruit juices so he can focus on her. Carlotta records the orders and keeps an eye on him.

"If you ask me, *Dr. Zhivago* is unparalleled," says Marta. "Such crying! I couldn't stop."

"I cried a lot over that book, too," another woman adds.

It seems calculated, and maybe it was all planned, because Cecilia ends the game and in her chirping voice starts reading the copy she brought from home, full of passages that have been underlined in pencil.

"Yuri Zhivago and Lara meet in a library: 'Now he noticed a change in the room. At its farther end there was a new reader. Yuri Andreyevich recognized Antipova at once. . . .'"

They recite and I ring up receipts. The river streams in, rests awhile, rises again, and flows out, not without having bought something. Oh, if only Alberto were here. Paper copy, whose death he regularly announces, is still with us. It's just that he decided to go fishing and won't be here until later. By seven, the proceeds are quite respectable: over a thousand euros, what with books and pastries, bitter orange drinks and lemonades "à la Pereira."

"Thank you, Emma, it's been a lovely afternoon. Unforgettable" is precisely what Emily says, holding the hand of the lady leaning on her like a cane.

"Come and see me again. I miss our chats so much. It was a pleasure to meet you, Mrs. Oldrini."

"I'm off to the gym. See you in a couple of hours," I announce, as if anyone cares. Manuele, dealing with panini and mini focaccias named after writers, is wearing a black cotton apron bearing the Sweet Dreams Locanda "logo," as they call it, and I feel like Queen Elizabeth, with the royal coat of arms. Outside in the piazza, a platform for dancing is being erected. It's hard to take a step forward or backward. A river is refreshing, but out here you just dawdle; it's stop and go. I need my yoga.

I return in time to enjoy the tempting leftovers from the happy hour, and Gaston's reading. He has chosen Casanova. He has never kissed a woman in his life, and I can't understand why he believes everything they say about the most overrated adventurer in history. The description given by Márai in *Conversations in Bolzano* is merciless, but he reads with an inspired tone, while I settle down at the cashier's counter and hear with my own ears that at age fifty-three, Casanova—who for some time had been driven to roam the world not by a youthful desire for adventure, but by the angst of advancing old age—was seized with such an intense nostalgia for his native city of Venice that he began to wheel around it like a bird coming home to die, descending from boundless heights in ever-tighter spirals.

The *advancing old age* disturbs me more than it should, after having gone through an hour and a half of asanas just to try to forget it. The unwitting literary conspiracy thrusts me into reality. Manuele is serving Franca, the young woman from the post office, and I have an urge to flee. What if it occurs to her to call me "the box 1004 booklady," as she usually does? She's spotted me. There's no way out.

"You're here, too? How nice to see you again," I say, feigning delight as I move toward her.

"I just got back from my honeymoon, Miss Emma. I felt like taking a stroll downtown. Oh, here's Guglielmo," she says, introducing her prey with the pride of a hunter at rest after the hardships of the chase.

The new groom has such a polished skull that you could see yourself reflected in it, and he doesn't look anything like a garage mechanic or gas station attendant—I can't remember which.

"So lovely to see you here, Franca. It's a pleasure to meet you, Guglielmo. The bookshop is at your disposal, and if you'd like to have something, stop in at the Locanda. White Night for us, too. . . ."

The time for thirtysomethings has arrived. Even the marketing people, the motorbike riders, the guys with a badge and a business plan are here. Wait, isn't that Fabrizio Lucchini sitting over there, looking dejected, at the only table equipped with a wooden chessboard? Wearing blue jeans, no pressed crease, he gets up and approaches the dais. I can't believe that those two have talked him into it, yet there he is. He clears his throat, thrusts out his chest beneath the burgundy polo shirt, and starts reading from de Maupassant's *Strong as Death*.

"His girl dumped him. I chose the text myself. He's not someone who reads a lot," Alice says, summing up the situation in a low voice as she hands me a copy of Barbara Pym's *No Fond Return of Love* to wrap for a plump bonbon of a customer who doesn't look at all desperate. "It seemed like a good idea. He's unattached, available, and has a permanent job. Now he knows de Maupassant. Wouldn't he be perfect for Cecilia?"

"If a few pages of a book were all it takes to find love, people would be lining up. Despite the text, he seems at ease, the little show-off. If you ask me, he doesn't even know what he's reading. What does he know about Guy de Maupassant? Something lighter, huh? Even people like Fabrizio suffer, and what do you give him, Alice?"

Yet he reads and does so fluently. The bookshop is full of narcissists: Put a microphone in a man's hand and he instinctively lets it go to his head.

Borghetti closed his shop; he's a snob and insists that his customers go to the shore on weekends, certainly not to White Nights, which are the opium of the people. He seems happy to be up on the podium, wearing his orange bow tie and Scottish vest. Borghetti is a dandy. He has chosen *A Love Affair*. Before reciting, he feels the need to indoctrinate the audience.

"Dino Buzzati portrays a respectable middle-class man, an architect, Antonio Dorigo, forty-nine years old, who in the winter of

1960 meets and frequents a sixteen-year-old prostitute passing herself off as a ballerina from La Scala. Her name is Laide. The architect falls in love with her, and she exploits him, takes him for a
fool, and betrays him. I am speaking of Buzzati, ladies and gentle-
men, not just any old hack," he says, lecturing the crowd before
beginning his litany of the architect. That may be, but poor Buzzati was orphaned as a child and in his early twenties saw his girlfriend suddenly die. Paying a woman, perhaps, is a way to avoid
becoming attached to her. That's how the poignant, outdated novel
was inspired. I have no desire to listen; for me, there's only one architect. I stay over here with Alice until the cavalier passes the ba-
ton to attorney Frontini, who steps up to the dais, as arrogant as if
he had attended the Actors Studio.

"I will read about the love affair between Josef and Irena, two
Czech émigrés. They meet by chance at the Paris airport, an acci-
dental encounter, which she mistakes for destiny. They had known
each other when they were young; he had courted her. Then, in
what is the age of ignorance, each had made the choices that determine the future. Josef moved to Denmark and married; now
widowed, he lives with the memory of his wife. Irena has also
lost her husband, Martin, and met Gustaf. 'That woman,' Frontini
intones, 'has never chosen any of her men. She was always the
one being chosen. . . . In her liaison with Gustaf, she thought she
was gaining freedom.' It's Milan Kundera's *Ignorance*. The great return to the homeland, however, is a disappointment: In Prague,
Josef and Irena seek and find each other, just before the final separation from that country to which nothing binds them any longer.
Irena samples the joys of adultery at last. At the hotel, she utters
obscene words in Czech, words that ignite the senses. Listen to
this; 'A total accord in an explosion of obscenities! Ah, how impoverished her life has been! All the vices missed out on, all the infi-
delities left unrealized—all of that she is avid to experience.'"

The seashell-shaped madeleine goes down the wrong way. Who
on earth chose this stuff? Who's the cretin of the day? Who said

reading is a reassuring activity? Kundera is a great writer, of course, but too much is too much. I escape to the bathroom. I lock the door and sit on the ottoman. I'm short of breath. It wasn't easy to convince Alberto, and not just because of the ottoman; still, there had been too many times when I was reading in a bookshop and had to drop everything to go out and look for a bathroom, "It won't happen here," I insisted. A bathroom equipped with every comfort for the reader. On the pale blue mosaic tile walls I hung yellowing postcards of buxom women draped in feathers and ostrich boas. To the right of the sink is a shelf of books ready to serve in case of boredom or lengthy stays. I don't think I even have Kundera's *Ignorance* in the bookshop. With all due respect to the author, I haven't read it, and I don't see why Frontini felt the need to slip us that particular book. He's happily married to his former secretary, Erminia, who ceased being his secretary decades ago. He seems composed, surely he's the faithful type, and my reaction—disproportionate—is a sign of exhaustion. This marathon is wearing me out. I go back to the counter and hope that Irena has finished panting. Mondo trots around me, panting for real, like an affectionate dog. I hand him a biscuit and he consoles me with a damp caress, up and down from wrist to forearm. Age makes us vulnerable, and he must have sensed it. The bells from the campanile ring out midnight and the numbers excite Alberto, who, having left his fishhooks, flies, and rods, is doing the accounts.

"We should organize more of these marathons, Emma. Are you okay, sweetheart? You look pale. . . ."

"I'm bushed, but I rang up receipts for one hundred and twenty-seven teas, sixty-two fresh fruit squeezes, ten hot chocolates with steamed milk, four hot chocolates with whipped cream—which, given the season, is a record—and assorted sodas and juices. Plus, I sold six SHHH . . . I'M READING cups."

"Hi, Camillo. Don't tell me they dragged you into the act?"

"I'm extremely ashamed, Emma. Alice persuaded me, but now that I'm here, I don't feel up to it. Damn, it's full of people. What if someone recognizes me? As you know, a married woman's lover is not very interesting, like in 'Good heavens, my husband!' By the way, who said that?"

"I don't remember; I think it was a movie. You could make a name for yourself and start a new career. They teamed you up with Margherita. Relax, no one knows who you are. What are you going to read us?"

"We're doing Chopin and George Sand, can you imagine?"

"As a doctor, you're the perfect choice to read about a sick genius."

"I was there with Laura, at their home in Majorca, when we were still together. . . ."

"Now don't start in with that same old story about your marriage."

"No, on the contrary, it's a literary anecdote; you might like it. Chopin and Sand were hated by the Majorcans. Just think, even the famous piano that can be seen in Valdemossa is a fake, as is the bed where the composer slept. As soon as the two left the island, their furniture, clothing, everything was burned, with the excuse that he was tubercular. Today in Majorca, they make money on what's left of the two people they despised. A tourism that sponges off of someone else."

Margherita and Camillo climb up to the podium, so awkward as to arouse some pitiful applause by way of encouragement. Gabriella gives me a hand wrapping packages. I have missed her, my "Little Voice." I need her now that I feel a clamp in my stomach and I don't know why. Or rather, I do know why. Everyone has stopped by today, and Federico is far away, drawing designs and overseeing construction workers. It seems unfair, and I can't seem to lighten my spirits on demand.

"I always thought that those who talk a lot about sex do so because they do it so infrequently," she says, without my having given her the slightest opening.

"They're not talking about sex; they're reading. It's not the case with me, if that's what you mean. . . . Since when have you become so good at wrapping packages?"

"Since I was a child, when we played store; it was my favorite role."

"Alberto was the cashier, I'll be."

"When we got together, we hadn't played that game for some time."

"Do you still play doctor, or did you stop?"

"Emma, after thirty years, it's not the quantity that counts, but the quality. You should know that."

"It seems that pleasure has become a duty. Look at Camillo. As intelligent and educated as he is, sex for him is a unit of measurement. When it comes to a woman, any woman, he loses his sense of reality. In some way, he has no faith in the mind, and only the body makes him feel alive."

"Valeria makes him feel secure; she showers him with attention. The body is real, Emma. Everything can be digitized except sex, illness, and death."

"I, for one, never think about death."

"That's why you like architecture, which is the physical construction of physical places."

"What time is it? I'm tired. I've got half a mind to skip out and go home."

"For you, it's the middle of the night; for most humans, it's half past midnight. Look at Mattia. . . ."

Manuele is slicing salami, Alice hands him the bread, and Mattia has made himself comfortable between two girls, one with chubby cheeks and gel-spiked hair, the other a white gloves and pearls type in jeans so tight, she can barely breathe. Two different worlds, the same smile. A pair of twenty-year-olds sit at the next table. She's drinking grapefruit juice; he sips a Coke with ice. He's gazing at her and she's gazing at him, but between them there's a third party, a pair of cell phones. The phones might ring; they might not hear them. And yet they're talking! In fact, they seem to be engaged in a real conversation. Byatt is right when she writes that if you put two people in a pub, sooner or later they'll begin telling their life stories. In the end, human beings have nothing but words to enable them to exist in this world. Dreams & Desires accomplishes a miracle. They've seen the sign; they turn off their cell phones. She slips hers into an oversized bag; he puts his in his jacket pocket. One thing leads to another. I am sadistically await- ing the grand finale, "The Budding Writers," along the lines of *La Corrida,* the bullfight show on TV. I can't leave just now, when the neopoets are arriving, the aspirants who have not yet been pub- lished. The underground practitioners of the word are entitled to asylum. Pablo Paolo Peretti, an Italian poet who lives in Copenha- gen, goes up to the podium. A romantic escape, I gather. He is ac- companied by a Danish guy, tall, blond, and handsome, like a tourist guide. Pablo Paolo reads his poetry.

"'Before my undoing you left me. Thank you. In the melan- choly of your memory I still think of you. The road to come, after you, has become clearer. Now I know you were just a lovely paren- theses. Life has returned to life and you are a part of it.'"

Pause. Reserved applause. Gaston, who has returned from din- ner with Borghetti, seems very interested—in the Danish guy more than the poetry, but it makes no difference.

"'I'd rather not love anyone. Because if you love, you have to com- promise; forgive, close your eyes to betrayal, scream in pain when the loved one disappears. If I were weaker and more cowardly, it would all be quite simple. She's calling me. I'll go make her mint tea!'"

I'm exhausted and I don't understand why someone so attrac- tive and healthy has to write such gloomy poetry. I say my good- byes and get ready to leave. "Kids, I'm going. Alice, will you take over? Good night, friends. Don't bother to get up. We're open till five. Warm croissants are on the way. Enjoy. Bye-bye."

I go out and take a deep breath. I look at the basilica (built in 1601, a magnificent example of Baroque architecture) and it's as if I am seeing it for the first time, but then I realize that I never see it at this hour, and I imagine I can hear treble voices at the back of the nave. Don Maurizio, who seems afflicted by the aftermath of a hangover—rather than walking, he's swaying in his cassock—is about to lead the chorus of the faithful.

"Hello, Emma. A marathon of a night, isn't it? Will you stay and listen?"

"I'm too tired, Father. I'm going home to bed, if I can manage to make my way through the crowds. Good night."

A man sitting in front of the church, backpack on his shoulders, is holding a baby; the baby's arms are wrapped around his father's neck, his head resting on the man's chest, his eyes sleepy.

•——————•

New York, September 29, 2003
Peaceful oasis number 7, Sutton Place Park

Dear Emma,

This city has no real center; sometimes it's like not having a stable reference point, so my oases become my makeshift centers. At the moment, I need one more than usual, after a day in which all hell broke loose at the Morgan, beginning with a fire that started at the construction site. It was like being in a TV show: The firemen arrived, tall and even more solid than the tree trunk, now useless, that they carried off like a defunct giant. I was sorry to see it go, even though I'm less of an ecologist than Sarah, who subjects everyone at home and at school to her anxiety over CO_2 and the "dying" planet. She's monothematic and hypersensitive—how could she be otherwise?—to the slow suffocation that they discuss in school, the teachers filling their minds with the projection of a future world (their world, Emma, not ours) in which the word *breathe* seems all too utopian. Sarah says it's our fault, and she's going to enroll in biology. I didn't tell her about the old tree that burned in the fire, because she would have cried. She's determined to have a dog at all costs, and when we said no (in unison, for once), she decided to protest by dog-sitting for the neighbors' three dogs. We're in full eruption; the pimples on her forehead make her irritable, resulting in constant bickering between her and Anna over the most idiotic things: the mess in her room, what she wears, the purple nail polish, and so on. When they start arguing, I leave. I get on my Vespa and go wandering. Now I'm in one of my favorite peaceful oases, Sutton Place. It's almost fall, an uncertain season, which has neither the stark lines of summer nor winter's contoured hills. I've calmed down, though I know very well that it's not those two who rattle me, but rather my shitty character and the heaps of insecurities that often hit me—these days all too often. I have to make decisions, and the construction site is the only place on earth where I feel free from anxiety (Belle-Ile excepted, of course). As I write, a chubby squirrel is feasting on an apple core underneath my bench. I remain motionless. And I think of you, my little squirrel.

Federico

P.S. Yesterday, Robert Morgan Pennoyer, J.P.M.'s great-grandson, visited his grandfather's house, stopped by the work site, and seemed very excited.

• ——— •

Milan, October 7, 2003
Sweet Dreams Locanda

Dear Federico,
It's contagious: I've been trying to make a list of peaceful oases amid the tumultuous confusion of Milan, like you've been doing in New York. I never have much time to walk, and the bookshop and the Locanda have made me even more lazy. I compose my list, a little skimpy but substantial, because while you have New York at your feet, we Milanesi have a glorious past to boast of, at least among ourselves. We can be close to antiquity in peace, without too much effort. In the cloister of Santa Maria delle Grazie, not far from here, I found two Japanese visitors sitting in the shade of the columns, in front of the fountain; in Sant'Ambrogio, under the four-sided portico, if you look closely, you'll find a peaceful oasis in the small park

of the Tempio della Vittoria; and in Parco Sempione as well, where de Chirico's fountain lies buried under a blanket of mold. I miss you. In every way. My heart is troubling me more than usual, and it's only October.

Emma

P.S. Mattia is enrolling in architecture. Can the unconscious be working unbeknownst to us?

. ———— .

Dreams & Desires's third anniversary falls on a Sunday and the balance sheet, to use a term dear to the Faithful Enemy, is more than positive. It's simply fantastic. Articles in three daily papers (the *Corriere della Sera, La Repubblica,* and *Il Giorno*) marked the start of a day on which autumn seems suspended. Just steps from all the chaos, from the maze of narrow streets leading to the bookshop, I come to this secluded, provincial little piazza. There are no cars and the peacefulness has an almost unnatural quality. The scene, viewed from the courtyard, is that of a private village; a climbing vine bearing a few ridiculously reckless little leaves announces the end of summer. It's only three o'clock, but they've already arrived. I see them from here and I am moved, picturing myself with Gabriella ten or twenty years from now, she and I sitting at a table in the winter garden, a cup in our hands and our hair inevitably white. My ladies have folded their pastel jackets and silk scarves on the chair. They are nearly deaf; I can tell from the way their necks turn sideways toward the mouth of the person speaking. They follow the thread of their own thoughts and, in fact, you get the feeling that they are not responding to each other; instead of having a conversation, each of them seems to pursue her own disconsolate monologue. Domitilla and Marisa are inseparable. Eating is their main activity. Lunch, afternoon tea, and dinner are the cornerstones of their day. Yet they keep saying, "You know, Emma, I eat so little." Coquettes. Besides cakes and Manuele's curls, they love books. They are readers to whom haste is unknown; they don't use

ATMs or give in to the temptation of credit cards. They have a silver card from Dreams & Desires: For every ten books purchased, one is complimentary, which does not mean succumbing to a discount policy, but showing them a little love. They give the impression of gazing beyond the horizon. They are retired.

"You'll be inundated with people who have nothing else to do," was Alberto's diagnosis when I showed him the schedule of readings.

"You're wrong. Retirees are the most appealing social category for a bookshop. According to data put out by the European Commission, the percentage of those over eighty will rise from the current four percent to eleven percent by 2050. My retirees are a resource. I read it in your favorite newspaper, *Il Sole 24 Ore*."

"And since when are you interested in economics?" he asked.

"Someone must have left it in the Locanda. Read this: Of the seven hundred people surveyed who are not engaged in any work activity, the perception of happiness was rated seven on a scale of one to ten. Postmodern elders, Alberto, not brains for the scrap heap. Look at Renzo Piano: sixty-six years old and irresistibly fascinating."

"I see you believe what the newspapers write, but I like this layman's approach to marketing. Since when are you also interested in architecture?"

I dropped the subject, but I blushed: Citing an architect, though famous and therefore above suspicion, was risky. Gabriella had sworn that the topic of Federico would remain between us.

They say that Italy is a country of old people. That may be, but I adore them. Deprived of real elders in my life, I've adopted them here. A memorabilia series, "Memorable Passages," is scheduled to mark the anniversary. "Readings," Manuele calls them to show off a little, partly because of the news crew that is filming a feature about shops that "make Milan come alive." They're exaggerating, but then again, maybe not. Today we'll stay open until ten. I sit at my counter and do what I love best: observe. I should be used to it, but I am still incredulous about the word of mouth that has spread from our longtime customers to the new readers who have discovered us. Dreams & Desires has become the island I envisioned, frequented by people browsing among the shelves, looking for books about love, who speak to each other as if they were old friends and who may perhaps fall in love. Steeped in the scent of the new candles, I like to think so. They arrived from Paris a week ago in a milk white cardboard box from Assouline Bookshop. Yuppie nonsense, says Alberto, unaware of the power that scents have over our lives. They are candles for bibliophiles and smell like a . . . book. I could never have imagined how many people would be willing to spend thirty euros for the "Bibliothèque" scent, but I've already sold three. You light it and the room smells of paper, leather, and wood, even if you're reading in an Ikea kitchen. Of course the French think about their own. So they printed a quote by Sacha Guitry, who—victim of a surge of self-pity and base humility—stated that he could write a book with everything he knew but could fill a library with all that he didn't know: *"Avec tout ce que je sais, on pourrait faire un livre. . . . Il est vrai qu'avec tout ce que je ne sais pas, on pourrait faire une bibliothèque."* Mr. Pedrini, who never misses an anniversary, likes the agarwood-scented Cuir candle.

"It smells like my office, Emma," he says, inhaling the aroma of leather as if it were a sprig of wisteria. He buys two of them.

"Ne prêtez jamais de livres; personne ne les rend": The flesh-colored band wrapped around the (recyclable toothbrush) glass warns against lending books, as no one ever returns them. Anatole France, whom I have never read and of whose works there is no trace here, went on to confess that the only books he had in his library were books he had borrowed: *"Les seuls livres que je conserve dans ma bibliothèque sont des livres qu'on m'a prêtés."* I light two wood-scented candles: cedar and copaiba from the Amazonian forests. The ecosystem is compromised by my nose's vanity, but an expert explained to me that the substances are synthetic (horrors!) and that no tree has sacrificed its bark.

The second novelty of the day is the radio. At the tables, a young man is fumbling with a recorder and taping everything

Manuele says; he's a journalist from Radio24 and has decided to do a live weekly broadcast from Dreams & Desires. There's a somewhat egocentric provisional title, "Afternoons with Emma"; it's not as if I were Bovary. It sounds a bit pompous. I can already imagine frustrated truck drivers on the Brenner Highway consoling themselves with Dickinson's poetry or the housewife listening to Quixote's delusional declarations to Dulcinea while busy cooking. Still, it's a great satisfaction, I must say, to think of all of Italy connected to Dreams & Desires via the airwaves. And it doesn't cost a thing. He does it all, the guy with the microphone, except for the feature "Words of Love," live in the voice of Emma Valentini. The books mentioned during the program can be ordered online by anyone who cares to, and from the radio's Web site as well; they then arrive in a special package, a yellow post office box with colored paper bearing my logo. They treat me like a business and have no idea how inadequate I still feel, but Alice and Manuele were so enthusiastic that I had to give in. I don't like to hear my own voice. I don't pause in the right places, my words come tumbling out, and to achieve an intelligible rhythm, I had to rehearse the spot six times. Then off we go, live, three minutes that seem like an eternity. Mattia is working a shift with Carlotta; he has to pay back money he spent on a phone call. "Mom, I'm an idiot," he confessed. "I made a twelve-minute call to Australia. Will you recharge my account?" Instead of recharging, I gave him a job. I don't ask whom he called in Australia because I'm terrified he'll disappoint me; things seem serious with Carlotta, I'm not even jealous of her, and I hope he hasn't taken after his father.

I go out to dinner with Gabriella and Alberto. I'm beside myself. I have to break the news, and find the words. My treat, pizza and beer at a corner table in Rosso Pomodoro.

"Those two are really sweet; I bet they might even get married."

"Manuele and Alice are the best thing that's happened to me since I opened the bookshop—not counting Mattia, who, miraculously, is taking all his exams. I don't know if they'll get married, but they really like each other. I invited you both here because I have something to tell you," I say, coming to the point as I bravely take a blistering bite of mozzarella di bufala.

"When you use that urgent tone, you scare me. What do you want now? What more do you need besides what you already have? Everything's going well, even the accounts," says Alberto.

"Why are you being suspicious and aggressive? Let her talk," Gabriella says, coming to my rescue.

"No doubt about it, the two of you together are deadly. Individually to be sure, not to mention as a pair . . . Okay, I'll be quiet. It's just that with Emma, you never know. I was protecting myself. Prudence, simple prudence."

"An apartment has become vacant, right above the shop."

"God knows what I was thinking . . . but why do you want to move? Well, I suppose the apartment is too big for you when Mattia stays over at Michele's, and besides, in a few years time he, too, will go live on his own. Or with his Carlotta. Yes indeed, the years go by, my dears, and we need less and less space."

"Thirteen hundred square feet is the ideal size for a small hotel. Boutique hotels are in vogue today." Naturally, I keep my eyes lowered as I say it, staring at the anchovy on the pizza as if it were an insect. I always do that when I fear other people's reactions.

"You want to open an hourly hotel? That's all well and good, but it's not as if people will buy a book and then go tearing upstairs for a quick fuck!"

"Who said anything about an hourly hotel? Just three rooms with bath, a comfortable hotel for writers passing through Milan. Publishers put them up in those big, anonymous, expensive hotels in the center, like the Manin. A press agent who shepherds writers around for interviews and book presentations told me so. I inquired . . . just to check it out. She explained to me that publishers have agreements with a couple of hotels; we could do the same and have a stable customer base."

"You're out of your mind. Where would we come up with the

money to buy an apartment in Piazza Sant'Alessandro? You don't expand a business if you don't have the expertise to do so. And you don't know the first thing about hotels."

"As far as expertise goes, I didn't know anything about book-shops, either. We can take out a mortgage. You're biased. It could be an investment."

"You'd be better off finding a man; that way, you'd stop filling your head with nonsense. Give me a break. The Locanda is suc-cessful. I supported you from the start. We're renting and we're making good money. A hotel is too demanding. You have to think about retirement, Emma. Retirement is the objective; that's the target we should be aiming for. Aren't you sick and tired of work-ing by now? I can't see Mattia being a hotel concierge. He'll make his own way and you'll be relieved of having to support him. A hotel! You are really insane. Why don't you just take it easy?"

"Or why not take a nice trip with Gabriella?" my best friend adds at the same moment I do.

We are so in sync that we think and say the same words at the same time. The saying "a single soul dwelling in two bodies" ex-presses exactly what I'm feeling right now.

·———·

New York, October 27, 2003
Peaceful oasis number 8, Central Park West

Dear Emma,
Central Park's 125 years can be read from the inside looking out. I can retrace its history and see its stratification by observing the buildings and skyscrapers that line the four sides of the park. Each one is different from the others, just like the trees around me, wear-ing various shades of red and gold. In the eighties, this place was in ruins: The lakes were polluted, children couldn't play here, and the park was invaded by gangs of hoodlums. Once again, it was a phi-lanthropist who took out his checkbook and told the mayor, "we must return the park to its original state." Central Park is back to

the way it was designed in the nineteenth century by landscape architects Frederick Law Olmstead and Calvert Vaux: 843 acres of
woods and meadows, lakes and stairways that today celebrate the
conception of a privileged space, protected and unique, created in a
large clearing carved out of Manhattan's schist. Just like our Morgan. New York is a city with a high level of allergens, and I am a
perfect casebook example of a guinea pig. What with the concrete,
dust, and 168 species of trees around me, I am perpetually sneezing: Could it be the maples, the oaks, or these horse chestnuts? I
keep trying antihistamines; there's not a one that works, but I would
never forgo my tree break in this urban forest. The woods are a
balm for me. In the atrium of the Morgan, we're going to plant trees
that will grow through openings in the floor, symbols of the irrational in the rational, the possibility of something that knows no other
rules but its own. Simple, right?

My beloved Emma, tomorrow I'm leaving for Paris. I am with
you. Always.

Today especially yours, Federico

P.S. The Strand has a kiosk at the entrance to Central Park. You
won't believe it, but even executives buy books there and sprawl on
the benches, reading.

· ——— ·

Milan, November 2, 2003
Via Londonio 8

Dear Federico,
I have so many dead I should commemorate today, on their feast
day, and I'm staying home. I don't like visiting graves, and the cemeteries are full of people. I need to be alone—today more than
usual. I have the day off. Mattia left with Carlotta. The bookshop is
closed, and only now do I realize that my passion for solitude can
have serious drawbacks. I miss you, a physical want. I can describe
it; in fact, I have to. I started to read, but even that usual antivirus

doesn't seem to work. Just think how we change, Federico, even
without intending to. As a girl, I used to read at the beach, under
the sun. Today I can't even stand light, much less a lounge chair and
oily suntan-lotion stains on the pages. It was only after my divorce
that I began to enjoy reading in bed. Michele liked a bed without a
headboard, and I defy anyone to read while balancing on an elbow
or lying supine—even Alfieri, who, in fact, had himself tied to a
chair. If I lie on my stomach, my neck retracts like that of a turtle
and my stomach tightens, making even the most compelling novel
indigestible. On my side with one hand pressed against my ear? No
way. The pins and needles start in less than ten minutes. Some
people read in the bathroom: Alberto asked Gabriella to put together a small collection for him, inspired by that famous tropical
swine Henry Miller, who wrote about reading in the toilet. Thinking about it coolly, here at home, I think that if I were able to
choose, my ideal place to read would be a train. As long as it's not a
rickety interregional, the rolling of the wheels rocks you and it isn't
distracting. I'd like to take a train right now, to come to you. Paris is
nearby, after all. After years of experimentation, I have perfected a
plan for peaceful (Michele calls it "neurotic") reading. In fact, I am
now on the couch, well supplied, with a pile of new books resting
on the low coffee table beside their companions: books loved for a
brief time, then never opened again; books that are tired and lying
down; unfinished books that never got enough attention. All within
easy reach of hand and eye. They are a secure berth whenever I feel
lost. Like now, in my favorite position; in the left corner of the sofa,
legs curled to the side, the light pouring straight down on the pages,
saving me from having to twist my neck, two pillows under the
lumbar region, the only vertebrae I can't manage to release despite
Pilates. Close by, a blanket, cocoa butter, a thermos of hot tea. In
summer, a bottle of water or a pitcher of iced tea. In any season, a
ten-pack of cigarettes, though after last April 10, I stopped smoking
and threw away the ashtray. When I forget something I need (like
now, when I can't find my glasses), I get rattled just thinking about
having to get up while I'm perhaps strolling through a narrow street

in London or while a policeman is talking—one who's in love. In short, Federico, while you're an active person, I'm at my best when indolent. And if I feel melancholy, I stay put. Patience marks the measure of my time; waiting is my indulgence. I read because I'm anxious to have something to do, and when I don't know what to do or what to decide, I pick up a novel. I open it at random and I forget; my anxiety dissolves into the pages and I'm grateful to the book if it can relieve this apprehension that has settled on my stomach like an undigested meal. I nurture my hope in patience, though I wonder what hope there can be for a love story made of words. As I sit here, what fascinates me about grappling with words (at one time, I would note them on a pad) are the places and smells that surround them, the snares that entangle them and that I like to unravel, because I feel at home in their company. In the end, it is they who have cured all my disorders. I show my appreciation by selling them to strangers. And I forget about all the rest. But not about you. Though I see less and less of him, I'm not sad without Mattia; a son is one of the few solid achievements one can realize with a creature of the male sex. I'll stop this whining. Write to me; otherwise, I'll have to rearrange your letters and reread them and let the past console me. I need the present. Or to stop time.

I'm about to cry, I feel a little dead myself. In solidarity with the souls.

Your Emma

· ——— ·

New York, December 8, 2003
Bar Veloce, 176 7th Avenue

Dear Emma,
In New York, the snow is back; millions of feet trample streets plastered in the white stuff that snow trucks try to plow away. The sign at Bar Veloce features a Vespa like mine. I'm on my way home, having a glass of white wine after a day that I can't resist telling you about. I'll use the present tense; I'm still excited. So then. This

morning, I enter 522 Fifth Avenue, a solid marble building, and go up to the third floor. Destination: J.P. Morgan Fleming, our friend's repository. Here, in the vaults of J.P. Morgan Chase, is where they've stored those items of the collection that have not been sent on tour or left to rest in the East Room's chrysalis—like actors who are too old and therefore cannot travel. I have to examine some manuscripts with an expert to assess the impact of light on these precious folios, which will be displayed in "butterfly cases" in the two rooms we have designed. Emma, I had never before seen a bank vault and I pictured it as a corridor with safe-deposit boxes. Wrong! This is a room as big as your bookshop . . . and the manuscripts are protected like gold ingots. They pull out a blue box with the Morgan's gold trademark. They give me a pair of white cotton gloves, which make me laugh. They're definitely too small for my hands. I should have known, I think; librarians and booksellers are petite women and know how to handle a manuscript. The Morgan will have natural lighting, modulated by that of the sky, but the display cases we'll install will be closed, so I have to consider how to illuminate the material without the light ruining it. I open the box. I pick up the autographed manuscript of *Lady Susan*, written by a "certain" Jane Austen in her own hand between 1793 and 1794, a text illegible to a layman, acquired by Belle da Costa Greene in 1947. As chance (?) would have it, it's an epistolary novel: Here, too, Emma, letters, letters, and more letters. The volume is bound in beige leather trimmed with gold. I am joined by Christine Nelson, curator of the Morgan's Literary and Historical Manuscripts collection, a kind of handmaiden with a charming smile. "They bound it well," I say, acting like someone who knows, and she looks at me too kindly, explaining that it was the collector who saw to the binding, according to his taste. In 1900, the person who bound the manuscript mounted each page in a cream-colored mat that obscures the words at the edges. You would groan at this treatment. "There isn't even one revision. Gifted, our Jane," I say, simulating competence and admiration for the lady. Christine gives me a withering look, though no less polite.

"In those days, manuscripts were recopied, Mr. Virgili. Jane

Austen likely revised it and then wrote out a clean copy." Touché. It's intact. Miss Austen's only complete manuscript, the hand-maiden informs me. Opening my Moleskine (in preparation for this letter), I transcribe the opening lines of missive number nineteen, written by Lady Susan to Mrs. Johnson: "You will be eager, I know, to hear something further of Frederica, and perhaps may think me negligent for not writing before . . ." I thought of you: Your last letters betray a sadness that I don't like to see and that I might know how to remedy. My beloved Emma, I'm sure that you would be ecstatic in the Morgan Chase vault; I've never understood the excitement, "this type" of excitement over a manuscript, but I held it in my hands with a physical pleasure that was new to me. And I wasn't thinking about the lighting. In retrospect, sitting in the bar's warmth, my glass of white now empty, I can admit it: It wasn't the manuscript; it was you. It was like holding you in my arms. "Finis," Miss Austen wrote. Finis-Terrae. Like the strip of land that we can see from La Touline's window in Belle-Ile.

I miss you. I feel like getting drunk, but I have to go home.

Your literate and faithful

Federico

P.S. Speaking with Christine, I discovered that among J.P.M.'s collections there are numerous love letters. Shall I look into it?

. ——— .

"How can you expect people to give a damn about Jane Austen's birthday!"

"For that matter, *people* wouldn't give a damn about our patron saint, Ambrogio, either, if it didn't mean a day off. There are dozens of Austen fan clubs around the world; if you look carefully you'll find them on *your* Internet."

"How tedious, Emma, that same old story. Will you get it into your head that the Net is democratic, that it doesn't belong to anyone, because it belongs to everybody? What's strange about Austen is that she wrote romantic novels, but there is no record of her own romances. A fine match—she wrote about a subject she knew nothing about. It's as if you were to write a biography of Bill Gates: absurd."

"Jane was poor, and once her sisters were married off, there was nothing left of her father's vicarage to leave her as a dowry. Destined to remain a spinster, she preferred to write."

On my knees with pushpins in my mouth, I must not be a pretty sight. At age forty-one, the poor thing died of Addison's disease—an illness that made every movement difficult for her—after writing six novels. Masterpieces. The map of Great Britain is in pastel tints; the blue of the sea is warm and gentle. I push a yellow-headed pin into Winchester, where Jane was born and where she is buried in the cathedral; one into Chawton, where she lived; and another into Bath, where she resided in the Georgian house at 40 Gay Street. In the center of the display window I place my walnut desk—well made, with sturdy legs—which I brought here because it's so very Austen. Manuele didn't agree, only because it was so much trouble to have to move it, but it's really impressive and, as the Faithful Enemy would say, saves us the cost of a rental. I emptied the drawers, as you never know. On a tray decorated with delicate-tinted roses I arrange a porcelain teapot, two tea-filled cups with saucers, a milk jug, a sugar bowl, and some cookies. To the left of the table I place a starched bonnet tied with a blue satin ribbon, bits of cambric and muslin, and ribbons of various colors: cream, beige, peach, light blue, pale yellow. As backdrop, two cotton "curtains" (the usual sheets from my trousseau) frame an imaginary window, in the center of which I hang a painting of a hunting scene, borrowed from Gabriella. Under the table sit a pair of men's muddy equestrian boots. Perhaps Darcy stopped by?

I display several copies of *Sense and Sensibility, Pride and Prejudice, Emma, Mansfield Park, Northanger Abbey, Persuasion,* which was reprinted with a preface by Virginia Woolf, and a brand-new edition of *Lady Susan* and *The Watsons.* I also add some unique items, such as the *History of England* and *Lesley Castle,* in paperback, examples of Jane's correspondence, defaced by her sister Cassandra, who burned many of her letters (it's an obsession, this passion for burning letters). The only complete work that contains the 154 letters that have come down to us today is *Jane Austen's Letters to Her Sister Cassandra and Others*, edited by R. W. Chapman in 1932, a rare volume, which I found at the antiques market on Portobello Road and brought from home.

"Why don't you post a birthday greeting on the Web site instead of arguing about it? I'll bet it would lead to a discussion group. Oh, and mention that the Morgan Library in New York has the manuscript for *Lady Susan*."

"I didn't know you were such an Austen fan; you're as excited as if you were talking about a loved one."

As usual, I'm overdoing it, but I can't explain to her that it's like having him here, and that it fills a void, which, in spite of myself, makes itself felt in the usual place, the diaphragm area, with the consistency of plasterboard. Thank God for the bookshop. I don't know what I'd do without this place.

"Listen to what that young woman was able to write: 'A person who can write a long letter with ease, cannot write ill.' Or this: 'One half of the world cannot understand the pleasures of the other'; 'Life seems but a quick succession of busy nothings'; 'There is safety in reserve, but no attraction. One cannot love a reserved person.'"

What about me, then? So reserved that I haven't spoken to Gabriella about Federico in weeks? Of course you can love a reserved person, but that's a different story. The display window is a "lark mirror" for my birdlike customers. Cecilia arrives, chilled and famished, and gratifies me with an exclamation of pleasure. "Wow, Emma, what a fantastic idea. *Pride and Prejudice* should be distributed in the schools, compulsory for both males and females. We're all potential Darcys and Elizabeths who revolve around the problem of love until we're exhausted."

"Hear that, Alice?"

· ———— ·

Milan, December 31, 2003
Via Londonio 8

Dear Federico,

I'm writing to you before sinking into the bathtub and getting ready
for dinner with a few close friends (I hate big New Year's Eve parties) at Gabriella's house. I went by the post office, crossing an unusually bleak Piazza del Duomo, what with Christmas just past and
the next one fifty-one weeks away. Five lightbulbs were burned out
on the streetlamp to the left of the facade. I retreated to the warmth
of the Galleria, the amber-tinted light reflecting off the wrought-
iron balconies, from which garlands looped like luminous spaghetti.
Even the pigeons were taking it easy, pecking here and there wherever they could, while a gold-plated man stood motionless under the
arch, sharing the donations of passersby with a boy plucking Gypsy
melodies on a violin. The tourists were snapping pictures. The others,
the Milanesi or those from outside the city who had come to take a
stroll downtown before the parties, walked along with no pushing or
shoving; a group of boys in low-slung pants came out of the megastore with a package of CDs and ducked into McDonald's for an
unhealthful burger snack. My dear architect, I thought of you while
walking through the Galleria with my nose in the air, gazing up at
the Octagon, where Christmas has left its traces in the explosion of
Santas pictured on the balloons that escaped the fingers of distracted
little children and rose over 150 feet to the highest point of the central dome, a jewel with its glass-covered iron framework, designed in
1865 by the architect Giuseppe Mengoni (by now, I've heightened
my sensitivity and receptiveness for design). An unfortunate man,
Mengoni: He did not live to see his work completed, but fell during
an inspection of that very dome on an icy winter day, December 30,
126 years ago. I was looking upward when I was distracted by a
small group of Japanese tourists. Like a troop of schoolchildren on
holiday, they had paused while their tour guide promised a year of
good fortune. She explained that if they made a half turn on their
heel on the "bull's balls" pictured in the mosaic there on the ground,

2004 would be a year when dreams came true. Obviously I tried it too, but I had to imagine the poor beast's balls, because in their place there is now a depression, and who knows if it will bring good luck just the same. I made my way along, hunched over, forced to run a slalom among cigarette butts, tram tickets, cards, and the wrappings of hastily opened gifts. I counted six empty bottles of every possible nectar, five plastic cups, a shoe without laces, and two glossy magazines. And filth, so much grubby filth. The dark brown trash cans were overflowing with paper and remnants of revelry. When I turned right, along the lateral wing, a hundred yards separated me from Piazza Cordusio, where your letter awaited me.

The bath is ready, my darling. I wish you a happy new year, and despite its worn balls, I hope the bull delivers the promised results.

Your Emma

· —— ·

What I'm fretting about are the returns. "Remainders," Alberto calls them. Leftovers, unsold copies that, according to him, should be returned and billed to the publishers. The word *remainder* implies that the book *remained* on the table or was shelved, with only the spine showing. An insult, a rejection, a watershed between living books and those ready to be made into pulp, sent to a used-book stall, or given to a prison or hospital library. A remainder book is not exactly dead; it's just feverishly moribund, weakened by indifference on the part of readers and booksellers. It is we, the medical examiners, who declare it deceased and return the body to the publishers. Sending it back is like killing a newborn baby, cutting off his breath before he's even had a chance to inhale the salty sea air, smell the fragrance of a rose or the scent of a lover's body. Being a bookseller is a destiny, not the foolish, unprofitable obsession that the Faithful Enemy insists it is; and, as everyone knows, even bad novels appeal to me, and no bookseller is anything but a friend to her books.

"You're not a collector," he's been telling me for hours as we do the inventory.

"As long as it stays on the shelf, it's alive; if you return to sender before its time has come, the book is done for. The classics should never be returned, Alberto; why else would they be called classics? It's publishers who are in a hurry, not booksellers. We've managed to extend our payment terms to one hundred and twenty days, which means they have faith in Dreams & Desires. A book should live a peaceful life and not be stressed by you."

When the catalogs with pictures of the newborns arrive, there's rejoicing in the shop. I leaf through them and at first glance I'd like to order all of them. Instead, I have to choose. I order a title and make a record of it in an 8.5x11 notebook.

"If I have only one copy of a book, I keep it. You never know. Take Fogazzaro's *The Little World of the Past,* for example. It's outdated, sure, but someone could always ask for it, or a teacher might assign it to his students to read."

"What imbecile would ask his students to read that book, Emma? For some reason, it reminds me of Alida Valli, a great beauty. Maybe she's already dead. Is Alida Valli dead, as far as you know? Anyway, I thought it was a story about the Risorgimento, a historical novel. What does it have to do with the bookshop?"

"It's the story of a marital crisis, Alberto. Luisa is a woman who considers her intellectual independence important. I keep it on the 'Couples' shelf. I don't think Alida Valli is dead; I would have read about it in the newspapers or seen it on television."

"The profitability of a bookshop is measured in square feet. If you spent less time seeing to your customers' comfort, you could increase your stock. You talk like a librarian. You can't hold on to books as if they are personal treasures."

"That's what my customers are used to, Alberto. They come here purposely for that. You insist on not getting it."

"Before the Locanda, they came for the free coffee, to sponge off you."

"It's rare for someone to leave here without buying anything. The café has proved to be an investment. And so will the hotel, wait and see."

"Talking with you is a waste of time. Take a look at the accounts: Despite your pigheadedness, agreements with companies for Christmas gifts have resulted in an increase in sales."

"Not bad, huh?"

"Of course we'll never know if your customers' love lives have seen improvements, but that's not our objective, right?"

Alberto pokes fun, but Dreams & Desires's balance sheets give him satisfaction. For him, an increment (what an ugly word) in sales proceeds is equivalent to what a well-healed scar means to a surgeon, an invisible filling to a dentist, or a smoothing leg wax to an aesthetician. He has his accounts. And Gabriella.

· ——— ·

Paris, January 12, 2004
Charles de Gaulle Airport

Dear Emma,

I'm in Paris; I'm boarding in twenty minutes. Whenever I sit in the Air France lounge with a small group of fortunate prodigals, I think about the fact that I'm just an hour and a half away from you, and that it wouldn't take much to break the villainous, masochistic pact I've bound you to. I can't change the past, but I want to be with you. Each day without you is like one day lost. When I left, a week ago, Anna had a long face. She can sense that I'm distant. I don't have the guts to talk to her about us, and, what's worse, I can't even talk to her about myself. Sometimes she looks at me with an unfathomable sadness, a kind of despair. I pretend not to notice and I feel like a shit, as Mattia would say. Anna doesn't judge. She's never hostile, doesn't ask, doesn't offer the slightest opening for a confession or disclosure, almost as if my mood frightens her. She's afraid of revelations she couldn't bear, as if the slightest change in our lives would be unendurable. Sarah is bright, intelligent, very pretty, and by now she completely fits in at school and with her friends. There's one boy who comes around the house regularly. It's no longer Ricki; his name is Francesco, an Italian from Florence, the son of some newspaper correspondent. I can't go on as if nothing has happened. I deliberately drown myself in my work. The construction site is the most kindred thing I know; the excavation is a symbol, but I'm incapable of delving that deeply into myself. That's the problem. They're announcing a delay for the flight to New York. I won't phone you; I'll go to the gift shop, buy a nice Liberté, Egalité, Fraternité vintage French stamp, and mail this. That way, this letter from a pathetic, weary soul will arrive sooner.

Read it with understanding.

Yours, you know that,

Federico

P.S. You and the Morgan are my entire world.

• ——— •

Milan, January 27, 2004
Dreams&Desires Hotel

Dear Federico,
New stationery. The blue Smythson of Bond Street envelopes are off to be pulped. I'm inaugurating the ones for the Dreams & Desires Hotel; it's actually still under construction, but I'm getting a head start. Can you imagine? A small hotel just for me and my writers! It's evening, the painter has just left, and I can sit here in peace and write to you. I have my personal construction site; there's dust everywhere, if you know what I mean. Naturally, I can't compete with you. I don't want a museum; nostalgia doesn't interest me. But we'll have three rooms, each with its own private entrance and names yet to be decided (any ideas?), a bathroom, and a small reception area. Each room will be furnished with restored furniture. At the antiques market in Navigli, I found porcelain doorknobs and handles, porcelain light switches, and—horror of horrors!—I had them install an Internet connection with a new system, almost without wires. Should a guest decide he wants to read his e-mails (Alice and Mattia thought of it), he can connect with his laptop. In my deficient imagination, a writer passing through Milan would have no desire to

write; he'd rather go see *The Last Supper*, wouldn't he? When will he have the chance again? Anyway, we have the connection and to each his own. Mattia is acting like a Niemeyer or a . . . Federico Virgili. He thinks he can impress me with his future architect's vocabulary. I invited the press agents (almost all women) of the major Italian publishers to the bookshop; I treated them to a light lunch at the Locanda and then I showed them the restoration efforts at the hotel (they were already familiar with the bookshop). Their reaction: enthusiastic. E-N-T-H-U-S-I-A-S-T-I-C about having their writers stay at the Dreams & Desires Hotel. I asked them to please let me know their authors' wishes, preferences, and idiosyncrasies from time to time so that I may accommodate them more adequately. They'll find good things to eat at the hotel; breakfast will be at the Locanda. The publisher is paying the bill, so I can afford not to skimp. I'll inquire about their favorite foods, and the books they'd love to find on the nightstand (besides the ones they've written). I've already taken the first reservation: five days at 150 euro per night, breakfast included, for a well-known British writer, who will be in Italy for a reading at the university and a series of interviews. It may not be the Morgan, my architect, but I'll have my writers in the flesh, not dead like yours! It won't be long till April 10. I am copying these lines of a poem for you, which I found while tidying up:

> April is the cruellest month, breeding
> Lilacs out of the dead land, mixing
> Memory and desire, stirring
> Dull roots with spring rain.
> (*The Waste Land*, by T. S. Eliot)

Your favorite hotelier,

Emma

P.S. I'm beside myself. And you know why.

· ——— ·

New York, February 15, 2004
42 W. 10th St

Dear Emma,
Today the boss quoted Yourcenar (another coincidence that con-vinced me to buy one of her novels, and to punish my ignorance as a late-blooming reader, I will force myself to read it in English), saying that when in darkness, you have to look about you with defiance, optimism, and rashness. I felt so close to him that for a moment I thought of telling him about you, but I refrained; I could never let my relationship with him, as meaningful as it is, cross the line into friendship. I can't treat him as an equal. He is the Master and my admiration for him precludes any type of intimacy. I wanted to mention this elective affinity between him and you just now, even though you don't know each other.

A kiss, on the shoulder, on your face, on your mouth. Wherever you like.

Federico

P.S. I look for you in my darkness, each night before falling asleep, but I'm not always able to be optimistic, much less rash.

· ———— ·

They've delivered the candles with the Dreams & Desires logo! The square blue box bears the bookshop's gold crest and a large amper-sand. The scent of paper, the aroma of ink, a bouquet of paste and glue. You breathe it in and it comes back to you, in a Proustian olfac-tory moment. A contradiction in these times, when everything is deodorized: a nasal taste of books. A retort to booksellers who keep books in plastic wrap so as "not to ruin them." A far cry from the digital revolution of online books, very different from the cyberen-thusiasm of those three—Alice, Manuele, and Mattia.

"If you ask me, they won't sell, Mom. Who would want a candle that smells like a bookshop in their house?"

"Candles don't smell, Mattia. The purpose of a candle is to be *fragrant*. Aromatherapy is one of the most popular alternative medicines. Books don't have an odor anymore—the glues are less noxious and more environmentally friendly, the way you like; inks are made with water-based pigments—and I'm convinced that lighting a book-scented candle makes reading more thrilling. I sold Assouline's candles and I'll sell these, too. And it's not like they have an expiration date. They're timeless."

I'm nervous and I take it out on him. It's unfair, I know, but his academic forays irritate me. Alice and Mattia are antennas in my relationship with the outside world, labyrinths in which I feel my way around like a dilettante, proceeding by intuition.

"Well, come on, then, give me a hand. I want to do a window display about gay romances. Will you help me choose?"

"Mom, I don't know anything about literature, much less gay fiction! Get Borghetti to help you, or Gaston, okay? I like girls, Mom. It's your bad luck to have a son who's straight. Besides, I have to go to the Poly."

He says "Poly," too. Generations change, but not nicknames.

"Don't be a homophobe. A-a-a-a-lice, will you come and help me, please? It's late and I have to get to the hairdresser."

"Why bother to go to the hairdresser?" Alice asks. "By tomorrow, you'll be soaking in a pool all day, in thermal waters. Having your hair done is a waste. Anyway, we have Forster's *Maurice;* a novel by an Italian newcomer, Ivan Cotroneo; Edmund White's *The Farewell Symphony;* and *The Hours,* by Michael Cunningham, who has just written a portrait of Provincetown, a village in Massachusetts, or is it Maine? I would also add *The Page Turner,* by David Leavitt, the story of a failed pianist who is reduced to being the page turner for a successful pianist, whom he obviously falls for. Then, let's see . . ."

"Mom, can you put in some condoms? Better yet, why don't we sell them?"

"Mattia, please beat it and give it a rest. Condoms! Can you just picture Lucilla's expression, not to mention that of her friends?"

"They fucked, too, when they were young. You sell candles and mugs; why not something that's really useful for love? It would show you were open-minded. Think about it: It could make news, the first bookshop to launch a campaign for safe-sex awareness."

APRIL 10, 2004

Falling in love was not gradual. It was not one of those considered, cautious romances that, assisted by a glance, a handshake, or a chaste decade-long friendship, moves from encounter to friendship and tumbles by surprise into unexpected (until that moment) erotic passion.

No.

It was what injudicious novels call "love at first sight." Or better yet, more in keeping with this region, a "blast of wind," a "slap in the face by a vehement seaman." It lasted thirty years, spanning the wars. Cupid's arrow was planted among the rocks on a sultry summer afternoon in 1893—a strange thing for Brittany, as sultriness is not a mood that characterizes it. She had yielded to the insistence of Georges Clairin, an introverted man with a goatee on his chin and a set smile, one of those figures who in Parisian high society were sought after for parties, dinners, premieres. Heir to his father's incredible fortune, he lived in Paris with a manservant. He was a painter. He had set up a summer studio in Le Pouldu, in Brittany, but the place was terribly lonely, and so, to avoid falling into depression, he invited friends to keep him company. They visited Concarneau, Benodet, Audierne, and that watery cemetery that intimidates even the more reckless sailors, Pointe du Raz. She was strolling along the shore of Finistère in her little silk shoes when Clairin suggested an excursion to Belle-Ile. The Union Belliloise's ferry would take them to Le Palais. Waiting for them on the dock was a horse-drawn carriage. The group of late-nineteenth-century lunatics stopped for lunch at the Apothicairerie, an inn planted on the edge of the cliff—as though to defy good sense—by a certain Ferdinand Huchet, who rented horses before switching to the hotel business. Nothing fancy, just a few simply furnished rooms, a favorite with the artists who came to the island in search of peace and quiet, inspiration, and the masochistic pleasure that came from living with storms that slammed spray in your face like the foam on a pint of beer. After lunch, the walk continued up to here.

She later said, "I was exhausted from a tour, I don't remember where, in any case by a thousand performances, and I had reached an age that seemed sufficient to me to put a stop to my hectic rushing around. It was then that I came upon that stretch of land so wild yet so civil, so violent and so gentle, called Pointe des Poulins. In front of me, embedded in the rock on a gentle slope, was an abandoned little fort. Dark and forlorn, scoured by rain and sea water, it displayed a sign: 'Fort for sale, inquire of the lighthouse keeper.'"

Set among the rocks and hidden from view, ignored by the French military and relegated to municipal property, there was nothing imposing about it. Light filtered in through narrow grated openings. All around, a barren moor scorched by wind, salt air, and sun. No life seemed able to withstand that forsaken place. She, however, could. Having recently turned fifty, the most celebrated and most headstrong actress in France was vital and beautiful and had the world at her feet. That afternoon, Sarah Bernhardt slipped through a side door into the darkness of the ground floor; she reappeared shortly afterward, proclaiming to her friends, "I announce to you that from this moment on, everything you see is mine. I am the owner of a fort." She signed the purchase agreement for the sum of three thousand francs, and the following summer she took possession of the fort, which in a few weeks went from anonymity to celebrity. And Belle-Ile-en-Mer, that "inaccessible, uninhabitable, cheerless" place, became the summer realm for the stage actress who could not bear to be alone. The tyrannical diva invited a court of poets, playwrights, painters, farmers, and fishermen there, in addition to Maurice, her adored only son, and Lysiane, her beloved granddaughter. Summer after summer, that barren corner was transformed into a paradise of indolence, fishing, sadistic lizard hunts, fatuous readings, and previews of plays performed for a few lucky spectators. Sarah's guests, Sarah's blitheness, her unconventionality, her passion for storms became legend. And the island lost its unprecedented ability to be left in peace, apart from civilization.

She said, "I was seized, at Belle-Ile, by a giddy whirl of planning and well-being that old-school Parisians, dismayed and sickened by the incessant hustle-and-bustle of city life, always dreamed of."

"Look at that rock down there. It looks like the profile of a lioness."

"You always see what's not there, Emma."

"It's a privilege we romantics have, my darling architect."

"They're restoring Sarah's property, the fort will be like it once was: a living room, nine bedrooms, a kitchen, and two bathrooms. She had other cottages built; two are still standing, those down there."

I turn toward two gray structures wedged among the rocks, each with a rooftop terrace and an external staircase leading to the upper floor.

"Somewhat ugly, I'd say."

"Bernhardt had so many fawning admirers that after she restored the fort she had a studio built for Clairin, a cottage for her son and his family, and a 'dependency,' which she called 'the house of the five continents.' 'Have you seen Maurice?' she'd ask. 'Yes, he's in Oceania,' someone would reply from the Africa window. Bernhardt was a megalomaniac when it came to being in the avant-garde."

"A true diva, not like today's inflated starlets."

"The only arrangement she wasn't able to pull off was the small island down there, Basse Hiot. She wanted to have her tomb built there, but the fishermen claimed it as a mooring for their boats and managed to defeat her. Sarah bought it, but they did not allow her to use it. You wouldn't be able to buy a house here, Emma, unless you were very, very wealthy."

"Why?"

"Because you don't know how to drive. How come someone like you doesn't have a driver's license?"

"Laziness, sweetheart. I don't like cars, I'm happy to walk, and I'm terrified of finding myself alone, in the dark, in the rain, with a nail in my tire. Do you think it's a flaw?"

"You have no flaws, Emma. Remember?"

"Federico, the level of our conversation is becoming pathetic, but you know what I'd like to shout to this sea? 'Who gives a daaaamnnn. . . . This is what happiness is.'"

"Happiness rightfully belongs only to children, and you are the most beautiful, most charming little girl in the world."

We are at the tip. The lighthouse behind us is a little white cottage with a bright red cap, sitting on a rocky spur carved with sea monsters. No one lives there anymore, not even the lighthouse keeper. The interior is bare; the slate tiles weave a checkerboard of blacks and grays. The moor is choked with hawthorn, thistles, bindweed, and saltwort climbing on the rock. A brood of plump black birds with red beaks feasts indifferently. I'm cuddled up in Federico's arms. His breath . . . his body, so warm, holding me tight for a few nights at least. The saffron-colored wool cloche is beside the basket, from which a sprig of broom peeps out. Picking flowers in this corner of the world, where the word *ecosystem* is not just a slogan for a few fanatics, is prohibited; and I, a slightly idiotic romantic who can't resist the tone-on-tone capped flower, am breaking the law. We are the only humans who have decided to defy good sense. Persistent frigid gusts chill the ears and tip of the nose; under these conditions, even kissing becomes complicated, due to the cocoa butter I smear on his chapped lips, making them slippery. The wind, a good stiff wind bracing as a sea chantey, is a barrier to dialogue. The tide advances and recedes, murmuring to itself, and I am in a decidedly cheerful mood. In a word, I'm happy.

"Emma, a few more hours and the lighthouse will be cut off, and us along with it. Want to stay here with me forever?"

"Forever and ever and ever? We have nothing to read, and you, what would you do without a drawing pad?"

He presses his lips on mine rather than tossing me into the sea, but it's clear that when you feel intoxicated in that silly way people have when they're in love or something like that, coming up with idiotic responses is a way of not admitting that with him I would go or I would stay, that I would travel anywhere and do anything, stand still or walk, fly or stand on a ledge, enroll in driving school, and let myself be carried away by the most lascivious thoughts without feeling a shred of guilt. With him, I would face the ocean and confront the mystery. From the way he looks at me, I think he's about to say something. He checks himself, however. When we're together, words become an impediment. In a perfect setting in a perfect world, we're afraid we'll regret what we may say, upsetting the equilibrium of a love that, logically speaking, is unsteady. I have no desire to rake things up, remember, discuss, detect, examine, analyze. I don't even want to make an effort to understand, to establish boundaries, much less rules. I just want to stay here and stop counting the remaining hours. Neither of us has a watch. He has no wedding band on his ring finger. It happens: Fingers swell with age and there's no way to slip it onto the place assigned by the amorous resolution, the marriage bond.

"What are we doing?"

"We're listening to the sea and doing a crossword puzzle, my dear lady."

"Stop it. . . ."

"I don't know, Emma. I don't know exactly what we're doing, but giving a name to all this is not all that important to me."

The birds with the red beaks are wheeling around in a circle. A crab as big as a serving platter scuttles away, limping. The tide rises in empathy with a nature that knows no weakness. Clinging to Federico, I feel safe. This sea is our infinite expanse, our stability. In fact, we are moored to this strip of land, letting our minds wander with Sarah Bernhardt, about whom I have acquired some information.

"She was eccentric, rambunctious, generous, endowed with a monstrous talent. Daughter of a demimondaine, which is a chic way to say prostitute, she had a miserable childhood. There was no trace of a father. When you're born like that, you have no choice: Either you die or you redeem yourself in a big way. I just wonder how she happened to get to this place."

"Bernhardt's arrivals in Belle-Ile were memorable, Emma. She started out from the Montparnasse train station, the same one where you arrive, in a sleeper, which took fourteen hours to reach Quiberon. The ferry awaited the passengers at Port Maria, and loaded the *Courrier de Belle-Ile* with dozens of chests, animal cages, dogs, a cheetah, chameleons, monkeys, parrots, hampers, baskets, hatboxes, suitcases, maids, lady companions, and those fantastic trunks full of drawers, hangers, and secret compartments. Everywhere she went, Sarah lived her lifelong motto, *Quand même.*"

Nevertheless. (Charming, this tragedienne.)

"She would never have been able to meet her favorite architect only once a year."

"Well, no. After an hour and a half on the ferry, she would land amid the islanders' cheers and endure several more miles of dirt roads. Grueling. Sometimes she persuaded the ferry captain to reroute the vessel; she would transfer to a dinghy and arrive at the beach down below. They would all be exhausted from the journey, all except her."

"My dear architect, your Emma is exhausted and would gladly return to La Touline."

"They don't make women like they used to! Come on. I'll take you to safety. What would you do without me?"

Indeed, what would I do without him?

The widow's garden is on the island's wild coast, at the junction of the impenetrable valleys of Bortinec and Pouldon. In the confusion of trees left to grow riotously and uncared for amid woods, rocks, and natural rubble, Véronique de Laboulaye has reconstructed paths, unearthed dry stone walls, and dug beds for streams that have begun to flow again, like veins that course with a certain moderation, thanks to a patient cardiologist. We stroll along on a guided tour led by the lady, a friend of Annick Bertho, crossing waterfalls and fountains, lakes and a pond where two frogs stare at us in bewilderment. A sculptor has created nests for birds using branches and has pruned the shrubs into squiggles. As we go up and down wooden steps bordered with white and pink rock roses, we are told about the willows, elms, red maples, and apple trees and led through a maze of asphodels—reminiscent of the crop circles in the film *Signs*—along with water irises, faded purple hydrangeas, gerberas, daisies as big as sunflowers, locust trees, tamarinds, and maritime pine. The widow is a lean woman with a shock of blond hair, dressed like a salesclerk in Harrods's gardening department; her paradise lost is a botanical handbook. In her bony hands, she holds gardening gloves and a pair of worrisome shears. The widow, before she became one, had one single objective: to bring this ruin of abandoned land back to life.

"Now that Rodolphe is gone, I feel 'called' to continue carrying on the dream," she tells us before saying good-bye and getting back to driving her riding mower. Extremely competent, learned, alone. After the slog through the gorge, we are at Grand Sable beach. We need the sea.

"Do you think it's possible for two people's sole purpose in life to be that of creating the most beautiful garden in the world?"

"It's a great project, isn't it? The wealthy little widow would make a perfect character for one of your novels. If you ask me, there's a studly gardener lurking somewhere in those bushes. Want to come for a swim?"

"I'd rather watch you from here."

"You should try it, Emma. Floating in the frigid water is a great feeling. Your legs become numb; the sun bakes your face. It's like a microclimate of contrasts. Good for the circulation."

My hero had had the idea of planning a picnic on the beach. Madame Bertho has prepared a hamper in perfect Bernhardt style: linen tablecloth, sailboat cutlery, crystal glasses, bottles of beer, a baguette with butter, cheese, tuna salad, bananas, and a lemon cake still warm from the oven. The sea, sand, and sky are more than enough for me, whereas the insane architect has decided to take a swim. Grand Sable is a spit of sand. No lifeguards, refreshment stands, ice-cream vendors, restaurants, or discotheques, just a barren stretch dotted with asymmetrically shaped rocks. There is nothing for the gaze to dwell on except for an isolated wave or two marking the surface of the Atlantic. It's the great calmness of the season that brings winter to a close, an almost worrying stillness, no tourists about, the water seemingly drowsy, though best not to trust it. Federico wades in with cautious, apprehensive steps, then waves for me to join him. No thanks. I prefer to be a voyeur, safe beneath my sunhat and sunglasses, observing that body I know so well. All bodies are similar, after all; Federico's resembles this island. Strong and seafaring, it is a body without bridges, swift as the clouds and flecked with gold like this sand beach. What matters to me, above all, is touching it. I have decided to end things, but I put it off. I'll tell him on the last day. Today is the next to the last. I'll wait until the last embrace and kiss at the airport. Of the two of us, I'm the talker. Federico swims and speaks little; his daughter, Sarah, is the only one he allows some space to, between us. We are no exception: Female brain circuits dedicated to communication are so refined that they can express 250 words per minute, compared to 125 for men. Like all shy people, I go overboard with words; I don't think before opening my mouth, but with him I feel uninhibited. "I love it that you're a talker," he told me, with the direct gaze of someone you can trust, with whom you can let yourself go without taking any risks. I talk, of course, but I don't *dare*. Until yesterday, I was sure I wanted to break free of the 360-day parentheses that separate our encounters. Federico, what are we doing with an affair—or rather, a relationship made up of bits and pieces, odd moments, and . . . You tell me: What's another word that explains how excited I feel at just the idea of seeing your eyes in mine? How will I find the courage now?

Behind me are a projection of granitic cliff and minute white houses tucked under the maritime pines like animals huddled against the cold. I could blame it on fate, the one embodied by my stone ancestor. Yes, that's it; I'll take him to Jeanne and I'll tell him that I feel like her—immovable, helpless, impotent. Literary. I, on the other hand, want to feel alive. Even without him. I will admit that I have crossed the line into addiction. He will laugh, with that smile that is both ironic and teasing. And he'll talk again about intimacy, the kind that only we two understand, that just *happens* as soon as we touch, that each year seems to evaporate between our letters, yet all it takes is nothing at all and there it is again. Without the scruples that age should dutifully suggest. We have no time to lose. We have no time, Federico. Basically, I like living this way; it took me years to restore the innocence of solitude.

"I'm starving," he announces, shaking himself off like Mondo and dripping on the beach table I arranged, like when I used to play with my Barbies. The only thing missing is a vase of flowers, but I did the best I could.

"Hey, you're splashing the sandwiches."

"Are you happy? *How* happy are you? Do you have everything a woman could want?"

"No. I don't have everything I could want."

The blue of the sky is darkened by a cloud overhead. Until a few moments ago, I was ready to tell him that this affair doesn't make sense, and now I have spoken without even thinking. I'm already regretting it. It must be that cloud's fault.

"We have to talk about it, Emma."

"All right, but without making a scene about it. Just to set things straight."

As if that were possible.

I open the bottle of Britt and fill the crystal goblet. They don't go together, the beer and the fine glass. You don't have to have taken a course for sommeliers to know that.

"That's how we were. You were the beer. You were wild; you didn't give a damn about appearances, form, your family. You were intelligent and studious; you stirred things up, shattered their plans. I owe you an apology," Frederico says.

"What for?"

"For being weak. I couldn't take the pressure."

"The pressure, of course. The pressure from the beer?"

"From my mother."

At the ocean's edge, the waves are still, like on a beautiful summer day. I dig my toes in the sand to uncover the mollusks. And to impose a certain composure, on my body at least.

"I never slept with a man I didn't love. That's why I've had so few. I thought it was your father who couldn't stand me."

"That means you're monogamous, but I'm like you, even though I belong to the unworthy category of males."

"When it came to sex, I knew almost nothing. Well, not that I'm a big expert now, you know. And here I thought it was my fault. That you dropped me because I kissed that guy the night we occupied the school of architecture. . . . I don't even know who he was. I tried every way I could to convince you that I was . . . that I wasn't aware of what I was doing. Instead, it was because your mother didn't like me. It's like something out of the Dark Ages. Why didn't you tell me before?"

"Of course, you acted like quite a bitch that night. We were waiting for the Right Moment. To do it. And there you were, making out in the auditorium with that pimply turd. I couldn't touch you anymore. For months, I was almost impotent."

"Not again! We didn't know what we were doing. It was what kids did, that's all. It was the time of the *sexual revolution*, Federico; we thought we had to 'do it.' And all I did was kiss him. I told you that."

"I believe Edgar Morin wrote that memory can also be tainted. Yours is, Emma. That's not the way it happened. It was *her*, Emma. She didn't want me to be with you; it's medieval, but that's just how it was. I couldn't stand the scenes, the long faces, the way she made me feel guilty about the sacrifices my father had made for us, how he had built his wealth with his own two hands, and on and on. She still hoped that I would take over my father's business, that I would meet a nice girl from Rotary. The night of the occupation, Daniele . . . Daniele was the guy you were sitting on the floor necking with, though it seems you've forgotten. . . . It was all an excuse, a bunch of crap. How could you not have known?"

"About your mother? I don't know; I just didn't. This is manipulating memory."

"You know, at the beginning, when you wrote to me, I believed the story you told me, sure; the fact that you didn't remember was an excuse, a defense mechanism. I thought you just didn't want to talk about it. When she died, I withdrew into a kind of no-man's-land, a world all my own. I never leave it. Except with Sarah. And . . . with you."

He's talking about an eighteen-year-old schoolgirl, I was that girl making out with Daniele (who knows what he looks like now and what he does?). I feel a surge of pain in my sternum, the spot relegated to the plasterboard, the sour taste of something that didn't sit well. It's an old story, the one between me and his mother. His mama. A momentous moment, it would be a true moment of glory if only I could accuse her of everything now, like in those novels where the mystery that has kept readers glued to the page is finally revealed. I was simply troublesome to her. She didn't like me. She didn't want her little grandchildren to go and visit a grandmother who sold fruit for a living. Still, things are better left unsaid at times. The truth is so obvious; invention, imagination, and distortion are so much better. Wouldn't it be more romantic to think that Federico, entering the auditorium at the Polytechnic, couldn't stand seeing that girl, *his* girl, smooching with that idiot? And that at that moment all his plans for their first time together—a moment dreamed about and meant to happen that night of the defiant occupation—fell apart, and that as a result he decided to leave her? But no, he has to go and blurt the truth out here, on a beach, over thirty years later, and it's all about his mother. In a novel, no one would believe it. Doubts, fictions, lies, betrayals are excellent subjects for a good book. But those were the seventies, in Italy. And there were kidnappings, and scions such as Federico were sent off to study in Switzerland, as though dispatched to a sanitarium: pathetic cowards that had to be protected. Deadly boring, Switzerland.

"I just remember that I felt awful. I don't remember anything about your parents, not their faces or how they sounded. Nothing. And I didn't want to know anything. I left for Freiburg. Quarantined. I worked as a salesclerk and studied. Boys disgusted me. I studied and cried. Gabriella knows. I think that's why she's mistrustful; she keeps warning me."

"For months I brought home girls who were disreputable, I would fuck them in my room. I introduced each of them to her. I told her I would knock up the first one who came along. I was filled with rage. I hurt a lot of people, except the whores. I paid the real ones. I enjoyed upsetting her. I returned from Geneva to take the exams at the Polytechnic. You were too . . ."

"Too penniless."

"You were 'too much' for them in every way."

"It's not as if you were the crown prince, just the son of a hard worker who got rich, and you let me get away because of money. And status. It's crazy; it's like you're talking about a good boy who took up with a worthless good-for-nothing."

"You're not thinking straight, Emma. Sure, you're right, but you don't realize what it means to be the only son in a family where money and appearances are almost all that matters. I was convinced that her happiness depended on me. She was depressed; she would lie in bed for hours. And it was all my fault."

"So you married someone just like her. Class differences were ironed out."

"I needed a convenient wife. The absurd thing is that my mother died before she could meet her."

It's the first time we've raised our voices. We need to. And so out with it, all the accumulated resentments, things left unspoken, unfair accusations. I've seen her only in photographs, his wife, and I have no right to take it out on her. There were no visible scars in this relationship until now, on this stretch of sand. We intentionally concealed them. It's easier to remain uncertain. To float. Even if the ocean is frigid and you can only feel the sun on your face. Rapid heartbeat, shortness of breath, trembling lips, flushed cheeks: Who said emotions are a mental phenomenon? It's the body that speaks for us. Federico provokes physical reactions. And I'm the sort of person who, in her fifties, still doesn't know how to handle shame. How much better it would have been to go on being happy.

"I've never been good at expressing my feelings. They call me 'iceberg,' even Enrico."

"You should be more lenient toward the two kids we were then. What happened happened. We made it just the same. You're an established professional. I'm a fairly successful bookseller. Let's leave it at that; it wasn't destined to be for us, that's all."

"We're the ones who determine our destiny. It's only when I'm with you again that I feel I'm where I belong."

I listen to him, my head resting on his shoulder. We talk to the ocean, in the not-so-secret hope that spewing out now everything that has remained trapped in some mysterious recess of our organism might relieve the pain that has gnawed at us for decades, like a mouse nibbling away at leftovers. It had to happen sooner or later. Now we have to face the subject, utter the word *future*. Except that it's no longer credible on the lips of two little-more-than-fifty-year-olds. If you don't grab it when you have a chance, maybe you don't even have a future.

"It's late. We met late."

"I never thought that writing to each other would lead to this. I'm naïve, shallow, and arguing with you . . . well, it's absurd and I don't like it. My father never wanted to talk about it. Nor did I. She died and that's that. I don't know the cause exactly; without being specific, they said it was heart disease, congenital. I never inquired further, nor claimed the right to know. I'm protecting myself against the risk of being abandoned again. I think that's what it is. Yes, I think that's it."

"You're not free."

"I'm all too free, Emma. I'm free to tell you that I want to be with you. I had to show my father that I didn't need his money. I didn't realize that I was demonstrating to her, to that mother I so loved and feared and hated, that I did not have to follow the model. Anna was instrumental in planning a life in which I was at the center. I've gone along with this state of affairs and nothing has ever interrupted the orderly flow of our lives. Anna wants to live in my shadow. Sarah is all there is for me now. I'm not sure where everything else falls."

"I'm your last chance, like at the book sales."

"The *only* one, Emma."

"Hold me close. Let's not talk about it anymore."

The salt on his shoulders, the hair falling over my eyes when I mount that body that is so much bigger than mine, my nipples stiff in the palms of those sensitive, gentle hands of his, as if our age prohibits the passion that dominates the body when it loses control, those gestures so ordinary yet never fully learned; his fingertips wipe away my tears with a delicate caress, from the inner corner to the outer, but the tears continue spilling down his chest.

"You're trembling."

"I don't know what's wrong with me exactly. Hold me tight and massage my neck, if you would. I can't understand why such an old story should have such an effect on me."

"Let's give each other a gift, Emma."

"What?"

"Let's try to live without the slightest suspicion of a lie. It's not up to us to determine what will happen. And maybe it's not even important."

Belle-Ile is an island of ups and downs. Rage. Fear. Pride. The Méhari is parked in the space below the house, next to the stone wall. Yellow this time, with a canvas canopy roof that barely protects us. The same fellow who brought us here awaits us at the port. "It rained last night; the sea is rough," he says. And we hadn't noticed a thing. We climb aboard the hydrofoil, continuing to hold hands. All this has to end, because it will end. The package is at the bottom of the suitcase. Federico almost forgot it.

"I brought you a present, because of the ink stains on your recent letters."

"A pen! My first Montblanc!"

"It's a bit masculine for you, but I couldn't resist. After all, he brought us good luck."

The limited edition of the "Patron of Art—Hommage à John Pierpont Morgan," with its silver cap, is in fact a fountain pen for males. The *M* engraved on the gold nib recalls the magnate's legacy: the Morgan Library.

"I'll use it only to write to you," I say magnanimously, and untruthfully.

Standing on the *Locmaria*, we turn to the low tide. The cove, to the right of the Sauzon lighthouse, is like a fingerprint in a cake. Sailboats and canoes are lopsided in the mud, like toys abandoned by a child who slipped away from his mother and is now distracted by a new whim. Relics of personal shipwrecks. Seagulls nose-dive into the tidal pools, domestic vultures looking for scraps of fish. A mahogany-skinned man in a blue oilskin, his bare legs sticking out of big rubber boots, is holding a net in his right hand and a bucket in his left, collecting snails for supper. A catamaran with a yellow sail is stranded in the mud. It, too, is waiting for better times. We gesture good-bye to Annick Bertho, who waves to us from the dock, and we seem to be saying farewell to a world that we are not at all certain we will see again.

The plague of middle-aged women has a disagreeable name, few synonyms, and it's not menopause. It's called "regrowth." We brunettes are fated to fall victim to it, certainly more so than blondes, who manage to disguise it by flinging their curls here and there in a *pseudo-tousled* look, which in reality is carefully calculated. The illusion of having eradicated it lasts a couple of weeks; then the white reappears like a pedestrian stripe freshly repainted on the asphalt. In ads, women dye their hair while they're cooking a roast, chatting with mom on the phone, or reviewing the text for a conference. I am not able to. When I tried, I managed to ruin two luxurious bathrobes stolen from some hotel, both of which ended up spotted like a Dalmatian. The person who sees to my hair is Dino, a young, tall, perpetually tanned *coiffeur pour dames* on via Mazzini. "Brown hardens your features, Emma. What if we tried a lighter tone?" he asks. Going to Dino seventeen times a year for 110 minutes each time is deadly boring, so when our regrowths coincide, I go with Gabriella, who is now sitting beside me, looking like a foil-wrapped fish ready to be baked in the oven. They've covered the strands of her hair with thin strips of aluminum foil to highlight her *natural* brown with lighter streaks. We are a pair of monsters, and I can't even read because I'd end up staining the pages of Anna Gavalda's *I Wish Someone Were Waiting for Me Somewhere*. Also, I can't ignore Gabriella.

"Well then? Don't you have anything to tell me?"

"I always have loads of things to tell you."

"What if we stopped? The latest trend is to let the gray grow in naturally. Look at Helen Mirren."

"In Italy eighty percent of women dye their hair. Why should we be the ones to lower the average? Helen Mirren's gray hair isn't natural; it's tinted. We wouldn't solve the problem."

"It would express self-confidence, show that we're not afraid."

"I'm terrified by time's passing; gray hair would make my life worse. I'm sure of it."

"Are you talking about hair to change the subject?"

"Are you expecting exciting, ironic, cute, or scathing stories, maybe spicy and erotic? Well, I can't think of any."

"Actually, I'd just like to know how you are, but from the aggressive way you're acting, I suspect things aren't going well at all. What are *scathing* stories, anyhow?"

"Seeing him again was wonderful, as always. We're happy together. When I come home, I'm irritable for a few days; then I get used to the same old same old."

"The same old same old."

"I planned to leave him the last day, tell him that when we say good-bye, it's as if something in my belly rips apart, but I felt pathetic, and you know I don't like that. If you think, *Now I'll end it,* it's like when you want to commit suicide: You tell yourself, *It's simple; I'll jump. It's quick and I won't feel a thing.* Then your courage fails. It's the same feeling. In any case, I said almost none of what I meant to tell him."

"Did he talk about her?"

"Who?"

"His wife. You know I'm interested."

"Yes, he spoke about her."

"And . . ."

"He doesn't love her anymore, but he feels responsible for making her live in his shadow all these years. We spent the last night talking about it. But the most important thing is that he told me what happened when he left me. Did you know that it was his mother and not his father who hated me?"

"Yes, though *hate* is a strong word. What a shame, to waste the last night talking. How do you know it's not all a bunch of baloney?"

"I can tell by his eyes that he's not lying. The bitch. Why didn't you ever tell me?"

"Mother or father, what difference does it make? He was a shallow rich boy and he gave in to class-conscious pressure."

"You think I'm an idiot and you're certain that this relationship won't go anywhere. I never write to him about my anxieties. When we meet, we hastily dispose of painful matters and close the door. We'd rather be happy."

"*Excusatio non petita, accusatio manifesta,* Emma. 'He who excuses himself, accuses himself.' I don't think you're an idiot. On the contrary, Federico is good for you; it's the circumstances that are odd."

"In a novel, you would be the narrator who disagrees with the protagonist. A disapproving author, that's what."

"Don't hide behind books, not with me at least. It's just that I don't understand what sense it makes to see each other once a year, not to phone each other. . . . It's a put-on. You and Federico are like that play—what was it called? You know, the one about the two people who meet once a year in the same hotel? We saw it at the theater some years ago."

"*Same Time, Next Year,* the comedy by Bernard Slade. Even your Degas rebelled against the telephone. He considered it vulgar because it allowed anyone to summon him as if he were a servant. Speaking of painters, are you familiar with a certain Clairin?"

"A late-nineteenth-century portraitist, a pupil of Delacroix and a rival of Ingres, a less conceited figurative painter than Boldini."

"He was the one who led Sarah Bernhardt to discover Belle-Ile."

"Okay, but what happened after he told you about his mother?"

"Nothing happened, Gabri. Things are the way they are and they're not going to change. The fact that he no longer loves his wife . . . doesn't concern me."

"Of course it concerns you. He says he loves you, yet he does nothing to change the situation. As if knowing were enough."

"'Loves me'? Are you sure? Racking our brains like teenagers over the meaning of the word *love* is a waste of time. I never feel like I'm competing with anyone else, much less with a woman I've never seen. I live each day as it comes, without making plans, and I like it that way."

"It's not true that you don't make plans. Why not admit that you don't know what plans to make."

In the time it takes to dye my hair back to its natural soft brown and highlight hers in luminous ash blond glints, I tell her everything, even though recapping Federico is like viewing vacation slides with someone who wasn't there. It's impossible to explain their magic; they remain soulless images.

"The last time I made love on a beach . . . I can't remember. For sure I wasn't coming to have my hair dyed. Not yet."

· ——— ·

Milan, May 18, 2004
Sweet Dreams Locanda

Dear Federico,
I'm furious with Mattia. *We* used to shout the pronoun *we*. *They* mainly know the word *I*. He lives in symbiosis with Carlotta (and that's fine), but he hasn't the slightest sense of what's going on around him; I don't mean in the world, but even in his own country, even in the city and province of Milan. His one magic word is *connectivity*; "being connected" is a condition that he cannot do without. The cell phone is his antenna, the iPod a curse, and if you ask him about the war in Iraq, he has no idea what to say. We used a Walkman and went to concerts. They stick their ear buds and emotions in their ears and experience them by themselves. They chase after the holy grail of communication yet have no sensitivity to what surrounds them. I don't understand them. Is Sarah just as un-communicative, surrounded by her clique of friends, not caring

about anything else? Forgive the outburst, but today was tense.
Mattia argued with his father, an ideological debate, simply because
Michele dared ask him what his intentions were for the future. A
legitimate question, since Mattia made up his mind to do an internship with the architect Monzini, whereas Michele wants him to just
attend classes and study. Mattia has done okay with his exams, but
I think that if he were to start discussing architecture with you, you
two would be far apart. He has no sense of mission; he told his father he's studying because he wants to make money. "I'll be an urban planner," he says; "I don't want to end up decorating the homes
of the ignorant rich." They talk about money too much, these kids.
I don't like it. Again, pardon my outburst, but sometimes being a
mother is much more complicated than being a bookseller. Today I
thought of the tree trunk with the arrows that stands at the tip of
Belle-Ile, on Grand Phare cliff, 3,432 miles from New York, 4,127
miles from La Cayenne and that sign, DANGER: SHEER DROP. And
don't ask me why that particular sign came to mind. You know why.

Your Emma

P.S. You're beside me at this moment; I'm sure of it. Lying next to
me as we listen to the sound of the sea. I can smell its salt spray.
You?

. ——— .

New York, June 1, 2004
Peaceful oasis number 9, Gramercy Park

Dear Emma,
We're wrong to look at them as if looking in a mirror, even though
it's impossible to distance ourselves from the sole example that each
of us has: ourselves and our own experience. It's highly likely that if
they knew that we write to each other and keep our letters in a post
office box, they'd think we were a couple of idiots, but we certainly
don't think that, so it all depends on your point of view. Sarah argues mostly with Anna; I still enjoy the privileged status of a myth.

But she, too, lives surrounded by her group of school friends; that's the only way she feels protected. The boys who come to our house are attractive and bright; they wear jeans and hooded sweatshirts that make them look like bank robbers. They don't want to be accepted and the aesthetic confirmation makes them feel different from us, their parents. We were that way, too, Emma. We had long hair and unkempt beards (at least I did, not you; you had a peaches-and-cream complexion) and wore those horrible bell-bottoms; I got pissed off every time my father gave me an order, and I thought I would change the world through architecture. So . . . we shouldn't talk. The latest studies on the brain and mind, as New York neuro-psychologist Elkhonon Goldberg writes in *The Wisdom Paradox*, reveal that the human brain, once past fifty, is more pliable and better able to change its pattern-recognition process than a young brain is. They see and change the tree in the forest; we see the forest and . . . we want to change that. As for technology, however, and the hold you think it has on our children, you're wrong: The idea that it limits us and affects the essence of our thinking doesn't stand up. Think about us architects. The first line of a building's design is drawn by hand and that sketch already says it all; even your beloved Morgan began that way. Technology saves us a lot of time, and I assure you that, compared to the past, it's a great way to work. What matters to me is to make sure that Sarah doesn't suffer any devastating depressions; I want to see her at peace and not drag her into my own state of mind—vacillating. If only I, too, could have your gift for forgetting! Since you're an expert, you could teach me how. Memories inhabit me, confuse and immobilize me. At the work site, I'm happy. I sit before the mandatory screening of a film; then later, in bed with the lights out, I have to metabolize, or face the "morning after" syndrome. Don't worry about Mattia: I, too, when I was studying at the Polytechnic, thought I would change the world, and that all the other architects, especially the females, would become interior designers. Let him dream about being an urban planner. The rest will come.

Federico

P.S. See how good I've become at translating and "defusing" your thoughts?

• ———— •

The first pages I read when the cartons of new books arrive are the acknowledgments. The dedications interest me less; they're too generic, oedipal, mysterious, a bit like gravestone inscriptions at the cemetery: reflections of virtuous lives, flawless deceased, righteous men and faithful women, indissoluble families. Fictions. There are even some dedications on the frontispiece that I am unable to decipher. "To Maurizio, who knows." Who is Maurizio and what does he know that we can't know? The author's declaration may be addressed to a husband, a wife, a legitimate child or the outcome of a casual fling, to a grandfather, a grandmother, a close friend who has reread the drafts several times and deserves gratitude, a literary agent who has negotiated a good contract, the baker, the blacksmith, a cousin or a former lover to whom he is sending a message in a bottle. The dedication is a genealogical tree of faceless people. Maurizio may already be dead, and in that case, why on earth are you dedicating a novel to him, if he can't read it?

I like the acknowledgments.

Terse (thanks to so-and-so, without whom this book would not have come about), or, better yet, torrential, ranging over several pages: radiographs of entire lives. The author thanks all those who made the work possible; there's no comparison to a dedication. Behind a thank-you, you can imagine any number of things: what the author's days are like, the room he works in, his notebooks, a computer or typewriter, his apartment, a library, an entire city, a desk, a table in a café, a park bench; you can see the still steaming cup, the ashtray full of butts, the cell phone turned off to avoid being disturbed, a little child's face as he knocks at the door and announces "Supper is ready; Mom is wondering if you want to eat." Behind a thank-you lie friends and advisers, the exhausted faces of those who read the first, second, and third drafts; there's the editor, who gave advice, made cuts, argued, suggested.

Family members are always thanked. Relatives are the raw materials used, their lives arbitrarily mingled with those of the characters, and they should be compensated. They have endured the writer's absence; the author hasn't been around for them for weeks, months, years. Acknowledgments are the Yellow Pages of a novel and give a face to the words.

It's half past eight. I am absently unpacking the new arrivals, engrossed in the acknowledgments, when Cecilia drops in to pay me an unexpected visit. Since she received her first marriage proposal, she's been nervous and irritable; she buys one novel after another to conquer her insomnia, but really all she needs is to vent with someone who won't delude her. That and a cup of tea.

"Can I give you a hand, Emma? I have about half an hour free before I have to go shut myself up in the cage."

"Of course, sweetie, I'm by myself and these cartons are heavy. Hey, let me look at you. You're so pale. If this is what it's doing to you . . . you're not obliged to get married."

It's useless to beat around the bush. With Cecilia, men of the same age don't work. Her father left and ran off with his secretary when she was five. A stock escape, which leaves a deep scar on a daughter.

"He's twenty years older than I am; I feel so safe with him, but at times I think I'm doing something foolish. When I'm his age, he'll be seventy, maybe paralytic or with Alzheimer's."

"It depends on how you spend those twenty years. You could even have a child. Look at Chaplin, or Picasso. There are many fathers of a certain age throughout history," I tell her, swallowing nervously as she helps me arrange the articles of an extinct family on the shelf beneath the window, salvaged for little over seventy euros from a junk dealer. Except for the candlesticks, vases, and bottles, everything was painted white, perhaps with an urge to annul or a need to erase any traces. It is the color of beginning, a premise from which all things are possible. White, like an offer of marriage.

"Roberto didn't have children with his first wife; he's already told me he'd like to have a baby right away."

"Well then? Cheer up. Everything will be just fine. You'll see. We'll have a big party. I like this romance with a widower, and then, too, do I look like I'm on my way to becoming paralytic?"

"You're special, Emma. Listen, has my *Pamela* arrived?"

"Yes, I set aside a copy for you. An inexplicable success, were it not for the TV adaptation."

"*Elisa di Rivombrosa,* the series on Channel Five."

"I even tried to watch an episode one evening, but it's really second-rate. Still, I adapt to current tastes. I put the book in the window. Come on, we'll have a cup of tea; the Locanda opens at ten today and I still don't know how to work the coffeemaker."

Pamela is the novel that was made into the TV serial that is thrilling the ladies, a mediocre tearjerker that for weeks has been at the top of the foreign fiction lists, though until a few years ago it would have ended up withering away on the shelf of some bibliophilic curator. Six hundred and twenty pages of letters written in the mid-1700s by a pensioner who, before discovering literature, was a printer and publisher, and for this alone it merits my full respect. The writer of the letters: a young servant girl, the *honest and dutiful daughter* of poor peasants, who confides to her indigent parents her agitation when her master—the pleasure-loving Squire B. of Bedfordshire—attempts to seduce her. The same old story and the usual repetitious solution: resistance. Pamela resists and will yield only upon the squire's atonement, when he will be brought to the altar, to the jubilation of all and the envy of many. The astute tenacity of the young servant transforms the nobleman's lust into love, virtue triumphs, and marriage seals it. The first modern Anglo-Saxon novel depicting a way of life to which the public of that time aspired, it was an unprecedented publishing success. With its peekaboo sex scenes— revealing just enough—the dramatization glues millions of spectators to their seats; it is fatuous to just the right degree and capable of transforming virtue, *that* virtue, into a timeless instrument.

"You could start a shelf 'In Love's War, He Who Flieth Is Conqueror,'" Cecilia says, greeting Alice, who, like her, doesn't miss an episode.

"Who's fleeing, ladies?"

"You two should both do what this Pamela does: Save yourselves," I reply, waving the hefty book.

"Too late," they respond in unison.

"I'll be a bridesmaid, Cecilia. Have you picked the date?" Alice asks.

"We were thinking about September fifteenth, a simple civil ceremony. Where's Manuele?"

"Never mind. We haven't seen him for a week; he's on an examining board in a high school in Brindisi. As if there were no unemployed, available teachers in Puglia."

"You'll have the whole month of August to enjoy yourselves. Distance helps; take my word for it. Think back to when he wrote to you on the forum site and you didn't even know what he looked like. It seems like ages ago, and now you two are happy. You get along well intellectually—and not just intellectually—Manuele is educated, intelligent, and has the patience of a saint. What more do you want?"

Federico is an obsession. How could I explain to these two that at eighteen we did not make love, and that now this is perhaps a rematch? They wouldn't believe me or they'd think I was crazy. To tell the truth, I never fully understood the power of sex. I do it and that's that. You do it if you love someone; otherwise, don't even think of it. This way of looking at it, somewhat simplistic, has always been my way. Today's young people, Mattia included, are like us, but they don't say it. That's where the difference lies.

· ——— ·

Milan, July 7, 2004
Via Londonio 8

Dear Federico,
This morning, I went back to our old high school and got in line with the kids going in to take the final exam. No one stopped me,

not even the porter, who, I'm sorry to say, no longer wears a smock. She's an attractive woman with streaked hair, nothing at all like ours. It's all changed, if you don't count the anxiety in the students' eyes. They no longer sell those greasy round buns; there are coffee and soft-drink machines, like they have in offices. The walls are still peeling and the world maps tacked up with pins don't take the wars into account. On those walls, time has stopped.

Emma

P.S. Mattia, who is filling in for Manuele these days, serves us creamy coffee drinks as if they were cocktails. He concocted one with chocolate and spices; it makes me shudder just to mention it. Naturally, he and his friends find it "wicked cool."

· ——— ·

New York, July 12, 2004
Peaceful oasis number 10, Metropolitan Museum

Dear Emma,
A stop at the Metropolitan, where they make an excellent creamy Italian-style coffee. I'm reading the *Corriere*. Have I ever told you about my favorite newsstand agent? His name is James, he's at University Place, between Eighth and Ninth Streets, and he sets aside a newspaper for me every morning. Speaking of newspapers: Architecture is dangerous, or so Renzo said today in an interview in the *New York Times*: "It is . . . a socially dangerous art, because it is an imposed art. You can put down a bad book; you can avoid listening to bad music; but you cannot miss the ugly tower block opposite your house." According to Renzo, a city should express joy. I leave you with that thought: Consider the responsibility and don't take offense at what he says about books. Renzo, who has the gift of levity, often cites Calvino in this regard. A city is made up of houses, streets, and piazzas. We are restoring the Morgan around the concept of a piazza. And we will plant a large tree in it. A fig tree, I think.

I've finished my coffee. Back to the work site. I have a meeting with Frank and the others, but you're all I think about.

Federico

P.S. My thinking is rock-solid, not like your pages.

．——．

The phone call comes early, though I should know exactly what time it is, since I am at the bookshop and have just finished dusting. Something is wrong, an anxiety as flavorless as vegetable broth from a bouillon cube.

"Ernesto is dead." I never noticed how heavy the receiver in my hand is.

"He was going over the material for Wednesday's reading," the voice adds, emotionless.

"What did he choose?"

"*The Crimson Petal and the White,* by Michel Faber. He talked about it for days; he was sure his audience would like it, and he wanted to compare it to some Victorian novel."

"Oh Lucilla, I am so sorry, Lucilla."

She says "his audience," meaning Ernesto's. And I'm not jealous. Why am I incapable of comforting her? But no, I go and say something stupid, so stupid, something a stupid women would say. "What did he choose?" was the most idiotic question I could come up with. When you are told someone you cared for has died, you always think about your own death, even though up till then you thought about it only occasionally. It's a human reaction, all too human. We're all afraid of *that* moment and feel compelled to imagine how it will happen to us. I am no exception, although as far as I'm concerned, everything is in order. I don't want a grave; I want my ashes scattered in the ocean. Mattia won't have to feel obliged to come visit me, to keep the gravestone clean and bring flowers; as for a gravestone, I wouldn't even know what inscription to choose. Dissolved in saltwaters. The sea of Brittany. Together with the fairies.

"And, in those dreams of flying, Sugar's old life has already ended, like a chapter in a book," Faber wrote.

I feature the prostitute Sugar's Victorian London in the window display, and slip on my wisteria-colored cotton sweater. I don't have the heart to tell Alice what happened. She's just arrived with a contented expression, her hair damp from the rain on this strange July day. I climb into a taxi. We reach the outskirts of town, walls offended by the senseless acts of jacked-up young guys who call themselves artists. Ernesto and Lucilla have lived here from the time they were married. Some children are bouncing a ball on a little soccer field, *ba-bump, ba-bump, ba-bump*—inside, outside, cut. The ball seems made of sponge; it flies high and lands on the grass: The mothers are chatting and smoking filter cigarettes, keeping an eye on the young athletes with their grimy knees and terry socks rolled around their ankles. Staircase A, third floor. Marble steps, landings. Simple surnames: Rossi, Solari, Benvenuti, Boschi. The door on the third landing is ajar. The lights are on throughout the apartment and in the bedroom, as well. Usually the shutters are closed, following some unwritten code, and I had already mentally adjusted my eyes for darkness. Instead, a pale sun filters in now that the rain has stopped, and it does not seem disrespectful to me. Ernesto is lying on the big bed, fully dressed in his dark blue suit. The double-breasted six-button jacket has the Alpine crest on its lapel. The shirt is pale blue, like his eyes; the tie is dark blue, with small orange giraffes. Lisle socks cover his feet, which are turned outward. *En dehors,* like a classic ballet dancer. He looks handsome. I can't tell her, though, that I'm at peace here, in this obscure calm inhabited by those who have gone who knows where, without giving you time to prepare for afterward. He seems more asleep than dead, if it weren't for his impassive face and the massive wooden coffin that awaits him on a wheeled metal pedestal. Professor Ernesto's surname was Boschi, and only now do I realize that for those of us in the bookshop, he never had a last name. But this is the effect that all the deceased have on me; they are nearby, yet in some corner of your mind you sense that they are very far away indeed and that they couldn't care less about what's happening around them. I've seen a father, a brother, and a sister under these emotionally distant circumstances. Not my mother, though. With her, I couldn't do it. I had had my fill of corpses; it had all happened so quickly. Michele saw to it, the acknowledgments, the funeral arrangements and obituaries.

Like an ungrateful daughter, I had a desire for sunlight.

He looks composed, Ernesto does, his thin legs stretched out on the bluish green chenille bedspread, displaying none of the agitated imperfection of the living. Lucilla has become smaller, on the other hand. Huddled up, she hasn't donned widow's clothes; she sits on the chair beside her husband, caresses his clasped hands with brief, rhythmic strokes. I can picture her on tiptoe, going to join her mate underground. She strokes him with a secular caress; Ernesto is not holding a rosary in his hands, nor a small crucifix. An oversight, perhaps.

"We can die at any moment. It just took him a second. He didn't wait for me, although he had promised me he would," Lucilla says. She consoles me and the neighbors gathered around the bed. The armchair in the small dining room, with its crocheted curtains and pink geraniums and peaches in a bowl, seems to bear the mark left by the body of that gentle man, who lived for physics and later converted to literature. Wire-rimmed glasses rest on a small table, along with newspapers and clippings, flash cards, sewing scissors, a notebook filled with jottings: objects of a life marked by the soothing rhythm of a carillon. It's the home of a couple who love each other, though childless. They are enough for each other; they don't need anything else. Or maybe a child doesn't come. And I'm still thinking in the present tense.

"Oh Lord, award to each his fitting death," Rilke wrote.

I feel like calling Ernesto. I always feel like phoning someone who has died and it takes me a few seconds to realize that the person will no longer answer. *People should die in winter*, I think as I head home. No, on second thought, I'll take a ride to Sant'Ambrogio. I need some silent time to meditate. It happens, and deaths are a

fitting occasion to reflect on people and everything else. The subway takes me to the front gate. My steps echo; the cobblestones
make even the most sober stumble along, especially with heels. The
basilica lies in wait for me; they do it on purpose, these churches, I
know it. I need a church, the smell of candles and the trace of in-
cense lingering in the air from that morning's service. I need the
austere, mute faces of the statues. There's a sign on the gate: HOURS:
9:30–12:00 AND 2:30–6:00. It's one o'clock now and I can't get in. Do
even saints take a lunch break? My dream is to pray. A murmured
prayer, whispered, not just a few words and off I go; I want to linger
in there. Maybe to understand. Or just to ponder. Instead, there's
that sign. Damn it, talking with God is a universal right, and they
close the church on me?

· —— ·

Milan, July 23, 2004
Sweet Dreams Locanda

Dear Federico,
Today I woke up with these words in my head: *I didn't take enough
care of myself. For you.* I don't really know what it means, or if it
came from a novel; maybe it welled up because of the funeral. Yesterday we accompanied Professor Ernesto to the cemetery, and in
the afternoon the kids organized a reading in his honor. There
wasn't an empty table in the Locanda. Lucilla never seemed to tire
of hearing people say over and over again how important Ernesto
was for their Wednesdays. We underestimate—at least I do—the
degree to which some individuals become indispensable, without
our realizing it. I had never thought about the importance of those
readings, and I don't claim any merit for them, but when Manuele
went up to the lectern wearing a light cotton blazer and shirt—he
even wore a tie—and started reading, I realized that for many of these
men and women, Dreams & Desires has clearly become a place where
affectionate attachments are formed. "Everything will be okay,
Lucilla," I told her. "It's very kind of you all to read the passages he

loved. Yes, it's really very thoughtful of you," she replied, intimidated by all those people.

"For a year now, every so often during his readings he felt he was meeting . . . other readers. Every so often, only occasionally, though more and more plainly, he would recall these people, for the most part strangers, who were reading the same book. He would remember certain details as if he had actually experienced them. Experienced them with all his senses. . . . In truth, when he reflected seriously on these strange phenomena, he himself came to the conclusion that his personality was vacillating dangerously, past the point of reason. Or was it all just an illusion owing to an excess of literature and a deficient life?" Alice and Manuele had chosen this passage from *69 Drawers*, by Goran Petrović, an author I was not familiar with. He seemed to be speaking about Ernesto, although his life was far from lacking; on the contrary, in fact. Lucilla's eyes were moist. We'll have to be there for her. Ernesto was her entire life. Obvious, right? Not necessarily. I know widows who seem relieved of every care, widows who are reborn and become even more beautiful.

I didn't take enough care of myself. For you. What a stupid sentiment. Maybe it means that we're wasting our time, that what holds us together—the letters—isn't enough. This is the first time that I've seriously thought about the fragility of our encounters. Today they seem too infrequent, brief, pointless. Diversions. Fillers. Surrogates for love. Because if it was love, we couldn't stand being apart. This morning, after seeing that woman who hasn't a doubt in her mind, my theories about our being, above all, friends fell apart. Because if we were only casual lovers, I wouldn't be feeling so chilled now, on a day when it's unbearably hot here in Milan, and in New York, too, I'm sure. You are not here and I am thinking about our dead, of how little we've talked about death, of how little I've told you about me. About the accident in which I lost them all and didn't cry enough to be able to tell about it with some semblance of composure. Standing in front of that grave yesterday, I was not crying for Ernesto, who died at peace and, most of all, quickly. His students stood around his coffin, an indication that physics formulas had left their mark: that of a schoolteacher who was not only a teacher but also a friend. I was crying for me, Federico, for us. I was frightened by the thought that I have no time, and yet I act as if I have all the time in the world.

Write to me. I need your words and your embraces,

Emma

. ——— .

New York, July 30, 2004
42 W. 10th St.

Dear Emma,

I'm at home. The girls are in the Hamptons; by now, they're an integral part of the New York practice by which each Friday at five Manhattan is left in the hands of the tourists. I'm not going; I have a lot of work to do and an excellent excuse to stay in the city. My allergies won't let up. My nose looks very similar to that of J.P.M., not its size, but certainly the cherry red color it has settled on. I duplicated for you a few photographs taken by Frank. The steel structure forming the future Morgan looks like a great big toy. Isn't it fantastic? You should have been there, Emma. A premounted protective cage was lowered by the cranes like a huge piece of an Erector set. I'm also including a photo of the restaurant area that we will create in Jack Morgan's former dining room, and one of the bookshop, which overlooks Thirty-sixth Street. The piazza is still not visible, but you can get a feel for it. The size of an Italian square, it will be the center of a village of European proportions. There was a meeting to decide the color of the entrance; rejecting Beaubourg red, we mixed a cream color with rosy pigments in order to obtain the "Morgan color," that of Tennessee pink marble, the same as the McKim building and the annex. The interiors of the staff's and curators' offices on the upper floors of the brownstone were also decided. I'm enclosing a group photo as well. In case you don't recognize me, I'm the one on the right, the hottest one. . . . Forgive the spirited mood; I know you understand how wonderful it can be to work without rancor or discord in a peaceful, enjoyable environment. Activist Frank, who is obsessed with coherence and saving the stone, is supervising the carving of the stone that is to match McKim's marble. You can see him in the picture (green arrow); he's the one to Renzo's right. "We will leave a reverent architectural mark on a corner of Manhattan that will recapture its history," he keeps saying, and woe to anyone who contradicts him. In fact, we will use the steel that Morgan produced, though he never wanted to use it for his home, naval sheet steel and steel pillars. The old and the new Morgan will kiss but will not disturb each other, a bit like the two of us. I'm teasing, but it's to distract you and tell you how close I feel to you. Your story moved me; reading it, I felt as if I, too, knew your customers. I repressed my parents' funerals and I rarely visit the family tomb: I wouldn't know what to say or even what to think. There are people who see to it. They didn't need me while they were alive, much less now.

I, on the other hand, need you. Always.

Federico

P.S. You must never cry, Emma, not for me and not for you.

• —— •

I've never worked so hard as in the last few days. I'm making progress on my depression and I'm recommending novels on how to survive in love. It's hot and the ceiling fan overhead doesn't cool enough. Alberto says I'm having menopausal hot flashes and refuses—still!—to install an air conditioner. Lucilla has begun coming to the store in the afternoons; she is a volunteer for culture, she says, and she won't go away on vacation, so as "not to leave him alone." She is choosing the volumes for the new window display, which she suggested: love stories written postmortem. She doesn't seem bothered by the subject, and I had never noticed how many there were, because, it's true, you become aware of novels when they speak about your own life, when they become mirrors.

It's curious, if you don't count Roth, how young the authors of these novels are, almost as if the older ones tend to want to keep death at a safe distance: There's the Irish author, Cecelia Ahern, with her *P.S. I Love You;* the French writer Anna Gavalda with *Ensemble;* Marc Levy, who, judging from the photo on the jacket flap, is a fascinating novelist specializing in lovers who return from the hereafter; and Guillaume Musso, underrated by us, the author of romances that surpass the barriers of death. Lucilla displays them and speaks quietly of Ernesto. Lovely.

"I could write a biography," she says, and the idea seems to seriously tempt her.

"Your marriage has the story line of a successful novel, Lucilla," I say as she hands me the books for the window display. We arrange them plainly, without showy decoration or frills. In the hereafter, everything is blank. Maybe.

"These last longer, Alice," she says, pointing to the books and allaying my assistant's concern. She is a strong-spirited woman, Lucilla is. She spent her life among her students; she could always console them with verses from the *Sonnets.* Yet I can't get out of my head the image of her leaving here and weeping softly so as not to be heard. The windows open to summer recommend a wintry death.

Afternoon, the final reading in the courtyard; the customers come by to stock up on their summer reading. Borghetti and Gaston are leaving for Thailand, and they're looking for lengthy novels for an intercontinental journey. Cecilia will test out a honeymoon with her widower, who is a really nice gentleman and who looks at her in amazement, thinking, *How did such good fortune happen to me?* Michele even stopped by and his girlfriend cleaned him out by buying three candles, two SHHH . . . I'M READING cups, and a dozen books: he's making her take a trip to Mexico, when she would have preferred a cruise in the fjords of northern Europe. Great success with the new ice creams; the gelato shop Del Biondo di Brescia produces an ice-cream pop, custom-made for the Locanda, that has the sweet flavor of childhood, and when you're done with it, you have the little stick with words taken from books. "Let the future sleep for now, as it deserves. If you wake it too early, you get a groggy present" (Franz Kafka). I was hoping for Woolf; today's postcard is still fresh from the mailbox.

· ——— ·

New York, August 3, 2004

Dear Emma,

I am sending you this postcard caricature of Virginia Woolf, designed by Mike Caplanis, an artist and illustrator whose work has appeared in the *Washington Post*, the *Los Angeles Times*, the *Philadelphia Inquirer*, and other American publications. If you like his drawings, I can put you in touch with Luminary Graphics, a small company that produces cards, bookmarks, umbrellas, bags, and other items illustrated by him. His subjects are writers. No architects. Let me know what you think. I'll be in New York until August 10. Then we're going to Hawaii, guests at the hotel of an Italian man who moved to Maui and has no intention of going back. Sarah is very eager to go; we're taking her "friend" Francesco with us. I have to get used to it: She's becoming a young woman. The other day, she chased me out of the bathroom because she was in her underpants. For her, now, I'm a man like any other. I have to resign myself.

Enjoy your vacation and happy birthday. I'm whispering it; no one will hear me,

Federico

· ——— ·

Milan, August 12, 2004
Sweet Dreams Locanda

Dear Federico,

Another twenty-four hours and we're off. I am so exhausted that the house in Roussillon seems like a dream, a place where I can do nothing but sleep, sleep, sleep. I can use the rest; it's been a grueling year and my creative capacity for planning needs a break. Although creating stories is the only way I know to construct a tolerable version of what happens to me, I have to stop thinking of the two of us so persistently. It happens to me even when I'm leafing through a magazine, like this morning when I took a test that urged people to "find themselves," while suggesting formulas for "how to overcome the past and live joyfully in the present" and proposing "rules for self-esteem." I hate taking stock, through the looking glass or not. I threw away diaries, letters, and business cards that I'd kept for decades, but your letters will go with me. At the end of the quiz, I didn't recognize myself in any of the descriptions. I always turn out to be midway between profile A and profile B. I am a woman with no identity and I can't wait to leave this place to its summertime fate. Three weeks without customers is all I want, besides you.

I'm thinking of you. Write to me if you can find the time, even in Hawaii. . . .

Emma

. ——— .

A warm, overcast morning. Milan is already clogged with cars and motorbikes. People have already started running here and there, and it's only September 4. There are some who insist on calling it progress. To me, it seems like senseless folly. Alice, tanned and with a trace of fat (she says) around her waistline, a sign that her vacation with Manuele was unsurpassed (all the food and sex they wanted), makes a virtue of necessity. She dreams of marriage and badgers us constantly about the project she developed during her vacation: a bridal gift registry. Before leaving, she had tossed it out on a few Internet sites with evocative names—Today's Bride, Everything You Always Wanted to Know About Marriage, How to Plan Your Wedding Without Getting Stressed—and already there are numerous requests. The idea that, besides pots and sheets, the bride's girlfriends might buy the couple books as gifts struck me as bizarre, but this morning a young woman came into the bookshop and chose a total of fifty titles, while another one ordered 150 cop-

ies of Austen's *Emma*, to be distributed as favors. A novel—and what
a novel!—instead of the little trays, plates, and doilies that you
never know what to do with. While Alice projects her desires and
sits at the computer with a friend of Mattia who is reorganizing the
Web site, I busy myself with the new flower nook. Like Eliza Doo-
little, I've decided to sell roses, thanks to Piero, the butcher, who
allows me to keep them in his refrigerated room at night. I've arranged them in zinc pots in the corridor between the bookshop
and the Locanda, unnoticed by most people. Roses only. Garnet
red, red velvet, red-gold, white, yellow. I—who thought I lacked a
green thumb—discovered Karen Blixen roses: The owner of the
nursery told me about them when he found out they were meant
for a bookshop. The bouquets from Dreams & Desires are simple,
but when I realized that a single rose, combined with a book, makes
a great impression, I started selling individual ones as well, at one
euro apiece. My ladies treat themselves to roses to raise their spirits.
A dozen roses costs ten euros, and when you figure that a bouquet
will last at least a week if properly preserved, it comes to less than
two euros a day: a respectable palliative against insensitive boyfriends and forgetful husbands. Today, close to teatime, I wrap a bouquet of twenty for a publishing executive who stops in supposedly
to buy gifts. He works for a major Italian publishing house and by
now he no longer treats me like an eccentric book lady, averse to bar
codes, a bookseller who doesn't push sales (because it's true that I
have no effect on proceeds). I listen to him, and even a book publisher needs to be heard. The woman in the purchasing department
at FNAC treats him haughtily, so whenever he's in the area, he
never fails to drop in and say hello. The roses, pale yellow, are for
his wife, who has just had a baby and is depressed.

"I can't seem to convince her that I'm the happiest man in the
world. The baby is very good, yet all she does is cry."

"It's normal for her to feel a little despondent, Giuseppe; you
just have to be there for her. Pamper her and take her this bouquet
of roses. Better yet, no, we'll deliver them to her at home. That way,
it will be a surprise."

"If you say so . . . and the hotel, how are things going with the hotel?"

"Just fine. Very well, in fact. We're booked up as far ahead as Christmas. There are only three rooms, but by now word of mouth has spread abroad. I have to accept fashion-industry people as well, but I manage to palm books off on everyone."

I ring up the order and he leaves, satisfied. Mattia will see to the roses: He's equipped the Dreams & Desires bicycle with a basket on the handlebars and makes home deliveries.

· ——— ·

New York, September 11, 2004
Peaceful oasis number 11, Partners & Crime, 44 Greenwich Avenue

Dear Emma,
I am in a small bookshop in Greenwich Village that you would like for its atmosphere more than for the books it sells: mysteries and thrillers, no romance novels. They don't serve great coffee, but the place is friendly and, most important, it's the only spot I found to write to you before going to the studio, where an interminable meeting awaits me.

This morning I couldn't resist. The newspapers and TV (which I watch very little, actually) have been writing and speaking of nothing else, and it seemed natural to go back down there. At eight o'clock, I got into a banged-up Ford sedan—I took a taxi; the Vespa seemed like a dumb idea. "Impossible to make it to there—the observances. I'll drop you off nearby," said the cabbie, an Egyptian named Aswan, like the dam. "Let me out wherever you can; I'll continue on foot," I told him. I'm writing almost as if I were transmitting live. I'm tempering my emotion for you, though anyone who hasn't seen this place can't fully understand what it expresses. So, my darling, this is how it went. The air conditioning in the cab was turned up to the max (the heat is still summerlike), the windows closed. When we got to Fulton Street, I paid the fare and got out in that surreal topography of sorrow; as I opened the car door, a sort of Gregorian chant struck me like . . . an embrace. I entered the narrow passageway that borders the chapel of St. Paul. The interior of the church, which for months was a center where volunteers gathered, is a grim reminder of human generosity, littered with photographs and objects: cots, blankets, mugs, keys, shoes, teddy bears, photos of firefighters, fragments of the skyscrapers' structures that will constitute a museum dedicated to the World Trade Center. Memento mori. Remains from just three years ago, yet it seemed like evidence from a world war; the pillowcases, sheets, and blankets seemed embalmed. I've discovered that I have an excessive attraction to craters; it may be because of the Morgan, or who knows what else. There might be a lot a psychiatrist could reveal about me starting with this mania for holes in the ground, and for heights, the more dizzying the better. Emma, I left the church and, walking like a zombie, approached the metal fencing surrounding Ground Zero. I then realized that the beautiful, ancient sound was none other than . . . the chanting of first and last names, reiterated in a gentle, sonorous sequence. It was nine something . . . I looked down and those little figures holding hands seemed like a circle of toy soldiers waiting to play ring-around-the-rosy. I was seized by a terrible, selfish sadness, I whispered my chant and intoned a prayer that had your name. Emma, Emma, Emma. I have such a need to see you. . . . In two weeks, I'll be in Paris. I'll spend a few days at the studio, and it would be the most normal thing in the world for us to meet there. I can't wait for another April 10; at this moment, in this bookshop, which you would like so much, I think it would be an unforgivable mistake. What do you say? Even just one day, in Paris . . . Think about it and tell me about the hotel: Can you keep up with everything and still find time for yourself?

Your Federico

.————.

It's seven in the evening and the October sky is still bright. I'm beside myself, nervously awaiting a famous guest. Mr. Patrick McGrath resembles his novels, in the sense that he couldn't be any different

from the way he appears, there at the end of the street, accompanied
by the young lady from the press office. He's big man, tall and burly,
with very pale skin and gray strands in his reddish hair. The son of
a psychiatrist, he spent most of his childhood in England, where his
father was the medical director at the Broadmoor psychiatric unit.
He has accustomed us to entering the minds of the insane from the
first pages, a practical method, perhaps, to overcome his own fears.
We all have them, let alone someone who encountered barmy people
each and every day. The large man is holding hands with a beautiful
woman, Maria Aitken, his wife, a professional actress. They stop in
front of the window display and a decidedly astonished expression
appears on his broad face. Alice has barricaded herself in the bookshop. She says I embarrass her. What can I say.

"Extraordinary, Miss Emma. And so welcoming, thank you."

"Not at all! In the history of literature, we have Tolstoy's Russia, Thomas Mann's Germany, the London of your colleague Ian
McEwan, and . . . McGrath's asylums. I tried to reconstruct a scene
in a psychiatric hospital as I imagined it when reading about it.
Your father must be proud of you for *Asylum*'s success."

My English is still quite good, yet I use the tone of a person who
is explaining herself.

"Unfortunately, he died shortly before it was published," he replies, with the easygoing smile of someone who, unlike me, has a
clear conscience.

Madness, as I imagined it, is chalky. I bought whitening powder
at the paint store, mixed it with water, and brushed it on the four
sides of the window. I spread a linen sheet stiffened with starch on
the rear panel. Two mannequins are wearing straitjackets borrowed
from Dr. Dominelli, who lives in my building and used to work at
the psychiatric hospital in Mombello. The mannequins are studying each other almost suspiciously; the two polystyrene heads are
covered with magazine clippings depicting eyes, attached with a
hat pin. Around them, on the floor, lie a comb, a cup, a plate, an
umbrella (because there is always an umbrella in novels about crazy
people); everything is whitened, even the books (four volumes that

will have to be thrown away, but it was worth it): *The Grotesque, Spider, Dr. Haggard's Disease,* and *Martha Peake,* which we will present tomorrow. In the center I stacked copies of *Asylum,* and attached other copies to the sleeves of the straitjackets: a tangle of gray-covered books. I'm satisfied and I watch him to see what effect it has on him.

"Stella isn't a bad woman, Mr. McGrath. She's a victim. Doing away with her is the only way to stop the degrading abjection that passion produces in her. The psychiatrist who controls her from the first page to the last or the unemotional husband who doesn't love her, doesn't touch her, doesn't caress her anymore, assuming he ever did do so tenderly: Who is the villain, Mr. McGrath?"

What's come over me? Wouldn't it be better to talk about the weather?

"Stella is a woman who is dragged down by sexual passion," he replies, and he isn't surprised to hear me talk about his character as if I knew her personally. He must be used to it, because he remains impassive. He displays the imperturbability of a true British writer. His wife doesn't leave his side as I accompany them upstairs to the suite named "The little Love-god lying once asleep." When he reads the inscription on the door, he laughs.

"Do you change the name depending on your guest's nationality, Miss Emma?"

"No, I use universal names. And Shakespeare works for anyone, Mr. McGrath."

I couldn't be happier. The madhouse writer is pleased with his reception; he likes the room and—despite having lived in an asylum—seems to appreciate the cast-iron radiator, the wooden plank floor, the window and door casings, the two small tables, the desk and straw-bottomed chairs, the sage green wainscoting in the bathroom, and the stack of books on the table, which includes a copy of *Asylum*: a bookseller's toadyism, courtesy of the Amsterdam airport bookshop. His wife describes my rooms as a "telescoping hotel."

" 'Telescoping' "?

"Yes, with rooms that are strung together; that's what it's called in England."

"Well, in that case . . . welcome to my telescope. If you need anything, we're in the bookshop until ten. Oh, if you need to use your computer, we have Internet access."

"Thank you, Emma, but I don't carry my computer with me when I travel. What time is the presentation tomorrow?"

"At five o'clock, teatime. There will be lots of readers, and I will personally act as your interpreter. It was my job at one time. Everything will be just fine."

How proud I am of myself! And I'm delighted at the idea that the great McGrath doesn't carry a computer with him. He's one of the family. Hurray.

"Alice, where did you disappear to?"

. —— .

Milan, October 16, 2004
Dreams & Desires

Dear Federico,

Alice is tapping away on the computer and I'm writing to you. She discovered a site, Maremagnum.com, with whom (a *site*, mind you; it's not as if it were a person) she corresponds regularly. I act like *No thanks, I'm not interested*, but in reality the idea that inspired it is lovely and reminds me of myself. Maremagnum was conceived by a bookseller who, like me, must live with a constant feeling of abandonment. How else to explain the fact that he sells lost books? Alice buys books from him, through the Internet, of course, although she could easily go and pick them up by car, since Mr. Book Rescuer lives in Milan. I don't gain a profit from it, just respectability in the eyes of my customers. It's possible to locate the unobtainable through this mysterious gentleman, and one of these days I think I'll invite him here. I still can't convince myself that you can love a book without touching it, like a long-distance love with no embraces—you know, those virtual relationships where he's on the other side of the screen and you don't even know what he looks like. Alice, prompted by Alberto, says that Internet purchases account

for 4 percent of the world's book sales; to me, it seems like an insignificant little number, but when I timidly pointed that out, she told
me that it's "destined to grow." So I bend, adapt, and don't argue.
It's just that online they give discounts and I, as you know, hate to
debase the value of books. I lower the shipping costs instead. And
people are happy just the same. "We have to give them the impression that we can satisfy every wish, Emma; otherwise, one day they
will end up no longer needing us. They can be their own booksellers,
choosing from the *mare magnum*, 'the great sea,' of titles on the
Internet." I can't resign myself. I feel superfluous; still, I'm happy
that Alice and Manuele are looking after the bookshop, along with
Lucilla, who comes in regularly in the afternoons, and Carlotta,
whom I hired part-time on a "project" basis, even though the project
is always the same: my books and my new passion, the hotel, booked
for the next six months. You read that right: six months. Of course,
I have to accept guests of all kinds, not just writers, but the mortgage
payment is covered and I'm not drowning in debt, despite what the
Faithful Enemy predicted. Your last letter was full of sadness and I
don't like to think of you that way, but I understand your fear.
Emma, too, is afraid. Write to me about the Morgan, which seems
like a vital antidote to the wistfulness of two former classmates.

Your Emma

·———·

New York, November 7, 2004
80 Spring St.

Dear Emma,
Here I am. I'm writing to you in the Moleskine (I'll have to tear the
pages out, alas, but I haven't got any other paper handy). I'm at
Balthazar, a bistro you would like, in SoHo. I'm meeting Renzo for
lunch. We must miss Paris, because we hardly ever meet in this
area. There are the same close tables like at the Latin Quarter; plus,
the kitchen turns out traditional French dishes and—the ultimate
pleasure!—serves baguettes warm from the oven of the Balthazar

Bakery. I'm early, so I'll bring you up-to-date on the project, because it's truly a fantastic time for us. We can begin to see what the
structure will be like now that the framework is completed. And
the light, Emma, I wish I could describe the light for you. The lighting will respond to the light's natural movements; the lamps will
track it. You'll be inside the piazza and it will be like being outside:
You'll look up and see Manhattan. . . . I'm thinking about the fact
that transparency affords greater certainty than opacity; each of
us can see what's happening behind a glass pane. I think the two
of us are transparent to each other. A little less so to the rest of the
world, apart from Gabriella. I haven't talked about us, not even
with Enrico, who, after spending two weeks here, left yesterday to
go back with his whole family. I'm not able to talk about myself, let
alone about you, and at my age this behavior can't be changed. . . .
Maybe it means that I don't fully trust those close to me, and,
though it may seem strange to you, I know what you mean when
you say you're afraid. It happens to me, too. I'll be walking down
the street and a kind of panic comes over me; I feel lost for no
reason . . . but I'm ashamed to talk about it. Enrico and I can stand
naked in a locker room (yesterday we went to the gym, and I can't
tell you how vulgar the jokes were), but confiding in him is hardly
likely. As I wait for Renzo, my cholesterol level is rising like mer-
cury in a thermometer: I spread an indecent amount of pâté on my
bread and I don't feel the least bit guilty about it. After all, I know
you like me even with a potbelly. But I'll get back to the Morgan,
since you asked me about it; sorry if I digressed. Some numbers will
give you an idea of our satisfaction: We extracted 46,000 tons of
stone ("our" stone); from the central piazza, a staircase will lead down
to an underground level, where a cherrywood auditorium will accommodate an audience of 250 to 280 people, and on the floor below
it, an armored, climatized submarine will enable "your" books to live
in peace. I gazed at it yesterday, and it was as if it had always been
there, that miniature city where everything will be possible, among
the stone megaliths and future elevators in tempered glass, whether

it's sitting down for coffee, lunch, or dinner, stopping to read, talk, listen to music, or watch a film, or simply relaxing among the trees and works of art. J.P.M. would have liked it; I'm sure of it. And you would, too, my bookseller, though I have the feeling that your new role as hotel keeper is taking you in hand, and it bothers me very much that I didn't lay my hands on you first. Send me some photos. That way, I can cast my vote on your architect.

A hug before I order a tartare and welcome the boss, who is just coming in,

Federico

• ———— •

It's bitterly cold, there is still half an hour to go, and there are at least fifty people lined up straight as an arrow, an unwitting homage to the nationality of the author whom I'm awaiting with some trepidation. Mattia is already here, for the only writer in the world he holds in high regard. Because of football and the Arsenal. It was not by chance that I invited Nick Hornby to the bookshop, and not because he writes love stories. I simply felt a surge of sincere irritation while reading one of his articles in *The Believer*, whose credo is unique: Write whatever kind of books you want; *length is no object.* They state that they "give people and books the benefit of the doubt." I managed to get an exclusive with him, overcoming competition from those overbearing giants Feltrinelli, Mondadori, and FNAC. Hornby didn't even object to the fact that this is a somewhat atypical bookshop, and he's coming. I will welcome him with the honors that are due a writer of rare skill and genuine charm, but I will not let myself be intimidated. "Mr. Hornby," I will ask him, "why have you publicly maligned Anton Pavlovich Chekhov and his wife? Mr. Hornby, you have attributed offensive words to a man who by your own admission is a giant of literature: 'She seems to have reduced the man to mush: "My little doggie," "my dear little dog," "my darling doggie," "Oh, doggie, doggie," "my little dog," "little ginger-haired doggie," "my coltish little doggie," "my lovely little mongrel doggie," "my darling, my perch," "my squiggly one," "dearest little colt," "my incomparable little horse," "my dearest chaffinch" . . . For God's sake, pull yourself together, man! You're a major cultural figure!'—as though it weren't common knowledge that at times we all become somewhat idiotic and lapse into words that we would never use in other situations."

Imagine saying "pull yourself together" to Chekhov, as if he were just any man, and only because he's in love! When I let the frozen fans into the Locanda, all my self-assurance vanishes. How dare I pick holes in a writer's work? Who do I think I am? Tonight I focused on the four hundred letters that Chekhov wrote to Olga (his "doggie") and I suddenly recalled my first and only time in Saint Petersburg, which had been relegated to some corner of my forgetful little brain. I was accompanying a delegation from La Scala. I stayed one day longer than expected because they had issued the wrong date on my return ticket. I had gotten it into my head to look for him there, Mr. Anton Chekhov, not knowing that his city was Moscow, not Saint Petersburg. I found him on a wall, however, purely by chance. I was searching for him and also for her, Olga Knipper, his beloved wife, a sensational stage actress, whose letters I had read in an English translation. It was June, the transparent sky was a prelude to the "white night," when the light resists the night's rightful insistence and fades into dark at a tiring pace. I reached the Alexandrinsky Theatre and from there headed to a building that was nearly in ruins. I climbed the wooden stairs. The door to the theater's museum, little more than an apartment, was on the third floor. A woman with a wrinkled face, wearing a gray uniform, opened the door. Another woman, with gray-blue eyes, her hair in a chignon, from which yellowish strands escaped, sat in the center of the room on a kind of throne, left over, perhaps, from the set of some nineteenth-century melodrama. Coarse cotton curtains hung at the tall windows. The walls were covered with playbills in Cyrillic, which I read as patches of color, signs, images. "Anton Chekhov?" I asked, certain that they did not understand, and they let me wander through the rooms whose care was entrusted to them. The two women, paid only a few rubles, kept the place tidy and allowed it to be visited by the few tourists who were familiar with the address. The display cases were overflowing with stage props.

"Chekhov . . ." I said, insisting. The lady with the chignon, without getting up from her throne, pointed to a wall, which featured a dozen black-and-white photographs: The poet and Olga smiled sadly at the photographer in front of the rural dacha; between them, like a bench between two trees, was a playbill for *The Seagull*. It was that photo that stirred my interest in those two; later, I found their letters in a bookshop in London—nothing you wouldn't expect from a love between a man and a woman made up of passions, stage performances, catheters, and cod-liver oil. In those letters, which Mr. Hornby panned, for Chekhov the man there was only her. He wrote that she was the most unexpected thing to happen toward the end of his years and called her the "last page of my life." They loved each other at a distance, with respect, admiration, and betrayal (on her part). It was a love nourished by absence, by desire, by the power of imagination—so imaginary that, not to break the bond, Olga continued writing to him even after his death, and Anton Pavlovich seemed to respond from the grave with *Three Sisters*: "Our suffering will turn to joy for those who live after us, happiness and peace will come into being on this earth, and those who live now will be remembered with a kind word and a blessing." Mr. Hornby defaced that love, failing to understand that those letters reconstructed the true story of that literary giant and of the couple: the first meeting, the friendship, the secret affair, marriage, and death.

"Perhaps the feelings that we experience when we are in love represent a normal state. Being in love shows a person who he should be": the words of Anton "Pull Yourself Together." Mr. Hornby came into the bookshop with a wool cap pulled down over his forehead, and he is now sitting beside me, with his beautiful bald head and his gentle, ironic eyes, and I'm ashamed of myself; it seems strange that he even exists, because although I see their faces on the cover flaps, I never think that writers physically exist. Mattia is ready to open some beers, but Nick prefers a cup of tea with a slice of carrot cake. He's a father, a family man who loves rock and football, which couldn't be further from my taste, but he is very likable, and warm toward the customers, who welcome him with a rock star's applause. He confides to me that he loves booksellers very much. He's gallant and generous, and my boldness vanishes. I'm nearly stammering, and it's he who sees to putting me at ease when I ask, protectively, if anyone in the audience has any questions. I don't mention Chekhov, and neither does he. The Locanda is full of young guys who probably want to talk about football or the league rankings—a feeling I can understand. Mr. Hornby, I, too, like results lists. To avoid embarrassing the author, I've adopted a system using slips of paper. I prepared some classic questions, such as "How do you come up with your plots?"and "What are you working on?" and "When you reread your work, do you enjoy it as much as we do?" I distributed these to the regular customers, who in that awkward moment of apnea (it always happens, trust me) now raise their hands and ask a question, sipping a cup of Earl Grey. Nick Hornby is courteous. He can't stay away from home for very long because of his son; he'll be in Italy for only two days. He disappoints the fans a little when he explains that no, he doesn't enjoy rereading his work and never laughs when he rereads it. He keeps the structure of the text in mind as he writes, searching for the precise words to express a given situation or a pun, but he's too absorbed to start laughing. "Writing is a craft," he says; "it's a difficult craft. And it's even more difficult to try to recount amusing situations that highlight complications in the characters' lives. It's best to avoid laughing about them. I don't care for comic novels. They never make me laugh."

Forty copies sold, all autographed. And along with this came the discovery that Hornby does not use the silly little phrase "with esteem" to inscribe his books, but finds the right words for each reader.

For me, he penned, "To Emma, the bookseller of love, who con-

vinced me that calling a woman 'doggie' is not a crime after all.
Yours, Nick."

· ——— ·

New York, November 27, 2004
Peaceful oasis number 12, Barnes & Noble, Astor Place

Dear Emma,
I'm on my way home. I'm treating myself to a stroll through the old-
est Barnes & Noble in the city, which you are familiar with, if I remember correctly. Rumor has it that it will soon close because of
the high rent. As you can see, you're not the only one who has to
argue with an accountant; even in opulent Manhattan they have the
nerve to eliminate a historic landmark because of . . . sales proceeds. There are three couples sitting at the tables and two out of
the three are of the same sex—nothing strange about that, but I
wonder if the owners realize the importance of this bookshop and
the hundreds of encounters and affairs played out within these
walls. You are infectious; not only do I keep finding hearts everywhere (the collection has grown with the addition of a white-streaked
gray stone found in Central Park, used as a paperweight after wiping
the soil off) but I view the couples I come across with new eyes.
Though naturally I can't reveal this kind of anthropological passion
to anyone but you, this inclination to analyze human beings and
make up stories about them: dramas, reconciliations, and breakups.
Because of you, I am losing my rationalistic vision—or rather, it's as
if I've sharpened my awareness of love and everything that in some
way has to do with human relationships. I look at Sarah with her
boyfriend—oh, yes, Francesco has risen in rank and is officially des-
ignated as such—and I find them fantastic, beautiful, healthy, and
so terribly serious in their exclusive relationship. I'm not jealous and
I like that she talks to me about it. Not sex—that's a topic I couldn't
bear to discuss with my daughter. I force myself not to even imagine her making love with her handsome Italian; that's Anna's department. I remain detached; besides, I can't ask too much of my

already-easygoing fatherly demands. Today I thought of you "acutely."
I was on Forty-fourth Street. I passed by the Algonquin Hotel and
you were there with me. I swear to you, Emma, you were with me.
They've refurbished it, not all that well, I would say, and the table
where your beloved Dorothy Parker once sat is gone. "It's been rebuilt exactly the same," the blonde at the front desk said, handing
me a postcard (which I'll include) that reproduces Al Hirschfeld's
drawing. The hotel has been rebuilt, not restored; it's a fake copy,
which even Frank would be horrified at. Your writer is the short-
haired brunette; seated to her left is a certain Robert Benchley . . .
and the entire group of unkempt intellectuals with whom she spent
her days, evenings, and nights. Obviously, I haven't the slightest
idea who they are, but you will be familiar with their biographies.
And if you don't know them, you'll find out about them. Thank you
for last week's letter. Reading your responses, I realize that at times
my sad, hopeless reflections are tiresome and that I'm the one who
poses problems, disproving the conventional wisdom that views
women as complicated and men as simple. I'm not making any
progress on the pathway to emancipation, and, strange but true, I
find myself becoming more and more bearish, almost withdrawn,
toward others. It's Sarah who saves me from ineptitude, who forces
me to keep up-to-date and constantly reflect. Perhaps children also
serve to keep us alert: With the excuse that we have to monitor
their upbringing, in the end we're obliged to scrutinize ourselves as
well.

After a very mediocre Starbucks-brand cappuccino, I have to go.
There are six couples now; I'm the only single. I'm off to mail this,
my darling.

A kiss, you know where,

Federico

. ——— .

"Alice, the bookshop smells like tangerines today. I don't see any
candles." She looks at me smugly, my flamingo.

"It's the tangerine peels I put on the radiator to diffuse the fragrance. We're terribly late with the December window display. You nixed my angel silhouettes, snowmen, gilded snowflakes, silver balls, wooden firs, bagpipes, music boxes, chocolate, candy canes, nougat, crèche figures, tailed comets, and stars without a tail. I'm all out of ideas."

"And stereotypes. I was thinking of oranges instead—oranges studded with cloves. And family novels. Christmas is a family holiday and there are some great family love stories, don't you think?"

I have scarcely finished pronouncing this rhetorical hymn to obvious good cheer when I realize that the only novels that come to mind, sublime though they may be, are chronicles of calamity.

"Well, *Buddenbrooks, The House by the Medlar Tree* . . . oh, and *What Maisie Knew*, by Henry James. It's the story of a marriage breakup that affects her especially, the young protagonist. Oh dear God, Alice, aren't there any novels about happy families? We could combine them with seasonal titles, such as *The Christmas Stories*, by Dickens."

I'm grasping at straws.

"Dickens doesn't write about love, Emma. Let's use Spark instead. We have three copies of *Memento Mori;* all those angry, wicked old folks would cause anyone to lose their desire to have children. Not me, though. I'll take David Leavitt's *Family Dancing* from the 'Gay Romances' shelf and we'll also include Catherine Dunne's *In the Beginning*. Oh, Emma, I just love putting up the window displays!"

She smacks a kiss on my cheek and peels me a tangerine.

"We'll do an antifamily display. And in the center we'll put a lovely Christmas tree decked with paperbacks instead of the usual ornaments. You aren't by chance pregnant, are you?"

"*In the Beginning* is about a bastard who leaves his wife; it doesn't seem like much of a tribute to the family. And no, I'm not pregnant, of course not. We're getting married first. . . . Wait and see."

She said "a bastard who leaves his wife," but not everyone who leaves his wife is a bastard. There are a great many wives who leave their shitty husbands. And there are husbands who leave their shitty wives. Amen.

"A secular display. To each his own, the family and the novel he deserves. Brava, my little assistant. Let's do it."

. ——— .

Milan, December 4, 2004
Dreams & Desires

Dear Federico,

I'm in the bookshop and he's upstairs. He's a customer, although calling him customer is not quite accurate. In reality, he doesn't buy anything. He reads and that's all. The man who reads comes here regularly on Wednesday and Saturday afternoons, usually around three, makes a quick tour around the tables, picks up two or three novels, sometimes leafs through even more of them, scans the jacket flaps, then, with his chosen copy, goes upstairs, sits in the only armchair left in the coffee nook, and reads until 6:00 or 6:30. He returns the copy to the exact spot where he found it. I've never had the courage to stop him or ask him anything. It's clear from his discreet, polite, silent behavior that he's grown fond of the store, but since he never opens his mouth, we don't know who he is or why all he does is read the books as if he were in a library. And in the end, he never buys anything. To me, it's touching; I think he feels very lonely and I like to think that novels are a kind of consolation for him. I don't know for what, yet I see no other reason for his behavior. When he leaves the shop, I'm left wondering whether he'll return the following Saturday or Wednesday. I've grown fond of the man who reads, but I'm the only one who feels that way. Manuele and Alice consider him a parasite, actually. . . . I find it difficult to even guess his exact age. Sixty? Seventy? He's not a bum; he dresses rather nondescriptly but neatly. It's hard to imagine what type of work he does or if he even has a job. I don't have the courage to approach him; I'm always cautious when I'm among unstable individuals, and I like to think that Dreams & Desires is a nicer refuge than an anonymous city library. I prefer not to ask because I think he feels at home here, with no one to disturb his rounds. That armchair with the worn-out springs is there for him. It was you who gave me the idea, with your letter from the bookstore. I really hope they don't close it, the Barnes & Noble. . . . You made me think about how many people wander around our cities and how little we notice these invisible inhabitants who certainly have worlds to tell us. Your two couples at the Barnes & Noble and my man who reads should be protected; this much, I'm sure of. As for young people like Sarah and her handsome Italian, you're right: They have charm and sweetness galore. I can see it in Mattia and his friends. They're beautiful, Federico, perhaps less fortunate than us, but they're sound. We did a great job.

Milan is clogged with cars, but this is nothing new. Our little piazza preserves and defends its stillness; our self-management of the neighborhood has intrigued the newspapers. Today the shop window was featured in the *Corriere della Sera*, in the insert "Events," dedicated to the opening night at La Scala, a showy affair that is punctually repeated each year as some kind of cultural occasion. I obviously adapted and decorated the window with recycled historical posters of La Scala, stolen by the theater's press office manager, Carlo Mezzadri, who gave them to me about twenty years ago: unique pieces like the Requiem Mass, conducted by Sabata, which has nothing to do with love but goes very well alongside Visconti's *La Traviata*, sung by Maria Callas. I displayed on a burgundy velvet backdrop texts that relate to singing and the playing of musical instruments. Françoise Sagan's *Do You Love Brahms?*, Flaubert's *Sentimental Education*, with the echoing notes of a harp (Manuele's suggestion), while Alice's deputy bookseller's repertoire yielded the spinet from *The Sorrows of Young Werther*, along with Pfühl's Bach in Thomas Mann's *Buddenbrooks*. I thought of Monsieur Verdurin's pianist, Roberto Cotroneo's lost score, and *The Kreutzer Sonata*, which Mr. Frontini likes. No rock, my adored architect, that's reserved for you, and you don't know how much I'd love to have you here now, strumming your guitar and kissing me gently on my left earlobe while the man who reads paces overhead.

Emma

P.S. Can you kiss someone while you're playing the guitar?

·———·

A woman around forty, though maybe not, maybe thirty-five (it's becoming increasingly difficult to tell a person's age), holding the hand of a delicate little boy bundled up in a bright yellow scarf and a coat with a velvet blue collar, distracts me from my desires, which fall in this order: a Caribbean getaway with Federico, a week at a spa with Gabriella (who is cheating on me with Alberto in Andalusia), and a miraculous potion enabling me to become a patient person. Today I was surly with everyone and I'm worried that this barbarization of my character may be irreversible. I can't tolerate anyone anymore, which, for a storekeeper, is definitely not a good thing. I always liked velvet collars, and this little boy looks like he stepped out of a sixties film; kids his age wear bomber jackets or padded vests, play with cell phones instead of teddy bears, carry backpacks, and get around on the trolley. I never took a trip with my parents. The word *vacation* was synonymous with Bellaria, on the Adriatic coast, and I envied the girls who went to Liguria and Forte dei Marmi. Summer after summer, they parked us there, me and my brother and sister; they stocked the rented apartment's refrigerator and went back to Milan. They remained in the store and closed only for summer break in August, the week of Ferragosto. Those summers were my apprenticeship for solitude. I would walk past the beach to the Bagno Milena, paralyzed by shyness. And so I discovered that I liked being alone.

"I'd like a book that you have in the window, the *Memoirs* of Casanova," the mother says.

"Bingo, Emma! You see, didn't I tell you? Never go by appearances. She looks like she just stepped out of *Peyton Place,* yet she loves the great writers, and I can assure you that this is one of the most interesting books she can read," Gaston whispers to me.

"Well, the expression 'great writers' is a bit strong," I reply to Gaston, the intended audience of the display. It's a farewell to him: He is moving to the Côte d'Azur with Borghetti. They are closing their wonderful shop permanently, since, as they said, "at our age there is no ocean that can hold a candle to the Mediterranean, Emma." The ocean is the fourth desire on my list. Gaston is officially here to keep me company, now that their shop has been dismantled, but it's clear that he is sorry to leave this place, so he lingers. The little boy is sitting on a chair. He dangles his legs and waits for his seductive mother. Gaston offers him a candy, certain that the boy is getting bored. The child reaches out and takes it, and doesn't even say thank you.

I head toward the window, followed by Gaston, who is bent on convincing me at all costs.

"Set aside your aversion to seducers and consider that Casanova was first and foremost a notable literary figure; he discussed literature with Voltaire on equal terms, putting him in some difficulty. We're not talking about *Don Giovanni*. . . . That child is rude."

"His mother isn't the epitome of cordiality. . . . I'm not ready for Casanova."

"You're biased. On the contrary, you would love him. His female conquests . . . they were mostly actresses. At the time, they were considered high-class prostitutes, and it was perfectly legitimate to offer them money in exchange for favors. There were about a hundred of them; any average playboy easily exceeds that number in a few years."

"Did you have many lovers before Filippo?"

"I'm a romantic, Emma, and romantics don't have many lovers. Now I no longer fall in love with young men. Filippo is really the last. Filippo is my husband."

"Of course, it's true, romantics like us fall in love instead. But then why are you so passionate about Casanova?"

"My first partner, Marco, introduced me to him. I've told you about him. The only gifts he gave me were books about Casanova; I bought the rest of the collection afterward . . . when he was gone. Here, let me do it; I'm a whiz at wrapping. Would you like it wrapped, miss?"

"Thank you, yes. It's a gift."

He refrains from asking whom such a proper lady can be giving his idol's memoirs to and wraps contentedly.

"There you are, Merry Christmas, miss. Bye-bye, little one."

The child with the coat doesn't say good-bye.

"Do you know what my only regret is in life?"

"No, what?"

"Children, Emma. I would have liked to have a child to raise, to see him become an adult. . . . There'll be nothing left after I'm gone. A void that cannot be filled . . ."

"Did Casanova's talent scout leave you for someone else?"

"He died of AIDS, in 1989. Marco identified with him; he showed me that Casanova was not a 'minor' figure, but one who represented the eighteenth century at its purest, a writer and philosopher, magnanimous and vindictive, a libertine and a moralist, a man who cheated and was cheated. Just think, in London he ended up filling his pockets with stones, determined to throw himself into the Thames, all because of his unrequited passion for some little actress. A fellow he met by chance saved him. A man who has no regard for women would never for a moment think of taking his own life over a prostitute."

Gaston wears death and grief, abandonment and old wounds with the beauty of pathos. I will miss Gaston and Filippo very much.

"He deserves justice because above all he loved love, Gaston. . . . Oh, who knows who will move in now, in your space. Nowadays, all they open are clothing shops. As if that's all people care about."

"It will be an antiques dealer, Emma; we even sold our license. You can rest assured that the piazza will not change, and from what I understand, she loves books."

"I'll miss you two just the same, Gaston. Ernesto is dead, you're moving away, and . . . It's just that I have to learn to detach myself

from welcome, established routines. I get attached to people, schedules, habits. Changes unsettle me. The year is ending; an era is
ending."

"We're not going very far, Emma, and it will do you good to
come and visit us in Nice."

Everything changes. Everything is changing all around me and
we've come to yet another December 25, with the shop half-empty
and the tables bare. The only one happy about it is Alberto.

• ——— •

Milan, December 25, 2004
Via Londonio 8

Dear Federico,
Here I am back at home. Tonight our extended family Christmas
was reminiscent of those of the large families of the past, although
nowadays less attention is paid to conventions and seating at the
table is no longer preordained by wealth and title, as in traditional
families. We were a congenial group at my in-laws' dinner, with
Michele and Marina, Mattia and Carlotta, Marina's parents (divorced), their companions, and their other child. I looked at us all
gathered around the table, skillfully arrayed in a way I could never
manage to do, and later, when it came time to exchange gifts, I read
an almost childlike joy on each of the faces, despite the fact that
Mattia had insisted that his grandparents convert to an artificial fir
tree. I watched us, as if I were someone else looking in, and I
thought that biology has nothing to do with it, that it was all about
shared affections, a hybrid of relationships and broken marriages, yet,
all in all, harmonious. I thought of you and—this is a confession—I
felt like the person who in novels and in life is called the "other
woman." There's no getting around it, even if I don't put it in capital
letters, Christmas is not a time for lovers, period. I'm pathetic: It
was little more than a pinprick, but when I thought of you so far
away, I threw myself at the food. It's only one day, after all, and after New Year's everything goes back to normal. The menu "rocked"

(Mattia lingo): agnolotti in broth, a capon the size of a turkey, pâté, and a pyrotechnic finale with gluttons' panettone, which is actually a panettone like any other, over which we drizzle melted chocolate. I'll close here. Know that, as a lover, you were with me even tonight, as people walked along the street, heads lowered, looking up only to whisper "Merry Christmas" when meeting other hurried feet. I say it—or rather, write it to you—with all my heart: Merry Christmas, my architect.

Your Emma

·——·

Milan, January 20, 2005
Locanda of Dreams

Dear Federico,

It's been two weeks since I've had a letter from you. You may be busy, you may be traveling, you may have the flu, or it may be the Morgan, of course. . . . What will be will be . . . like the song by what's his name, I told myself. I'll mail this postcard depicting a caricature of our Jane Austen, drawn by Mike Caplanis. They are new items for the shop: bookmarks, cards, and refrigerator magnets dedicated to women writers. They're selling well and I got an exclusive for Italy. Waiting hopefully,

Your Emma

·——·

Books are meant to be touched, picked up, and held, in bed, on a bench, on the bus, on the couch, on the floor, lying on the grass, or even while strolling down the sidewalk. People read while they're waiting. Novels are enjoyed in the early-morning hours or at sunset on a lounge chair at the beach. In the dentist's waiting room, reading relaxes the tension; I even do it at the aesthetician to make the pain of the mad waxing bearable. I read Lewis Carroll at Disneyland as Mattia spun around in the Mad Hatter's Tea Cups or reveled in perilous roller-coaster rides with his father. My favorite places are trains, the most enormous multilingual reading room in the world, on every continent. Those who don't suffer from nausea read in the car, like some women who illuminate their pages with a miner's helmet lamp while their husbands drive along listening to the opera. A book is fantastic; it doesn't require plugs, chargers, batteries; it patiently tolerates ballpoint pens, pencils, notations, and dog-ears. The book is my parallel life; it makes me feel blessed with relatives and friends even if they are dead. When I read, I forget who I am. I don't remember who said that reading books is like smoking, and that the best part is that there is no need to quit. And if this shop has become my home, I owe it all to those books. Yet today, on Virginia Woolf's birthday, books do not console me.

Manuele arranges finger sandwiches of prosciutto and sweet bread on the counter as the audience members for "Afternoons with Emma" take their places at the tables. Lucilla baked a raspberry tart and was officially appointed his adviser. It seemed like a tender strategy: Her husband is irreplaceable, but Manuele is also a teacher, and therefore a natural successor to Ernesto. He has talent galore, he's a consummate reader, and Alice is proud of him, since she feels she discovered him. He introduces the authors (even the dead, who can't talk back) as if he had just left them at their door a few hours earlier. He's lively and antiacademic; he comes up with bizarre digressions about the writer or the cultural environment around him, using gossip and anecdote as his weapons. The result is that no one in here feels ignorant or judged because maybe he or she hasn't read much, and literature is reduced to a lava flow of chatter, a parlor conversation, while enjoying a sandwich, a slice of cake, and a cup of tea. The word *menu* was recently eliminated from the colorful listings on the tables, now replaced by *"Madamina, il catalogo è questo,"* "My lady, this is a list"; after various attempts, the words from the aria of Mozart's *Don Giovanni* were appreciated even by those customers whose tastes are strictly Wagnerian. Manuele gazes out at his devotees, who are all here. Decidedly on in years, they love their ailments, but when they come into the bookshop, it's as if he rouses them from their lethargy. They prepare to listen to excerpts from Marguerite Duras's *The Lover* and Isak Dinesen's *Out of Africa,* selected by Lucilla and approved unanimously. Alice looks at him adoringly, today more intensely than usual. They're hiding something from me, but I would never admit it.

"Excuse me, sweetheart, but why not passages from *Mrs. Dalloway, To the Lighthouse,* or the classic *A Room of One's Own*?"

"Emma, you already did the window display, and Woolf cannot be recited."

"Perhaps you're right; Kidman is the only one who was able to. . . . You look especially happy; today, in fact, you're luminous. Your skin looks lovely; your eyes are bright. . . . Did you have a facial?"

"Think so?"

"They're shining. . . . You know when you have the impression that a woman is especially . . . something? Well, you're especially . . . I can't think of the word."

"Happy, Emma. Especially happy. He asked me last night."

"What?"

"To marry him. He didn't actually ask me; he left a ring under my pillow. Maybe I look especially something or other because it's the first time that a man has decided he wants me to be with him for a lifetime. It seems like a historic turning point, at least in my life. He made me feel worthwhile, important, I don't know if you can understand. . . ."

"Honey, it's wonderful news. We have to celebrate! Oh my God, we have to start planning! And how about money? Will you be able to get by?"

"Emma, we already live together, and my father will pay for the ceremony. Don't worry. You're the one who's the culprit. If Dreams & Desires hadn't been born, if you hadn't refused for months to open the community blog and if you hadn't left it to me to manage the site, he and I would never have met. We said so last night: We owe our marriage and our happiness to a bookshop and the Internet. You've already done all you needed to do and more."

"Shhh . . . we can't hear. Can you lower your voices?" a woman complains; my enthusiasm is such that my tone must have risen. Alice and Manuele are getting married! But what am I getting so excited about? Clearly they should marry, right? Who knows when Mattia will marry and when Sarah, *his* Sarah, will get married. There's nothing better than marriage to make you feel important. And Gabriella, who promised a pizza for us all, still hasn't come.

"Oh dear, Alice, I feel like giving Manuele a hug."

"Calm down, Emma. You're more flustered than I am. Better not—he gets embarrassed with you; you know that."

"I'm not flustered, sweetie. I'm not flustered. . . . On the contrary, it's the first good news in a long time."

"Sometimes we forget the obvious, Emma. Why don't we recycle Jacques Prévert? Some of his poems are gems, like 'Cet Amour': 'This love / so violent / so fragile / so tender . . .' et cetera. What do you think? Shall we plan a reading for that marvelous day in February?"

"Please, Manuele, I understand the emotional state you're in, but Saint Valentine's Day, absolutely not! Think about those poor men and women like you were before Alice rescued you from the brink of bachelorhood, the poor souls who don't have a girlfriend, a sweetheart, a lover, not even an admirer. I'd rather do a display about alternatives."

"What alternatives?"

"Friendship, for example."

"And where the devil would I find a novel about friendship between a man and a woman? Sooner or later they end up in bed or something happens."

"I'm not in the mood for such a commercial holiday. A trumped-up sham. Plus, I feel too tired today to create a special display. Speak of the devil, here comes Camillo. Let's try it out on him," I say.

"Camillo, do you think it makes sense to do a public poetry reading on Saint Valentine's Day, what with all those unfortunate souls who have no one to give a flower or a book to, no one who will give them a flower or a book—in short, to those who are desperate and maybe lonely or even solitary and maybe content? Manuele has rediscovered Prévert's poetry."

"When I was twenty, I received bundles of love letters—some of which I've kept, despite my wife—from Christine, a beautiful girl from the cold north, the Pas de Calais. She wanted me to go and live with her forever, and I had spent only one night with her. . . . *'J'aime quand tu me regardes, quand tu me caresses, et surtout quand tu me fais l'amour.'* 'I love when you make love to me,' she would write. I still have the letter. However, I agree with Emma; Valentine's Day just means business for restaurants and pizzerias. No readings. Emma dear, I have to talk to you, though. I don't want to take up your time, but I ducked out of the office. . . . It's imperative that I tell you what happened to me. Please understand that I am trying to remain calm only because of an antiquated heritage of good breeding, which does not allow me to get pissed off and shout, but I am very, very, very pissed off."

"Let's go into the Locanda, where we won't be disturbed. Everything is all right with Valeria, isn't it? Please don't give me any bad news, not you at least."

"It's all going so well that I told Laura I thought it was time for us to divorce. I like being with Valeria. And Laura likes being with that Sandro, who seems like a prick to me, but if she's happy . . . And you know what my darling little wife told me?"

"No. What did she say?"

"That she won't divorce me. She *won't* divorce me. Not now or ever."

"Because of the kids?"

"The kids? Of course not! Our children are more savvy than we are, and this idiocy is just fine with them; they have a great time when the house is left to them. Emma, you see it with Mattia, don't you? As soon as you leave, it's party time. They have an empty house. They do what they want."

"And you're pissed off at Laura? The hell with her. Stay with

Valeria and sooner or later she'll give in. Maybe the prick will ask her to divorce you. Give her time. What's your hurry?"

"You can't imagine what she did to me."

"No, I can't guess. Tell me and don't keep me on tenterhooks."

"She did a horrible thing."

"She ran off with the funds?"

"Worse, much worse. But I want to tell it to you properly, what your ex-girlfriend Laura did, so you'll realize that I have been sharing my life with a mentally unstable person and didn't know it."

"Is it something so terrible that you can't say it?"

"She flooded the house."

"Flooded the house . . . your house?"

"Her former house. Fortunately, a neighbor noticed the stream on the landing and called me at the hospital."

"Was there a lot of damage?"

"Well, the parquet floor swelled up like a bubble, but that's not the worst of it."

"Of course, you'll see, it will dry, and with a fresh coat of sealant it will be as good as new, Camillo. Don't make it into a tragedy."

"Before flooding the house, she committed a crime that cannot be remedied."

"Which is?"

"She filled the bathtub with my books; she tossed them all in there, and I mean *all* my books, from your novels to my medical texts, even the ones from university. She piled others around the tub and turned on the tap. Then she left."

"My God, that's horrible! It's murder! They'll have to be thrown away!"

"Waterlogged, Emma. A horror film. I'm going to raid the bookshop, but the medical texts are so expensive, I'll never be able to repurchase all of them. It would have been better had she burned my clothes. You go to the store and you replace your wardrobe. But not books! I told you: She's insane."

I embrace Camillo as lightly as possible, on this day for lovers

that is absolutely hopeless. My poor, poor friend. If someone did
something like that to me, I could kill. In fact, his nostrils are quivering.

"You can't go back home under these conditions. Pack a bag and
stay at my place until the parquet is refinished and someone re-
moves the books from the tub. Go back to your little mothers now.
You're a doctor; you can't let yourself slump into depression this
way."

I go home—or rather, I decide to take a walk. I need to walk, just
walk. I'll prepare supper for my new housemate. In these weeks of
sadness, a lump forever in my throat, even just comforting someone
to whom a horrible incivility has been done (drowning his books to
drown him) can offer safe passage toward a certain normality. Valentine's Day, what an idiotic holiday. I couldn't bear to see those happy
little lovers come into the bookshop and smooch in front of my
shelves. I just couldn't. Sorry, Emma passes. At least for today.

I'm becoming a solitary figure. And I don't like it one bit. Milan
is full of *solitary figures,* and I opened the bookshop to remedy all
this. I was presumptuous, arrogant. It's not possible to be a Red
Cross worker and save souls by hopping and skipping from word to
word. It's not true that novels save lives, at least not tonight.

It takes more than that to save ourselves from what happens to
us when what we desire is the exact opposite of what happens.

APRIL 10, 2005

The TGV bullet train left the outskirts thirty-seven minutes ago and is devouring the rails to Quiberon. From the window, the hills look like the humps of a weary camel. The colors waver between what they really are and what they should be in the mind of a former romantic: The yellow of the sunflowers inches toward ocher, the green has lost its intensity, and the tree trunks are streaked with mold. The windowpane is lined with drops as fine as a child's eyelashes. I place my bag on the seat, where someone left a copy of *Madame Figaro*. The train's lullaby is a song that has been committed to memory. Alternating flow: I think, I read, I whimper. The letter is safely tucked away. It's a brief good-bye, effective immediately. Rereading it yet again would be like going back to a novel you've wasted entire nights on, letting the warning signs scattered between the lines escape you. What is a letter if not a crossword diagram, the words set down, side by side, with marginal notes, strung like beads on a necklace? What use is a letter except to kill time? I hate time, it never feels like what you expect it to, and I've always detested that expression. It's not funny, lady, and don't look at me that way; have a heart. You'd force me to explain everything and I wouldn't know where to start.

·———·

New York, January 22, 2005
Barnes & Noble, Union Square

My love,
I am in our bookstore. The same coffee, the same tiled floor, and your flamboyant writers on the walls. I would rather be drawing than writing. If someone with greater talent hadn't already done it, I would do a pen-and-ink sketch of the concrete-and-iron span topped by stately brick arches that crosses the East River and connects Manhattan to Brooklyn. I would draw a bridge. Ours was interrupted while still under construction, for reasons beyond our control. There's corrosion on the Brooklyn Bridge and the Transportation Department officials routinely overlook it. They announce its restoration at regular intervals; years pass between one warning and another and nothing is done. Too expensive to tackle a symbol. As I write, I can hear your comments and your breathing. You wouldn't say a word. I know it. But you would think of everything and the opposite of everything. Except the truth. Because there is an objective truth, imposed by the facts. The last time, with you, I would have liked hour hands and meridians to be nonexistent; I didn't want to hear the anger that was and is directed mainly at myself. I would cry, if only I were capable of it. It was a love story. Nothing more, an ingenuous, fashionable cynic would say. Just a love story. The story, our story, ends here and it hurts me just to write the four letters that make up the word *ends*. Four, like the letters of your name. The love will be forever. That's where the difference lies. Every story has a beginning, a middle, and an end. You taught me that; it's the first rule of a good novel, which must unfold according to coherent dramaturgical canons. Because we owe this to the readers. *Love stories end when you no longer love each other*, you're thinking, Emma. There is no justification for my behavior, no logical or reasonable excuse, and it's not cowardliness. It's inability. That's what you're thinking. I'm not immune to the extortion of fear and sorrow, and the error, my error, remains relegated to the past. At night, it roams and

finds no peace, pursues rest, won't let me breathe. Your architect has caved in. He did not endure the slow corrosion of convention; it happened without sovereign proof, as the scientists say. I have no proof—or rather, I have just one: You are not at fault. This grave digger's talk makes me sick, but I have no other words. Just this. I know what you're thinking about us, about our encounter: for the shelf "Possible but Hopeless Loves." Because of the protagonist. Incapable of saying the only words that would make sense, today, in a New York as cold and sterile as a hospital room. These: I love you.

Federico

· ——— ·

I should have known. An island born of tears leads to tears. If I were a true bookseller, I would have been able to read between the lines. Everything seems to be going along when the whistling of the ax neatly severs the pages and certainties of the narrative. Not so for attentive readers: It's hard to surprise them with shabby plots. They know how it will end and they mete out the pages, waiting for it to happen. I'm a superficial woman. "And they lived happily ever after" is a bunch of baloney they feed us as children, forgetting that children know perfectly well that a happy ending only serves to put an end to any questions. Like when mommy and daddy are half-asleep or there are friends at the table, and the storyteller is hungry and wants to get back quickly. The fairy-tale-reading parents believe that a straightforward ending will let the child sleep without nightmares. True love stories have to end badly. A story with a happy ending is worth two that end tragically; a novel whose main character is a male villain is exchanged for two with a contemptible female protagonist. I've always heard this. And I thought it had nothing to do with me.

You'll get used to it, Emma.

Rails. The station. The *Locmaria*. The island's silhouette. Wild and fierce, the intended destination seems almost like revenge.

Serves you right.

The drizzle continues. I drag my bag to the steps of La Touline. I'm not in any shape to get dressed, put on makeup, or stand upright. Plain to see, Madame Bertho. I approach the desk in the hall, set within thick walls that, before welcoming lovers, housed an apothecary, a shoemaker's shop, and a sardine-canning plant. I rummage through my purse for my ID papers. The rain lashes the window-panes, and this makes it easier to lie.

"Everything is fine, thank you. No, I won't be dining. I'm going to rest now."

She doesn't want my ID papers and doesn't ask me anything. It may be just my impression, but she studies me as if she were x-raying me. It's quite different for her, too; she loved chatting with Federico on the sloping grassy terraces in back.

"Do you have everything you need, Emma?"

"Thank you, yes."

Everything I need hasn't changed his mind. Up until the last moment, I kept hoping that he would come to meet me on the dock, that he would embrace me, explaining that it was all a misunderstanding. Or a bad joke.

I waited for you. And you didn't come.

I would have punched him; I would have showered him with abuse, letting him know that it was like telling someone he has a tumor, only to later apologize for having read the wrong medical report. Doctor, someone took it upon himself to tell me that Federico would disappear from my life. I would claim damages for the suffering unjustly caused, although there is no suffering that is justly caused. Suffering is unjust, period.

I waited for you. And you didn't come.

It was instinct that thrust me into this affair and now instinct requires me to be here, on the date determined by my idiotic personal destiny. The fog descends upon me and I am unable to oppose the decrees of its agenda. Among the constellations, which I cannot decipher, a single star shines more brightly than the others. I suspect it may be an effect of my presbyopia, but I am here in search of signs, answers, revelations. I start with the sky. I close my eyes. I reopen them and I feel like I have been gone for hours. Room number 5 is empty and tidy, like a hotel room should be before being occupied. From the window, I glimpse a steely grass carpet on which God is bestowing His decorous tears and a mournful dirge. A blue fishing boat, down at the port, is unrigged, the dock is deserted, and the Café de la Cale has no customers. The Mozartian "Lacrimosa" of raindrops is stifling, exactly as I had imagined, self-inflicting the punishment of spending five days at Belle-Ile, *l'île où on vient pour se cacher*: "the island where one goes to hide."

Marcel Proust went in search of lost time, only to find that it was always different from what he had imagined. I don't want to think about the time I lost, and this is why I willingly forget. I came here with a purpose. I am here to regain the benefits of solitude. I had learned to enjoy it, that feeling of freedom, when you know you're able to cope with the silence, when you make it to evening without the hollowness breaking you, when you're proud of yourself for not needing someone to talk to. The solitude of this welcoming womb is the sum of free and easy moments, in the absence of human contact. I experienced the weight of solitude as a couple. "I sensed that the time had come to make myself a solitude again," Michel Tournier wrote: a sentence read years ago, one that immediately stuck in my head and that comes back to me now, because novels can be useful when you least expect it. Though I would gladly have avoided getting a taste of it again. Somewhat like measles, once you've had it, it doesn't come back. I had been heading serenely and obliviously toward old age without a husband, imagining myself as a grandmother. And at last I could breathe. No dependencies, just books to keep me company, those creatures offering bounteous vistas. I had safeguarded it, that luminous solitude of mine, holding it carefully in reserve. All it took was his handwriting in that green ink to shatter all my certainties.

Sitting on the bed, I spread out the last trace of our correspondence, the centerpiece for an old ladies' tea party. Its watermark harbors the senseless reasons for a decision. Solitude. There are those who mistake it with being antisocial.

According to A. S. Byatt, women are always inside, looking out the window, wondering how to get out, how to be free.

I look out the window and I don't know how to take advantage of the freedom that rains down on me, now that I no longer care about it. The tolling of a bell announces the hour, but I don't know which one. I open the window a crack and the scent of the sea invades my nostrils, smelling of salt and sunlight chilled by the night—a complex scent that many writers have tried to describe. *The Sea, the Sea,* five copies sold, two in stock. The remaining two will sell; that's why I haven't sent them back. The rosewood chest needs some personal touches. Methodically, like when I arrange the new books on the shelves (usually on Wednesdays), I set out jars of antiwrinkle cream, night cream, vials of eye-contour serum, cocoa butter, an earring stand, and Chanel black mascara and eyeliner, purchased at the airport, like in the good old days. Never let yourself go to pot, even if a man has dumped you. The room remains anonymous and there's not even a minibar.

Enough.

On the bedside table, *The Garden Party and Other Stories,* by Katherine Mansfield, an old edition belonging to my mother. I had looked for it assiduously—I was sure I had it—among my books at home and shoved it into the suitcase, on the assumption that perception and reality might be reconciled, that it would all prove to be a mistake, like in the story "The Singing Lesson." The lesson takes place soon after the teacher has read a letter from her fiancé, who is breaking off the relationship. The notes are desolate—"Every note was a sigh, a sob, a groan of awful mournfulness"—until, summoned by the headmaster, she is handed a telegram: Her fiancé begs her to forget that letter. The lesson resumes and the student's singing becomes joyful and harmonious.

I know this floor inch by inch; I could describe the pattern of its grain with my eyes closed, draw the curves of the wood, but not even the added touches—the clothes, the cloche resting on the small table, the familiar book covers—manage to lend a hint of warmth to these two hundred square feet. Time for a bath. Lavender salts, and the soul's abrasion is washed away. Birds are squawking out there, a harrowed sound, doleful and furious. They're demanding attention, like me. When I fall asleep in this unfamiliar French bed, I don't mourn my twenties. I am under the hypnotic effect of novels. I feel like Jo, heroic Jo, the best of the little women, witty, intelligent, captivated by literature; instead, I'm a middle-aged woman who is surely starting to suffer from arthritis.

In the morning, I wake up with stiff joints, and merely straightening my fingers is painful—especially the thumbs. I go down and I'm ready to challenge myself. I rent a bicycle, ignoring Monsieur Moulinc's astonished look. It's silver and has huge mountain-bike wheels, nothing like my black Bianchi with its straw basket and flowers around the handlebars, perfect for a proper Milanese lady, as Mattia says. Monsieur Moulinc reminds me of what I know all too well: Belle-Ile is made of steep rises and "daring descents," like in the song by Lucio Battisti. Ups and downs, and I hadn't considered the wind, a sonorous wall that penetrates everywhere, plunging into the valleys, passing over the slate roofs, then subsiding between the spokes of the bicycle as it struggles along the road. Around me, the tops of the cypress trees are wearing monkish cowls. Everything is gloomier than I remember—and it was only a year ago. I hold on tight at the first bumpy hole, pushing down on the right pedal with a superhuman effort. When I make it through, the satisfaction is incredible; every pedal thrust is a victory in my personal war of independence. Like a cyclist *in surplace*, I stop, my calves racked by cramps. I balance, going neither forward or backward. I'm about to fall, and I remember Annemarie Schwarzenbach, the rebellious feminist, who died at age thirty-four from an injury sustained in a bicycle accident. I have to pedal. A flea-ridden dog runs alongside me and I'm terrified that he might bite me. The kindly beast ignores me and settles down in front of the wheels. Then he gives me permission to pass with a languid look. He pities me, of course; for him, too, I'm as predictable as a plot when you already know at page 20 whether the story will turn out well or not. It's the kind of novel that sells the best, a novel with no surprises. Readers enjoy it when just what they expect happens, ignoring what the critics say.

Like a grown-up Gretel, I retrace the crumbs of a romance, following the credo—Jungian or Freudian, I can't remember which— that states if you relive a painful experience, there is a good chance that you can erase its memory. Shredding, chopping, and dicing it makes it easier to digest. In my case, there is also the insane desire to try to rewrite the story, to rewind the tape recorder and dash off a new version. A bit like children do when they get tired of a story or find it scary: They change the book's plot to suit their liking. I want—or rather, have—to be sad. It's part of the therapy. It's so damn obvious in this situation, and the herculean effort not to be sad isn't productive. Better to sink into the hole, describe the pain with a little imagination, change the adjectives here and there, rearrange the words, set the story at the sea or in the mountains, amid grimy city streets or the brightness of a blue Formica kitchen.

For a woman who is not all there, whose lover has traumatically abandoned her by mail, for a woman bereft of good sense, her thoughts predictable, not at all witty or particularly intelligent, the first station of the cross is those two: Jean and Jeanne, two stones that have a story because man's fantasy wanted to give them a beginning, a middle, and an end. Without those, the plot unravels. I wear myself out on the ascent. The road cuts through fields of poppies; if only they had an opiate effect, I would smoke them to alleviate the anguish. I trudge along, my muscles taut as a wire; my lungs expand as I inhale and exhale deeply; my legs are contracted with lactic acid. I approach the inanimate figures.

Stones, Emma, they're stones. They don't think, they don't speak, and they don't feel anything.

My cloche pulled low over my forehead, almost as if I am afraid of being recognized, I reach out a hand. There she is, my stone counterpart. I see a young blond girl emerge, who lays anemones bound with wisps of straw at my feet. Strange, these flowers. I've never seen them here, among the slate and granite. The figure of the young Jeanne is not an ankou, but a hologram for reckless lovers who yielded to the unknown. I should hang a reproduction of her in the bookshop and quit pitying myself. The young girl is thin, with blue eyes and small, rigid breasts. She's wearing a little tunic and a cap over her hair—a uniform, like the one I wore at school. With her hand, she motions me to come closer. It is an invitation to a private ceremony, a frugal funeral. Oh, of course: The little corpse must be buried quickly so it won't stink. She holds out her child's hand. My hand joins with hers, palm to palm, fingers entwined. A memorial is inscribed in the stone:

> HERE LIES A LOVE
> THAT DIED NOT BY CONSUMPTION
> BUT THROUGH IRRESPONSIBILITY

Once the funeral is over, I'm able to cry, thank God. The plasterboard girdle is back, obstructing my breathing. What if I were to die here, in front of her? The *bellilois* would wonder what the Italian tourist was doing in the middle of a field on a weekday in April. They would sift through the room, pry into my clothes, rummage through my bag; they would find the letter, the little notebook in which Mattia's words mingle with those of Woolf and other sorrowful ladies. The police would cite the legend of the ankou that has no face but has power. There is no Breton village that does not have an ankou. It is not a personification of death or the devil; it is an entity that forewarns, whose duty it is to alert people to what will happen. At the island's headlands, it warned the seamen's wives, heralded shipwrecks, storms, and misfortunes. I, instead, don't see the ankou; I can't feel its presence. And because of this inadvertent negligence, the old pain gushes out without proper notice.

For old times' sake, the doctors of zoology had driven out of town that Tuesday afternoon to make a final visit to the singing salt dunes at Baritone Bay. And to appease a ghost. They never made it back alive.

They almost never made it back at all. They'd only meant to take a short nostalgic walk along the coast where they had met as students almost thirty years before. They had made love for the first time in these same dunes.

I brought with me the notebook in which I jot down opening lines. This one seemed fitting. I climb back on the bicycle. The sky above Belle-Ile is one single cloud mass. I must censor this insane passion. *It takes application, Emma, diligence. Day by day, you'll have to delete a passage here, omit a phrase there.* When it comes to leaving memories behind, I'm an ace; I can re-create like nobody's business who I thought I was and who I've become. Just as Polonius, observing Hamlet, exclaims, "Though this be madness, yet there is method in't," so I, too, need a method to eradicate love. I continue along, pushing on the pedals, comforted by the sound of the *Locmaria* coming into port and tying up at the dock. From its hold, it spits out some cars, two vans, and a few frozen people. I sit in the park in front of the port of Sauzon. It's cold, but that, too, is normal. The two zoologists in Jim Crace's *Being Dead* were murdered. In a few months, I sold three copies that had been ordered. Monsieur Moulinc takes back the bike and asks me how it went.

"*Très bien, merci.*"

I'm sweating under my seventies-era denim jacket and I feel like singing "April Come She Will," by Simon and Garfunkel, a song dedicated to the most foolish month of the year, which begins with a joke and keeps going senselessly. La Touline is empty and dismal, like mornings in the bookshop when it's raining out. I go upstairs to number 5. I can sleep sideways now, spread out like a starfish, hands and feet like points.

I spend the first two days working through the bereavement, and each draft must be repeated with precision, written in pencil, before making a good copy with the fountain pen and its emerald green ink. Contemporary novels mock love with their cynicism: The stories that work are those in which the female protagonists are wary of men and scoff at tragedies related to abandonment. A bookseller adamant about twentieth-century literature, I surrender to the new millennium. Alice thinks I am happily enjoying thalassotherapy. Manuele loves her and has asked her to be his wife. I don't have the heart to warn her.

It's raining now. The water is pouring down like an accent grave and the sky is spitting out squalls like flocks of angry birds. I'm hungry; I prepare myself for the pilgrimage to the restaurants where we would stuff ourselves with charcuterie and mussels and prawns—making love makes you hungry, and Federico is as voracious as a teenager. At the Café de la Cale, two young couples are squeezing lemon wedges and swallowing oysters, picking them up with their hands from a two-level serving platter. *What are you looking at? Haven't you ever seen a woman order a carafe of vin blanc?* I have to try everything, and I won't end up an alcoholic like Duras, with young lovers and pimps. I know how to deal with shyness now. All I have to do is pour myself a drink.

I could easily be your mother, damn it.

The day's special is entrecôte in a red wine sauce. I'll try intoxication, eliminating the stigma of being a teetotaler from my curriculum. The polished floor recalls that of a drowsy tavern. Every seaside town has one. Facing the waves that smear the restaurant's window with sea salt, I drink and I feel cheerful, even, amused by the young people and a fatalist all of a sudden.

"To watch the end of all was not much different from watching the beginning of things, and if you weren't ever going to take part anyway, then to watch the end was far and away better." The words of Maeve Brennan, a writer who died alone a few years ago, after a brief marriage that ended, due to her husband's alcoholism.

Exactly.

Waking up is precarious. It's the last day and I feel better. I sleep soundly at Belle-Ile, even without the herbalist's infusions. I have a good supply of emotions to ponder over during the entire return trip. Working through things is proceeding nicely. I haven't even become bitter. On the contrary. I should go to Madame Bertho. I don't feel like explaining; it's part of the script. This is probably the last time I'll get to talk to her, and I've appreciated her discretion; she hasn't asked me anything during my days here. Only "Everything all right, Emma?" knowing that it isn't all right. I spent time looking at things that weren't there, listening to a voice borne on the wind.

"You're going out early today. Put on a sweater, Emma; it will be cold. I'll expect you for supper. The fisherman promised me a monkfish. That way, we'll have time to say good-bye."

It rained during the night. On the road, there's the scent of woods. The island rewards my devotion with a mustached smile from Monsieur Moulinc, who gives me a discount. He doesn't rent many bikes this time of year and he seems to have taken a liking to me. He likes my little hats, he says. And he gives me a flower. Arzic Point is a few miles away. I should be able to do it in an hour, which is equivalent to three hours of Pilates; it firms the thighs and turns your glutes into buns of steel.

You don't need it anymore, Emma.

I'm removing the boundaries of the territory I marked. Naïve, oblivious Emma. *You've never been a good catch.* The father of that fabulously wealthy young man had an infallible nose for making money. Like J.P.M., like the stockbroker Alice was infatuated with. Never trust writers and billionaires. Or guys with tangled dark curls and long, muscular legs. Never trust anyone who lowers his head and looks down. Do what rabbits do: Instead of standing still when chased, they dash off. Never believe anyone who wears Eau Sauvage and who knows how to draw a straight line. I'm angry, and every pedal thrust is a breath of freedom. If he had never entered the bookshop, I would not have known the beauty of this island. Love is useful for learning geography, but you can get fed up with beauty.

Et tant pis pour lui, as the French say—"so much the worse for him."

The guidebook states:

To communicate from one end of the island to the other, in the eighteenth century the military built simple structures on tree-tops. In 1805, the navy replaced them with a kind of telegraphic apparatus called a semaphore; in 1859 they decided to restore four electrosemaphoric stations at either end of the island, intended to serve a dual purpose: communication with ships at sea and surveillance of the coastline to signal possible enemy attacks. Of the semaphores put into service in 1862, only the one at Arzic Point has retained its original appearance. The house included two living quarters for two semaphorists and a garden surrounded by stone walls. Occupied by the Germans during the Second World War, it has now been abandoned by its owners.

I wanted to go to the seashore with my mother. And I never told her.

I follow the path lined with rosemary; thistles threaten my delicate ankles with their usual sting. I walk quickly, as if late for an appointment, afraid the person waiting for me will be gone. The semaphore, the deserted house, there it is. The door is open. The windows have been scraped and painted blue; the back porch is supported by logs positioned like columns, still covered with bark. Not unlike people, houses, too, tend to become eccentric when abandoned, and this one resembles an old slipper that has lost its mate. Two pickaxes and three shovels are propped against the wall; nearby is a copy of a Monet. On the floor, there's a flashlight that works. I shine it around, illuminating a pile of bricks and the shutters of the back windows, which are hanging off their hinges. I've seen enough. I pull the door shut behind me; a few drops begin to fall. As I hurry off, pushing the bicycle by the handle-bars, I feel like whimpering. I have four empty hours to fill before suppertime. I pedal along, singing at the top of my lungs.

The rain is coming down in buckets and Monsieur Moulinc looks worried and astounded at the sight of the drenched Italian lady who returns his bicycle with a kiss on the cheek. Supper lies ahead, the last stretch of the road to redemption and freedom.

Adieu, Jeanne.

I go up to the room, pull the curtains, and lie down on the bed without removing the cover. I'm waiting for something, and slowly, like in the pause between one labor pain and the next, between one sharp contraction and the next, my chest expands and the vise-like grip releases. The only sound I'm conscious of is that of the seagulls, screeching and circling over the seawall that encloses the harbor. At seven-thirty, the insistent whistle of the *Locmaria* pierces my heart. Better to soak in the tub before facing Annick Bertho's likely questions and my probable lies. I'll stick to generalities.

I dress with care. No heartache justifies a slovenly appearance.

It's time to reminisce. I realize it when I enter the dining room. She is waiting for me in a navy blue pantsuit. On the jacket is a brooch of white-gold filigree with small pearls woven into the metal. The table is set for two; the white tablecloth is embroidered with sea-shells. It's clear that Annick—she wants me to call her that and drop my lame "madame"—has prepared the meeting thoughtfully. I count on her courteousness. I'll be reserved.

"I'm sorry you are leaving without having enjoyed even one full day of sunshine. We have not been fortunate this year. Hope-fully, the summer will be better."

"Belle-Ile is magical in any kind of weather, Annick. I rested and took some nice bicycle rides," I say, trying to avoid the only topic I'm concerned about. The monkfish is exquisite, and by now I'm a master at drowning my embarrassment in a glass of wine.

"Federico is a shattered man," she says, and her eyes seem to tear up like small lakes. "I heard from him two weeks ago; he's still stunned, shocked. He's very worried about his daughter."

My jealousy and resentment toward this good-natured, affec-tionate woman are overwhelming. She watched me all these days, knowing why I looked like a star-crossed heroine, and didn't say a word until now, decked out like an old woman in greasepaint.

"He wrote me a letter, yes," I stammer, mortified. I hate her. I detest this woman who pours tarragon sauce on the fish and brings the glass to her lips, smearing it with lipstick. I'd like to run away, pack my bags, and never see her again. I hate her because she knows, she's known all along, and she treats me as if I were an extra with a walk-on role. While my thoughts are spinning in a *danse macabre,* Annick begins talking, without considering the possibility that I have no knowledge of the facts, as they say in detective novels— which are not my genre. I don't know what she's talking about.

"Sarah has problems?" I bow to ignorance; I don't know what I could say that would not let on that I am unaware of the cause of Federico's "shattered" state, though it costs me to admit this to yet another female figure in my life whom I cannot decipher. And this condition is unbearable to me: not understanding.

"Annick, I don't understand."

I quickly drain my glass; that way, my head will spin and I'll abruptly fall asleep. I have to get drunk. I am entitled to now. Who gives a damn about the humiliation I feel rising up like the surging ocean. I've never taken up seafaring and I don't intend to start now. Repetitions, in life, are a terrible thing. Recurrences are usually disappointing. It's like rereading a novel you loved as a girl: Now you find it boring, overly sentimental, or badly written. Incomprehensible. What does she mean by the adjectives *shattered, stunned, shocked*? Really. Over a furtive, senile romance? Come on, Annick, let's not exaggerate. Affairs end. We were only long-distance lovers, commuters. Sporadic and foolhardy.

"Tell me."

Annick looks at me gently and understands my embarrassment, because she, too, is embarrassed. Biting my lower lip, I wait for her to speak. Instead, she gets up, goes to the desk—I can see her from here—opens a drawer, rummages in it, then comes back and sits down at the table.

"Here," she says in a whisper, and puts a letter in my hands. Written with a fountain pen, it's in black ink. I turn toward the fireplace, like when you're on a train and you look out the window so you won't have to make eye contact with the person sitting in front of you. I'm not handling this well at all, and I hold Federico's letter as if it were a sacred icon from a church.

. ——— .

New York, February 7, 2005

Dear Annick,

Forgive me for not calling again, after your e-mail. Writing to you will help me sort things out after the chaos of these past weeks. I'm at home. It's late. Sarah fell asleep beside me on the couch. "Now what will we do, Dad?" she asked me while we were having dinner, she and I, at Julien, a restaurant she likes, the closest to French in New York. A simple question, the most obvious one that a child who has lost her mother can ask her father. I told her that we'll get by somehow, although I don't exactly know what "getting by" means. Back home, I held her to me with an intensity meant to at least try to banish her anguish, that lost feeling when faced with death. I, however, cannot rid myself of the shame of being alive, and it comforts me to write to you here, sitting on the same couch where we found Anna. Her hands were clutching her chest as if wanting to protect what that chest held, Annick, as she lay here. A sudden dizziness, the couch, her clenched hands. And those eyes that were imploring something as Sarah ran to the phone. "Can you see me?" I asked her. "I see your shadow," she replied in a whisper. Then nothing more. Anna was a healthy woman. They carried her to the ambulance and took her away. I waited in the hospital hallway, and when the doctor came toward me, his arms hanging limply at his sides told me all there was to know. I slumped to my knees like a puppet whose strings have been cut. A visceral grief filled me. I should get up *from this shameful position*, I thought the doctors came over and spoke to me in a confusion of voices; they kept saying they knew what I was going through and that I had to be strong. But strength was nowhere to be found. I was unable to get up, frozen there, the pain stored away, concealed under my knees or the palms of my hands there on the floor. A migraine, or something like it, started pounding in my head. Sarah came toward me like a doll in teenager's clothing, a little yellow sweater, low-rise jeans, and combat boots, ready for battle. I was so embarrassed to have her see me like that, yet I couldn't move. To discover what love and pain are at the same time, all at once, is an indescribable feeling, a vertical descent into the unknown.

I asked to see her. They had placed her on a bed, removed the respirator and nasal tubes. Everything was shut down. Darkness inside. Darkness outside. I asked why Anna had died that way, without having time to even realize it, to say good-bye, to give us the chance to tell her how much we loved her. I felt like a fool. I should have asked about the "technical" cause of death. The rest was my own private affair, but the words came by themselves, strange for someone who doesn't usually get personal. The bureaucracy of death is like the bureaucracy in a bank or in any office. The bureaucracy of death has nothing to do with death. A paradox, right? "Her heart, Mr. Virgili, but it wasn't a heart attack. To understand what happened, we have to do an autopsy. Do you authorize an autopsy, Mr. Virgili?" Anyone would want to know what caused a revolution in his life, what the medical report about a mystery might reveal to a stunned man and a young girl. Anna died of an illness that has an unusual name, Annick. My wife had a broken heart, a shattered heart. I listened to the kind doctors. *Heartbreak* has an exaggerated, comic-book sound to it, yet it's a disease. It's called "Takotsubo syndrome," and I had to laugh, because some syndromes are lexically ridiculous. A female syndrome, they explained, almost as if wanting to reassure me that it couldn't happen to me. I hardly think that one heart is different from another, although I'm convinced that men and women use it differently. They love in different ways. They die in different ways. Takotsubo syndrome is the result of emotional stress. The brain produces a surge of so-called fear hormones, which stagger the heart; the left ventricle becomes deformed and comes to resemble—so the cardiologist explained, his tone suggestive of someone telling a fairy tale—an ancient Japanese flask-shaped pot, used by fishermen to catch octopus. Hence the absurdly funny name. My wife had a broken heart and I didn't know it. Caught in time and with the proper medications, the heart "readjusts" itself and no traces remain of the emotion that broke it. Anna was home alone. Sarah was with me, shopping for Christmas gifts. I didn't get there in time, Annick, and I can't find peace because of it. I spend my days at the Morgan construction site, which has become my buffer. Renzo Piano is of great comfort to me, and my colleagues bend over backward to find excuses to invite me and Sarah to dinner. Her classmates' mothers have practically adopted her. Only in the evening, at night, like now, do I permit myself to let go.

I could use your help with the semaphore. I phoned the company. I'm not able to oversee the restoration work and I don't know when I'll be able to travel to Belle-Ile. Could you keep in touch with Posieur and the engineer Vauvan for the time being? They already have the complete plans for the job. I don't think there will be any problems. I would be truly grateful to you.

I'll call you. Please feel free to do the same if there's anything you need. Affectionately,

Federico

· —— ·

Suddenly, it all makes sense. A real broken heart, not like the ones found on the bookshop's shelves.

I can't compete with a blameless corpse. His wife. Now I understand: Federico had bought the semaphore, and used to come here from Paris—to this island his mother loved so much—in order to see to the restoration. Evidently, he would stay here at La Touline. Apparently, Annick knew about it. And she said nothing when Federico and I came here together.

I can't compete with a blameless corpse.

Federico's wife was always invisible to me. She was so absent in her absence, and now all of a sudden she has a body. The little bird flaps its injured wings, asking to be rescued. He slumped to his knees in the hospital corridor; he certainly wasn't thinking about how I would take it. I wept. This is the second time I've cried over a relationship that has ended. It never changes. I finally have a reason to get over it.

At daybreak, I am calm. Belle-Ile-en-Mer goes back to being what it was: one of the world's most unique settings. The backdrop for a romance. Someone I loved.

Something will happen, and when it happens, I won't be here.

Old and visibly moved, her face chalk white, her eyes heavy-lidded, Sarah Bernhardt waves good-bye to the fishermen lined up on either side of her on the dock at Sauzon harbor. Without the cries of joy that always accompanied her arrivals and departures from the island, the silence weighs heavily on the crowd jammed among the cars being loaded onto the ferry. The whistle urges the last passengers to board. On August 13, 1922, Sarah had sent a letter to Sauzon's notary, announcing her decision to sell the property for 450,000 francs. Belle-Ile's climate was not good for her, she had said, lying. She is seventy-nine years old, alone, her right leg amputated; she is carried to a special chair. The years have etched a web of deep wrinkles on her rouged face. Her body, hidden beneath blankets, is huddled over. The amputation forces her to remain seated or lying down, like the injured and maimed who have returned from the front. The crowd observes the scene with a mixture of sadness and admiration. A man kneels before the "Divine Sarah." That departure is a farewell; they both know it. The weather is fine; Sarah's chair is placed outdoors, on the deck. The boat moves away from the shore. On the forward deck, passengers wave their handkerchiefs, while a circle of friends watches over the old tragedienne, who is half asleep. The ferry leaves the island, heading for the mainland. It turns left and disappears beyond the breakwater, leaving a plume of thick gray smoke behind it.

On the trains, to save themselves, they would read. A perfect balm. The fixed exactitude of reading as a suture for terror. The eye that finds in the tiny switchbacks dictated by the lines a clear shortcut through which to flee the blurred flux of images imposed by the window. . . . Perhaps reading is never anything other than fixing on a point in order not to be seduced, and ruined, by the world's uncontrollable slipping away. No one would read anything, if it weren't for fear. . . . The truth is, we read to avoid looking up at the window. An open book always certifies the presence of a coward—the eyes glued to those lines to prevent their being ravished by the world and its burning desires—the words that one by one force the clamor of the world into an opaque funnel until it drips into the little glass molds we call books—the most refined form of retreat, to tell the truth. Repulsive. But *utterly delightful*. . . . Who can understand anything about delightful things if he has never bent his life, all of it, over the first line of the first page of a book? No, this is the only and the most delightful casket in which to keep all fears—a book that begins."

I found these words in an envelope made out to me without a return address, slipped under the door of the bookshop. And now, standing here motionless in front of the post office for a good half hour, like a poor imitation of Marcel Marceau, I don't know who wrote them. They're simply beautiful, and I put the note in my pocket. I take my time, watching the people passing by—or rather, racing by (everyone around here is always running)—like one of those pious women who sit out on their balconies, hands folded in their laps, smiling distantly, spectators of a promenade that has nothing to do with them. I don't see anyone; I don't *really* see anyone. Milan's gritty dust sticks to my hair; it sounds like wind, but there isn't that longing for freedom that the wind has. It's more like the melancholy sound of the surf's undertow when a wave retreats and decides to hold back the sea.

I wrap the bicycle chain around my usual, favorite signpost. The sign is upside down now; the white arrow on a blue background points to the sidewalk, and no one has thought about fixing it. My body is aching, like when I exercise too much and run into what the trainer calls "forgotten" muscles: a body with disconnected compartments. I know the first thing I'll do when I get to the bookshop is change the label on the "Broken Hearts" shelf. I've been mulling over it for months. Alberto won't notice, and to think that it was a product of my *imagination,* not a syndrome that kills wives. "Amorous Disasters" is not disrespectful to anyone. Belle da Costa Greene, before her death, burned Bernard Berenson's letters and asked him to do the same. A despicable act. Burning letters is like destroying lives. What do I do now with this heap of paper that smacks of New York? I walk down the metal-lined corridor to Box 1004, greeting the young lady behind the window as if she's an old friend. Actually, I've never seen her before; Franca is on maternity leave. All the better, as she would have asked questions and wondered why I was taking the letters; there's still room in the mailbox and they're so tidy, a maniacal archive of feelings. So many letters, almost as many as those of Anton to Olga. I open the mailbox and the missives are there waiting for someone to carry them off. Alice would compare me to that crackpot Aleramo. And she would be right. I shove them into my backpack. I'll have plenty of time to sort them by subject and maybe give them a title.

A Man and a Woman Meet Again after Thirty Years. Too long. A simple *Encounter* or maybe *A Paper Romance* would be better. Terse chapters, with brief titles; "Milan," "New York," "Belle-Ile," "Sex,"

(though out of decency, we included very little), "Memory," "Sema-
phore," "Novels," "Morgan Library," "Belle da Costa Greene," "Book
Lists," "Window Displays," "Melancholy," "Grass," "Waves," "Cliffs,"
"Rocks," "Menhirs."

The two of us, in a novel of our own . . .

There's the usual Milan sun: It's there, but you can't see it. But
the bicycle is nowhere to be seen, either. The chain is dangling
from the post. Who could possibly want a bookseller's broken-
down bike? That's all I needed, to have it stolen. Or maybe that's
just what I needed. A new life, a new bike; life is made up of symbols. I take the tram to Rossignoli, in corso Garibaldi. I choose a
strawberry red bike and spend almost more for the accessories, but
now I have two lined baskets in which I can cram the shopping
and at least twenty volumes.

I would start sobbing at the cash register if the bookshop
weren't filled with customers. Just today. Just now. Why is it that
on an ordinary June afternoon everyone feels the need to buy a
romance novel? The sight of a middle-aged lady weeping while
ringing up a receipt is indecent; plus, there are those two: Manuele
and Alice would immediately figure it out. I put it off until tonight,
maybe a nice crying jag with Gabri, who doesn't yet know the details. I banned the subject of Federico even with her, because talking about a failure, even with a friend, makes you feel ashamed.
"Friendship is certainly the finest balm for the pangs of disappointed love," Austen wrote. I phone Gabriella, then arrange the
window display for the week: "Treachery." I frame it in a box, lining all four sides in black velvet, to the left a red stool, where I stack
books with traitorous characters: *Vanity Fair*'s Becky Sharp, the social climber who ends badly yet has the sharp intuitions of true
malice, and Erika Kohut from Elfrede Jelinek's *Piano Teacher,* a novel
of horror and desperate violence. There's Rebecca and then Nara,
the Creole dancer who leads Michele to murder in *The Kiss of a Dead
Woman,* chosen in deferential homage to Invernizio, whom critics
basely ranked among the "minor" writers. A genius instead. She
wrote three novels a year and did so for forty years, a prodigious

output. I possess these volumes in the first edition, thanks to Mrs. Donati: genteelly perfidious titles such as *The Atrocious Vision, A Talent for Evil,* and *Dora, the Murderer's Daughter.* On a shelf I place a silver tray with a red apple impaled by a dagger whose elaborate handle is studded with precious stones (fake). Snow White and the Wicked Witch. Spread out on the velvet are other books, along with overturned glass bottles dripping red nail polish. In the center of the wall, a mirror, the vanity that has a lot to do with women's treachery. *Mirror, mirror on the wall . . .*

Mattia is in his room. Judging by the greenish light filtering under his door, he's watching television. "Hi, sweetie. How come you're home?" Silence. "Mattiaaaaa! Your mother is back."

Not answering is a fixation with him. I open the door and an acrid smell assails my nostrils. He's sitting on the floor, his back against the wall. His ears are sealed up by cushy headphones and he's staring at the screen, where an agitated group, dancing on the roof of a garage, is brandishing electric guitars as if they were weapons. You can't see a thing.

"What are you doing in the dark, sweetheart?"

Mattia looks up, turns toward me. His face is streaming with tears.

"What happened? Why are you crying?" It's too late to take back my question. You never ask someone who's crying "Why are you crying?" Seeing a young man almost six feet tall shaken by sobs has a devastating effect; it makes you imagine the most terrible scenarios, especially if you're a mother. It makes you think of drugs. Who knows why we mothers all think that sooner or later we'll find out our child uses drugs. Or that he's done something really serious, committed a robbery, or run someone over with his motorbike, or something like that. Definitely something tragic.

Mattia's eyes meet mine, as if searching for a solution. He pushes his shoulders back with a painful grimace.

"Nothing, Mom, nothing's wrong."

"What do you mean, 'nothing'? Did something happen?"

Of course something happened; otherwise, he wouldn't be crying. But a mother becomes a babbling idiot when she sees her son crying. I approach at a respectful distance; sometimes when I try to hug him, he pushes me away, and I couldn't stand feeling useless right now.

A brilliant flash. "Carlotta?"

"Yeah."

"Did something happen to her?"

"You could say that."

"Damn it, Mattia, can you be a little clearer? What's wrong with her? Is she ill? Oh dear God, she's pregnant. You two are expecting a baby."

"A baby! Of course not, Mom. I wish. I don't even know if we're really a couple," he says.

"You wish? And how would you support a child? You're both students and you're penniless. Then, too . . . either you're a couple or you're not. You've been inseparable for a good number of years and you mean to tell me you're not a couple? It's impossible that you're still at that point . . . but why are you crying?"

I'm tempted to take him in my arms, but given our sizes, if I sit down instead of standing up like a soldier, he'll be the one holding me in his arms. In the end, I, too, sit on the floor. I tilt his face up. He forces himself to look at me as if he didn't care, but he wants answers from me. What are moms good for if they can't ease love's heartache, which hurts them as much as it does us, and is just as pitiless to them?

"How do you know if you're a couple and if someone is thinking of being with you? I can't very well ask her, Mom."

He acts as if I'm a past expert, but I don't fully understand what he means. They have the courage of their feelings, these fragile twentysomethings, but the question is complex. Indeed, how do you know if you're committed to someone? I can't think of any men with broken hearts apart from Petrarch, who still found it hard to make people believe he was sincere about suffering for the sake of love (I remember reading his reply to someone who accused him of inventing it all for purely literary reasons). The men of my generation don't like to show their vulnerability in this area, and they have never made love the subject of literature in and of itself. For women, on the other hand, suffering as a result of love is almost essential: Women don't love if they don't suffer; they don't enjoy it if they don't suffer. You've never heard of a woman in the world who hasn't suffered for love, and if a man doesn't make a woman suffer, she leaves him to his fate as an unfortunate loser. Suffering over love is described by women; men keep quiet, and if they suffer, they do so in silence. Not Mattia. He's learned, despite his father.

Why do I feel like a caricature holding my young son in my arms, part mother, part woman, part lover, and even a part-time bookseller? Why can't I manage to find happiness and independence after preaching about them so much? Federico, damn it. Where are you?

"Honey, you know you're a couple by telling each other so, repeating it until the other person has understood. You have to believe it. But if Carlotta is uncertain, don't be insistent. Allow her the freedom to be unsure. Someday she'll be grateful to you. And be hopeful. I'll make supper. Go take a shower; then come to the kitchen and we'll talk some more."

"Okay. Thanks, Mom. I'll take a shower and then smoke a joint. Better yet, let's smoke one together. What do you say?"

"I've never smoked a joint in my life, Mattia."

"It's time you did. I'll take care of it. You'll see, it will relax you."

"Oh, but I am relaxed. It's pathetic, a mother smoking the first joint in her life with her son. . . . Do I really have to?"

"Mom, it's only a little grass, just to snap out of this heavy mood. I'll go wash up. I smell of Carlotta and I don't like it."

I get busy at the stove and try to remember what little I know about cooking. Dinner will be spaghetti with olive oil and *bottarga* that Gabriella brought from Sardinia. Smoking one's first joint at my age is a definitive step toward emancipation.

We talked a long time that night. We talked at length about him, about her, about his dreams and his aspiration to become an urban planner rather than an architect. I tried to comfort him. Maybe I was able to, thanks in part to that joint, which had no effect whatsoever on me. I hadn't smoked a cigarette since the blizzard of 2003. I stopped in to say good night, to tell him I was proud of him. That's how I felt about that boy who was growing up unafraid of feelings, lacking the fear needed to avoid being hurt too badly. But he was already asleep.

Before becoming a bookseller, I thought writers felt honored to present their novels in public. Over time, I started to see them as having more commonplace needs. Even writers have to make arrangements to leave their children with relatives or neighbors when they're traveling; female authors also have baby-sitters who run off at night, leaving them in the lurch with husbands who treat them like ordinary wives, muttering "That's your problem" as they leave the house with a quick kiss; even writers have mortgages to pay and relationship problems, and their novels aren't necessarily autobiographical.

Today I set aside the roses and filled the baskets with white tulips. I lit vanilla-scented candles to lend the petals of these flowers a fragrance that nature has not given them. I discovered that tulips have no scent. They're just gorgeous to look at, like those well-endowed musclemen with no personality who appealed to Borghetti before Gaston. The reading with Catherine Dunne has just ended and I'm quite satisfied: sixty-two copies sold and a homey, almost surreal discussion. My customers were as insistent as a marriage counselor and asked questions that were somewhat embarrassing.

Her *In the Beginning* is a kind of manifesto of an abandoned wife, caught between stovetops and teakettles, reflections and bursts of independence. She could have bragged about the bestseller and blown her own horn a little. Instead, the writer is a simple woman ("Do call me Catherine," she said as soon as she went up to her room, where I had left her a teakettle), with fine blond hair and fair skin sprinkled with freckles. She dresses like a middle-class lady, and it is easy to imagine her in the garden of her cottage in green Ireland, pruning the roses in a cotton smock. A gentle woman, like her novels. She signs copies dutifully, has a phrase for everyone, and does not write "with esteem." I ask you, how can a writer have esteem for a reader just because he buys one of her novels? Esteem is a serious matter and comes after years and years of knowing someone. Catherine was deluged with questions about Rose's future. She promised a return appearance in her next novel.

"Will she fall in love with someone else?"

"And what about that bastard, Ben, how does he end up?"

"And the children: Do they turn out all right?"

Catherine remains unruffled; perhaps it seems natural to her that her characters are treated as though they were next-door neighbors. That would not have happened with Shakespeare; it just goes to show that contemporary fiction can be profoundly moving and offer solutions, more so than any essay on couples relationships, and all for only thirteen euros.

"Hmm, I can't reveal the ending. I would spoil your surprise. It was Rose who brought herself to my attention again; she asked me why I hadn't finished telling her story."

We serve tea and biscuits in her honor. The bookshop smells of vanilla, and romances in progress.

The months go by and my armor, infallible, is a short memory. Though there are only a few days left before Christmas, today won't be a big day; maybe no one at all will come in, but the appropriate adjective to describe these conditions in Milan is *enchanting*. It

snowed all night, the piazza is a frosted tea cake, and my situation
is getting out of hand. In a word, my life is zigzagging along. I've
just started *Gilles' Wife,* by Madeleine Bourdouxhe. It is about a
masochistic wife, overly in love with a husband who betrays her by
having a sordid, sick relationship with her seductive, fickle sister. It
will end in tragedy. I can feel it, even though I'm only at page 12,
sitting at the counter, doing absolutely nothing. I'm waiting for the
kids, who for some weeks have been pestering me about a playlist,
which I continue to call a sound track, seeing no reason to change.
I find background music annoying in bookstores and in cafés, too,
where you can't even talk to the person next to you unless you
shout and let everyone know your business. Megastores that blast
out music remind me of hotel lobbies or airport waiting rooms. According to Manuele and Alice, who, since they got married, have
been lording it over me, conspiring with Mattia, Dreams & Desires
absolutely must have (they used this expression, literally) *its* music.
Its, which is not mine. Good-bye silence, and this soothing solitude
that I find healing. I have no intention of compromising. As long as
I am the proprietor of this place, I will not allow music, not even in
the Locanda.

"The pages create the music. Pick up a book, leaf through it
quickly, and you'll find that it breathes, that it has a sound: the
pleasing hum of newly bound sheets."

"Huh? What do you mean? Books don't make any sound. . . .
We'll start with a playlist of love songs and see how it goes. A stereo
system costs very little. . . . Come onnnn, Emma!"

"Out of the question. As long as I'm alive, you'll never succeed
in turning this place into a discotheque. The answer is no."

"Who said anything about a discotheque? We're talking about
background music, famous love songs, maybe some classical music
like Chopin, Debussy, Ludovico Einaudi. Certainly not rock or even
pop songs . . ."

They seem high, or, as Mattia would say, completely zonked.
Alice especially. I attribute it to her being overworked these past
few weeks. There are five of us in the shop, and apart from today's

unnatural stillness, the pace has been exhausting. I even sold those beautiful photography books that never sell, which these days are going like hotcakes, along with the candles, cups, and flowers. The new room fragrances, Les Liaisons Dangereuses, imported from Paris, have already sold out. If I carried detective novels, I'd sell those, too. Exceptional proceeds in the Locanda, too: a gourmand's emporium, which we've been renting out for drinks and receptions since company parties have come back in style. The guys with the name tags are booked for this evening, thirty-five people. We'll even serve them alcoholic beverages, such as a delectable Donnafugata wine—the most literary I could find, which I sell coupled with *The Leopard,* a perennial. Also available on DVD.

APRIL 10, 2006

I'll take care of everything, you just worry about the video re-corder," she said on the phone with a know-it-all tone and a fluty voice that wasn't her usual.

It's Monday. I feel calm. I filled the bathtub with the usual lav-ender salts and lay there soaking for half an hour, waiting for Ga-briella. She's taking care of the food, after all, and I certainly don't know how to use the damn VCR, which belongs to Mattia; he's been gone for a week and left without leaving instructions. I never use it, actually, since I prefer seeing films in the appropriate place: a movie theater. We'll be just the two of us, like in the good old days. A nice evening by ourselves in front of the TV. Alberto is busy with income-tax returns, a slave driver who makes his office clerks keep ungodly hours. He comes home late at night. Who knows if he's telling the truth. By now, I've even become suspicious of those above suspicion.

"We'll tape it just to be safe, in case you want to watch it again. We might fall asleep and miss a critical scene," she says, placing an elegant package from Zen Sushi on the books (uh-oh!). "I spent a fortune, but at least we don't have to deal with pots and pans. It's all ready, delicious, and plentiful. I'll dish out. Would you mind moving the books at least?"

As if I could fall asleep tonight, of all nights, given such a coin-cidence: one of those situations that life throws at you and it's up to you to decide whether to ignore it or face it squarely. I, who have the courage of a lioness, never ignore a coincidence, and I'm sitting quietly on the sofa in the living room, waiting for the plot to my story. Apart from exceptions such as live opera from La Scala or some old black-and-white Bette Davis movie, television does not produce any devastating effects on my emotional state. In a word, it doesn't move me. It's *only* a TV show. Of course, one might wonder why they scheduled it on this very day, but when I receive a sign, I don't ask questions; otherwise it wouldn't be a sign, but a TV listing. Charlie Rose's *Cold Fusion:* sixty minutes dedicated to the new Morgan Library & Museum, whose inauguration will be held in two weeks, at 225 Madison Avenue, New York, USA. It will be an exclusive tour, a preview for subscribers of the Leonardo Channel, broadcast on Sky Italia. I surf around a little with the remote control, but the other broadcasters are all talking about national politics, and this year it's a huge mess. It's not clear who has won the elections, and they'll go on well into the night. I feel like I'm at the rail of a vessel, watching a sailing cup final. We have twin Ikea lap trays with pistachio green plastic feet on our knees and are ready to celebrate: sushi, sashimi, soy sauce, four cans of Sapporo beer, and a basket of strawberries. Gabriella truly did think of everything.

"They're the first of the season, Emma. You shouldn't slice strawberries, much less season them with sugar and lemon; it's best to eat them whole," she says with a new indulgence in her voice, not knocking my incompetence as a slatternly homemaker.

"Hey, it was your idea to have dinner in front of the TV, and I have no intention of getting drunk. One can each is more than enough."

I'm lying. At least a little. Actually, I'm anxious for it to start, and the beer will offset my agitation. It's just that the newspaper lists it at 11:30. The clock reads 11:42 and the program still hasn't started. Arrhythmia, intermittent. This must be cardiac arrhythmia. I'm not very hungry; food is mainly an accompaniment, like when Alberto watches a game with Michele and Mattia. They eat to console themselves or to celebrate. We try to fool time, but it's not fooled. Instead, it moves more slowly. I listen for a rhythm and hear only a fluttering.

In sweater and tights, I'm at home, and I don't have to measure up to anyone.

"How do you feel?"

"Like someone who has been revising the proofs of her own novel for five years and who is now about to receive the bound copy." I was prepared for the question because I'd been asking myself the same thing all day.

"I'm curious to see how he looks now; maybe they'll interview him."

The little bricks of rice with tuna and salmon are stacked up; it's almost a shame to eat them and ruin the symmetry. Gabriella entertains me with an account of the recent school trip she took with her students last week: She escorted thirty-five of them to Petra, Jordan. Heroic.

"Us, they took by bus to Florence. Remember what a madhouse it was? Crowded, into those pitiable boardinghouses. Singing all night with that—what was the name of the guy who played the guitar with Federico? It seems like yesterday, Gabri, yet it was decades ago. Every so often, I think about organizing a dinner for the veterans of fifth-year section B."

"For the love of God, Emma. I know people who did that, and it was worse than a funeral, what with those who had died, the depressed failures, or, worse yet, the ones who had become successful and put on airs. For me, all it takes is Alberto to remind me of the school trip of my life. It took me two more years to get to know him seriously after that time. This morning, when I told him that I was coming to your place, he made a jealous face. He realizes that we sometimes leave him out and he doesn't like it one bit."

The opening theme. We cross chopsticks; the trays wobble on our knees despite the invincible Ikea design. The room is dark; you'd think we were in a movie theater. Mondo sighs and turns around on the couch beside us, docile and seraphic.

"*Cold Fusion*, what a chilling title! And Philip Glass and Roberto Cacciapaglia as background music, a somewhat banal choice."

"America and Italy, it's intentional. Want to create feeling in a

newscast? Go with the piano. Glass's music is perfect for a documentary; too bad that this is the sound track of *The Hours,* and
there's not one line by Virginia Woolf at the Morgan."

The ceremony begins with a POV shot—you know it's a cine-
matographic creation—then the usual yellow cab that stops in front
of the entrance (as if to say, Here we are in New York), the journalist
who steps out (without paying the fare; it's obvious that it's staged).
Architect Piano awaits us on Madison, pushes open a glass door,
and invites us to follow him into an enchanted place, a light, transparent space (having had it described to me, I feel as though I've
actually been there). The camera turns toward the sky and frames
the tops of the buildings, the windows of the houses in Murray Hill.
Life flows while mine stops. Just for an instant, though. A brief moment of wonderment. The proofs have become a book and the author with the ascetic face opens it to the frontispiece, his eyes clear
and confident, his slim hands manicured; he's wearing a blue shirt,
a tie with horizontal stripes, and a wool jacket.

"Being here will be like living in a huge Italian piazza," he begins, and then welcomes us as if he were at home (but then the
Morgan is somewhat like home to him), while a painting gradually
appears in the background: J.P.M. in a tailcoat and frilly collar, his
big nose prominent. I recognize him. It all started with a piazza, a
place for socializing, for meeting people, a space that opened toward the city.

"When you enter, I'd like you to forget that we are in a library
that houses the world's third-largest collection of books from the
past and feel as though you are in a light-filled piazza."

I already know what I will see. The camera cuts to an artist's
hand touching the button on a glass elevator. Gabriella looks at me
sideways, uncertain whether to comment or take me in her arms.
Protective, she fears a collapse. It doesn't happen, and I don't even
force myself to watch for him. The architect host has the class of a
sailing master; Federico used to say that his boss talked about complicated things as if they were simple, as if that austere mass of
glass and steel had been created in a few hours, as if it were utterly

natural and obvious that McKim's marble and Piano's steel had been placed in frames and hollowed out on the sides to evoke the technique of fusion. As if there were no secrets in that box, no obstacles or barriers, and thought were able to flow, free to express itself without censure. One is connected to New York, yet at the same time magically distant, as if one were sitting in a garden.

"Steel is Morgan, the founder, who built his fortune on that very steel. America is a nation that has roots. We don't have to look for fake ones by turning to heraldry; all we have to do is use the real ones. The steel beams we used are the kind that could support industrial buildings; the walls are made with sheet metal used for ships. There is also wood, in the reading room and in the auditorium, while the vaults where the manuscripts are kept were carved into the rock like the compartments of a submarine."

Exactly.

He speaks with the gentleness of a monk. You know, architect, I'd like to tell him, I understand everything. I laugh and nod; I understand everything he's saying, despite my limited knowledge of architecture. I mentally dedicate a "Romantic Spaces" shelf to him, because what he is ushering us through, with Bob Dylan in the background, thank goodness, is a place of love. And don't think I'm being mawkish; I seriously think so, architect Piano. A place where you can lose yourself and find yourself in the truth of transparency as the elevator descends and slowly drops into the well, that pit I recognize as if I had been confined there forever. The architect walks along the light-filled path that separates the white vaults containing the treasure. "There's no better place than Manhattan schist to preserve books forever. The past is a good refuge, but the future is the only place where we can go," he affirms, his tone that of a genius who doesn't take himself too seriously. He seems to be talking to me personally. It's an honor, maestro. "Here we have the auditorium, two hundred and eighty seats, the wavy ceiling in cherrywood." I seem to hear the husky voice of an actress performing Austen for me, as if Jane's wit had remained dozing in there and were speaking to me again, in the familiar, mysterious act of turning the page.

Federico is sitting on the floor. He did that exactly three years ago, when there was only a crater in the ground at that spot. But this is just my imagination. And a man who is crying would look like a fool, let alone in a documentary. Federico isn't there, but it's as if he is.

"It's beautiful," my friend says.

"A little wanting as a comment, from someone who teaches art history," I reply, and I despise the bitterness that slips out of my mouth.

"If you ask me, he's not there. How do you feel, Emma?"

"Morgan wasn't an art expert; sometimes he got swindled and paid too much. But lucky for him he could rely on the services of the greatest experts in the world. It seems like a magical place; they did a sensational job. He was right to fall head over heels for it."

"I'm asking what effect it has on you."

"What effect it has? Well . . . it's like an outfit you saw in the paper, you kept the clipping, and now you finally put it on. I'm proud of him. I can't imagine how he feels, what someone feels when they've played a role in the rebirth of a place that's so . . . unique, that's it. I'd just like to know how he is. It's likely he won't be able to enjoy the Morgan's success, that it will always be linked to the memory of his wife."

"You really loved him, huh."

"I still love him, even now. I can't be angry with him. I never could, and it's too late to start now."

After all those letters, three thousand drawings, and $106 million, it's completed. "See you at the Morgan," they'll say, the furtive lovers, the ladies who meet for tea and gossip, managers who want to read the newspaper in peace.

"Architecture is a tangible activity, because it must provide a solid defense for people," my Virgil concludes, "but it is also spiritual, the most spiritual of the arts."

"How come you have some left over? You always liked sushi. He's really down-to-earth, this Piano. Maybe Federico . . . will arrive for the grand finale."

"Imagine if he were to see me in this getup now, with sticky hands and ballerina flats. Architecture changes the world. . . . Mmmh, it's the architects who change it."

The camera scrolls down the list of names and the sushi goes down the wrong way. They skim by like the names of building residents on a brass intercom. The cast of a colossus. Piano bids us farewell to the strains of Franz Schubert's *Death and the Maiden*. That, too, is in the vaults. The camera pans out to focus on the rosy-colored cube—oh, sorry, the cube in Tennessee pink marble. The color of the past, the color of the present. I watch it on TV and it's as if I had always been inside it, just as it is now, a city of glass in which everything seems possible: sitting down to enjoy coffee, lunch, or dinner, to read, talk, listen to music, see a film, listen to a concert. In the piazza, you can sit among the trees and works of art. Who knows where Federico is at this moment?

"He would have liked it."

"Who?"

"J. P. Morgan. You should read his story."

"Maybe we'll go there someday. . . ."

"Mattia is superexcited; from what he says, he never sleeps. The first time in New York has that effect on everybody."

"It's late, Emma. I'll send Alberto a message and sleep here, if it's okay with you."

Of course it's okay with me, and how well I know her. She doesn't trust my little jokes and my nonchalant air. She didn't see him. But she knows perfectly well that it's as if Federico had been sitting here on the couch between us.

Cold Fusion really is a bad title—even for a science fiction novel.

A man is walking down Madison Avenue. It's drizzling on this damp April night, but he just doesn't feel like taking a taxi, and the Vespa is already on the container ship. The city seems deserted; his American venture is over. Suspended for a few months, maybe a year or more, it couldn't have ended better than it did: in TV spotlights all over the world. "Night, boss. A huge success. Congratulations. Wonderful," everybody kept saying. The man walks along, his body bent slightly forward. He calls his daughter on the cell phone, says, "Everything's fine, sweetheart, and you . . . how about you?" "I'm fine too, Dad. I'm sorry I had to pass up the celebration— I'll bet you were fantastic—but tomorrow I have my art exam and I can't miss it. . . . Yes, Katherine is with me; we're just about to go to bed. I'm proud of you, Daddy. Give my regards to Renzo and Frank. I'll call you tomorrow to tell you how it went." The man can't tell her that he's worried about her, that it's like always being sleepless. The thought of leaving her at the college torments him, but he doesn't say anything. Those miles are too great a distance; he's the only one who misses Paris. Then, too, you don't always feel like talking to someone, and he prefers silence. She has a future. The man who gets in a taxi and tells the driver to take him to 42 West 10th Street thinks he no longer has one. He slumps on the seat as if it were a sagging armchair, his temples pounding. He received the world's congratulations, but he couldn't wait for all of it to be over. He has to shake off the suffocating affection of those around him, as though he were a risky case; they don't understand that he just wants to be alone, to go home and find a way to stop his head from throbbing. He climbs the stairs. He turns right at the landing, unlocks the door, and enters the living room, where the stacked boxes give the room a sense of anticipation. All that's left are the books, piled up in the corner, their titles forming a sequence of poems. Sentences. He'll pack them up tomorrow. Anna's clothes have already been folded away in some trunk in Italy. Her mother will be there every morning to stroke them like fetishes; that's what you do with the clothes of the dead, divested of the body but not of orphaned memories. He has kept the art books—he had never realized how many Anna had bought—along with the CDs and photographs and those notebooks he hadn't wanted to read. Anna wrote—there are so many things we don't know about the people who live their lives beside us. Sarah kept for herself the earrings and brooches that still bear her mother's scent. The good-byes, yet another party tomorrow at the studio, three more days, then he's gone. It's over. He'll be back—there's the Columbia University project—but for now he feels the need for Europe, for familiar faces, friends he left behind, his furniture and his own four walls, a refuge where he can breathe a little or find some air—it makes no difference. He pours himself a whiskey thick as honey and stands under the shower as Bruce sings about not being able to sleep and he follows along, strumming an imaginary guitar. Packed up, the guitar, too. The apartment phone rings. *Who the hell would be calling at this hour?* he wonders. He immediately thinks of Sarah, with that anxiety that, despite the pills, never loosens its grip, but why not on his cell phone? He hates phones, no matter what they say. "Hello," and the receiver grows damp. The male voice on the other end of the line is an electric shock, a foghorn in a brain already clouded by liquor, but he knows he heard the name right. He recognizes Emma in that voice. "Good evening, Mr. Virgili. I'm sorry to bother you at home at this hour. I'm Mattia Gentili, I'm in New York, and I'd like to meet you." Her son. A boy with a man's voice. How old can he be? Twenty-four, twenty-three, a few years older

than Sarah. In his haste, he overlooks the consequences of his reply: "Of course. I'm free tomorrow; we can meet at the Empire State
Building. Is one o'clock all right with you? Do you know where it
is?" Everybody knows the Empire State Building, the most predictable spot in the world to meet in Manhattan and eat somewhere
nearby; he'll find a place for that strange encounter. What is that
boy doing here, tonight of all nights? He's getting used to people
upsetting his plans; in fact, he's learned that planning is a load of
crap, a way to pretend that everything is all right. He crawls into
bed, exhausted and damp from his shower. Springsteen sings a
rough lullaby on the stereo, but he doesn't feel like getting up and
turning off that friendly voice. Tomorrow is already here. There's
no time to regret his rash action, and he's curious, even excited,
when the taxi drops him off in front of the line of tourists waiting
to go up to Manhattan's most popular observatory. He recognizes
him in the crowd. The spitting image: delicate features and down-
turned eyes that seem almost imploring (though it must be the effect of the light); an iPod nano on his wrist, metal chin stud,
short-sleeved T-shirt worn over a red long-sleeved tee, the All-Stars
a bit faded, the swinging stride that comes naturally to guys over a
certain height. He feels flustered and confused and nettled, as if
surprised at seeing her materialize again. He walks toward him the
boy, but without a doubt. He doesn't need to confirm his identity,
and when he's standing in front of him, they are the same height;
his instinct is to hug him. What is he thinking? "Good to meet
you," Mattia says, and he shakes his hand with the identical smile.
The man stammers something about the skyscraper, which in a
few weeks will celebrate its first seventy-five years, tells him that if
they went up to the 102nd floor they could see New Jersey and
even Connecticut. He's speaking too quickly; he'll seem like a
know-it-all, and if there's one thing kids can't stand, it's when an
adult acts too chummy. He makes the same mistake every time
Sarah brings home a boyfriend, slipping into the usual grotesque
authority of an adult. He can just hear her: *Dad, you're acting like a
cretin. They know you're my father; it's better not to pretend to be*

something you're not. How many times she's told him and he still hasn't learned how to act. He feels tired, as if he hadn't slept; the effect of facing that familiar face is devastating, the shock of a journey without maps or guides. It's not really longing, but the usual guilt hammering away inside him, like an echo, reproaching him for his mistakes, the mishaps, a destiny derailed. The man and the boy go into a Japanese restaurant rather than stand out on the street; the boy studies him a little, occasionally smiling that forthright smile of his. He, at his age, would not have dared defy the taboo. Meeting his mother's lover: unthinkable to even imagine her in the arms of someone other than his father. On that male face, the eyes slanting toward the temples make a certain impression, but they are hers, the eyes and ears and profile of that face he knows so well. The lady in the brightly colored kimono hands them the menu as if it were a business card, holding a small hot towel with a pair of bamboo tongs. "For washing your hands," she suggests, her face expressionless. The boy crosses his arms; dark hair peeks out of his sleeve. He seems to be looking at him defiantly, but it's only an impression and it must surely be shyness. He's just a boy and things shouldn't have gone this way. Now he thinks of it, when the merry-go-round has stopped. "Sushi or tempura?" he asks. "Sushi is good. I like raw fish." The young man leans back in his chair, a sign of relaxed submission. The man does the same, failing to come up with an interesting topic other than the Empire State Building. Yet he likes being here; the experience is less painful than he had imagined. Because he dreamed about Emma all night. There's a silence to fill. "How come you're in New York? Would you like me to help you find a job here? I could talk to my colleagues at BBB; it's an excellent studio, and everyone is very friendly." "I don't particularly care for Piano's style, no offense. I have a job. They took me on for a six-month internship. I'm an architect, like you, Mr. Virgili." A broad smile full of youthful pride. "Even though I'm old enough to be your father, please call me Federico. We're colleagues. . . ." "I called to talk to you about Mom."

He tells him that and it sounds true, natural; there's no affectation, no reserve. He's sincere and not at all impulsive. "How is she?" And his heart starts pounding so loudly in his chest that he thinks he can actually hear it hammering, a dizziness and confusion that leaves him limp yet relieved. He wants to be polite, as he normally is, but seeing the young man in front of him is like viewing a scrapbook, the kind from back in school. From his backpack the carbon-copy boy pulls out a photo of a beach trip more than thirty-five years ago. It has a certain effect. Some people, Enrico certainly, would call it bad luck; better to drop it, he'd advise. "And her? Is she all right?" "No," he replies, his voice almost flat, and skewers his sushi as if to sidestep the question. Or so it seems. "And the bookshop, her hotel?" "Doing great. They've opened a similar one in Rome. . . . It's none of my business, but yesterday I went to the opening. I hated you; forgive me for saying it. Yes, I know what happened; I'm sorry for your daughter." *For your daughter,* he says, not for you. He's right: Young people close ranks, even if they don't know each other. They can't believe that a grown man can suffer. They can't stand to see us that way; they don't want vulnerable parents. "I called you to talk about her." "She's all right, then?" "She's fine, if it's her health you mean. It's just that . . . she's changed. She walks differently, as if she weren't really sure which way to go. She takes her time, whereas I was used to seeing her rushing around. In the evening, she stays home, reading or watching TV; oh, sure, she's always done that, but I hated the idea of going away, leaving her all alone. Maybe I'm wrong, but I got the idea you had a lot to do with it, so I went to the opening, meaning to talk to you, but I couldn't do it. You might have told me to get the hell out, and I didn't want to spoil your celebration." *Spoil the celebration,* he says. What celebration? He can barely contain himself. "I found this among the letters. Mom keeps them in a box. I was looking for some journal issues in the bookcase at home and . . . I couldn't resist. I got curious. I don't usually do that, because I don't like her snooping around in my room. In fact, she never does. You know how she is; she's pretty special. But don't worry, I only read a few of them. It's none of my business, but . . . well . . . I came to tell you that personally I think . . . well, you could at least call her. I convinced her to buy a cell phone; now that I'm here, it's the only way we're able to talk to each other. Basically, she only uses it with me. It's . . . It's just that I hate to see her so sad. Your letters are beautiful . . . and so is the Morgan. . . . Excuse me, miss," he says, signaling the kimonoed waitress, "can I have another beer?" Emma has a cell phone. He can imagine how she must hate it, and he pictures her fumbling with the keys as she calls her son. Emma slow— hard to imagine his tiny wren walking slowly on her heels. "She writes text messages, too. . . . If you call her, it might make her happy. I don't know if I've done the right thing. I changed my mind about it a thousand times. . . ." Federico smiles, thinking about all the precautions, the secrets, *the feelings they held back,* and about mailbox 772. The letters are all still there; he'll stop by tomorrow to pick them up. Shit, how embarrassing. Who knows what he'd written. . . . The boy read only a few of them, or so he said somewhat knowingly. He feels cold, now that it's his turn and Mattia has finished what he had to say. He has to say something. He watches the boy eat like a ravenous wolf. Kids are like that. They don't eat; they devour. It's like a crazy dream; his old life lies beyond the restaurant's walls. In here, a man and a boy talk as if they have known each other forever. The grown man stares at his plate. He feels relieved; he has the impression that someone has given him back something precious. A thought fills him. She is there, he pictures her in the big bed, and the only word he can think of to express what he would like to tell this fine dark-haired young man is *gratitude.* A mirror reflects the image of a man and a boy. Ten years from now, Mattia will be a man and someone else will continue the love story. God, how he envies him. He would like to talk to him about Sarah, a subject other than Emma. Reserve, that's all it is. He gets up and leads the way. The number is tucked in his pocket. A passport to reentry. "Thank you, Mattia.

Thank you, and if you need anything, please call me and I'll put you in touch with the studio."

He would not sleep that night; he already knew it. He walked off, then, after a few steps, turned around. The boy was walking hurriedly, the iPod buds in his ears, walking with that swinging stride typical of guys over a certain height.

FINIS TERRAE

Seen from behind, petite, my white hair in a layered pageboy down my neck, I'm a decidedly romantic vision. I could be the heroine in the final pages of a romance novel, if someone could see me here in the meadow, among the wild rosemary bushes and thistles, the creeper embroidered on the walls of a nineteenth-century weather station. I'm holding a glass of Sancerre; my jeans are rolled up above my knees, my bare feet slipped into a pair of aubergine Repetto ballerina flats.

I'm making progress: I gave up the heels, I drink all kinds of alcohol, and I don't dye my hair anymore, though this doesn't mean I've stopped going to the hairdresser once a week. I gaze at the ocean, while he, tanned beneath a short beard sprinkled with white, walks along the planks with the confident step of a captain on the deck of his ship. The semaphore has been restored; its walls are whitewashed, its windows cobalt blue. I've transplanted my heart here: the desk, the beige-and-burgundy-checked armchairs, the butcher-block counter, the ottoman, and a Colette with ruffled hair tossing grains of rice to the pigeons at the Place du Palais Royal. A baby seagull glides to a landing at my feet, looking for a friend. It's August and today is my birthday. It's almost dinnertime, and the throaty voice of Carole King sings about love that's possible.

"Emmaaaa, come and see," the captain calls.

"There's no need to shout. I'm not deaf yet. You come here instead. You don't know what you're missing."

"Come, I'm telling you. This is too good."

"What is? What's too good?"

"You've got mail."

"Who knows what I was thinking. *Will you still love me tomorrow?* Hmm . . . shall we dance? I'm on my first glass and already my head is spinning."

The "New Message" light is blinking on the screen of my MacBook. Subject: "Here we are." Oh, it's not a text; by now, we're into video. This is what people do nowadays and I no longer rebel at this insane method of communication; instead, I've taken to it with a deference due to modernity. A double click of the mouse and it's like having them here in the flesh, and I'm idiotically moved to see her linen shirt stretched tight over her big belly, while he nods his head and waves his big hand, like so long ago. They're beautiful and in love and in a little over two months I'll be a grandmother. A quasi-grandmother, if you consider that Alice is the daughter I never had, and Mattia is proud to become a quasi-uncle. The shop is different now that Federico set his hand to it and with a couple of felt-tip pen strokes turned it into a *concept store* (horrors) that sells books and candles, flowers and perfumes, and even wallpaper with texts from the great writers. I left it in good hands and I certainly can't complain. The accounts are in order, the hotel is steaming ahead at full capacity, and the books on the new cherrywood shelves are still divided according to types of love. Of course, the new wood and metal chairs are a bit minimalist for my taste and I have a hard time swallowing the new English name, Emma's Dream—the Italian name, Dreams & Desires, was "too local." They kept the Sweet Dreams Locanda in Italian, a commemorative plaque to the memory of the original owner, as if I am already defunct. The video message even has sound, but I'll never understand how the devil it works and they'll never persuade me to talk to myself in front of a camera that feels like an informer.

"It's an island, Federico; that's what you've done. You turned the shop into an island. I hadn't quite realized it yet, but I finally just got it, how brilliant you are, my darling architect!"

"Happy birthday to you, happy birthday to youuu, happy birthday, dear Emma, happy birthday to you!" the two sing from the monitor.

"How sweet they are. . . . I feel like crying, Federico. Will they be able to handle it all, the baby, the shop, and all the rest?"

"It's no longer your problem, Emma. And I really think they're managing very well. Stop feeling like you're indispensable and think about the fact that today you're an old woman. Almost as old as me."

It's not cold, here on the Atlantic, which confronts its towering shores like a rebellious child. Federico holds me in his arms with the care of one who has learned to choose. I bury my nose in the crook of his elbow and breathe in the scent of that skin I came to know in a past whose memory no longer needs to be recovered. I carry your heart in my heart; you carry my heart in your heart. Now let's love each other. And go on loving.

ACKNOWLEDGMENTS

It is my pleasure to thank a multitude of people. I'm sure that if she were reading this, Emma would enjoy imagining the personalities concealed behind the names and, most important, she would understand.

My gratitude goes to the following:

First of all, to the architect Giorgio Bianchi, partner in charge of the Renzo Piano Building Workshop. Trusting and generous, he contributed stories, emotions, and insights related to the project, both in the studio and at the construction site, as well as some exclusive anecdotes that allowed me to "construct" the character of Federico.

To Francesca Bianchi for the photographs, notes, and explanations concerning the Morgan Library, and for the time she spent with me.

To Renzo Piano, who encouraged me with a letter written in green felt-tip pen.

To Frank J. Prial, Jr., of Beyer Blinder Belle, who disclosed the secrets of a truly special work site.

To Charles E. Pierce, Jr., Brian Regan, Patrick Milliman, and Christine Nelson of the Morgan Library & Museum of New York, who kindly and professionally allowed me to poke into the private affairs of John Pierpont Morgan and his library.

To Fabio Fassone, who was the first to support my passion for the Morgan.

To Fabrizio Ferri; he knows why.

To my "personal" readers, who recommended titles and love stories and who loved Emma even before they met her; above all, to Diego Arquilla, for the wines, titles, and detailed e-mails—without him, Dreams & Desires would have many lacunae.

Also to Pablo Paolo Peretti, Anna Pia Fantoni, Elena Albano, Paola Peretti, Valeria Palumbo, Marco De Martino, Veronica Bozza, Mita Gironda, Gianfranco Pierucci, and Manuela Campari.

To cardiologist Stefano Savonitto, who led me to discover "broken heart" syndrome.

To Corrado Spanger, who believed in this book from the first synopsis.

To Laura Galletti, bookseller, who educated me in the "science" of bar codes and shelving in a proper bookshop.

To attorney Fulvio Pusineri because, though it may not seem so, this novel had great need of legal advice.

To Alessandra Gentile, who designed Dreams & Desires' window displays with me.

To Luca Barbareschi, to whom I also owe the first shot: that of a helicopter flying over the menhirs of Jean and Jeanne.

To Gianmario Maggi, who led me to discover Brittany; to Giulia and Guido Venturini, thanks to whom I came to know and love Belle-Ile-en-Mer.

To Giulia Ichino, my editor. She knows how to listen; she's patient and reasonable, yet endowed with impeccable tenacity. Exactly what an author needs.

To my son Davide, who gave me the character of Mattia.

And, as always, to Vicki Satlow, who is much more than a literary agent. She is an accomplice and friend, and knows how to manage my crises with intelligence and love.